THE MAKING OF ANNIE-MAY

Books 1 & 2

Alana Davies

·

Unabridged

Awduresau Cymru Publishing

Awduresau Cymru Publishing
58 Victoria Avenue
Porthcawl
CF36 3YU

1

This book is dedicated to everyone's daughters
including, and especially, mine.

CONTENTS

BOOK ONE

4

BOOK TWO

PROLOGUE
Jessie's Story

1957

Sorting through the bags of clothes had become monotonous work, even with the small-talk.

'Part of being Lady of the Manor, eh?' Peggy's tone was light, but Jessie resented it nonetheless. She was very aware of how she was perceived in this little seaside town, despite its being her childhood home. She smiled.

'It's nice to be able to give something back, you know?'

'Yes' said Peggy, arms outstretched in the process of folding a vast jumper. 'It's great that so many people have given us their cast-offs for the Jumble. I'm sure that all the poor people will love them.' This time there was no mistaking Peggy's tone.

When the doorbell rang it was a welcome distraction for Jessie. Peggy opened the door to two police officers.

'Mrs Hughes?'

'No, I'm Peggy Morris, the housekeeper. I'll fetch her.' She turned, and started towards the drawing room when she saw her young employer walking across the hall.

'Jessie, it's …' she began.

'It's ok Peggy, I heard.' Jessie turned to their two visitors. 'How can I help you?'

6

'Mrs Hughes? Mrs Jessie Hughes? May we come in?' Their ID badges were flashed briefly.

'You'll have to excuse the mess – we're sorting some donations for tomorrow's charity sale' Jessie said.

She led the officers into the spacious drawing room, where several boxes stood, carefully stacked. A neat pile of folded clothes lay on a large polished table, and the sunlight streamed through the two tall casement windows. A magnificent dollshouse stood on an impressive stand in a corner, and a toddler was playing, very gently, with its contents. Jessie noticed their glances around the room, and became aware that this was not the sort of "mess" they may be used to. She sat on one large sofa and motioned them to another.

'How can I help you?' she repeated.

'Do you want me to stay, Jess?' asked Peggy.

'Yes please Peggy - can you keep an eye on Anya for me? She's due for her nap soon.'

'Mrs Hughes' the constable began. She cleared her throat. 'I'm afraid we have some bad news about your husband, Michael Hughes.'

She hesitated. Then,

'I'm sorry to tell you that he's been found dead in his car'.

Jessie was silent for what seemed a long time. Doris Day was singing *Que Sera, Sera ... Whatever will be, will be* on the radio.

'What?'

'I'm afraid …'

'Dead? Michael? Dead?'

'I'm sorry, yes.'

Then,

'Would you like a glass of water?'

Did she look as numb as she felt?

'Dead?'

The officer looked at Peggy, standing near the door, now covering her mouth with both hands, horrified.

'Could you fetch Mrs Hughes some water, please, Mrs …?

'It's Miss. Morris. Peggy Morris' she whispered.

'Yes of course.'

Jessie heard her daughter, oblivious to the earthquake around her, offering tiny pieces of china to the mannequins seated in the dollshouse. 'Cuppa tea?' she was saying.

'Do you feel up to answering some questions Mrs Hughes? Or can I call you Jessie?'

Jessie nodded.

'When did you last see your husband, Jessie?

' … um … this morning, early. About eight.'

'Did he say where he was going?'

'No, not really. He was going to the office I expect.'

'And did he do or say anything unusual?'

The door opened again, and the officer waited while Peggy handed over the glass of water with shaking hands.

'He said his usual goodbye stuff – have fun, take care, enjoy your dollshouse … love you …' Jessie swallowed. She took a sip of water.

'Enjoy your dollshouse?'

'Yes. Family joke. He called this...' she waved an arm around the room '... my dollshouse.'

"Ah, I see. Jessie, I'm afraid I must ask you to come with us to identify your husband's body.' Her voice was gentle but firm.

She nodded.

'Is there anyone we can call for you?'

She shook her head. Then,

'He said *things aren't always what they seem*'.

The sergeant looked up sharply.

'He said that?' he asked. 'This morning? What did he mean?'

Jessie shook her head.

'I have no idea' she whispered.

In a quiet but steady voice, she asked Peggy to finish folding the clothes.

'And can you look after Anya for me please?'

As Jessie was leaving the room, the child ran to her, holding out a scrap of paper.

'There y'go Mummy!' she said, beaming.

Jessie bent to kiss her, hug her, willing herself not to fall apart.

'See you later Sweetheart' she said. 'Be good for Auntie Peggy.'

She allowed herself to be escorted to the black car waiting at the top of the long drive.

Jessie looked down at her husband. She felt strangely distant, removed. This wasn't real. This couldn't be her Michael. She'd kissed him this morning. Said goodbye, went about her day. And now this. No, this wasn't happening.

'Why is he so pink?'

'Can you confirm that this is the body of your husband, Michael Hughes?'

'Yes. Why is he so pink?'

'If you follow me to my office Mrs Hughes, we can talk there.'

She walked after him, stiffly, conscious of putting one foot after the other. She sat on the hard wooden chair in front of his desk. Who was he?

'I'm from the Coroner's Office, Mrs Hughes.'

As if he'd heard her. Had she said it aloud?

'I will try to answer any questions you have.'

'Why is he so pink?' she asked again.

He took a deep breath.

'We'll need to wait for a post-mortem before we can be certain about the cause of death, Mrs Hughes. But your husband's pink colouring leads us to believe, at this point, that your husband may have died from carbon monoxide poisoning. He was found alone in his car. The Coroner will ask the police to gather the information about his death. I'm so sorry Mrs Hughes.'

Jessie sat, hands folded in her lap. She tried to take in what he was saying, but her mind was numb, foggy, full of cotton wool. This was harder to grasp than being told he was dead. Eventually she spoke.

'He committed suicide. That's what you're saying.'

'As I said Mrs Hughes, we will need to wait for a post-mortem before we can be certain ...'

"No. No. He wouldn't do that. He couldn't. He wouldn't choose to leave us. He wouldn't ...'

She bent her head, but not before she saw the glances between the people in the room. Even in her state of utter disbelief, of shock, of horror, she knew what they meant. She guessed that all the wives said what she had said. They all thought their husbands loved them too much to do this terrible thing. The fog cleared.

'My husband didn't kill himself. And your post mortem will prove it.'

'Mrs Hughes.'

A new voice. She looked up.

'Mrs Hughes, I'm Inspector Daly. Would you like to come with me? There are a few questions I'd like to ask you – and you may have some for me.'

Another name. Too many names. She'd never remember them all.

She sat in his office.

Rob Daly looked across at her, not unsympathetically. Pretty woman, he noted. She wasn't looking her best, naturally – no tears yet, but her eyes were reddening and her blonde hair looked dishevelled. Quite a bit younger than her husband, he guessed. An affair? Maybe. Jealousy? Too hard to live with? Or corruption? Bribery? Time would tell.

'Mrs Hughes, can you tell me something about your husband? About Michael?'

She nodded.

'OK. When did you last see him?'

'This morning. When he left for the office. About eight.'

'Did he have any money worries? Work worries?

'No. He had a big contract coming up. It was a lot of work; he was a bit distracted, waiting to hear whether he'd got the job.'

'And what job was that, Mrs Hughes?'

'A big contract with the council. But he has other jobs on – smaller ones. He's a building contractor you see, my husband' she said proudly, lifting her head.

'I mean – he was …' Her head dropped again.

'And did he have any problems with colleagues that you know of? Or with neighbours? Friends?'

She shook her head, not raising it. After a pause, Inspector Daly stood up.

'That's all for now, Mrs Hughes. Thank you for being so helpful. We may need to be in touch again. Is there a relative or friend we can contact for you?'

Jessie realized she had no relatives now, no friends. Not here, not in her home town. She shook her head again. She left the office and the building, sat in the waiting car, was barely aware of the drive back home. Home? Not now, she thought. Not ever again.

The next few days were a whirl of activity and nothingness. Peggy stepped up and helped. She changed from being the often critical, wordlessly disapproving and sometimes downright sarcastic creature she had been since she had started working for the couple. She took over the arrangements for her widowed employer, making phone calls and answering them, contacting the funeral director, protecting Jessie from curious journalists. She came into her own.

12

Then on week two, the nothingness stopped, to be replaced by a series of small explosions. Explosion one - the police had carried out their routine checks and found that Michael had made a large withdrawal of cash a few days before his death, and had virtually no money in his account. Explosion two - he was suspected of bribing council officers.

And so it went on. He had recently taken out a much larger mortgage on their house than she knew about. The news that the insurance company wouldn't pay out if the cause of death were confirmed as suicide.

There was a shame attached to those left behind after a suicide. A guilt. And, she now knew, an anger that he could have done this to her, left her with nothing – not just the money, the house, but her dignity, her memories, her security, her feeling of being loved – all gone. Just like that. And without saying goodbye.

CHAPTER 1

THE COLLEGE

1982

'How was she then?'

'Er – sorry?' Anya was thrown for a moment.

'Lucy's first day today, wasn't it? How was she?'

The low brick building with its multi-coloured windows came back into focus. She was standing on the small square of concrete separating the two blocks of the school.

'Oh sorry – of course. Miles away!' She brushed her hair out of her eyes. 'Yes, she was fine – she's been looking forward to joining her sisters for a long time. How about your little one?'

'Well he's a big boy now – in Class two already' said Veronica proudly, as
the row of mums stepped back in a well-rehearsed move, almost knocked off their feet by the sudden stream of children pouring from the door marked *Infants*.

'Mum!' shouted Anya's youngest. 'Mum! I made a picture for you! And I did a wee on the tiny toilet like you said!' and she hurled herself at Anya's knees, to be engulfed by a laughing hug. Francesca ran to her, close behind, confirming that her little sister had been fine.

Then the mothers turned, as one, to face the *Juniors* door on the opposite side of the square, and settled to wait ten more minutes for their older offspring. Emily,

14

at eight, had insisted she didn't need to be met, but endured the embarrassment for the sake of her sisters.

'So' continued Veronica, 'You finished that course you were on?'

'I have indeed!' replied Anya. 'A fully fledged teacher now – better late than never! But no jobs around at the moment, and now the school year's started, there's not much likelihood of anything coming up, for a while at least.'

She cringed inwardly at the memory of the only job interview she had managed to secure so far. In desperation, she had applied for a post in a secondary school even though she was trained as a primary teacher, and was amazed and thrilled to be short-listed. After all, this was not the best time to look for teaching posts. But it all went downhill from there. She found she wasn't at all prepared for the experience. The full day, the expanse of school governors she was confronted with, the list of three questions she was handed with such a short time to digest them, and the awful, embarrassing experience of drying up a few minutes into the allotted time, having to sit there in silence as the clock ticked. It had almost convinced her to call it a day for a teaching career, and look for a nice safe office job. Almost.

'That's a shame. It's taken you – what – three years?'

'Yes.' said Anya. 'Three years'.

Three years. Not the easiest of times, but she'd stuck at it. Now she wasn't sure it had been worth the hassle.

'Well I don't know if it's any help,' Veronica was saying, 'but my neighbour was telling me that they're looking for someone to teach biology in the college she works at. Biology's your subject, isn't it?'

'Yes it is' said Anya, surprised. 'But what college is that?'

'Haven't a clue, sorry' said Veronica. 'In the backwoods somewhere, I think. Not local. I'll ask Elaine to give you a ring, shall I?'

'Anya? Hi. It's Elaine Walters. Veronica gave me your number. Is now a good time?'

Clutching the phone and glancing from the hallway back into the kitchen, she saw that the dinner was simmering contentedly on the stove; David was sitting in the lounge opposite her, can in hand, and she could hear the girls laughing upstairs.

'Oh, hello Elaine – thanks for calling me. Yes, now is fine'

'Veronica tells me you may be available for some teaching.'

'Well yes, I am – but I'm primary trained – and I don't know anything about college teaching.'

'FE. Further Education. "Second chance" college. Don't worry, I can fill you in. We all can. We're a friendly bunch.'

'I don't know …'

'The science woman has left. After seven years, she suddenly decides to pack it in at the start of term. So the Head of Department is pretty desperate. Call in tomorrow – I'll set it up'

16

'Science? Oh, I…'

'Don't worry. Glyn will tell you all about it.'

'It all seems a bit informal Elaine!'

'Yes, that's FE for you! This would be part time, hourly paid. No holiday pay, no pay if you don't turn up. Full time? Permanent? Well that's another story. But it's a start isn't it? Anyway, call in about ten if you can. And remember – whatever he asks you, say you can do it. You'll be fine.'

Giving hurried directions to the college, Elaine signed off with 'You can't miss it!'

Anya stared at the phone. Did that just happen? She glanced into the lounge. David hadn't moved. He stared at the TV. He hadn't had his dinner yet.

'I think I've got an interview' Anya said to the room. 'For a teaching job. At a college.'

'That's good.' He didn't look up.

The spaghetti was bubbling and the sauce starting to spatter over the cooker as she went back into the kitchen.

'Girls! Tea's ready!' she shouted, and hungry footsteps came running down the stairs. The three little girls didn't need telling twice. They sat at the big wooden table in the cluttered kitchen, and chatted, and laughed, and ate gratefully.

'I'm just taking your dad's dinner in' she said automatically as she lifted the tray.

'Mum, why is Dad's called Dinner and ours is Tea?'

Anya laughed. 'Good question Lucy! I'll think of an answer in a while!'

'It's because he's an adult and we're not' answered Fran knowledgeably. At six she knew these things.

'And why is Dad allowed to have his tea – I mean dinner - in the lounge and we're not?' Lucy continued.

'Well, Dad's a bit sad you see, Luce' explained Emily. 'He used to have a job and now he doesn't. So he stays in the lounge.'

'And he's a bit grumpy' added Fran helpfully.

Anya carried the tray into the lounge, where David balanced it on his lap without looking up from the TV news.

'Ta.'

As she was leaving the room he suddenly asked 'A college? What college?

'Um … I'm not really sure. It's FE apparently'. She felt wrong-footed at his uncharacteristic show of interest. She should have asked Elaine more questions.

'It's up the Nantllai valley.'

She turned to leave the room, then,

'Nanty Tech you mean?'

'What?'

'Nanty Tech. That's probably not the proper name, but lots of the boys went there. Did motor mechanics, engineering, that sort of thing.'

'Engineering?' She was confused now. 'No, I don't think so. They want a science teacher.'

David returned to his dinner and his lager and the news.

Anya wasn't sure if she'd remember Elaine's directions, so she left early the next morning, straight after dropping the girls off. Lucy was an old hand at this school business now, having spent a whole day there. Emily and Fran assured their mum they would keep an eye on her. She drove the battered Vauxhall Viva towards the west, along the coast road as far as she could, before turning inland, and made her way to the little town of Pontarafon. She reached the square with its impressive-looking community centre which dwarfed the shops, post office and single estate agent's surrounding it, and headed up the road ahead of her. Was there really a college up here? She'd lived in the seaside town of Port Haven all her life, and had never heard of such a place. There again, she rarely – if ever – ventured this far west, and then only to head towards the Mumbles or one of the bays along the Gower coast. And now she wondered why. After half a mile, after passing the ugly square building of the sewing factory, and the parallel rows of shops selling saddles, ropes and tractor equipment, the view was transformed. The mountains on her right reared up, dotted here and there with a few houses and outbuildings. Lanes and tracks snaked across the landscape, hardly making any impression on the patchwork of grasses and hedges. To her left, the drop to the valley below became steeper and deeper with every mile. The river blinked between dense patches of trees, and the mountains beyond climbed high above. This was spectacular, she thought. But a college? Here?

After half an hour, she passed a colliery on her left. Of course! The colliery! She knew about this. It was one of those on the news these days, threatened with closure. She'd heard that this was a big deal, although it didn't affect her. Apparently large numbers of people in the area relied on the mine for work, and just as many relied on the miners' business. She could see the great wheel turning slowly as she drove past, men walking through the gates, heads down, silent, preparing for their descent into the Welsh mountain. She drove on till she came to a fork in the road. A small black and white sign told her that "Dref y Nant College of Further Education" was to her left.

She didn't have to drive far. The college was brick-built, and seemed to be set at an angle, so that the entrance was in one of the corners of the squarish building. It was low at the front, with a two-storey tier rising up at the rear, the whole thing neatly surrounded by a wide driveway, a grass verge, and high railings. The gates stood open and she drove in, parking in a signed and conveniently-placed visitors' area. She walked up two shallow steps and through double doors and was met by a smiling receptionist.

'I'm here to see Mrs Walters' she said. 'I'm Anya Gethin'.

She listened to a brief phone call, and having been assured that Mrs Walters was on her way, she sat in the small waiting area. True enough, Elaine wasn't long. She swept down the staircase, blonde, slim, elegant in a fitted dress and flowing scarf. Anya thought of how she must look. Her untamed bouncing red curls, the green suit she'd bought for her first teaching practice and worn for all the following ones, the handbag she'd borrowed from her mother last night. No padded shoulders and power dressing for her. For some reason she thought of Veronica – neat and tidy Veronica, with her hair in that tight little bun, her sensible shoes and her serviceable cardi. She felt better.

Elaine welcomed her and marched her briskly up some stairs, along a corridor and into a large, airy room full of comfortable chairs.

'Staffroom' she announced unnecessarily.

Large windows on either side of the room gave a pleasant airy feel. In one corner was a small kitchen area, comprising a counter covered in assorted cups and mugs, and an old water geyser on the wall. A few people were sitting in a huddle in another corner, seemingly engrossed in something on the coffee table in front of them.

'Don't worry about them' Elaine said. 'They're the bridge fanatics. They try to get here early for break.' She glanced at her watch. 'Hmm. A bit too early I think!' and she walked over to the back of the room where she made two cups of coffee in record time, and brought them to where she had left Anya.

'OK – why don't you sit? – this is the deal. Glyn John – head of department - is desperate for a science teacher. It's not rocket science – excuse the pun – so just say yes to whatever he asks you. Now …'

Anya interrupted. 'About that - did you say science? My subject's biology, not the other sciences. I don't think …'

'Don't worry, it's all pretty basic stuff I think. I teach sociology so I know nothing about that side of things. But there'll be plenty of books. Come on, drink up – I told Glyn we'd be there at ten.'

Anya gulped down as much as she could of the steaming coffee, stood up, and followed her. Another quick-march along corridors, up and down stairs, across an open area that gave onto another building, and they were outside a door marked *'Head of Caring and Personal Care'*. Elaine knocked quickly and walked in.

'Glyn, this is Anya I told you about. I'll leave you to it', and she was gone.

'Come in Anya. Take a seat. I'm afraid I don't know your surname – Elaine gave me the minimum amount of information about you.'

She sat in front of the huge wooden desk, and looked at the perfectly round glasses on the perfectly round head, the shiny black skull-cap of hair, the intelligent eyes and the smiling mouth.

'It's Gethin, Mr John. Anya Gethin.' Her breathlessness was more to do with racing along corridors than being nervous – she hadn't had time for that.

It was the strangest interview she could imagine. Glyn John told her about the course – which turned out to be hairdressing – and the need for the students to have a sound understanding of chemistry and a little physics, as well as human biology. He told her that all the students would be girls, that the rest of the staff would be helpful, and that she would have a parking space. He chatted about the history of the area and of the college, established to educate the young boys starting work in the mine. Anya could see that he must be, or have been, an inspiring teacher. She was taken aback when he suddenly said,

'So does that sound ok to you? Happy with all of that?'

'Umm ...'

'Just a couple of questions ...'

This was the bit she was dreading. Experience? None. Subject knowledge? Biology, yes. But chemistry? Physics? The prospect of having to speak on any of these threw her, although she should have been prepared. She felt panic beginning to rise. But the question, when it came, was more personal.

'So, Anya – tell me a little about yourself. What would you say are your strengths?'

Strengths. Anya composed herself. This should be easier that chemistry or physics questions. Strengths. She should say "I'm a team player". But where was the evidence for that? She'd just spent three years studying on her own, not letting herself be part of any group, rushing home after lectures each day to children, cooking, housework, husband. No, no team playing there. The thoughts went through her head in a flash, and flew out just as quickly.

'Umm - I'm enthusiastic. And I'm well organised. I'm punctual....'

'Lovely, lovely. Let's see – today's Tuesday - could you start tomorrow?'

'Mr John ...'

'Glyn, please!" he said, smiling.

'I haven't done my probationary year yet' she blurted out before he could go any further.

'Probationary year? Oh, we have none of that. Not in FE. Now, about tomorrow...?'

'Umm …'

'Maybe a bit too soon, eh? OK – how about Thursday?'

Anya found herself nodding. She wasn't sure what she was agreeing to, but it seemed rude not to. A knock on the door made her jump.

'Ah, Ethan, right on cue. Ethan Lowe, this is Anya. She'll be taking the hairdressing science – years one and two. I thought you'd be relieved!'

Looking back at Anya, he added, 'Ethan has been stepping in for us. On loan from Engineering.'

He stood.

'So Ethan, can I leave Anya in your capable hands? To show her round and fill her in?'

Anya turned and saw a tall, slender young man wearing a khaki overall, his fair hair falling over his eyes.

'My pleasure Glyn. Come with me Anya, and I'll give you the grand tour!'

The "grand tour" was an extended- and considerably more leisurely - version of the route-march Elaine had taken her on, this time with commentary. He showed her the various departments, the laboratories, the workshops. She was sure she would never find her way around this place. He opened a door in the middle of the ground floor corridor, and they walked into a small classroom with high windows, bare walls, desks in rows, table at the front, and a large grey steel cupboard. Nothing else.

'Here we are. Survey your domain!'

Ethan had been so helpful and friendly that Anya at last felt able to ask some of the many questions that had been building in her head since leaving Glyn's office. She was already thinking of him as Glyn, and she recalled Elaine's words "They're a friendly bunch". But her first question was about the dismal little room they were standing in.

'It's very – bare' she said timidly, not wishing to criticize this world of which she knew nothing.

'Bare? It's appalling!' he said. 'How on earth can you inspire youngsters in a room like this? They don't want to be here anyway. They want to be in the salons - I'll show you those in a minute. They didn't expect to be learning science, and doing exams. They aren't exam material, Anya. Well, most of them. They want to get away from all that. So – you'll have your work cut out just to get them to turn up, never mind engaging with you. Sorry – not putting you off am I?' He grinned.

'I must come clean' he went on. 'I haven't made any effort here. I've been covering the science– mainly doing the physics and hoping like hell that someone would come along and rescue me before I had to learn the rest. So you are a very welcome sight! Term only started last week and I've been treading water. So it's up to you – do what you will! That cupboard is full of bottles and packets of chemicals I've never come across before. Use them or don't use them – up to you.'

She turned to face him and took a breath, knowing that the admission she was about to make could mean the end of her career in further education before it started..

'I don't think I can do this Ethan. I haven't done any chemistry or physics since my school days. I'm not trained to teach sixteen and seventeen year olds – I'm a primary school teacher. I don't know what they need to know, and I'm sure I won't know it anyway, and I don't know what exams they'll be doing ...'

'Oh bless you love, I'm sorry. I'll be giving you the syllabus. And I'll give you a textbook – it'll be your bible. It's written especially for the course. The students won't have a copy, so you can impress them with your knowledge! And I'll give you your timetable. You'll be doing sixteen hours a week I think. Thursday is quite a light day. You'll be fine. Come on!'

And she followed him out into the corridor, somewhat reassured but still decidedly anxious. He took her to the practical areas, fully equipped as working salons, and introduced her to the staff teaching the hands-on elements of the course.

'Come down one Wednesday afternoon love, I'll sort that hair out for you!' offered one, not unkindly, as she ran her fingers through her own purple spiky hair.

Anya had her first sight of some of the students she would be teaching. They looked so big. Tall. Grown up. Made up and coiffured, more like Bonnie Tyler than her idea of students, they looked so much more stylish than she felt. Anya remembered the informal advice they had received on her teaching course: "the class will listen to you because you're standing at the front and you're so much bigger than they are." Well that just went out of the window, along with everything she had learned about teaching, it seemed.

They walked through the rest of the small college, noting the canteen, the office, and the staff workrooms. Ethan introduced her to staff as they went, she forgetting

26

names and subjects along the way, but everyone seemed pleasant and approachable. They ended up back at the main entrance, taking a detour for him to pick up the paperwork and book he had promised her.

'Well, welcome aboard Anya. I need to go now – I have the mining apprentices next, workshop theory. Always a joy! Any questions or worries, you'll find me in room A12. See you Thursday. You're a lecturer now. Good luck!' and he too was gone.

She drove home in a daze, listening to *Come on Eileen* and *Goody Two Shoes* on the radio. What had she done? Surely this was insane. A lecturer? Was he serious? Teaching grown women subjects she knew nothing about, for a career she knew nothing about, in a sector she knew nothing about? And starting on Thursday! She was scared. And excited. She had a job!

They certainly needed the money. She thought of the bills she had hidden under the sofa cushions, retrieved from the postman before he reached the front door, as she not-so-innocently hovered by the gate each morning to waylay him. It solved nothing, she knew, but coward as she was, it at least delayed another row, another outburst. It's not as if he doesn't know we're broke, she thought. How could we be otherwise? The odd day's labouring didn't bring in enough to cover the bills, never mind clothes and shoes for the girls. She had made all their dresses and skirts, and even coats, but vests, knickers and socks had to be bought. And the mortgage – she went cold at the thought of losing the house she loved so much. But logic seemed to have left David since he'd been made redundant.

It was four years now. Her eventual decision to train as a teacher had started one of their biggest rows yet. Three years to train? Ridiculous, he'd said. She needed to take any job she could, get some money coming in, he'd said. But she'd stuck to her guns, though trembling inside. She'd tried. Over and over, she'd tried to find a job, but slowly she'd realised she must look at other options. Then - they needed to take a long-term view, she'd said. With hours that would fit around the school holidays for the girls, and with decent pay. Jobs were scarce anyway, and she had no office or retail experience. She could do this. But it wasn't until she told him about the grant and the travel expenses she'd receive that he'd calmed down. She'd promised him – with fingers crossed behind her back - that nothing at home would change. Nothing would change for him, at least. And with help from her mother, she had done it. She had been exhausted. Just the planning involved in running the home, ensuring the children were cared for, and the travelling to and from the college, often by bus, nearly wore her out. She was sometimes in tears after putting the girls to bed and starting to write essays and lesson plans, but she had done it. And now she had a job.

As she turned into her road, she realized she hadn't asked how much she would be earning, or when she would be paid. How stupid! She knew that David would expect her to know that vital piece of information, that he would start shouting, advancing on her as he did in that intimidating way. She took a deep breath and put her key in the door.

CHAPTER 2

WEDDINGS

1973

'Annie-May, quick! She's throwing her flowers!'

'Don't call me that, Esther! I'm an adult now!' but Anya laughed as she ran with her friend, and several others, to reach the bride as the bouquet flew over her shoulder. 'Oops! Never could catch!'

The wedding of their friend and schoolmate had been hurriedly arranged to accommodate the imminent arrival of the next generation. As they kissed her and congratulated the new bemused-looking husband, Anya was half envious of the excitement and celebrations, while thankful that she didn't have the responsibilities the couple had to look forward to. But the event had meant a new outfit, even a hat, and she was determined to make the most of the day. Wedding breakfast over and the happy couple on their way, the two girls made their way back inside the lounge bar.

'Lucky bitch, she's missing a whole three weeks of school' grumbled Esther 'And she didn't sit the last two exams either!'

'Somehow I don't think that was the main reason she got married' said Anya, and they giggled.

'Does this mean we're on the shelf now, Annie?' asked Esther, tottering on too-high platform shoes. 'After all, she's younger than us.'

'Only just, dafty! She'll be eighteen too, in a couple of weeks' said Anya as they sat at the bar. 'And of course we're not on the shelf! I'm not thinking of settling down, far from it. I've got plans – exciting plans. College first, then travelling. After all, we're in the Common Market now – whatever that means. Though I wouldn't mind meeting someone for the summer, just for some fun before the term starts.'

'They say weddings are good places to meet people – boys that is.' Esther grinned and looked around.

'I just wish I wasn't so, you know, medium.'

Esther laughed out loud.

'Medium? Medium? What is that, for God's sake?'

Anya laughed too.

'You know, medium height, medium build, medium brain …' she tailed off.

'That's just stupid, Annie.'

'Easy for you to say. Clever. Tall and blonde – "leggy" as my mother describes you.'

'Well that's very nice of your mum. But there's nothing medium about you. You're a gorgeous red-head with a curvy figure, and you're going to make a wonderful teacher – when you eventually come back from your travels. Now' Esther said as she turned in her seat, 'stop fishing for compliments, and put these poor boys out of their misery!'

'Come and join us, girls.'

The group of half a dozen young men sat around a corner table, presumably all friends of the groom. They wore suits with flared trousers, their shoes were shined and so were their faces – scrubbed and starting to show signs of the free bar. A couple of them shifted up and patted the banquette seat between them. Anya and Esther looked at each other, shrugged, and stepped daintily across to the vacant spaces. Anya took off the large felt hat she had accessorized with a pink artificial rose. She laid it tenderly on the shelf behind them, shaking out her long red curls to a background of *Tie a Yellow Ribbon*, and sat, smoothing the skirt of her floor-length flowery dress self-consciously.

'Drink, girls?'

Having run through everyone's name, one of them, older than the rest, stood up. 'Anyone else empty?'

As he went to the bar, Anya heard one of them say 'Fair play to Dai Gethin, he's always first to get a round in.'

They spent a pleasant couple of hours chatting, laughing, flirting. While Esther seemed to divide her attentions between the group, clearly enjoying the banter, Anya was aware that it was David she was drawn to, and he to her. He didn't seem to be the sort of boy she usually went for. He was older, and seemed quieter. And not a boy at all. This one was a man, and that seemed quite exciting. He was tall and blond, with broad shoulders and the slim hips she had always been attracted to. His suit was beautifully cut, his shirt sparkling white, although by the way he ran his finger around the inside of his collar, he didn't feel entirely comfortable wearing it, and soon dispensed with his tie and his top button. So when, at the end of the afternoon when most guests were getting ready to leave, he asked her to stay, she was quite pleased.

'There's an evening do later, you know' he said. 'Fancy hanging on? We could have a bite to eat – they do a decent curry here.'

Anya glanced at Esther, who gave her the thumbs-up.

'See you later, Annie-May!' she said, winking, as she left with a crowd of boys.

School was over at last. Forever. Exams sat, results awaited, college course confirmed and books bought. Her A levels would be nice to have, but they weren't essential.

It was supposed to be a summer romance, nothing serious, nothing long-lasting, no commitments. But David was a bit intense, and Anya was rather taken with his solicitude, his attention, his generosity. He was ten years older than she was, divorced, no children, working in the local steel works, and hoping for a promotion very soon. This she gathered on their first date, when he had offered to take her anywhere she wanted, to buy her any meal she wanted, any drink. He had a car, which was a plus, and he had picked her up from her house.

'He looks a bit old for you, Annie' said her mother as she waited on the doorstep for her daughter to leave.

Anya laughed.

'Maybe he's nervous. Perhaps it's you, Mum – maybe it wasn't a good idea to run out to the car and shake his hand through the window!'

'Cheek!' said her mother, but she smiled. 'Make sure he treats you properly. And don't forget you're going to college in September – that's only a few weeks away.'

'I won't. And it's actually eight whole weeks away!' shouted Anya as she ran to the parked Consul, where David was sitting patiently.

As the weeks went by, David was the perfect gentleman - so much so that Anya began to think he didn't fancy her, particularly when he called her 'my dear'. It seemed such an old fashioned term to use, but she supposed it was endearing in its way. It was a late evening after a drive to the Mumbles and a meal of steak and chips with too many glasses of Martini Rosso, that they parked up at Blue Cove and David showed his passionate side at last. He told her he loved her, that he worshipped her, that he would do anything for her. And then things progressed very quickly.

Anya had occasionally had sex of a sort on the back seat of a car before, but this seemed different, not as uncomfortable and cramped as she remembered. David was gentle and patient, he said all the right things, making her feel safe and loved. He was more experienced than she was, and she was pleasantly surprised at his skilled lovemaking, but her pleasure was more to do with the idea that she was pleasing him than anything physical. She had yet to reach that elusive climax that some of her friends prized so highly, but it didn't bother her. In the drowsy glow afterwards, they listened to Donny Osmond singing *The Twelfth of Never* on the car radio, and talked in hushed voices. She allowed herself to be carried away by the moment, answering his despondent '...but you'd never marry someone like me' with an encouraging 'Of course I would!' And they were engaged. As easy as that.

In the cold light of day, Anya was in two minds about her rash promise. She was only eighteen, she had a three year college course in front of her – plenty of time to change her mind, to let him down gently. But a part of her was excited at the idea of having a fiancé, and of planning a wedding, no matter how far off. He was such a kind attentive man, she told herself. He loved her. He would make a good husband. Even the revelation that he couldn't have children had seemed manageable, doable, maybe something to worry about in the dim and distant future, but not now. When he picked her up the following evening, she half wondered whether he had taken last night seriously. It was clear that he had. He kissed her as she got into the car.

'So how's the future Mrs Gethin?'

She felt herself squirming inwardly. She wasn't ready for this. She needed more time to think about it. She didn't want to hurt his feelings, but she persuaded him that it wasn't a good idea to broadcast their engagement yet.

'That's ok, we don't have to rush' David said. 'We can take our time. We can plan. And while we're waiting, d'you fancy a holiday?'

'A what?'

'A holiday. Jersey. You'd love it. Loads of beaches, loads of things to see, but small enough to drive round in an afternoon.'

'Well – yes! That sounds wonderful!' Anya had never been on a proper holiday. Day trips and picnics were all her Mum had been able to afford when she was growing up.

'Good' he said, smiling, as they drove away. 'So – where to tonight, my dear?'

David was as good as his word. The flights from Rhoose airport were booked, and her Mum was assured that they would have separate rooms. Oh the innocence of parenthood, Anya thought, and would have felt guilty if she hadn't been so excited. She bought a plain gold-coloured ring from Woolworths for five shillings, and Mr and Mrs Gethin set off to the little island, where they registered in the Merton Hotel. The honeymoon hotel, David told her. They hired a sports car, and spent the week exploring the island, the beaches and the bars. They visited Gerald Durrell's zoo and the German underground hospital, ate delicious meals in fabulous restaurants, and slept in a huge bed in their luxury hotel. David was the perfect guide – he had been to Jersey many times, mainly on darts or snooker trips, and he enjoyed showing Anya the sights. He was chatty and playful, doing handstands on a deserted beach just to entertain her. She was delighted. And when he suggested buying an engagement ring on the island, she agreed enthusiastically.

OK, so she didn't feel that excitement she'd expected to feel when she met "the one". She didn't have butterflies in her stomach when they were due to meet, or get breathless at the thought of him. She didn't know why. He was good looking and treated her so well. But did anyone feel like that, really? Or was it all made up to sell books, magazines, films? He loved her, she had no doubt. He was protective and she felt safe with him. And maybe she did love him. She wanted to. He was a good man, and she cared for him. But love?

They chose a pretty diamond solitaire, although Anya was adamant that she wouldn't wear it till she'd told her mother. Technically, no need to ask her permission now – she was officially an adult, the law of a few years ago said so. But she wanted her mother's blessing all the same. She was as excited about going home to tell everyone about her new status as she had been about going on holiday for the first time. As they reached her gate, she jumped out, grabbing her bag.

'Call for me later, Ok? I need to talk to my Mum first.'

David smiled and nodded. She could see he was disappointed at being sent on his way like this, but he made no fuss. As he drove off, she thought *that's the man I'm going to spend my life with.* And she felt – excited? Scared? She ran into the house, shouting for her mother.

'All right, all right!' Jessie laughed, running down the stairs. 'You'd swear you'd been away for six months, not a week!' But she hugged her daughter tightly.

'Guess what Mum!' Anya said breathlessly. 'Guess what!' Deep breath. 'David and I are engaged!'

Silence. No squeal of delight. Then,

'Are you? Really?' Jessie looked at her daughter's smiling, shining, uncertain face and tried her best to look happy for her. 'Well that's all a bit sudden, love! When was this decided?'

Anya exploded into a non-stop list of all the wonderful things she could think of about David, about how kind he was, grown up, sensible, caring ...'

'And do you love him?' Jessie asked quietly.

The hesitation was tiny.

'Of course I do Mum! I wouldn't be marrying him if I didn't!' She rattled on. 'It'll be ages before we get married of course. I've got College, then I'll want to get a job, and he'll need to save up enough for a deposit on a house...'

Jessie smiled at last.

'I'm thrilled for you Annie' she said. 'Just don't rush. There's all the time in the world.'

But it turned out that there wasn't. When her period was late that month, Anya put it down to a change of routine, the excitement of the engagement and the prospect of starting her college course. She wasn't that regular anyway – was she? But two weeks late? Three? By the beginning of September she had missed her second period. And she knew. But how could she be? Hadn't he told her ...?

'David, you said you couldn't have children.' She was crying, sitting in the front seat of his Consul with him.

'I thought I couldn't, my dear.' His voice was tight. 'I was married to Marion for almost a year before she went off with that lifeguard. All that time, we didn't take any precautions, didn't use anything. She wanted babies straight away. But nothing. Not a sign. Then as soon as she started her affair, she was pregnant. So I assumed ...'

'You assumed? Is that it?' Anya's voice was broken, angry, scared. 'I thought you KNEW. When you said we didn't need to use anything, I thought you KNEW!' and she burst into a fresh bout of sobbing.

It didn't seem real. Oh, her mother's shock and disappointment, though well hidden, were real enough. But Jessie soon rallied. As Anya had known she would. They stood in their tiny council-house kitchen, and she held her daughter tightly, wiping away her tears.

'Come on now, there's nothing to cry about. This is wonderful news. A new life! This is something to celebrate!'

No college, Jessie thought. No teaching career. Tied down at eighteen to a man she barely knew.

Anya gave a huge sigh as her sobs subsided.

'Thank you Mum' she whispered.

'You don't have to marry him, you know' Jessie said gently. 'We'd manage. We always have.'

Jessie knew about managing. Widowed with a small child at twenty two, she had poured all her love and energy into raising that tiny scrap into the beautiful woman she held now. She had never remarried, never needed anyone else. And she had never regretted it. But she also knew what a struggle raising a child alone can be, both financially and emotionally. There had been times when she had felt scared, inadequate. When her precious daughter was sick, or naughty, or late home from school. But she'd managed. They had each other, and Jessie had revelled in seeing her daughter grow, make friends, do well at school. She was thrilled when Anya had been accepted at the teacher training college only twenty miles away; she knew that she may not see her from one term to the next, but she wasn't going to be one of those clingy

39

mothers, she wasn't going to guilt-trip her daughter into coming home every weekend. She rejoiced in Anya's future independence, knowing that she'd done her job, knowing she would miss her dreadfully, but proud, so proud of her.

And now …

Anya smiled and kissed her mother's cheek.

'Of course I want to marry him, Mum. Of course I do.'

David behaved impeccably. He called to see Jessie, looking nervous for all his years, and formally asked for Anya's hand in marriage. Jessie respected him for that, and of course gave them her blessing. Then everything happened in a blur. College course cancelled, a rushed autumn wedding planned – and all before Anya's pregnancy was confirmed. She went to the GP's surgery, and had to tell the receptionist sitting on the other side of the little hole in the wall, in the hearing of all the waiting patients, why she needed to see the doctor. Then a two-week wait. The result was positive of course, she really was pregnant, but it still didn't seem real. Even though she was becoming excited at the thought of getting married, setting up home with David, having a baby - it didn't seem real. She felt as if she were conning everyone, tricking them. Was this really happening? Could she really be pregnant? She felt a fraud.

The registry-office wedding and the reception at the small hotel was a modest affair, with a just handful of guests. David had paid for everything; he had also compiled the guest list, conspicuously leaving out his parents and his two older brothers. So just her mother, a few of his friends and one of hers – Esther had made the mid-week trip from London where she was studying Law, and Anya was thrilled to see her.

'You don't think I'd miss this, do you?' Esther said, hugging her friend tightly after the ceremony. 'I'm Matron of Honour, aren't I? Ok, so without the hideous long dress and bunch of flowers, but in my head I am!'

Anya laughed and felt some of her tension easing.

'So – what happened to this Summer Romance you talked about? Turned out to be the real thing, did it? You didn't hang about!'

Anya patted her stomach.

'No!' whispered Esther. 'You dirty dog!' She laughed. 'That's wonderful, Annie-May. And I expect to be Godmother, of course. To this one and to the whole of the brood you're bound to produce! And don't forget, if you should ever need a lawyer ...'

Too soon, they were off on their honeymoon. They would spend two nights in London before returning to their newly-acquired flat over a corner shop back in Port Haven. Anya found herself feeling surprisingly shy as they prepared for bed that night in the clean little B&B in Camden. There was no excitement, just an awkwardness that hadn't been there during their love-making in Jersey, or on the back seat of his car parked in a country layby or secluded car park.

She couldn't wait to go home. Not because she didn't enjoy the time they spent seeing the sights, eating in restaurants, or even rolling around self-consciously on the creaking bed. No. She simply wanted to start her new life – their new life, she corrected herself – as soon as possible. She wanted to put her stamp on their little flat, which she had yet to see. David had arranged it all, she hadn't needed to do a thing. And she wanted to start preparing for her baby. She felt a thrill each time she thought of this, even though it still didn't seem real. Her skirts were a little tight, but she had no visible bump to speak of. She had left the doctor's surgery with no information apart from a due date in April, and she had hardly discussed the pregnancy with her mother or her friends, so wrapped up had she been in wedding preparations. So when they left London after two days, Anya was alive with anticipation.

David didn't make any attempt to carry Anya over the thresh-hold as was the old-fashioned custom, and she was relieved, thinking of the embarrassment and indignity this would have caused, given the layout of their flat. The entrance to the building was off a small lane, and opened into a long hallway, lined with boxes of crisps and large packs of toilet rolls. David walked ahead of her up the stairs and turned right on the landing, which led straight ahead to a WC at the end, its door open. On their right in this short corridor was their own front door. David turned the key and opened it, and in they walked.

The little self-furnished flat consisted of three rooms. One corner of the small living room was curtained off as a kitchen, complete with cooker and sink. Through this area was a door leading to the bedroom, which was filled with a double bed. "Filled" was not an exaggeration – they would have to climb over the bed to reach the wardrobe on the other side of the room, the doors of which would have a struggle to open without bumping into the metal bedstead. A large curtainless window on the opposite wall let in plenty of light.

A door in another corner of the living room led directly to a tiny bathroom with no loo - they would have to share the one at the end of the corridor with those in the other flat across the landing. Anya had no idea how many people that might involve, but accepted it as a fact. The living room itself held a two-seater sofa, a fold-down Formica table, two wooden chairs and a small television. An ornate fireplace at one end hinted at the building's former, grander life, as did the two high sash windows.

Anya took it all in. She was not at all dismayed. She walked around her new home, examining everything, while David looked on.

'I can bring my candlewick bedspread from home. I'm sure Mum won't mind. It's only a single, but it will cover the bed, just about. She might have some curtains for the bedroom too.' She stopped by the sofa. 'And if she lends me her sewing machine, I'm sure I can make a new cover for this.'

And so married life began. Anya settled into her role of wife and expectant mother. It felt like playing house. Every week David gave her just enough for the rent, electricity and food. She knew that he was saving hard to buy a house for them, so she didn't ask where the rest of his pay went. She also knew that he was waiting to hear about the promotion he had applied for, working in a different part of the giant steelworks. He was already earning quite a lot more than many of his friends and it didn't occur to her to question the fact that, while the money he gave her was strictly rationed, he went out to meet them regularly – very regularly - in the Surf Rider bar.

But Anya started to worry about his lack of conversation, his many evenings away from home. He no longer chatted, or went out of his way to make her laugh. Where was the man who walked on his hands along the beach, who kept her in fits of giggles at his stories of his workmates? Was he regretting marrying her already? Had she disappointed him in some way? After a month, she summed up the courage to ask him, and his answer was meant to reassure her.

'No my dear, of course you don't disappoint me. And why would I regret marrying you?'

'It's just that – we don't talk, Davey. About anything. About the baby, or the flat, or about us. I've even learnt the rules of snooker, but when I try to talk to you about it when it's on the telly, you don't seem to want me to.'

She stopped, not sure if she had gone too far, offended him. But no. He smiled.

'We're not a courting couple now, my dear' he said. 'We're married, and we've settled down. And there's no need for you to bother your head about snooker – I can talk to the boys about things like that. So stop worrying!'

She kept herself busy with her sewing and her attempts at knitting. She bought skeins of cheap pearlised white wool from the town's famed Bon Marche Haberdashery Store, and made tiny cardigans and matinee coats. She didn't follow a pattern – her mother never had, and how hard could it be? Jessie tried to compose her face when she saw them, but didn't quite manage to hide her amusement.

'Have you ever seen a baby, Annie?' she asked.

'What? What do you mean?'

'Well love, these would be great for your Tiny Tears doll, but not for a real baby. I mean, there's tiny, and there's tiny ...'

Anya's efforts at sewing were a little better. With a housewarming gift of a few pounds from her mother, she made an acceptable cover for the sofa out of a remnant from Williams the Drapers, and her first maternity dress was a success, even though she had very little bump to conceal as yet. Christmas came, with lumpy gravy and a turkey with charred legs due to the fact that the giant bird David had bought was actually too big for their oven and had to be wedged tightly inside. But Anya was proud to be serving the food to her mother, who joined them for Christmas lunch, bringing a folding chair with her. No sign of David's parents of course – they had moved back to north Wales soon after he and Anya had got engaged. Devout Catholics, they had struggled to come to terms with their youngest son divorcing his wife, to whom he would always be married in their eyes, but marrying someone else was a step too far. Their absence wasn't mentioned, and everyone was relieved not to have their disapproval spoiling a happy day.

*   *   *

A new year. 1974. Now things were speeding up. Her bump was well in evidence, covered discretely with a selection of full, flared or gathered dresses. Her initial experience at her first ante-natal appointment at the general hospital in nearby Trefni Bridge was the source of embarrassment to her. No-one had told her that she should have worn a full-length petticoat. And surely the sergeant-major-like nurse could have allowed her a little more dignity than to send her into the examination room wearing only her bra. She would have felt more at ease if she'd been completely naked. But just a bra? The doctor showed a little more understanding. At least he handed her a flimsy garment that opened at the back.

'Put this gown on Mrs Gethin, and pop up onto the bed.'

The rest of the appointment may have been uneventful to doctors, nurses and midwives, but it was all new for Anya. She was weighed and measured, prodded and peered at, and eventually had a card which would record her weight and the height of the fundus – whatever that was – each time she attended the ante-natal clinic back in Port Haven. She was given a little information about classes, a leaflet about a maternity grant, and a large book w2s   apparently containing everything she needed to know, which she sat reading on the homeward-bound bus, absorbed but increasingly terrified. So much to know, so much to learn. She wasn't sure she was up to this.

As the months went on, she started gathering items the baby would need. She received £25 maternity grant and with this she was able to replace her little knitted samples with proper cardigans and matinee coats from Peacocks. She bought terry nappies, and her mum gave her a large galvanized tub in which to boil them atop the cooker. She had bottles and dummies, lotions and talcs, all put away carefully at the bottom of their over-sized wardrobe.

Then a day she'd been looking forward to – she went to buy a pram. Ideally, a pram the baby could use as a cot too, so it would have to be a small one, small enough to carry up the stairs to their flat. She had become friendly with some other young mums-to-be at the clinic, and she went along with a small group of them to Ashman's, the only shop in town which sold the larger baby goods. She saw such beautiful things there! Not only prams and pushchairs, but cots and carry-cots, highchairs and baby baths, all displayed to tempt them. But the prices were way too much. The cheapest, smallest pram was a lovely green one with a rounded hood. It had a removable body and a folding chassis, so could be used as a carrycot too. But £30? Even if she'd used all her grant she couldn't have afforded it, and she only had £12 of it left. As she saw her friends pointing out the prams they had chosen, had paid monthly for, she deeply regretted not doing the same. But how could she have done that? There was nothing left over each week after buying food and household stuff. She began to feel panicked. She did what she had always done – she ran to her mother.

'I've only got 4 weeks to go, Mum. What am I going to do?'

A cup of tea and a piece of toast later, sitting in Jessie's tiny kitchen, Anya was calmer.

'Have you asked David? I'm sure he must have some savings put away. After all, it's his baby too' Jessie said.

'He's saving for a house, Mum. And he already thinks I shouldn't be spending so much on food ...'

'What?' said Jessie, suddenly angry. 'I've seen your food cupboard, Anya. It's not exactly stocked with luxuries! I think I need to have a word with him!'

'Oh Mum, please don't!' Anya's returning panic was clear to see. 'I do buy too much stuff. Tomato sauce, crab paste. We don't really need those ...'

Jessie sighed, torn between telling her daughter what she thought, and not wanting to upset her further.

'Ok, ok, I won't say a word' she said. 'But promise me – you will talk to him about a pram.'

That evening, after dinner, Anya did just that. As they sat at the table, David listened to her stumbling description of the cost of prams, her promises to cut down on the weekly food bill, her anxiety about the imminent arrival of her baby – their baby – with nowhere for it to sleep, to walk out with. Then she waited.

'No need to get into such a state my dear' he said kindly, kissing the top of her head as he got up and walked around her, opening the door to the landing. 'The baby shall have a pram, of course. But perhaps not a brand new one.' And out he went.

So it was that the next day found Anya and Jessie browsing the small-ads written on postcards pinned to the inside of the book-shop window.

'Here's one Annie – *Carrycot, bath and stand, like new, £3.*'

One call from the nearest phone-box later and they had reserved the lot, promising that David would collect them the following weekend. They walked back to the ads for a final look.

'What about this Mum? I'm sure this one wasn't here earlier. *Silver Cross Coach-built pram, £8.* What do you think?'

'Silver Cross? That's the Crème de la Crème! And it's just around the corner - certainly worth a look!'

It was. A huge cream carriage with leather suspension straps, a black hood and apron, over-sized wheels, and a bird-of-paradise on either side. Big enough to act as a pram, a cot and a play-pen. Too old-fashioned for most, but Anya fell in love with it. She paid for it there and then, and they proudly wheeled it back to the flat, happier than she'd been for a long time. Ok, so it was far too big to get up the stairs, but there was room to keep it in the downstairs hall alongside the boxes. And the carrycot they had reserved would give the baby somewhere to sleep for a while, at least.

The icing on her cake came a week later. Their landlord – the owner of the shop below – asked if they would like to move into the larger flat across the landing, as the tenants there were moving out. It was £2 a week more, but Anya didn't have to persuade David that their current rooms weren't going to be big enough for the family they were about to become – he could see that for himself, and though the rent would be more, it was still very reasonable.

The move to their new flat, just a matter of feet away, took no time at all. A morning with her mother, while David was at work, and it was done. Their new home overlooked the main road into the town; it used the same entrance from the lane at the side of the building as their previous accommodation, turning left instead of right at the top of the stairs. Anya and Jessie closed the door behind them, and walked to the end of a long hallway to find a big living room with bay windows on two sides, a drawer-leaf table, and both a regular sofa and a large bed settee. A door further back off the hallway gave onto the bedroom with room for a cot as well at the double bed, wardrobe and chests of drawers that were already there, and then there was the kitchen. It, too, was large, and housed a bath – an unusual arrangement Anya thought, but liveable with. They would still share the toilet at the end of the corridor. Old-fashioned and tired though the decoration and the furniture was, this flat seemed like luxury indeed.

And just in time. In early April, two weeks earlier than she was due, Anya went into labour. David drove her to the hospital in Trefni Bridge, and after a surprisingly short time, she lay looking at the little person in the perspex cot opposite her in the delivery room. The midwives had left, and she was alone with her daughter for the first time.

'Hello' she whispered. 'Hello sweetheart. Aren't you beautiful?'

Two big blue eyes looked back at her, trusting, curious. White-blonde hair clung to her perfect little head, still sticky from the birth. And she knew her life had changed forever.

CHAPTER 3

A CHRISTMAS SURPRISE

1982

Thursday. 10am. Anya was out of her depth and she knew it.

'We'll come back to that. Just copy down the list for now, please' she was saying.

The piece of advice to "start tough and ease up later" had come back to her, and was one that she was trying to apply now in her first lesson. Or lecture. That's what she had to learn to call it. Well, she was being tough. Wasn't giving an inch. Wasn't even smiling. She couldn't if she tried.

Walking around the room between the single-seater desks, watching the fourteen young women dutifully copying down the chemical symbols from the blackboard, her footsteps sounded like a teacher's. And there, she thought, was where the resemblance ended. She had read the syllabus, studied the text book, followed the advice from Ethan to start with a new topic, and planned her lesson down to the last minute. She had talked, and written on the board, and dictated some notes, but questions? She wasn't prepared for those! She could hazard a guess, but a guess wasn't good enough. She'd be caught out, she was certain – caught out by the eighteen-year-old girls of class 2X, made a laughing stock, unable to stand in front of a class ever again. So she kicked their questions into touch. For now.

She surreptitiously glanced at her watch. Ten minutes! Still ten minutes left! And all explanations given, all notes dictated, nothing else planned. The knock at the classroom door was more welcome than she could have imagined. Ethan's head popped into view.

'Excuse me Mrs Gethin, could I have a word please?'

A relieved Anya made her way out of the classroom, and let out a sigh.

'That was good timing! What can I do for you?'

Ethan laughed.

'You don't think it was a coincidence do you? I came to rescue you! I've been in your shoes. But actually I do have a message– the principal wants to meet you. Before break. In his room. But here's a tip – don't let him close the door!'

Anya didn't have time to ask what he meant before a stream of girls came tottering on their high heels out of the classroom.

'Can we go now Miss?' asked a tall student whose name Anya, to her shame, couldn't remember.

'It's nearly eleven, and we might be able to get to the front of the canteen queue …'

Anya glanced at Ethan – for approval? He shrugged and smiled.

'Yes, alright. Just this once' she said. And her first lesson was over.

Hugo Larsson rose from behind his desk as she entered his office in answer to his *'Come in!'* He was a big man, tall, broad and rather shapeless, Anya thought. His face was big too, surrounded by course-looking greying hair. But his smile seemed genuine enough, and as he held out his hand to her, Anya smiled back.

'Welcome to Dref y Nant College, Anya. Or Nanty Tech as it's affectionately known. Are you finding your way around? Being looked after?' He was holding her hand for rather longer than was necessary.

She assured him that everyone was being very helpful. She was pleased to see that this wasn't any sort of interview, more an informal chat, and a short one at that. Having excused herself, Anya doubled back down the first floor corridor to find the ladies' toilet. As she retraced her steps to reach the staff room, Hugo was standing outside his office door with another man. This one looked more interesting, Anya thought. Not as tall as Hugo, and slightly built, he stood resting against the door frame, hands in his trouser pockets, one foot crossed over the other. Completely at ease. Her brief glance took in his curling dark hair that reached almost to his shoulders, his brown eyes appraising her as she walked past. She gave a small smile, ostensibly to the principal, and to her annoyance, she felt her colour rising.

'Now there's a breath of fresh air' she heard him say under his breath as she reached and opened the staffroom door.

She took a deep breath. The room was full. Full of strangers. This time it was Elaine who came to her aid, beckoning from amid a sea of faces.

'Over here, Anya.'

53

Two rows of comfortable chairs, facing each other and separated by a series of low coffee tables, ran the length of one side of the room from the door to the kitchen area, and Elaine was indicating a seat halfway along.

'Let me introduce you to everyone. Don't worry – you'll forget all our names at first!'

She wasn't wrong. Anya hurriedly tried to make mental notes so she would at least remember some.

'We all teach the nurses' said Elaine. 'Well, I say "nurses". They want to be nurses, but don't have the exams they need, so that's where we come in. I teach Sociology. You won't find anyone else up here who teaches the hairdressers, other than you – they tend to stay in the salons. But I'd recommend having coffee here, with us – we're much more sociable!' The other women laughed and nodded in agreement.

'Up there' Elaine continued, pointing to the group of men sitting further along the row of seats, 'are some of the engineers. Ethan I think you know.' The men nodded or smiled in turn as Elaine named them.

'Then on the end there's Paul Falder – VP. Vice principal' she elaborated as Anya looked blankly at her. 'He's also head of the Engineering department.'

Anya took in as much about the group as she could without staring. Ethan, his brown overall contrasting with his peers' jackets and ties, gave a little wave. The group of bridge-players sat, engrossed, on the opposite side of the room, as if they hadn't moved in two days.

'Ah, and here comes lover boy. I mean Byron. Byron Jones. Engineering. He's a bit of a ladies' man, but lovely with it.'

And in walked the man from the corridor.

'Have I missed the introductions Elaine?' He smiled at Anya. 'Hi, I'm Byron. And don't believe a word they say about me!'

'Anya. Anya Gethin' she said.

'Anya's teaching science to the Hairdressers' Elaine told him.

'Oh dear! Well good luck with that!' He must have seen her expression. 'I'm joking, of course. They aren't a bad bunch. I'm sure you'll be fine' And he smiled again as he went to sit with his fellow engineers.

Left to herself when the buzzer went, Anya checked her timetable for the umpteenth time that morning. No, no more classes till after lunch. She sat back and drank the coffee that Elaine had put in front of her, and read through her lesson plan for her only afternoon's lesson. Class 2Y. So the same lesson as this morning's, to a different group of students, but she would be better prepared this time. She crossed out sentences and added scribbles, arrows and asterisks. And it was twelve fifteen. Lunch time. Another hurdle to jump over. Another opportunity to pretend she was something she wasn't. Why hadn't she brought sandwiches?

The canteen was teeming, the noise deafening. A long queue of students snaked along the side of a counter, where ladies wearing white overalls and tiny trilbies were dishing out food. The row of students ended at a till that seemed a very long way away. She joined the back of the line, only to be pulled gently to one side by Ethan.

'I suppose no-one told you about signing up for lunch, did they? Staff can do that at break time, saves us queuing with the rabble.' He laughed at her expression. 'I don't mean it. I love them all really. It's just that we'd never get back for afternoon lectures if we all had to queue. Don't worry about not signing up – the ladies will forgive you this once. Follow me.'

And he steered her to the till, passing the waiting youngsters. Faggots and peas bought, he led her to a long table at the back of the room, already almost full.

'Staff table' he said. 'One of the few perks of the job.'

'Don't forget the toilets, Ethan!' said one called Dan. 'We don't have to share those with the students – yet!'

Everyone laughed, and carried on with their lunches. The staff she had met smiled, nodded or said 'Hi', while those she hadn't introduced themselves. She was aware that she was the only woman at the table.

'Most of the women bring their lunch in little plastic boxes' said Ethan, seeing her look. 'They take them to the staff room, or their classrooms, for some reason.'

'Good riddance I say.'

It was Byron Jones.

'They all voted for Thatcher, I bet. All comfy in their expensive houses with their wealthy husbands ...'

'Come on Byron, you don't know that. He gets like this' Dan said to Anya, not lowering his voice at all.

'He's obsessed with Arthur Scargill – sees a conspiracy at every turn!' The rest of the table laughed; Byron was clearly used to this reaction, and seemed not at all fazed by it.

'I'm right. You'll see. That woman's castrated most of the other unions. It'll be the miners next. They're the only ones left with balls. Excuse the language Anya' he suddenly turned a beatific smile on her 'but we're all engineers. If you're going to be eating lunch with us, we'll make you an honorary one if you like, but you'll have to cuss and swear like the rest of us!'

Before she could respond, he returned to his theme.

'And she'll get in again of course. After her little stint as Britannia-cum-Boadicea in the Falklands. God, it makes me sick.' He continued eating his meal.

Anya was confused. The TV was one thing, but she wasn't used to hearing such open political comments, not up close, not over lunch. She felt a little uncomfortable. And yet … his passion seemed genuine. And not a bit like her first impression of him, which had been that of a rogue, a sweet-talker. So she stayed, she listened, the table emptied of diners one by one, and still she stayed. He talked, asked her questions about her politics she couldn't answer, told her stuff, made her think of things she'd never considered before. And she stayed each lunch time, listened to him, asked him questions, began to understand his anger and his frustration.

So the term passed, quickly. Anya's lessons improved and she found she quite enjoyed talking to the girls in her classes. She found her way around the college and got to know the staff. And she even took up the offer from the hairdressing staff one Wednesday, emerging self-consciously from the salon with a glossy bob instead of her wavy locks, defying the current big-hair fashion.

Her shining hairdo didn't last long, the bob reverting to her usual bouncing curls as soon as the air turned damp, but work was becoming a good place to be, and some staff becoming friends. Things at home were falling into place too, thanks to her mother and her three lovely, happy, obliging daughters. They fitted into their new routine easily, proud of their mother and happy with their grandma. Anya may not have as much time to make them new clothes, but was able to buy some instead, and they were thrilled.

Not so with David. He was as surly as ever, worse if anything. Instead of appreciating the money coming into the house, it was clear to Anya that he resented her and her new career. She soon gave up telling him about her job or the people she worked with. She didn't need to hear him say *it's a man's place to provide for his family*, she saw it in his eyes, heard it under his outbursts. She gave him the bulk of her pay to manage, so he would continue to be the one paying the bills and making the mortgage payments each month, an attempt to boost his ego, a sop to his masculinity. Whatever it took for a quiet life.

Last day of term. Any students present were those loath to leave their friends for any more than the absolute minimum, and certainly no-one was expecting to be taught. The staff were in festive mood, with two bowls of Sangria and several plates of sandwiches laid out in the domestic science room to help the workers as Christmas decorations were taken down from the staff room.

'Nothing worse than coming back in January to find tatty trimmings still up' Ethan told her cheerfully as he balanced precariously at the top of a step-ladder, determined to reach the last hanging tinsel star.

It was after lunch, when activity was dying down and everyone was getting ready to leave for the Christmas break, that Hugo Larsson popped his head round the staff room door.

'Anya, could you pop into my office for a moment please?'

Ethan made a face behind Hugo's departing back.

'Be careful' he mouthed.

She had no option but to follow. He was the principal after all, but she dreaded being alone with him. It was bad enough when he "accidentally" brushed against her in the corridor, or she felt his hand against her backside as she was climbing the stairs. Helping her, he said, when she looked round, shocked. And he was unabashed, grinning at her. Letting her know that, yes, he was the principal. He was the boss. What a relief then, to see Glyn John seated in the room.

'Anya! I feel I've been neglecting you this term!' He rose and took her hand. 'I'm hearing great things about you.'

'Really?' Anya couldn't keep the surprise out of her voice. Who had he heard this from, she wondered?

'Yes indeed.' Glyn smiled. 'Please, have a seat.'

'And that's why we' he indicated himself and Hugo, now sitting behind his desk 'would like to offer you some additional hours.'

'The Nursing course is very popular' went on Hugo before she could reply. 'Too popular in some ways. Our class numbers are just too big. We like to have no more than fifteen per class, but some are way over that.'

'And as you may imagine'' continued Glyn in this double-act, 'some staff are not happy at having to teach such large classes. Mrs Crick, biology, in particular, between you and me! So – we're splitting the O level Human Biology classes. Just the first years to start with. We'll have to see how the numbers stack up before we decide to make it more permanent, and do the same for both year groups. Well Anya' he finished, 'what do you think? Are you willing to take the extra classes from next term?'

It wasn't just the extra money – although heaven knows she needed it. It was the faith they had shown in her. They really thought she could do this. And O level teaching too! She'd be teaching more hours than a full time member of staff. Back in the staffroom, Ethan hugged her, and she was on a high as she drove home, singing carols on top of her voice.

The children had finished school at lunch time, and they were waiting for her, with her mother, at the front door.

'Mum! It's nearly Christmas!' screamed Lucy as the three hurled themselves at her.

'And we're on holiday!' yelled Fran

'And we've made you cards and presents!' shouted Emily.

Laughing and hugging them, Anya made her way into the house, giving her mother a quick kiss on the way.

'Thank you Mum' she whispered. 'I couldn't have got through the term without you.''

'Don't be daft Annie, I'm happy to help.' Anya knew how much of her life Jessie had given up or put on hold for her daughter, and was more grateful than she could say.

The next few days flew by in a whirl of tree decorating and present wrapping, excitement rising to fever pitch by Christmas Eve. The girls had begged their grandma to stay over, and she had allowed herself to be persuaded. Of course they were convinced they would never get to sleep. And of course they did. The stockings filled and the veg peeled, Anya and her mum sat in the kitchen over a pot of tea.

'I was chatting to your friend Veronica at the school gates the other day' said Jessie, helping herself to a Christmas jaffa cake. 'She asked how you were getting on at the college, and I told her you loved it.'

'Oh, right. What did she say?'

'She sniffed'

'She – what?'

'She sniffed' repeated Jessie, laughing.

'What's that supposed to mean? Sniffed?' said Anya, affronted.

'I wouldn't worry about it love' she said, still laughing. 'I think she likes to feel superior, being a full-time mother, as she put it.'

'But she's the one who told me about the job in the first place!' Anya was affronted, amazed at her friend's reaction to her working.

'Ah, but you're not supposed to enjoy it, are you? Forget about it, Annie. I'm sure there's a bit of jealousy in there too. She tells me that she could have been a teacher if she'd wanted to. Apparently she didn't. You'll always get it, Anya. You know what they say – a Welshman can forgive anything except success. And the women can be worse. Well, some of them.'

They sat for a while, sipping tea and nibbling biscuits, deep in their own thoughts. Then,

'David not joining us then? Or is he in bed?' said Jessie, glancing at the wall clock.

'No, he's still in the lounge. He goes to bed quite late these days.'

'Things not good between you then, love'. It was a statement.

'What do you mean Mum?' Anya hid her face behind her mug.

'Come on Annie, I'm not stupid. I can read the signs. I've kept quiet all these years, but now …'

'What do you mean, *all these years*?' Anya put her tea down.

Jessie was quiet for a moment, then she, too, placed her teacup on the table.

'You've never really been yourself when he's around, have you love? You used to be so bubbly, such fun. You still are sometimes. But not when David's around. It's as though you're afraid of him. And it's got much worse since he lost his job.'

62

Anya stared at the table. What could she say? Although she'd been trying to deny it to herself for such a long time, she knew her mother was right. She sighed. It was a relief to talk about it. And talk they did. By the time they went to bed it was late. Anya didn't feel as if anything had been resolved, even though she had unburdened herself. She had talked about his resentment, his bitterness, his shouting and his finger-wagging. She talked about the panic she felt when she was a little longer at the shops than he thought necessary, or a bit later at work, worried about his mood when she returned, a tight little knot in her stomach. She talked about how she did her best to hide any tension from the girls, and how she wasn't sure she was succeeding any more. She talked about his drinking. And when her mother asked her if he'd ever hurt her, physically, she dismissed the idea. She didn't talk about the occasional bruise on her arm from a too-tight grasp, the spilt hot coffee that could well have been an accident... No, nothing had been resolved, but putting it into words had made her see that this was something that couldn't go on. She would have to talk to him, make him see that they must work on their relationship. She would do it straight after Christmas.

Christmas day was as magical as Anya could make it, as her mother had always made it for her. The shrieking with excitement, the laughter and hugs, all made the planning and the expense worthwhile. Christmas lunch eaten, games played, gifts from under the tree handed out by the children for their parents and Grandma, and then it was bedtime for them, hometime for Jessie.

Anya wasn't expecting a pleasant evening of togetherness with her husband, so she started to clear up, collecting discarded wrapping paper and cardboard boxes, when David turned off the TV and stood up unsteadily, knocking over his glass of brandy.

'So how much did that little lot cost then?' he said.

'What?' Anya turned.

'The presents, the food. How much?'

'As little as I could manage without ruining Christmas for the girls' she answered, the sight of him swaying in front of her making her more defiant than she usually was.

'Well it's too much. We can't afford it.'

Anya stopped in her tracks.

'We? Did you say "we"?' she said. 'I paid for. All of it. How else do you think we'd have had a Christmas? When did you last bring any money in?'

She knew she shouldn't have said it. She knew it would rile him further. She backed away as he lurched forwards.

'And how can I do that then? You tell me!' He shouted, standing over her.

'You find me a job! The bloody unions, they're the ones that brought all this on us. On me. Strikes and more strikes – work-shy bastards. They ruined this country, took my job.'

'And which union did you join, David?' Her voice was raised too now. 'Oh yes - you didn't, did you? You didn't need them. Well who did you think would fight for you? When they threw you out? Ever wonder why so many others kept their jobs? It was those "work-shy bastards" that fought for them. But oh no, you knew better, didn't you? Put your family at risk, put our home at risk. If I hadn't been able to pay the mortgage these past few months ...'

'Well, Miss Perfect, you were too late' he shouted. And he drew a handful of crumpled pieces of paper from his pocket, throwing them at her, looking triumphant.

She picked them up, sat down on the sofa, flattened them out. Letters with "Port Haven Urban District Council" headings, dates going back over months, the most recent standing out: '... *failure to make agreed payments ... failure to contact us with alternative payment arrangements ... have no option but to repossess the property ...*'

She sat. David stood, defiant, still swaying.

'How could you?' she whispered. 'How could you? I gave you the money. Where did it go? What ...?' She looked at the brandy glass. 'Of course' she said hoarsely. She stood, turned, and left the room.

CHAPTER 4

HOUSE & HOME

1976 – 1982

Their own house. It had been her dearest wish. David's weekly pay had improved considerably when he had at last been promoted. So despite the ever-increasing interest rates and reluctance of building societies to lend money, they had managed to raise a mortgage from the local council. The house they chose was a huge three storied terraced monster in the centre of the little town, and in need of some TLC. The price was surprisingly low. Newly built bungalows were all the rage, with their fitted kitchens and showers, and no-one wanted big town houses any more, especially those that needed "substantial refurbishment". But Anya loved this higgledy piggledy mansion as it was.

So many rooms, she thought they would get lost. Such high ceilings, with beautiful coving and ornamental plasterwork. Sash windows with coloured glass above, William Morris-style ceramics in the entrance porch, patterned quarry tiles along the floor of the hallway – she loved it all. The kitchen was huge, with an enormous Belfast sink, and the previous owners had left a wonderful variety of mismatched free-standing cupboards and dressers. She could make this their home, she knew.

While they waited for the purchase to be finalized, she was able to borrow the key, and would spend hours wandering from room to room, a two-year-old Emily in tow, planning room layouts, seeing cosy bedspreads and fluffy rugs in her mind's eye, and hoping against hope that they could move in before baby number two made an appearance. And they did. Just.

Francesca had bounced into the world just weeks after the move. She was born at home, Anya's mother close by and David in the next room, while a cheery midwife giving a series of encouraging exhortations in the form of "Good girl!" and "You can do it!".

As dark as Emily was fair, this new little one had the same big blue eyes and enchanting mouth, and Anya knew that she needn't have worried about not having enough love to share between two. She knew that this one came with her own package of love, and Emily's portion needn't be lessened. As she lay on the big bed, with her newborn in her arms and her eldest at her side, she couldn't imagine being any happier.

Anya had managed to clean and put up curtains before baby Fran had been born, but decorating was postponed for a little while. Then she had stripped walls, pasted and papered, sanded and painted, until every room shone. Life was good. David may not have been the greatest conversationalist, but he was considerate and kind, and she never resented his nights out. She was happy to stay at home with her little ones. She had everything she wanted.

It was unusual to see David at home mid-afternoon. A heavily pregnant Anya met him in the hall, Fran on her hip, Emily at her side.

'I've been laid off' he had announced abruptly, turning away from her to walk into the lounge. And so it had started. The silences, the outbursts, the drinking. There were no jobs, he said. Just an occasional day's labouring when a friend found him some work.

When Lucy was born a few weeks later, Anya's joy wasn't to be overshadowed by the anxious atmosphere that had hung over their home since David's announcement. Once again, a home birth. Once again, her mother on hand. But this time, no David in the next room. He sat downstairs, brooding, waiting for opening time so he could drown his sorrows, blot out his misery and his bitterness, be one of the boys again.

But Anya was able to rejoice at the miracle that had delivered her of yet another beautiful daughter, a new life joining her and her girls. She sat, surrounded by her little ones, and laughed as her mother had said,

'A redhead this time, Annie! One of each now – well done!'

The reality of their situation soon hit home. Anya did everything she could to eke out their meagre dole money, all the time trying to boost her husband's confidence, allay his fears. She cut down her clothes to make new ones for the children. She made stews that would last for days. Thanks to her mother's offer to look after the girls, she was able to apply for jobs – office work, shop work, factory work, anything. They told her she was over-qualified – *girls with A levels don't stay the course'.*

She was terrified they wouldn't be able to keep up the mortgage payments, would lose the house she loved so much. So she took in sewing, fitting the work around the children, stitching long into the night, turning up hems and replacing zips, all the while worrying that she would ruin someone's garment. And after a year, an exhausting, soul-destroying year, she came to the realization that she had to make her exam passes work for her, not against her. She applied for the college course she should have started six years before. And she'd done it – she was a teacher, and she had a job, they would keep their house, and all would be well.

CHAPTER 5

A MAN'S WORLD

1983

'Happy new year!'

Anya opened the door to her mother with the traditional greeting. Trimmings still up, Quality Street tins with just the toffees remaining, the no-man's-land between Christmas and New Year's Day was ending at last, with just this one more Bank Holiday to get through. It had been an interminable few days for Anya, her mind in a whirl, waves of terror threatening to engulf her. Her house. Her home. All slipping through her fingers …

'I can't forgive him, Mum.' Her voice was low as they sat at the big battered kitchen table. 'He's let this happen, and I can't forgive him. I don't know what to do.'

Jessie waited.

'I used to catch the postman, you know. Every morning. Just so he wouldn't worry about the bills. I couldn't do it when I started my course, or when I got the job, could I? Looks like he did it instead. Kept it all from me. And now … now…'

Anya's voice cracked.

'I mean, we'll have to find somewhere else to live. To rent, I suppose. Back where we started nearly ten years ago. But with three children. And I don't know what to do.' Anya put her head in her hands.

Jessie swallowed hard. It hurt her to see her daughter so distressed, and she felt a violent hatred towards the man who had done this. But instinct told her this was not the time to show her feelings – not all her feelings - towards her son-in-law.

'It's going to be up to you now, Annie love' she said. 'You're going to have to be the grown-up, take control, make decisions. You've done it before – you knew it was right to go to college, to train as a teacher. You stood up for yourself. And it's paid off.'

Anya looked up. 'Well, I'll be working more hours from now on, that's something. It's a start. But Mum, I'll need …'

'I'll help, of course' interrupted Jessie. 'Whenever, whatever you need. And by the way – if you need somewhere to live, you can move in with me.'

The new term should have been full of excitement and anticipation for Anya, and sure enough her low mood was lifted as she walked through the college doors. Despite the daily worry over losing their home, waiting for the eviction notice, and pretending to the children that everything was fine, her work was a refuge for her. Armed with a syllabus, a timetable and carefully prepared lesson notes, she felt far more confident in her new classes than she had just a term ago with the hairdressers. Those, too, had settled down, and Anya tried hard to make the lessons interesting and relevant. She had learned more about the details of skin and hair, and the effects of various chemicals on them, than she had ever known before, and although she was often only a few weeks ahead of her students in terms of what they needed to know, she managed to give the impression that she was an expert in the subjects. She felt much more at home teaching the nursing students. No surprises here – the human body hadn't changed since she had studied it.

Ethan continued to be a huge support to her. He was her go-to man with any questions she may have about the workings of the college, or whom she should trust. Their timetables often coincided, which meant that they were both early to break on at least three mornings each week, and he had given her lessons in what was expected of her, now she would be there every day.

'Most of the staff have their own mug – use one of theirs at your peril!' he told her, lining up a range of crockery on the worktop. 'Some are easy – they have a name on them. But you'll need to remember whose is the dragon and whose is the smiley face.'

He handed Anya an unremarkable mug of greying liquid, and she sat in the seat that had become her own, as he joined her.

'They won't expect you to know everything yet, mind' he went on. 'They'll give you time. You're new, you're young, you're part-time. So they won't expect too much at first.'

Anya enjoyed her chats with Ethan. She felt at ease with him. That wasn't the case with all of her male colleagues. She wasn't sure how she felt about some of their comments – comments about her legs, her hair, her clothes. Maybe she should have been flattered. And if she were honest with herself, she knew that her feelings were very much related to how she saw the men themselves. With some she felt slightly uncomfortable when they made their clumsy lewd jokes, although she rarely felt offended and never threatened by them. But pleasant and friendly as they were, she was often on edge, afraid she might be sending out the wrong messages, wary in case she would be seen as encouraging, them, giving them the "come on". Hugo Larsson, on the other hand, she found repulsive, and objected, although silently, to his blatant overtures. His advances were obvious, non-apologetic and held an underlying menace. But Byron was a different case. He was charming and flattering to all the women, but somehow he never offended them.

Anya confided her worries to Elaine one rare lunchtime when all the women had decided to stay in the staffroom, Tupperware much in evidence. Elaine laughed.

"Anya, it's time we extended your education'. She addressed the rest of the small group. 'Ladies, Anya's getting the Hugo treatment, and wants to know about the men.'

'No, I ...'

'Don't worry dear, we know what she means' said Marjorie Crick kindly.

'Now ... Hugo is a predator' began Elaine. 'He never stops. He's had a go at every woman on the staff.'

'Except Marjorie!'

'Who feels very hurt!'

'Come on ladies' interrupted Marjorie 'This is serious stuff.'

'Yes, she's right' said Elaine. 'We shouldn't have to issue warnings to new staff. Female staff, that is. The truth is, we've all had to learn to cope with it, one way or another. Me – I slapped Hugo on his crotch after putting up with his groping for months. I made out I was being playful, but it was a harder slap than he was expecting. His eyes watered and his grin was rather fixed ...' laughter all round as she continued.

'But – and here's the point – I took a risk. A double risk. He could have taken me up on my "playfulness", seen it as an ok for him to carry on, go further. Or I could have lost my job. He could easily have made up some reason or other – the governors, the council, he has them all in his pocket. Well, they look out for each other at any rate. All men. It's the local Labour party that runs the education system around here, and he's a big noise with that lot.'

'And the Masons. Don't forget them' added Marjorie.

'Masons?' asked Anya.

'Freemasons' explained Marjorie. 'Very powerful. Of course, Labour people aren't supposed to belong to them, but this lot are a law unto themselves.'

'And don't forget the Catholics' piped up Jean Rossi. 'They're the up and coming force to be conjured with – at least that's what Bruno thinks.'

'Bruno?' enquired Anya, aware that she was doing nothing but ask questions of the women.

'Sorry love – Mr Rossi. My other half. For now at least ...'

'Anyway' said Elaine loudly, bringing the informal meeting back to some kind of order. 'As I was saying, Hugo is a predator. And there's nothing we can do about it. No-one we can complain to. We just have to find ways to avoid situations where he could take even more of an advantage. Now, some of the others, like Dan, they're just would-be Lotharios, who think a bit of flirting is flattering to us. But they're just not very good at it, bless 'em. So they come over as a bit creepy and sleazy. And I bet they wouldn't know what to do if one of us flirted back. Run a mile, I should think.'

'And then there's Byron' said Jean, with an exaggerated sigh. 'Lovely sexy Byron. I think he would know what to do …' They all laughed.

'Jean, stop it!' said Elaine, laughing. 'She's had a crush on him for – well, forever!' she said to Anya. 'I wish I could say he's all talk, but the rumours of his affairs seem pretty believable. He plays the part of a gigolo very convincingly, with his wavy hair flopping over his eyes and his beautiful smile. His mother named him well!'

'He'd never leave Claire though' said Marjorie. 'He may mess around, we're not sure, but she's got him well and truly where she wants him – under her thumb. She must have some mysterious power over him. Maybe he really is devoted to her.'

Jean gave another extravagant sigh and a mock sob, which had them all in fits of laughter.

'And Paul? The VP?' Anya was surprised at the ripple of amusement – or was it embarrassment - that ran around the group at the mention of his name. She looked at Elaine.

'Ah, we don't talk about Paul. Do we Jean?' Jean flushed. 'That's a story yet to unfold, Anya. Watch this space'.

'Oh. Ok.' Anya was keen to move on. 'And Ethan? What about him?'

'Well now, Ethan's another matter altogether. Such a nice guy. And a brilliant teacher. No Anya, he's no danger to you. To any of us in fact. He'll never try it on with you, will he?' Elaine elaborated, seeing Anya's blank face.

'You do know he's a homosexual? Although I think he'd probably prefer the word Gay.'

And now a conversation came back to Anya, one she'd had with Ethan as they sat together over coffee at the end of last term, when he'd laughingly said to her 'Hey, if we keep sitting with each other, people will talk!' and she had blushed with embarrassment at the thought that he would think such a thing. Had she been sending signals, in all innocence, about some non-existent feelings for him? He reassured her immediately.

'I think most people would know you're not my type, Anya.' he had said, putting his arm around her.

Now it made sense. At twenty eight, she was still such a child, she thought to herself. Such an innocent. So naïve.

'Oh yes, of course I knew' she lied.

Elaine smiled. She wasn't fooled.

'Mind you, we don't talk about it' said Marjorie in a low voice. 'Not outside our little group. The men know but try to ignore it – they seem threatened by it.'

'Daft buggers' said Jean. 'As if he's about to pounce on one of them. But he could lose his job if the students knew – or rather, their parents.'

'What?' Anya burst out. 'But he's a lovely man. He's the only one I can talk to without feeling …well … pressured. I can be myself with him'

'And now you know why' said Jean. 'But the reason he could lose his job is because of some ill-informed, prejudiced people who think that being gay is catching. That a gay teacher will ravage their sons – or even turn them gay. There's talk about making it illegal to discuss homosexuality with students, even in the personal tutorials. And he'll never be promoted of course.'

'It's the men who are afraid.' Marjorie lit a cigarette. 'They like Ethan, but some are scared to get too friendly with him. There are some influential parents about. Powerful even. And some male staff don't want to be "tainted" by an association with someone the parents see as abnormal.'

'So' said Elaine, her face grim, 'while we have to live with perverts like Hugo Larsson leering at us, groping us, rubbing up against us at every opportunity, we can't possibly approve of a nice, clever, decent guy like Ethan, who just wants to do his job. Someone should do something about it.' And they all took another sip from their coffee cups. The buzzer buzzed and the conversation was over.

The day came, as she knew it must. Evicted from their home on the first of February. David hired a van and moved what essential pieces of furniture they could squeeze into the modest three-bed council house that was the home of his mother-in-law. So many pieces they were forced to leave behind. No time to advertise and sell them. Another spur in Anya's side.

They kept their distance from each other: she, determined not to make matters worse by telling him how she felt about him, and he, quite sure that Anya told her mother every little detail of their marriage, and resenting it. In that, he was wrong. While Anya had told her mother the gist of what was happening at home, she hadn't told her about the increasingly long silences, the icy, cutting remarks and the sarcastic comments he made to the children about her. She understood why David was so angry, so bitter about being unemployed, but by the same token, he seemed to show no understanding of how she felt, having to leave their home when it could have been avoided. And her understanding and forbearance didn't make it any easier to live with him. She hadn't told her mother how he had fought with her, wanting to rent somewhere, anywhere, rather than live with Jessie. This, too, Anya understood. She knew it was going to be difficult, and especially for him. But rented properties were expensive when your income was so low, and they needed somewhere quick.

She hadn't told her mother, or David, that she had seriously thought about moving without him. The thought alone gave her a sense of release and optimism she couldn't feel around her husband. She acknowledged to herself now that she had probably never loved him, but she knew she had been a good wife, and she didn't think he had ever doubted her feelings for him. A new life with her daughters was tempting. But she knew she couldn't go through with it. She felt pity for David now, as their roles seemed to be reversing. Where would he go? Could she really take his children away from him? And she wasn't sure if she had the courage to raise them by herself. She wasn't sure she had her mother's courage.

CHAPTER 6

DAVID'S STORY

1967

The church was full. Everywhere, roses. Bridesmaids, flower girls, groomsmen, incense. Young Davey Gethin knelt alongside his beautiful bride, veiled, demure, virginal in white lace. He stole glances at her, hardly believing she could love him, utterly and completely besotted with her as he was.

The service was long, much of it in Latin, despite the edicts that made this optional. Marion – his wonderful Marion – had converted to Catholicism. He had told her how important it was to him, that they should have the full Catholic wedding service, complete with the nuptial Mass, and she had agreed to postpone their wedding for nearly a year to allow this to happen. And here they were, listening to the intonations and incantations of Father O'Connell, occasionally responding, chanting, singing. He knew that many of their guests – and there were hundreds – would be feeling restless. But Davey didn't care – he would have stayed like this forever, frozen in time, capturing his joy, his pride.

He was sad for Marion that she had no relatives to witness their union. One of the many things that made him feel close to her was the fact that she had no parents, no relatives, no-one. No-one but him. By contrast, his family had turned out in force. Having moved to Port Haven from north Wales when Davey was a small child, they were now stalwarts of the Catholic community, and they weren't going to miss the chance to put on a big show. The wedding groups that were lined up for photographs outside St Brendan's church made for an impressive sight: a wide row of bridesmaids and flower girls in a delight of white flourishes, frills and ruffs, dotted with red roses, bordered by morning-suited men, and centre stage: the bride and groom, she radiant if overwhelmed, clutching the huge bouquet of red roses, he beaming happily. The best day of his life.

David had always been considered the runt of the litter. His older brothers, ostentatiously academically minded from an early age, passed the eleven-plus exam with flying colours and made their mark in the local grammar school. Luck – both good and bad – came to play in young Davey's life. At ten years old, a cycling stunt, urged on by a group of cheering friends, resulted in a stupendous crash when Davey and his bike both disappeared under an oncoming delivery van at the bottom of the hill near his home.

It was his good luck that he wasn't killed; nevertheless the multiple fractures in his leg left him in hospital for several weeks and absent from his convent school for several more. In his wisdom, the headmaster decided that David would have no chance of passing the scholarship, and therefore would not be entered for it. His mother – a virtuous woman more emotionally connected to the Church than to her sons – concurred. His father took little interest in the schooling of his children, other than the use of his belt on the backsides of any of them who gave cause for criticism of his family. David had seen more than his share of the belt. He had been a lively, curious little boy, more at home riding a gambo down a dangerous hill with his friends or turning on the paraffin taps at the back of the local ironmonger's store, than reading or studying of any kind. And yet he was bright. So he begged to be able to sit the exam, promised he would work hard in the few weeks left, all to no avail. His tears threatened another beating, so he dried them. Only sissies cried, he was told. Big boys didn't snivel.

His parents, the priest, the nuns, all told him that this was God's will. That he was meant for something else, something that didn't rely on education. At the same time he was told that this was all his own fault, that he shouldn't have been mixing with such a gang of hooligans, that he shouldn't have been so reckless. David struggled to see how both of these assertions could be true. He couldn't. So he decided that the church was a lie, giving convenient, but illogical, reasons for events that were affecting his life. But the church, and his parents, won. He wouldn't sit the exam. That was his bad luck.

And so he was branded a failure. In 1955, that was the general consensus if you didn't pass the eleven-plus exam. He knew he wouldn't be moving in the exalted spheres of the grammar school with his brothers, so he gave up trying. He misbehaved for the remainder of his primary school days, and continued in the same vein in the secondary modern school he went on to. He was bored, and angry, and for two years he spent more time in detention than any other boy in his year. His teachers despaired of him. His parents were called in to the school, resulting in cold looks from his mother, and another lashing from his dad. It seemed that he was heading for the juvenile court, when help arrived from an unexpected source.

No-one seemed to notice how the white lines got there, Davey mused as he stared out of the window onto the soccer pitch. But he knew. He had seen that old man push the wheel along the ground, dragging whitewash with it, making the rectangles, the arcs, the central circle. Davey didn't care for soccer. Rugby he could tolerate, giving him an opportunity to vent some of his pent-up anger and aggression, but he missed most PE lessons and of course was never chosen to play for a team. Now while the Wars of the Roses droned on at the front of the class, he watched as the faded lines grew bright again, and envied the old man his solitude, his quiet. And as if he heard his thoughts, the man looked up and smiled.

He was still there at break time.

'Hi.'

'Hello young man. I saw you through that window earlier, didn't I?' The old man was in his early forties, and spoke with a soft Irish lilt.

'Yes. I was supposed to be listening to a history lesson, but it was too boring. So I stopped listening.' Davey glanced up, waiting to see the familiar frown of disapproval he had become accustomed to on every adult's face. But not this time, it seemed.

'I know what you mean. I was never a fan of history either.' He passed the handles of the wheel to Davey. 'Want to have a go?'

So a friendship grew. Davey stayed on after school on the days that Tom worked, and they talked. Together, they cleared the pitches of bits of paper, they moved stones, they mowed the grass. And all the time they talked. All the things that Davey had been feeling, for all these years, came pouring out, and Tom listened. He listened to the anger, the resentment. And he heard the sadness and the loneliness.

'You're a good little worker, young Davey' he said one Friday afternoon. 'How would you like to help me with a bit of building work tomorrow?'

'Building work? Yeah!' Davey's enthusiasm was clear to see, and his eager face became that of a child again.

'OK, good. It's on Old Road, where the allotments used to be. Shall we say eight o'clock? Or is that too early?'

'Not too early for me, Tom!'

The work was hard and Davey loved it. No-one else was there, just him and Tom. He carried bricks and stones, learned to mix cement by hand, swept dust from the ground, all the while chatting, asking questions. Why? What? Who? All the things he hadn't felt able to ask his parents for all these years. He never let his patched-up leg slow him down, and bit by bit his limp became less pronounced. He saw the building grow, week by week. He always left before ten o'clock on a Saturday, Tom insisted on this. He never saw the builders working on it during the week, so it was always a matter of some excitement to see how high the walls had become.

'What's this building going to be then, Tom?' Davey asked one morning as he moved some stones from a mound nearby.

'Ah, that's a good question. An important question. And now that you've asked it, I'm going to tell you. But not yet.'

'When?'

'I'll tell you at ten o'clock today.'

But Tom didn't get the chance to tell Davey as he'd planned. As the nearby church clock struck ten, a woman walked past the entrance to the building site.

'Morning Father' she called out. And Tom raised his hand, before looking back at Davey to see his stricken face.

'Father? Why did she call you Father?'

Tom sighed.

'Because ...'

'Because you're one of them? You're a priest?'

'Look Davey, there's a reason I haven't told you' he said as he removed his dusty brown overalls to reveal a well-worn pair of slacks, an old jumper – and a priest's dog-collar.

'You tricked me!' whispered the boy as he turned. He walked away.

'No Davey, I didn't' called Tom after him. 'Davey! Davey! Please! Let me explain.'

He took some persuading but eventually Davey agreed to sit down on a cold stone wall with his friend. Other people were coming on to the site, each one greeting Tom respectfully. Davey could see now why he had to be rushed away before ten each Saturday. Before Tom's secret came out, he thought bitterly. He felt betrayed. He'd thought he had a friend, and now – this?

'So' he said. 'Explain. Explain why you told me you worked at the school when you don't. Explain why you left out the bit about being a priest. Explain what your real name is. And then I'll explain that I HATE the church, I HATE priests. And I hate you.' His voice cracked and he swallowed hard. He could say no more. But Tom could.

'Ok. I know you're angry … let me finish' he said, as Davey turned to him, ready to speak. 'First – I didn't tell you I worked at the school. I volunteer there. You assumed I was some sort of caretaker – and yes, I let you think that. I didn't put you right. But be honest, if I had told you my real job, would you have stayed to talk? So I didn't tell you at first. And then when you told me how you felt about your past few years, I knew you wouldn't take kindly to a priest hearing about it all. But I could see you weren't afraid to work. And I could see a door opening for you, Davey. A real door. And I liked you.'

'Just priest talk, that is' said Davey grumpily, more like the thirteen-year-old he was than the man he pretended to be. Tom went on.

'The work we do here is really important. I said I'd tell you what we were building, didn't I? I was going to tell you today, because you asked. You haven't asked before, and I was waiting. Up to now, you've been happy to do the lifting and carrying, following orders, never lifting your eyes higher than the next row of stones. But today you wanted to know. You looked a bit higher, and I knew you were ready. It's just a shame that one of the parishioners had to come by and salute me, spoiling my great unmasking moment!'

Davey didn't find this amusing, so Tom went on.

'We're building a church, Davey. A new one. The one across the road is falling down. The roof is beyond mending, and it's full of dry rot. The only thing that works is the clock. I don't think you've been to church for a while, have you Davey? It's ok, don't look at me like that! It's just that, if you had, you'd know we've been holding services in the council chamber all this year. And you'd know about the money we've managed to raise – well, the money that the Monsignor has managed to raise, over many, many years. But he's going to retire quite soon – I'll be taking over as parish priest when he does – so we really want to get as much done as possible before he leaves. And now we have enough to get started – though we need to do some of the rough work ourselves. We rely on volunteers. And we're using stones from the old church.' He stopped, and put his hand on the child's shoulder.

'That's what you've been doing Davey. You've been helping to build a new church. And hasn't it felt good? Even though you didn't know what it was, didn't it feel good? Don't you want to carry on helping? We need you, you know.' He smiled.

'And my name IS Tom. It's Father Thomas O'Connell. But you can call me Tom.'

He owed a lot to Tom. He had worked alongside him, talking, arguing, thinking, for another two years, until the church was built – a wonderful edifice in the centre of the town, modern, full of colour and gleaming steel inside the walls that were a homage to its predecessor.

Davey loved it. And he used it. When his parents saw him take his first communion at the age of fifteen, their restrained pleasure was just a little added bonus, not the reason he was doing it several years later than his brothers had. He could have said he was doing it for Tom, but that wasn't strictly true either, and he knew the priest would have been delighted that he had found a real comfort in the teachings of the church.

He had learned to value what he could do, what he had learned, what was important, and he had learned to let go of the bitterness that had swamped him for so long. Tom had helped him get his first job – a lowly one, but a respectable one, working for a local builder. And so he grew into the strong, muscular young man who stood in front of the church he'd helped to build, a respected figure, always willing to help, to fetch and carry for his own family and for others. It had been his special pleasure to ask Tom to officiate at his and Marion's wedding, and he was overcome with gratitude and love that day.

Davey couldn't quite put his finger on when things started to go wrong with their marriage. He knew that Marion didn't really like living with his parents, even though they had their own lounge as well as a bedroom. He didn't like it either. So Davey had found them a flat – a small one with sloping ceilings, at the top of a three story town-house, but they had it to themselves. He had to work extra long hours to pay for it, but he didn't mind, except that he saw less of Marion.

'I'll work all the hours God sends if it makes you happy, poppet' he'd told her.

'Why do you call me that childish name, David?' she snapped one day. 'I'm not a baby.'

He felt he could do nothing right. He could see that she was bored, frustrated, but he didn't know what he could do for her. She flared up at the slightest thing, told him he was boring, criticized everything he said and did. He was desperately unhappy, and finally confided in Tom, who was at a loss as to what the problem was. Unless …

'Davey, could Marion be pregnant? Sometimes women behave irrationally when they're with child – or so I've heard.'

'I only wish you were right, Tom' David said sadly. 'We were hoping to start a family straight away. We don't use any contraception, of course, but no, she's not pregnant.'

During the increasingly brief times that David was home, he felt he was walking on eggshells. He tried to give her everything she asked for, but it was never enough. He seemed to be constantly apologizing, and the strain was telling on him. What was he doing wrong? He encouraged her to go out with her friends, to enjoy herself, even though their evenings together were short and rare. Her outings became more frequent, but he dared not object. She seemed happier lately, and he didn't want to spoil that.

The knock at the door downstairs was completely unexpected. It was late – almost eleven o'clock, and David had been dozing in his chair, waiting for his wife to return. He was alarmed when he saw a police constable standing there.

'Sorry to bother you, sir, but I have to inform you that your wife is being held at the local station.'

'She – what? What did you say?' He must have misheard, must still be sleepy. 'Is she hurt? Has there been an accident?'

'I'm afraid your wife has been arrested, sir.'

'Arrested? What for? There must be a mistake … my wife is out with her friends …'

'She's been arrested for' the constable referred to his notebook 'outraging public decency contrary to common law, sir. Can you come down to the station to vouch for her, sir?'

David's world was turning upside down. The constable was telling him that she had been seen with a man in the local park, both scantily clad and clearly intoxicated, behaving in an indecent way, he said. Having sex on the grass, he added.

He didn't know how he got through the next few weeks. He didn't know what to do. The worst thing was that Marion didn't seem to know what to do either. He tried to talk to her, tried to understand. She was remorseful, apologetic, but she made him feel that it was all his fault. If he had paid her more attention, if he had spent more time with her, if he had bought her a house …

Maybe they could try to sort things out together, start again, maybe move away. At first, Marion agreed. But when she told him that she was sorry, she didn't love him any more, all the spirit went out of him. Then he discovered that she had continued to see the burly lifeguard, continued to be unfaithful to her husband, while living under his roof, accepting his protection, his affection, and the hope he cherished each time he looked at her.

When he snapped, it was a restrained affair. He knew she had nowhere else to go so he told her she could stay in the flat, that he would move back to his parents' home. He guessed she had no idea what such a move would do to him, to return to live in that oppressive atmosphere once again, having known what it was to be free of it. But he also knew now that she didn't really care. Maybe she never had. He packed his things and walked out. They had been married for ten months.

David had not needed to move out for long. Marion was installed in her boyfriend's place within weeks. And was pregnant within months.

He had never felt so low. He moved back to his attic refuge, and friends rallied round, but they were embarrassed. They didn't know how to help. They couldn't. Tom did his best, and it may have been some comfort to know that he was there, but nothing eased his pain and his bitterness. David's parents said little. Never ones to delve into the innermost feelings of their sons, they encouraged prayer and hard work, while his brothers seemed not to have expected anything less from their younger brother, and didn't speak about it. In his head he was back at eleven years old, the runt of the litter. Taller, stronger, but good only for fetching and carrying, fixing and mending, the brawn to his brothers' brains.

Even after a year, two years, the events surrounding his marriage left a raw, gaping wound in David's character. His friends encouraged him to file for a divorce, but he would have none of it. His faith was one of the few things he felt he could cling to. Of course Tom supported him in this, and he knew his parents would not have been able to bear the thought of such a thing. His friends did their best to help, especially Colin and his fiancé Gwyneth. She comforted him, and he enjoyed her company. In fact she started spending more and more time with him. But when one day she ran her hand up his leg, fondled him, started to kiss him; when despite himself he began to feel aroused for the first time in a long time, he asked her to leave. He would not do to his friend what Marion had done to him.

Life went on. Slowly, David seemed to mend. He left the building site and went to work in the local steelworks. After three years, he divorced his wife. It shook the catholic community in the town, his parents, Tom. He was sad to let his friend down, but there was a hardness about him now. He knew he needed to start his life again. He wasn't looking for a girlfriend, let alone a wife, and he wanted to put all thoughts of marriage behind him. And so he did. Until that day, six years after his own wedding, when he attended another. And met Anya.

CHAPTER 7

AND SO IT BEGINS

1983: March

Glyn John was rarely to be seen in the main staffroom. His hairdressing staff, along with those in the business department, tended to use small offices and workrooms near their classrooms for their break-time coffees and their lunches, although Glyn was usually to be found in his own office. So when he headed towards Anya at break one morning with a sheet of paper in his hand, she was surprised and not a little wary.

'Anya – glad I've caught you! Something that might interest you, hot off the press. It'll be in the paper at the end of the week. Pop over to my office when you have a minute if you like, we can have a chat.' He handed her the paper and left. She scanned it anxiously.

Vacancy ... Lecturer in Biology and Science ... Full time ... Permanent ... The words jumped out at her. Elaine leaned over.

'You ok?' she said quietly. 'Not bad news? You've gone a bit pale.'

'No ... it's fine' Anya answered. 'More than fine – I think!' she added, smiling happily now. She handed the paper to her friend, who read it through.

'Well yes, this could be good news. Excellent news.'

'Could be?'

'Well, yes' she said again, 'Hopefully you'll get the job, but …'

'But?'

'Well' said Elaine yet again. 'This is the job you're doing now, isn't it? So, if someone else gets the full time post …'

She didn't need to finish.

'I hadn't thought of that' said Anya. 'I'd love to be full-time – and permanent. Of course I would. But if I don't get it … I need this job Elaine. Part time or not, I need this.'

'Go and see Glyn, Anya. Maybe there are two posts. Maybe I got it wrong.'

Glyn wasn't able to put her mind at rest, although he did his best. Yes, it was her post that was up for grabs. Yes, if she weren't the successful candidate, then there would be no job for her. And worst of all, it would be a formal interview in front of the full governing body. No cosy informal chat this time. Her heart beat fast at the memory of a previous disastrous interview, only last year, but seeming so long ago now, almost another life.

'But Anya' he said, 'you've been doing the job for two terms, and doing it very well. You're bound to be the front-runner. Now, you've had advance warning. Don't waste it by worrying – use the time to prepare yourself. I can tell you that the interviews will take place in the first week or two of the summer term – the council's education department is anxious to get it all done and dusted before the cut-off date in May. That's the time when those teaching elsewhere would have to hand in their notice. All the classes are winding down for Easter– you should do the same.' He smiled at her. 'I'll be giving you a reference of course. A good one.'

Term over, Easter holidays. The tension at home was almost unbearable. There just wasn't room for all of them – and David's presence seemed particularly large and oppressive. This was a house unused to a man's occupation, and it showed. The bad blood between him and Jessie bubbled close to the surface on too many occasions, and the children seemed subdued. Anya took them out as often as she could – for long walks, picnics, paddling on the beach, anything that didn't involve spending money. She made the most of her time with them, playing games and laughing, anything to raise their spirits. Fortunately the unseasonable snow that was devastating the north of England wasn't in evidence in south Wales, although it was a cooler Easter than everyone had hoped for. She tried not to show her distraction to her daughters – her mind was in a large formal room full of grim but faceless people firing incomprehensible questions at her, while her body was building sandcastles and filling moats as her excited girls ran around her.

The expense of birthday parties was something she could do without, but how often was a daughter nine years old? So it was going to be an old-fashioned jelly-and-blancmange party for Emily, with pass-the-parcel games, Duran Duran and Spandau Ballet providing the musical background. Anya's main worry was the lack of space in her mother's home. And this problem would be repeated, with two more birthdays to come in the next couple of months. It was Emily herself, who was only too aware, even at her tender age, of some of the mother's worries, who came up with the solution.

'Why don't we just have one party, Mum?' she asked over breakfast in the cramped little kitchen. 'We could share it – Fran's birthday's in the middle, so we could have it then. I wouldn't mind waiting. And...' she added, seeing her mother was about to interrupt, 'we could have it in the church hall. They let it out for parties – my friend Magda told me. I don't think it costs very much.'

Anya hugged her. How blessed was she, to have such a daughter? Three such daughters, it turned out, as the other two joined in.

'Yeah, good idea Em! We'd have loads of people then! And loads of room to dance!' Fran jumped down from her seat and started twirling to her hummed version of *Total Eclipse of the Heart.*

'And bags me *Farmer in his Den* first!' shouted Lucy, clearly approving the idea, and starting to sing the song from the game. Anya laughed delightedly.

'Well, I'm glad you're all enjoying your breakfast so much!' said Jessie as she joined them. She, too, thought it an excellent idea. 'So we have another six weeks to plan it' she said. 'You'll all be back in school by then – and I'll have a bit of peace, thank goodness!'

As her three grandchildren leapt at her, hugging her and kissing her, she knew they didn't take her words

96

seriously. She loved having them and Anya around her, even if it was a squash. If it weren't for David …

As the Easter holidays came to an end, Anya became increasingly anxious about her application. She had submitted it on the last day of term, and now the closing date was very close. Perhaps no-one else would apply, she told herself, knowing how unlikely this was. Perhaps no-one else would have any experience of the particular groups they would be expected to teach, she thought. But this hope was dashed early on the Monday morning.

'Ah, Anya – just the lady!' Glyn met her in the foyer. 'Do you have a moment to come to my office, I wonder?'

She followed him along the now-familiar corridors.

'Nothing to worry about' Glyn said once they were seated in his room. She wasn't reassured by this, not one bit.

'Just wanted to mention that we've had quite a few applications for your post. I mean – THE post. Not surprising really – permanent jobs are at a premium at the moment, aren't they? And – um – one more thing' Glyn went on. 'You should know – your predecessor, who taught science to the groups before you joined us – she's applied too.'

Well that's that, Anya thought. She'd heard a bit about this woman. It didn't seem as if she was very well liked, but she certainly had the experience needed for the job. She'd been doing it for years. Anya couldn't compete with that.

'But don't let that put you off' Glyn was saying. 'Don't forget – she walked out a week after the term had started, left us in the lurch.'

She looked around her as she walked back to the staffroom. She loved it here. This was her safe place. In such a short time, her colleagues had become friends, and she would miss them. She glanced into portholes and through open classroom doors, where the young and the not-so-young were learning, talking, getting involved with their subjects, lecturers not lecturing but teaching, walking around, sitting on desks, laughing, showing. Teaching. She loved it all. Not what she trained for, but so much more. A second-chance college, Elaine had called it, and that's exactly what it was. And a second chance for her, too. She lifted her head. She was damned if she would give up yet.

That morning's lessons weren't her best and she knew it. Her mind was wandering, wondering who might be teaching future groups of young women the finer points of atomic structure, and whether the girls would be bothered one way or another. They looked bored, and she wasn't surprised. She stopped mid-sentence.

'Ok girls, I get it' she said. Heads went up, surprised faces stared at her. 'I get that this is pretty boring when all you want is to be in the salon and dye each other's hair. And I know you're wondering what on earth this has to do with hairdressing.'

Pens went down.

'And I have to tell you' she went on 'that I have absolutely no idea. I've tried to find a practical link to cutting, perming, colouring – and I've failed. And for those of you who are doing Beauty Therapy too – no, I still can't find any reason for you having to know about atoms and protons and electrons.' She paused.

'So I'll tell you why I'm teaching it, and why you need to learn it. It's in the syllabus. It'll be in the exam. No other reason I can find, I'm afraid. Now I've been taking a look at some different exams you could be doing. Without atomic theory. And there is a really good one. I'm going to try to get the college to change the examining board, so that in future, hairdressing students will study what is useful to them.'

Smiles all round.

'But – and I'm sorry about this - it won't help you. Your exams are just a few weeks away, and I have a feeling it will take quite some time to make a change like that. I may not be able to do it at all. I'm going to try. But in the meantime, we need to get this topic – boring and useless as it may seem - finished with, so you'll all have top marks, and never have to hear the word *atom* again. Can you do that?'

They looked stunned. Maybe they weren't used to such honesty from their lecturers. Maybe she'd gone too far, misjudged the feeling of the class. Then –

'Ok Miss' said the self-appointed class spokesperson. 'Fair enough. Let's do it.'

Anya felt a huge relief, and a pride in the group. She went on with the lesson, re-energised, newly enthused, drawing diagrams on the smudged blackboard and illustrating her points with coloured chalks, anything to illustrate the theory they all found so obscure. She knew she may not have the chance to make the changes she had told them about, but that wasn't their problem, and she wouldn't make it so.

Over coffee at breaktime, she told Elaine and Jean about the possible return of the previous post-holder, and they groaned, giving her some comfort at least. They were discussing all the reasons why this woman shouldn't, and wouldn't, be successful, when Marjorie came striding in.

'Anya, you're with me next lesson, ok? We'll combine 2A and 2B nurses for a bit of revision. My lab.' And she strode out again.

Anya stared at Elaine.

'We don't argue with Marjorie' Elaine said quietly. 'She's been here forever, knows everyone and everything. At least she thinks she does. She'd have made a very good headmistress of a girls' school – or maybe a hospital matron!'

And so Anya made her way to the laboratories. Her classes didn't warrant such a luxury as a lab, having to make do with borrowed models and equipment in her dingy classroom. She knocked on the door marked *Biology* and walked in. The huge workbenches with a sink at each end and gas taps in the middle, the uncomfortable wooden stools, the array of stuffed birds and animals adorning the windowsills, and the grubby skeleton hanging in a corner, all reminded her vividly of her own schooldays. And there was Marjorie, ensconced behind an enormous desk on a raised dais, surveying Anya over her half-glasses.

'Up here' she said, and pointed to a stool she had placed alongside her. 'Now' she went on, as Anya took the proffered seat, 'I thought we'd go through a past paper with them. Not long for the exam now, and they ought to be up to scratch. 2A have covered almost everything, and 2B will have covered quite a bit with me before we split the class. What have you got left to do?'

'Um –the liver. Yes, just the liver.'

'Pff! Liver indeed. Won't take you more than ten minutes. Just show them where it is and give them a list of what it does. Ten minutes.'

Anya wondered at her teaching methods, but had no time to ask questions before the eighteen-year-olds walked in, a silent straggling line of fashion-conscious would-be nurses.

'All right, all right!' said Marjorie loudly, as if they were making a noise. 'Mrs Gethin and I will be doing some revision with you today. So bring up your stools and gather round. No need to sit at benches today.'

An untidy semi-circle formed around Marjorie's desk.

'Now' she began, holding up a small sheet of paper. 'There are eight questions on this exam paper. You will be expected to answer five. Just five. But you should be able to answer every one of them, is that clear?'

Silent nods.

'So – Mrs Gethin, would you like to take the first question?'

Anya looked down and gulped. The kidney. Structure and function. She hadn't covered this topic with them – they had done that last term with Marjorie. She had expected to have time to revise it herself, plan it, prepare for it, before she taught it to a new class next year. But here she was. And she found that once she started talking, asking questions, getting the girls to draw diagrams on the board, it all came back to her. And so the lesson went on, topic after topic. Anya stopped feeling as though she were being observed in one of her training college teaching practices, and started to feel like the teacher she was, the lecturer she had become. Nevertheless, she breathed a sigh of relief when the lesson was over.

Heading back to the staffroom, her optimistic mood dimmed as she saw Hugo approaching her.

'Anya! Just the person! Come in, my dear, come in.' and he led the way to his office.

That '*my dear*' unnerved her. It was what David used to call her, when he was besotted with her. He had said it lovingly then. No longer. He still used it sometimes, but nowadays it was sarcastic, bitter. Anya followed the principal reluctantly. But it seemed he had some news. He sat behind his desk and motioned her to the seat opposite.

'We have the date for the interviews, Anya' he said. 'The third of May. Day after the bank holiday, just a couple of weeks away. So you don't have long to wait.'

'Thank you Mr Larsson' Anya said, her mouth dry.

'Oh, Hugo, please!' He leaned forward across his desk, folded arms resting on the polished wood. 'After all, I call you Anya, don't I? Anyway – of course we'll be drawing up a shortlist first. You'll be on it, naturally. I'll make sure of that.' He smiled broadly at her.

'Been a very good response, over twenty applicants...'

'Twenty?!' she burst out. She had only thought about her predecessor. How stupid of her.

'Yes, as I say, a good response' Hugo continued, making no reference to her short outburst. 'And there's no doubt you'll be shortlisted. Unthinkable not to – the incumbent and all that. And with my backing of course. Well Anya, I'd like to help you if I can.' He smiled at her again.

'As you know, the interviews will be by the whole of the governing body. All nineteen.' He paused for this to sink in. 'It would be good to have someone on your side, wouldn't it, my dear? Good to have someone rooting for you.' He paused again. 'Voting for you.'

Anya said nothing. She had an idea where this was going, but couldn't for the life of her see how to head it off.

'I'm a governor, you know.' Hugo sat back in his leather chair, his broad face glowing, his eyes alert.

'Yes' she whispered.

He leaned forward again.

'If I were to help you – would you be grateful?'

How could she answer this? If the question were as innocent as it seemed, she could answer "yes" without a qualm. She knew he meant more than this. What exactly would she be agreeing to? He was waiting for her answer.

'Of course, Hugo' she said.

103

'Good!' He sat back, clearly satisfied. 'Well, I won't keep you for now. I'll let you get on. I'll give you a call over the weekend.'

He was as good as his word. Saturday morning found Anya juggling the washing and cleaning, preparing lunch in between. Her mother had taken the girls to the park, and David was ensconced in front of the TV, making the most of Jessie's absence. When the phone rang, she switched off the vacuum cleaner and went into the tiny hall. Hugo's voice was chillingly familiar.

'Anya! How are you?' he boomed down the phone, as if he hadn't quite got the hang of how the instrument worked.

'Glad you're in' he continued without waiting for her answer. 'Playing the little wifey, eh? Got a pinny on? Anything else?'

A slight pause followed her stunned silence.

'I'm joking, of course. Just my little joke.' He said, laughing at his own humour. 'Anyway. Anya. How would you like to have dinner with me? This evening? Or tomorrow?'

'Oh … that's very kind of you Hugo. I'll see if my husband is free …'. Anya was aware she was using her position as a married woman to stall him. She didn't think it would work too well. She was right.

'Husband? I didn't say anything about your husband, now did I? I certainly won't be bringing my wife!' He laughed again, clearly enjoying what he saw as some sort of game. Or foreplay.

104

'It would give us a chance to talk about your interview, won't it? About how I can help you. You do want me to help you, don't you Anya?'

Was it her imagination, or did his voice have a threatening edge to it now? She knew what she had to do.

'Of course Hugo, I'd appreciate any help you can give me. But dinner ...' she lowered her voice slightly, hoping to sound conspiratorial rather than sexily husky. 'Now, I know, and you know, that it would all be completely innocent, above board, nothing inappropriate going on. But other people ...'

'Completely innocent?' he said quietly. 'Not quite what I had in mind.'

Then,

'You're not refusing are you Anya?'

'It's going to be difficult to leave my daughters this weekend, Hugo. I've promised I'll spend time with them, planning a birthday party. So I'm afraid I won't be able to accept your invitation' she finished, a little stiffly.

Silence.

'Very well. I'll see you on Monday.' And he was gone.

Oh well, she sighed to herself, that's that. No job for me. But at least his pestering will be over.

Wrong again. Monday morning saw the principal waiting in the foyer as Anya entered. He nodded to staff and students as they came through the doors, staff wondering why he was here, students wondering who he was.

'Morning Mrs Gethin' he said amiably, their conversation from Saturday forgotten or ignored; he fell in beside her, his hand on her waist, slipping down to her behind as she started to climb the stairs in front of him. Should she say something? Tell him to stop? That this wasn't acceptable? And yet no-one else made a fuss. No-one said a word, and most of the female staff had received the same treatment. Were still getting it. His hand slipped lower. He was a few steps behind her, lower than she was. She felt him touch her leg, his hand moved higher. This was too much. She stopped. Suddenly. And turned. His head was a little lower than hers.

'Don't do that, Mr Larsson. It's not appropriate, and it's certainly not wanted.' She spoke quietly but clearly.

Hugo did stop. He said nothing, but walked quickly up the remaining stairs, brushing against her as he went.

Sitting in the small ante-room, Anya looked around surreptitiously. Three more candidates still to go, including herself. Four had been called in, one at a time, and must have been shuffled out through a different exit. They didn't seem to be called in any particular order, certainly not alphabetical. Her main rival, as she thought of her, had been the first one in. What Anya wouldn't have given to be a fly on the wall for that one! Or any of them in fact. She glanced at the other two women. Yes, they were all women. She had been surprised at this when Glyn had told her that it would be an all-female shortlist of seven.

'Didn't any men apply? For a science post?' she had asked.

'Oh yes, there were some applications from men. But the classes are all girls. Hairdressers, nurses. Obviously a woman would be best for them.'

Anya had kept her mouth shut. Who was she to argue, when the policy was benefitting her? Even so, she felt uncomfortable about this. It didn't seem right. But now she looked at her fellow candidates, her opponents, her rivals, noting the over-large shoulder pads and slim skirts, big handbags, pointed toes and high heels. Almost a uniform. She had thought about buying something new for this, but money was still tight, even with her slightly increased wages, and she had a feeling that a new outfit wouldn't really influence the governors. Including Hugo, who, she was sure, had already decided she was not the one he would support. Not compliant enough. So she'd worn the old green suit again. She promised herself that she would treat herself to a new one if she got this job. She sighed, and waited.

She was the last to be called. She walked, stiff-legged, into the impressively large conference room, where over a dozen people sat around an enormous rectangular table. At the far end of the room, at the head of the table, sat a middle aged, thin faced, steel-haired woman. When she spoke, it seemed to Anya to come from a million miles away.

'Mrs Gethin, please take a seat. Sorry to have kept you for so long.' Her voice was well modulated, and helped to bring Anya back to the present. 'I am Councillor Geraldine Mainwaring, Chairman of the Governing

107

Body.' She smiled. 'Yes, an archaic term for a woman, but we're working on it.'

Anya smiled too. She took her seat and looked quickly around the room. All men. No faces she recognized, of course, except for Hugo Larsson, who looked back at her with equanimity. In a corner sat a young woman with a notebook on her knee.

Geraldine Mainwaring was speaking again, telling Anya about the procedure to be followed. Then the prepared questions came, one at a time, from some individual governors. They gave her time to answer, did not rush her. And the questions weren't difficult for her to answer. Why did she want this job? What experience did she have of teaching teenagers? How did her qualifications equip her for the post? and so on. She started falteringly, quietly. One elderly man furthest away from her asked her to speak up, and she tried to. But gradually her confidence grew and her voice grew stronger.

She talked about the classes she had taught over the past months, some of the challenges she had faced and how she had overcome them; she told them about the girls who came to her for advice, to confide in her, and how much she valued that. She told them about the plans she had to re-organise her classroom and involve the students; and she talked about the excitement she felt in being able to use her knowledge and her education at last. She stopped, suddenly aware that she had been talking for quite a while. Blushing, she apologized.

'Nothing to apologise for, Mrs Gethin' said Cllr Mainwaring, smiling. 'Well gentlemen, I think Mrs

Gethin has answered all our questions pretty fully, don't you?' She didn't wait for an answer.

'If you'd like to wait next door, Mrs Gethin, we will deliberate amongst ourselves. Or you could leave, of course, and we will telephone you with our decision later this afternoon. I believe most of the other candidates have done that.' She indicated a side door that Anya hadn't noticed.

'Thank you' she said as she rose. She walked past the principal on her way out, and realized that he hadn't asked her any questions. Well, neither did some of the others, she thought. But now he would have his chance to scupper her future.

Anya sat in the side room, alone. She was the only candidate to have stayed. What message did that send? Desperation? Arrogance? Complacency? But it made no sense to leave, she told herself. She was the last to be seen, so maybe they wouldn't take too long to decide. Nevertheless, she settled back, preparing for a lengthy wait. It was only ten minutes later that the door opened. The young clerk with the notebook popped her head around.

'Would you come back in please, Mrs Gethin?' she asked.

Anya followed her, not knowing what to expect. Were there more questions for her? Was she to go through the ordeal again? She didn't have long to wait. Geraldine Mainwaring was speaking.

'I'm delighted to be able to offer you the job, Mrs Gethin' she said. 'I hope you will accept.'

Anya barely contained her excitement as she gratefully accepted the offer; she heard information about when she would start, what documents she would be receiving, all the while wanting to jump up and down, singing. Cllr Mainwaring said she would call to see her in the next few days – Anya half registered some surprised looks from the other governors at this, but was only too happy to be able to leave the room, making an effort not to skip. She ran up some back stairs she had not used until today, and found her way to the staff room. It was empty. She glanced at her watch. Of course! Afternoon lectures were over, and this was the no-man's-land between day and evening classes. She made herself a cup of coffee, noting that she would now need to buy herself a personalized mug and grinning at the thought. She sat in her usual chair, and marvelled at just how happy she was, how much this meant to her, more than she had been able to admit. She was permanent! She would get paid through the holiday! Not the up-coming summer holiday of course – her contract wouldn't start until September – but all future vacation times. And the job was hers! She could stay!

She had one niggling worry that shouldn't be a worry at all. She had promised David that if she were successful today, they would get a place of their own. Rented of course, as he was unemployed and she was still officially a temporary part-time worker. They would buy a house again one day, but not yet. Even so, she should have been thrilled at the prospect of more space, an extra bedroom for the girls. A place of their own. But she wasn't. She secretly dreaded living alongside her husband again, and she longed to stay where she felt safe. Their marriage had deteriorated since they had lost their house – since HE had lost their house, she thought, still angry at the thought. And still he didn't talk, didn't tell her how he was feeling, didn't apologise, or explain. She would have listened. If only he would open up to her, she would make an effort to put the past behind her.

Anya jumped up. What was she doing? She had just been made permanent! Time to celebrate! Smiling to herself, she walked lightly along the empty corridor and ran down the stairs, to come face to face with Byron in the foyer below. She stopped dead.

'Oh, hi!' she said, flustered. 'What are you doing here?'

'Evening duty manager' he replied. 'But I could ask you the same. You don't take a night class, do you?'

'I got the job!' she blurted out. 'I got it!'

He laughed at the sight of her happy, radiant face.

'Well done you!' he said, and he hugged her. And then he held her a little away from him. And then he kissed her. Quickly, softly, on her mouth. He stepped back, his hands still on her shoulders. He looked as surprised as she was.

'Congratulations Cariad. You deserve it' he said quietly. And he was gone.

CHAPTER 8

TAKING A STAND

1983: May

The pleasure, the excitement, and in the case of the adults, relief, was shared by everyone that evening at what had become the family home. The children were thrilled because their mother was, but also, she was sure, because they had been promised slightly bigger presents for their joint party, now only a week away. David was visibly pleased, knowing he would be able to hold Anya to her promise that they would find a place of their own, move in, be together. Jessie was happy because her daughter had been recognized, and rewarded, for her hard work, although her pleasure was tempered with the knowledge that this would mean reverting to her previous single existence, which she didn't relish, having enjoyed the company of her family for these months.

Anya herself was, of course, delighted. They would have some security now, would be able to plan ahead – although what those plans might be, she didn't know. And while she was celebrating her appointment, re-telling the day's events to her mother, what was foremost in her mind was a touch on her lips, so swift, so gentle that she could almost believe she had imagined it. Almost. The image of his stricken face, shocked at his own actions, was with her still. She had not reacted in any way. Standing stock still, it wasn't until he had disappeared that she had allowed herself to breathe again. And now she still felt that kiss, making her tingle, making her blush in the darkness of the bedroom she shared with her husband, not fully exploring what emotions she may be feeling, just savouring the memory and not wanting to let it go.

Everyone in the staff room seemed to have heard of Anya's good news before she arrived the next morning, and she was taken aback at the number of well-wishers.

'All down to my report, of course!' said Marjorie, great pride in her voice.

'Report? What report?' asked Anya, confused.

'Well you don't think I invited you in to teach with me out of the goodness of my heart, do you? No. The chair of governors asked me what I thought of you as a teacher. So I said I'd find out.'

Elaine and the others burst out laughing.

'Marjorie! You didn't!'

'I did indeed! I wasn't going to put my good name to someone when I had no evidence one way or the other, was I? But you turned out to be quite good, Anya. So – well done.' and she walked serenely away.

Anya tried to go about her daily schedule as usual, but two things held her back. Firstly, Hugo was standing in the doorway to his office as she started down the corridor. She gave a slight smile, as non-committal as she could manage, and went to walk past, but he addressed her.

'Congratulations, Mrs Gethin' he said, an emphasis on her title. 'I see you've teamed up with the Mainwaring woman. I suppose that's what happens when they put a dyke in charge.' And he closed the door behind him.

Anya was shocked, and stopped in her tracks, only to feel a slight pressure in the small of her back.

'Keep walking' hissed Elaine from over her shoulder. 'Don't let him get to you. Don't forget – you got the job, and he hasn't had you.'

The second thing that was stopping her from getting on with her day with equanimity was the fact that she hadn't yet seen Byron, and that she was aware she was relieved and disappointed in equal measure.

However, an hour with class 2X was enough to distract anyone. The would-be adults were child-like in their excitement at the prospect of qualifying and ending their college life. The fact that they still had exams to sit – and pass – seemed to by-pass them, and it was all Anya could do to calm them down and to attempt some revision. The other classes she taught that morning were much the same, even though there was a good six weeks to go before the first years' courses would finish. By lunchtime Anya was exhausted, and as she carried her tray of shepherd's pie to the staff table, her only thought was on the hour of respite she could look forward to, so it was with a start that she realized she was standing across the table from Byron.

She put her meal on the table in front of her, placed her plate carefully to one side, and carried the tray to its shelf near the door, all the while doing her best to compose herself, and to control her breathing, which seemed to her to be too loud and too fast. By the time she had dropped into her seat, she was able to look up and

114

smile, before appearing to start on her meal. She moved the food around her plate. She couldn't be sure her hand wouldn't shake if she lifted the fork to her mouth.

'Hi' Byron said lightly. 'We thought you weren't going to make lunch today – you're usually earlier than this.'

'Yeah, we were laying odds on which of the local taverns you'd be celebrating in' said Dan.

Anya looked lost.

'Your job? Your interview?'

She laughed.

'Oh sorry! Yes of course! Been partying non-stop!'

'Seriously though Anya, well done' added Dan. 'It must have been hard. No wonder you look so exhausted'

'Students been playing up, I bet!' said Ethan from the far end of the table. 'Always the same this time of year – end of term euphoria seems to start from Whitsun!'

It was all so normal. Anya felt her breathing slow down, quieten.

'Yes, they're de-mob happy already!' she said with a laugh, and started eating her lunch. What had she been so afraid of? She was being very childish, she knew, making something out of nothing. A little peck, that's all it had been. It meant nothing. It had clearly meant nothing to him. And how stupid of her to think it might. To spend a night lying awake next to her husband, unable to get this man's face out of her head.

Although interspersed with humour and his perceptive observations of his students, the conversation around the table was, as usual, dominated by Byron's dire forecasts and angry outbursts. These were accompanied by the studied disregard of attempts of the rest of the staff to change the subject. Their topics included holidays, their families, exams, and particularly difficult, or particularly gifted, students. His included the miners, Margaret Thatcher, and the upcoming general election.

'… and of course' he was saying, 'people are so stupid, so easily swayed, so willing to believe whatever the latest headline tells them, that she'll get in again…'

Everything was as always. What had she been worrying about? But she didn't stay to argue, discuss, debate with Byron as she usually did once the others had left. She couldn't quite manage that. So it was with the group of her colleagues that she went back to the staffroom, only to find, waiting outside the door, Geraldine Mainwaring.

'Councillor! Hello!' Anya said, surprised. 'Can I help?'

'Just the person' the older woman replied. 'Can we talk?' Without waiting for a reply, she said 'Walk with me. And please, call me Geraldine.'

Anya followed her down the corridor and into a small room she had not noticed before. It was furnished in a surprisingly informal way, with floral wallpaper rather than the obligatory cream pain that was everywhere else in the building, with two sagging armchairs covered in a chintz fabric, and a low table between them.

'Some perks that go with the job' Geraldine said. 'Chairman of governors, I mean. There's always this little room available!'

She poured coffee for them both from a pot sitting on the teak-coloured sideboard, and sat down, leaning back comfortably, and indicating that Anya should do the same.

'I'll come straight to the point, Anya. May I call you Anya?' She went on as Anya nodded. 'I couldn't help but notice that you were glancing at Hugo – the principal – throughout your interview. Was there any reason for that?'

Anya sat up. She hadn't been expecting this!

'I wasn't aware that I was looking at him' she said, surprise evident in her voice.

'Ok. I just wondered whether he had been – shall we say – putting any pressure on you? About the interview? Or the job? Or ... anything else?'

How could she possibly know, Anya thought. And as if Geraldine had read her mind, she said,

'You wouldn't be the first attractive young woman he tried to get into bed with the promise of a job, Anya. He even tried it on with me – yes, hard to believe, I know, but I was young once! I brought my knee up, and brought tears to his eyes. After that, he convinced himself I must be a lesbian. After all, what other possible reason could a woman have for turning him down? He wasn't the principal then, so he couldn't do me much harm professionally. But I've seen enough of this behaviour, and it has to stop. I don't know whether he managed to trick you into doing anything you regret ...' Anya shook her head vehemently '... but I think we owe it to other women to do something about it.'

117

Anya found herself telling this woman of Hugo's groping and touching, his conditional promises of support, and his veiled threat to withhold his vote. She knew that Geraldine understood the pressure she had been under, and it was a relief to talk about it to an outsider.

'Thank you Anya. Pretty much as I suspected. Now, there are two things I'm going to ask you to do, and you may choose not to do them. That's up to you. First – can you ask your colleagues – your female colleagues that is – to tell me about their experiences too? You can reassure them that anything they tell me won't be divulged to anyone else unless they give me permission to do so. That goes for you too of course.'

'Well, yes, I can ask them' said Anya after a little thought. 'And the second thing?'

'Good. Thank you. The second thing is a bit harder. Will you go on the record? Be willing to stand up and say what you've told me? To governors? Councillors? The courts, if necessary? None of that may be needed. The threat of it may well be enough. But if it should – would you come forward?'

Anya was silent. This was just what she didn't want. To risk her job, her privacy, even her reputation if her version of events weren't believed. Hugo had some powerful friends, she knew, and she was sure he would have no compunction in twisting the facts to suit himself.

Geraldine leaned forward.

'And that's what he relies on' she said earnestly when she heard Anya's reservations. 'That's what happens. Most of the women he targets – seriously targets, not just a quick touch on the stairs – they either give in to him, and have to suffer the humiliation and fear that their actions will be found out by a husband, a boyfriend, a parent, or they refuse him, give up, look elsewhere for work, withdraw an application for a promotion. I've seen it happen, Anya. And it has to stop.' She sat back in her chair, looking tired.

Anya was silent again. Then,

'So why now, Geraldine? And why me?'

'Why now? I'll tell you. I've been a councillor, and a governor, for many years. I've been lucky – and persistent! So many women – good women, clever women – have given up. It's not worth the abuse and the insults, and, worse, the contempt and ridicule they've come up against. They have lives to live, and get sick of banging against a door that's firmly closed to them. Now I'm a stubborn so-and-so. And I had my own reasons for wanting to stand for election.

'I've seen people put into roles they weren't equipped for, and jobs they weren't suited to. I've heard rumours and whispers about bad behaviour of councillors, headmasters, senior public servants, all ignored, swept under the carpet, laughed about, but never acted on. All protected by the equivalent of the local mafia – which includes the Labour party boys' club. Do you know how many women there are on the county council? Three. Out of sixty five. And how many women chairmen of governors? One. That's me. But things are changing. The Labour boys are up against a new opposition. Not a political opposition. A new faction that's as old as the hills.' She paused and took a sip of her rapidly-cooling drink.

119

'The Catholics?' asked Anya. Geraldine's face showed her surprise.

'Yes, the Catholics. Do you follow politics then? Local politics?'

'Not really. Just what I've heard in conversation, in the staffroom, the canteen …'

'So what are they saying, these staffroom politicians?'

'That the Catholics are the next force to be reckoned with' Anya replied, and Geraldine laughed.

'Well someone's got their finger on the pulse!' she said. 'Yes, there are growing numbers of us on the council now, elected two years ago. And slowly, bit by bit, we're starting to make a difference. It's still very much a Labour council of course – and it is possible to be a Catholic and a member of the Labour party, as I am. One thing we've managed to do is to get the previous chairman of college governors to resign at last. He should have gone years ago. Kept falling asleep in meetings. We managed to vote him out and me in. He's still a councillor of course, but it's not quite so bad when he falls asleep now. At least he's not chairing a meeting!'

Anya laughed at that, but although Geraldine laughed too, it was clear that she was serious.

'So that's the answer to your 'why now?' question. Now is the first chance we've had to try to right some of the wrongs that are going on in schools and colleges, and I'm starting here.' She took another sip. 'Don't get me wrong, Anya. They're not all bad. There are some very good councillors, working hard, doing a great job. But a handful of powerful men at the top are stopping them – and us – from doing some things that should have happened a long time ago.

'So - why you? I saw something in you, Anya. At your interview. I guessed that he'd been sniffing around you.' Anya made a face. 'Not a nice term, I know. I apologise. But the sentiment is the same. I saw the way you kept glancing over at him, looking nervous, and the way he studiously ignored you. I knew you hadn't given in, either to his pestering or to his threats, and then there you were, standing up to him, telling us what you feel about teaching, about your subject, and most of all, about your students. You forgot he was there, didn't you? You were passionate, excited, committed. You were brave. That's why you.'

Anya drew a deep breath and drank the remains of her stone-cold coffee. She didn't know what to say. She was flattered of course, and surprised. But where was she to go with this? Brave? Was she? She thought about the next woman. Maybe younger, more frightened. Maybe one of her daughters one day ...

'If it comes to it ... if I have to ... Yes, I'll do it. But please, try to sort it out without my having to speak out.'

'Thank you Anya.' Geraldine stood and walked to the door. Then she turned back and said,

'By the way, he didn't have a vote, you know. Hugo. He didn't have a vote.'

At break the next morning, Anya spoke to the women in the staffroom. A few agreed, albeit reluctantly, to meet with Geraldine, but refused point blank to go on the record. After a hurriedly eaten lunch, she ran over to that unfamiliar territory, the Business department. She gave a quick knock on the door to the room she knew acted as an unofficial staffroom, and walked in, to be met with a dozen disapproving faces, clearly shocked to be disturbed in this way. Anya had discovered in the first few weeks of her job that there was no love lost between the two departments, and newcomers were made to feel less than welcome in B block, particularly those traitorous women who belonged to one department and drank coffee in another. Anya had decided to ignore all that this morning. She appeared to breeze in, grateful that her quickening pulse and no-doubt raised blood pressure weren't visible.

'Hello ladies' she said, smiling around the cramped room. 'I've come to ask if you'll take part in a meeting.' And she told them what it was to be about.

To be fair, they didn't dismiss it out of hand. They considered Anya's request to meet with Geraldine; they talked quietly to each other, heads together, before saying no. Except for one. Ruby Harcourt was petite and pretty, with a mop of dark curls that bounced when she talked.

'Come on girls, we all know it happens. You've all been touched up by Hugo, haven't you?' She didn't wait for an answer. 'Haven't you wanted to tell him where to get off? Or to slap him? Except you were too scared of losing your job?'

By the time Anya left her colleagues in Block B, Ruby and three others had agreed to come to the meeting the next day. She was delighted. As she drove home that evening, she planned what she would say to them all. If she needed to speak up, then speak up she would. She was buoyed by the support she had garnered so far – not all the women, of course, but enough to demonstrate that there was a pattern, and a long-standing one at that. By the time she reached the council estate where they now lived, she was feeling optimistic and enthusiastic about the difference her voice could make, but she was surprised to see David waiting for her at the gate, looking more animated than usual. More animated than she had seen him for a very long time, in fact. He met her as she got out of the car.

'Good news' he said abruptly. 'I've found us a flat'.

Her heart sank. She'd decided to put off finding somewhere else to live for a while. After all, her new permanent status, along with her increased salary, wouldn't come into play until September, and she wouldn't be paid during the long summer holiday. That was the excuse she was giving herself, and would have given her husband if he had raised the subject, but it seemed as if he'd taken matters into his own hands. She didn't relish stalling his plans by giving him these practical reasons, but neither was she looking forward to a move away from what had become a comfortable arrangement with her mother. Before she could point out her monetary objections however, David forestalled her.

'And something else. I've got a job.'

His obvious delight at telling her this made her soften, and she smiled at him.

'Davey, that's wonderful! Here, hold my bag, and you can tell me all about it inside.'

Seated around the tiny kitchen table, David told her how he had bumped into Tom.

'You remember Father Tom? I've told you about him. He turned my life around once. And he's done it again.'

He went on to explain, in his laborious way, that Father O'Connell had put him in touch with a friend of his, who was looking for local men for some building work.

'It's like history repeating itself' he told her. 'It's only labouring work, but it's work. And we'll be able to afford to pay rent now. So it's all good news.'

Anya should have been happy for him, and tried to look it. She agreed to look at the flat at the weekend, but she knew it was a done-deal. Whatever it was like, they would have to take it. She'd run out of reasons not to.

The following morning all thoughts of their upcoming move were dispelled as soon as she arrived at the college. One advantage, she thought, of having a long journey to work – plenty of time to leave home issues behind and look forward to the day ahead.

She had told the girls and her mother about their new home, and thought she'd done quite a good job of looking excited at the prospect. Her daughters, as always, took their cue from her, although when Lucy asked if Granny could come with them, her voice faltered. Her mother had come to the rescue.

'Well, I'm looking forward to coming to visit you' she had told the four year old. 'I can't do that if I live there!' Lucy seemed to accept her grandmother's logic.

'And don't we have a party to plan this weekend?' she had added, mercifully taking the conversation in another direction.

The informal meeting with the women staff had been planned for lunch time, and Anya had arranged to use an empty classroom which hopefully would be seen as neutral territory by both departments. Ten women assembled after eating lunch in their several hideaways, and she was pleased to see that two of the hairdressing staff had joined them. Geraldine had arrived earlier, and was sitting at the front of the room, behind a desk, looking for all the world like a teacher awaiting her new class. They, in turn, trooped in, looking variously embarrassed, anxious and annoyed at having agreed to be there at all. When they were seated, Geraldine rose, walked in front of the desk, and started speaking.

'Ladies' she said, looking round. 'Thank you for coming. I know your free time is precious and in short supply, so I'll keep this as short as I can, although it's a big subject we'll be discussing.'

Some expressions softened.

'My name is Geraldine Mainwaring. Pronounced Main-war-ing. The proper Welsh way. None of your *Mannerings*.'

A few more introductory remarks, and she had them eating out of her hand. They listened attentively as she told them, as she had told Anya, why she had asked to meet them. She told them what she planned to do with their evidence, and assured them that they would not be identified unless they wished to be. Most of all, Anya saw, she gave them hope. A future where they would not need to watch every word in case it were misinterpreted, where their attire wasn't seen as an invitation, and where they weren't afraid to challenge unwanted advances, seemed a possibility. Opportunities for promotion would be opened up, the possibility of a woman in a management role a real prospect.

After that, the stories came thick and fast. Anya had agreed to take notes, freeing Geraldine to continue her face-to-face conversations. There was no shortage of examples, from snapping of a bra strap to downright fondling. Lewd and suggestive comments were clearly just as unwelcome as physical acts, and made for a similarly uncomfortable atmosphere, although it seemed that many of the men concerned were blissfully unaware of this. It was noticeable that the vast majority of stories revolved around Hugo, but Anya was shocked to hear of such inappropriate behaviour from other male members of staff too.

Forty minutes later, it was time to bring the meeting to a close. Anya rose to thank Geraldine, and her colleagues, for attending. She decided to add a plea of her own.

'…and as Geraldine has said, your evidence may be used, but not your names. Unless you want to go on the record. That's a big step, I know. But it may be necessary if we – Geraldine and us – if we are to make the changes we want. The changes we deserve. So if anyone thinks they could do that, let Geraldine know.'

'Are you doing it, Anya?' asked someone from the back row.

'Yes, I am' she said simply.

'In that case, so will I'. Elaine said clearly. 'Put my name down, Geraldine.'

'And thank you, Anya. You didn't need to do this' said Ruby as they started to leave. 'Don't suppose you fancy a post in the union, do you?' she laughed. 'We need a new secretary – I'm stepping down.'

'That's not a bad idea you know!' said Geraldine.

Anya was buoyed up throughout the afternoon, the success of the meeting only enhanced by Geraldine's parting comments.

'I see a future for you, Anya. In teaching, yes, but elsewhere too. Secretary of a union can be a powerful role. Don't let the name *secretary* fool you. It's not about perching prettily on the boss' knee – although that's how many members see it. It's the secretary who receives all the information and invitations, and most importantly, sets the agenda. You won't have to say much, unless you want to, and if you do, then the sky's the limit. Chairmen come and go, but it's the secretary who does all the work, and wields all the power, if he – or she – wants to. Here, it's always a woman who's voted on, a woman from the Business department. We're back to the image of a secretary again. So the role has never been used as it should. But you could make it your own, Anya. And you never know where it may lead.'

She thought about Geraldine's words over the weekend, even though the two days were very full. Saturday was taken up with preparations for the joint

127

party on Sunday, and by mid-morning they were well underway. The girls were happy to be left with Jessie, stirring melting jelly, rinsing out rabbit-shaped blancmange moulds, and licking cake mixture off wooden spoons, while Anya and David went to see their new home.

Their walk to the little street on the other side of the town felt awkward to Anya, although David didn't show any evidence of having similar reservations. She realized they hadn't been anywhere together for a long time, and instead of falling into an easy and familiar step that a couple with ten years of marriage behind them should be able to expect, they walked a foot apart and spoke politely but little; what conversation they shared she felt was stilted and focused purely on practicalities around the apartment they were going to see – the lease, rent, the neighbourhood. Thankfully the uneasy and self-conscious walk didn't take too long. But when they reached the address in the narrow cul-de-sac, Anya's worst fears were confirmed.

Their property was on the first floor – something David had failed to mention – and the entrance was via a metal staircase that looked for all the world like a fire-escape. They clanked up the stairs, and on opening the front door, she had the feeling of stepping back in time.

'It's not bad, is it?' asked David as he walked in ahead of her.

Anya turned her head sharply, looking at him, checking if he was being sarcastic. He wasn't.

'Be nice to have our own place again' he said. It was a statement, and didn't require an answer.

The style was reminiscent of the first flat they had rented, albeit this one had a bathroom, a separate kitchen and an extra bedroom. It even had a telephone in the small hallway. But it, too, was furnished, as their first flat had been. No room for anything of their own, even if they had them. The basic table, sideboard, beds and wardrobes, reminiscent of 1950s utility furniture, were no worse than those they had lived with before. But Anya's remembered enthusiasm, in the aftermath of the news of a forthcoming baby and their hurried wedding, wasn't matched at the sight of yet another run-down flat nearly ten years later. She thought they had moved on. They had owned their own house – a house she had loved. They had filled it with pieces she had chosen, carefully, lovingly, his contribution being the providing of the finances to do so. The memory of losing that home still smarted. And here they were, almost back where they started. The bitterness Anya had been feeling towards David for so long was now dangerously close to the surface, and threatened to spill over into an outburst that would set back their fragile relationship once again, perhaps fatally.

She held her tongue. She told herself – this is temporary. It's not forever. I can do this. She couldn't articulate, even to herself, what change might allow her to leave this dismal place, what circumstance could precipitate such a liberation, but she knew that something would. It had to. So now she said the right things, the non-committal things that were needed to keep the peace. She knew she would have her work cut out to persuade the girls that this was a good move, as they had already made it clear that they were happy to stay at their grandmother's. The couple walked back in almost total silence. Anya hoped that David viewed it as a companionable silence rather than realising that she didn't trust herself to say anything. They would move next weekend and she felt panic welling up in her. She didn't want to go.

Party time the next day couldn't fail to be a success. Anya thought the girls enjoyed carrying the platters and bowls over to the nearby church hall as much as they would enjoy the party itself – but she was wrong. The party was even better, and they had a wonderful time. It was good to see some of the mothers she used to meet at the school gates, even Veronica, who looked suitably smug at the news, widely circulated, that Anya and David had lost their house, but Anya found that she didn't really care what the great and the good of Port Haven thought any more, and smiled sweetly while handing round the egg sandwiches.

Having gorged on the home-made party food, the games of pass the parcel and musical chairs, and a final half hour of disco dancing, filled the afternoon. By the time the other parents arrived to collect their offspring, children and adults alike were pleasantly exhausted. Anya and Jessie carried bags of discarded wrapping paper and used paper plates as they led the three girls, laden down with presents, back to the house. David hadn't joined them at the party, but there again, Anya couldn't remember a time when he had. In the early years, it was due to his long work hours, but he hadn't had that excuse for the past five years. He spent precious little time with his daughters, Anya thought to herself as they walked along. He didn't know them. And they didn't know him. So maybe it wouldn't be such a wrench …

'A penny for them!' Her mother's voice brought her back to the present.

'Oh! Nothing!' she laughed.

'So no need to look so guilty then' said Jessie, but she too laughed and, walking on, said no more.

CHAPTER 9

A NEW HOME

1983: June

Anya heard nothing back from Geraldine for the rest of the month. She supposed there was no reason to expect her to keep in touch, but somehow she felt a little let down. Despite her initial nervousness, she had become excited at the thought of making some changes, and now everything seemed a bit flat on that front. But other aspects of work were anything but dull. External exams to prepare for, and internal end-of-year tests to write and print, not to mention getting ready for next term. This was only her first year of teaching, yet so much had happened, and now she was preparing for her first year as a permanent, full time lecturer. She said that to herself, under her breath, several times a day, hardly believing her good fortune.

It was with an air of reckless enthusiasm that she had attended the next union meeting. It had been Geraldine's suggestion, along with her lunch-time discussions with Byron, that had piqued her interest. So she found herself volunteering to take on the role of secretary, and without a murmur from the other members, there she was. The other women members were glad not to have to do it themselves, and the men saw it as a woman's job anyway. She had a lot to learn, she knew, but she was keen.

She had been relieved that Byron made no reference to their brief kiss on the day of her interview, and she found she could talk to him as she had before, as if it had never happened. After all, it was just a "congratulations" kiss, wasn't it? His appetite for political debate had increased considerably as the day of the general election drew nearer. She never tired of hearing him talk in his passionate way about fairness, equality, the oppression of the working class, although her appreciation was not shared with other colleagues.

'Give it a rest, By,' sighed Dan over lunch a week before the election. 'We know you don't like her, but doesn't Mrs Thatcher deserve some credit for getting somewhere in a man's world? First woman Prime Minister – that's something, isn't it?'

'I don't give a damn whether she's a man or a woman – it's her shit policies I object to!' Byron came back angrily. 'Sorry about the language, Anya.'

He smiled at her, an unexpected ray of sunshine in a stormy sky, then he continued, as forceful as ever.

'And you should care about them too, Danny boy. Think about it. Why was this place built? Why is it still here? To train the mining apprentices. Oh yes' he went on, as he saw Dan about to correct him, 'Oh yes, we train people for hairdressing, nursing, office work too. They come here because it's close to home, convenient. And because we do a bloody good job at teaching them. But do you think there aren't other colleges not a million miles away who could offer pretty much the same courses? The only reason they haven't tried to take them all is because they can't get their hands on the mining apprentices. They are the ones keeping us going, keeping us open. Other colleges would give their eye teeth for them. But they don't have the workshops, the tools, the instruments, the heavy equipment. Oh, and yes - they don't have a colliery within spitting distance as we do.'

The staff around the table were listening to him now.

'So – think about it. Thatcher and her Tories get in. Hammer the unions again. Hammer the miners. Close down the mines – yes, Scargill is right, that's what they'll do. So what then? No mine. No apprentices. No college. No job.'

Byron's words went around Anya's mind as she drove home that evening. Politics was real. Why had she never seen it before? Was it because the consequences of government decisions didn't seem to affect people like her? But no – they had already affected her. Wasn't it politics that had resulted in the recession? The high levels of unemployment? The impossible interest rates? Hadn't her own family suffered as a direct result of these? Isn't that why David had lost his job? It was as if a light had been switched on in her head. She saw it clearly now. Politics was real, and all around her, and she'd never seen that. And she realized just how many other people thought the way she had – until now. The ones who didn't vote, the ones she'd heard on the TV saying "They're all the same". No they weren't. They couldn't be. There had to be a choice. She had a choice.

As she drew closer to Port Haven, she brought her mind back to their living situation. It wasn't great. As she had suspected, the girls were less than enthusiastic about their new home, and it was all Anya could do to inject an element of excitement and adventure into the move. She now saw that her mother had done the same thing, over the years, whenever money was tight and things were bleak. Make it into an adventure, hide your own fears. Leaving her mother, and her old childhood home, would be harder than she could have imagined. Even after having moved out so long ago, she knew she would miss it.

On the Saturday they were leaving, she and her mother went around the house, children trailing behind them, checking they hadn't left anything. Anya had a feeling that Lucy had hidden a few things that she would have to come back for, and she smiled at the thought. The girls ran ahead and stood outside Jessie's room.

'Granny, can we play with your dollshouse please?' begged Emily. 'Just one last time?'

'Of course you can' laughed Jessie. 'Just be very, very careful …'

'We know, it's fragile!' finished Fran.

They stood in front of the impressive structure, not a toy, but a re-creation of bygone years.

'It can go back into the spare room later' Jessie said. 'I've liked having it here, but it does clutter it up a bit.'

'Tell us about it, Granny' asked Emily, using her usual delaying tactics. Anya rolled her eyes while Jessie laughed.

'I'm not sure I can tell you anything new, Em, but ok, a quick version.'

The three girls huddled round the magnificent dollshouse they had known all their lives, and listened to the story that was fast becoming as familiar to them as it was to Anya.

'Your grandad made this for me when we were first married. We had moved a long way away, and he knew I was a bit homesick. He promised that one day we'd move back home and live in a great big house, just like the one on the hill outside the town. So he built this one exactly the same - on the outside anyway. He made all sorts of secret passages and cupboards, and hid little secrets for me to find. He gave it to me on my birthday, the day I found out I was expecting your mum. It was very special.' Jessie paused, waiting for the next question.

'And what happened next, Granny?' pleaded Fran, jumping up and down with excitement, knowing the answer.

'Well, we did move back home. And guess what?' They didn't need to guess.

'You bought the huge house on the hill!' all three shouted.

The story was part of their family folklore, known so well. And yet Anya knew that it was a bittersweet story with an unhappy ending to her parents' time together.

'And did Mum play with it when she was a little girl?' asked Lucy, right on cue.

'Yes she did, even though she wasn't supposed to. She would toddle over to it when she was quite small, pretending to make tea for the dolls, using those tiny china cups and saucers.'

Her mind ran briefly back to that fateful day, her little daughter offering round a "cuppa tea", Peggy gently pulling her away, the police officers sitting uncomfortably on the lavish sofa …

She shook herself.

'And now I'll have it all to myself again for a while! What a relief!' and she hugged her precious grandchildren.

So they had moved into the flat, making new arrangements for Jessie to take and fetch the girls to and from school. David had already started his new job with a building firm a few miles outside the town, and Anya was pleased he seemed to have settled there. He got on well with his workmates, who picked him up each morning in the mud-spattered works van, and they invited him to go out with them in the evenings. The receptionist at the firm was someone called Gwyneth, whom he hadn't seen for many years, and he had met up with some other old friends too. Rekindling his old friendship with Father Tom, he started to get involved in church life again. As an ex-communicant, he didn't take part in the services, but he had offered to help out with any odd jobs around the ecclesiastical grounds. At first, Anya felt a pang of irritation at this, as for five years he had done nothing to improve their home, not the slightest bit of DIY, even though he'd had the time, heaven knows. And the place they now lived could certainly do with a face-lift. Even some shelving would have improved it. But another part of her, the part she wouldn't reveal to anyone else, was only too pleased that he was spending more time out of the house, besides his work hours. Spending more time away from her.

She parked the car in the side street and mounted the clanging steps to their front door. This was temporary, she told herself. They would live somewhere better than this.

June 10th. Conservative win. Landslide victory. Michael Foot set to resign. The atmosphere in the staffroom ranged from celebratory and triumphant to glum and fatalistic. Anya had no doubt the same would be the case at the lunch time staff table, and she was right. But if she had expected Byron to be in the depths of despair, she was wrong. He appeared to be the same as ever – alternating between cheery and argumentative.

'No surprises' he pronounced, as the staff took their seats and got stuck in to the steak and kidney pie special.

'It's what we all expected. And what some of us hoped for.' He looked pointedly along the table to Dan and the others, and winked at Ethan.

'Come on Byron, you know we're not Tories' protested Dan.

'No, I know' admitted Byron. 'But you're not sorry about the result, are you?'

No-one answered for a while, all keeping their heads down, concentrating on their meals.

'Well, after your little pep-talk the other day, I think we're all a bit worried' said Ethan eventually, and the nods around the table confirmed this.

'I mean,' he went on, 'I know we may all be worried, or pleased, about different things, but we all have one thing in common. We work here, and we want to carry on working here.'

The discussion continued until the buzzer rang for the first of the afternoon's classes, when Byron made a hasty exit.

'First year Motor Vehicle boys' he explained as he walked quickly out of the canteen. 'They're likely to wreck the workshop if I'm not there first!'

'Oh bugger! I didn't realise the time!' said Anya as she jumped up from the table. 'I was going to do some printing after lunch. It'll have to wait till the end of the day now – thank heavens I've got a free.'

'You're joking, right?' said Dan. 'You won't get near the printing room this afternoon. All the sessions will be fully booked – exams start Monday, remember?'

'What? Oh no! I was going to put the papers together over the weekend! What can I do?'

'Well, maybe next time, don't leave it till the last minute!' laughed Ethan, who was howled down by the others.

'Only kidding Anya' he said apologetically. 'That's what everyone's done. That's why you won't get in. You might have a chance after five o'clock though. It's Friday, no night classes tonight, so all the staff shoot off as soon as they can. Have a word with the caretaker. He'll moan at you, but he'll keep the place open for a couple of

139

hours if you ask nicely. The office should sort it. But do it quick!'

She ran to her first class, gave out a prepared worksheet, and told them to make a start.

'I'm putting you on your honour not to talk to each other' she told them, knowing full well that this particular instruction would be completely ignored as soon as she left them, then dashed to the office

'Can I use the printing room at five, please?' she asked breathlessly.

'You'll be lucky!'

This most unhelpful of the College secretaries never missed an opportunity to exercise her authority over lecturing staff.

'Left it a bit late I'm afraid. And it's not called the printing room any more. It's "reprographics" now.'

'Come off it' called her boss from the inner office. She was the most senior admin person there, and managed to hear everything through a seemingly closed door. 'You know there'll be no-one in the printing room at five on a Friday!'

'Well as it so happens' she answered triumphantly, 'there is someone booked for five. So the only machine available is the Gestetner. And I hope you're not expecting one of us to type out your questions for you!'

Anya breathed a sigh of relief.

'It's the Gestetner I need' she told her. 'And it's ok, I've handwritten the stencils. Thank you. Can you book me in please? And how do I get hold of the caretaker?'

'No need. Someone's already booked so the room will be open. Just don't leave it in a mess!'

Returning to her class, Anya checked the worksheets with her students, trying to keep a straight face when the answers of all of the girls were identical. And word perfect. Almost as if they had been copied from the notes she had dictated during the term. She didn't mind. She knew that the very act of finding the answers and writing them out was a form of revision in itself.

It was during the afternoon break that she realized she needed to contact her mother. As the phone rang, she prayed that she hadn't missed her – she glanced at her watch. Ten past three. Crossing her fingers, she listened to the ringing, until,

'Mum? I caught you!'

'Only just, love' said Jessie. 'I was out of the door! Be quick or I'll be late for the girls.'

'I have to stay late, Mum, to do some printing. Can you hang on and tell David he'll have to sort out their tea? I should be home by sevenish, seven thirty at the latest.'

'How about I bring them back to me, Annie? They could stay the night.'

'Oh Mum, that would be wonderful!' Anya said delightedly. 'What about …'

'Don't worry – we'll call in to the flat, pick up the jim-jams, and leave a note for David if he's not home. Now I really have to go!'

A load off her mind, Anya's last class of the day flew by. She managed to buy a bread roll in the canteen before it closed, then went to the workroom to pick up her precious papers and stencils, and made her way to the printing room, located in a remote corridor that seemed like miles from anywhere. Her arms full, she kicked open the door and it went flying, crashing against the wall.

'Oh, sorry!' she exclaimed as she realized someone was in the room. 'I didn't mean …'

'No I don't suppose you did! Here, let me take those for you.' And Byron was lifting the pile of documents out of her hands. 'Are you on the Gestetner? I really hope so! I've got a load of stuff to print and I certainly don't have time to make those blasted skins!'

Anya found her voice. She made a conscious effort to steady it, as the surprise of seeing him there, unexpected, unprepared for, had somehow taken the wind out of her.

'Er … yes, I'm on the Gestetner.' She walked to the ancient machine and started looking for the ink bottle in the cupboard above it, anything to hide her blushing cheeks from him. 'You on the litho machine?'

'You mean The Beast? Yeah, I'm trying to tame it!' He turned back to the huge machine which filled half of the small room.

It had taken her a little while to master the old, hand-cranked machine in front of her now, painstakingly making stencils or "skins", feeding them onto the roller, covering them with just enough ink and turning the handle at a nice steady pace, and it suited her to continue to use it.

'Are those handwritten questions?' Byron was looking over her shoulder. 'I'm impressed! You must be more organised than I am – and not as lazy! I'm afraid I get the office staff to type my papers out.'

'Well, I don't know about organised' she replied, keeping busy, keeping moving, keeping talking, trying to ignore the smell of his aftershave. 'So many of my exam papers are made up of diagrams, it's easier to draw them onto the skins than to ask the office to leave spaces for them!'

She was calmer now. She had surprised herself by her reaction to seeing Byron, but they chatted easily as they went about their work, stacking papers, sorting them, stapling them where necessary. They didn't talk about anything personal. They never had. They talked about the election, politics in general and the miners in particular. They talked about the college, its future, its threats. And they talked about the unions, strikes, and picket lines. Anya had learned a lot from Byron, enough for her to be able to disagree with him, argue with him, put another point forward, all of which he seemed to relish, pushing her to make her case, think logically and not be drawn off track. Time flew by.

'Done!' they exclaimed simultaneously, and laughing, they both turned, only to find they were face to face, inches away from each other. Neither moved. She could have stepped back against the table. She should have. But she didn't. She looked into his eyes. His brown eyes. They seemed to see so much more than she wanted him to. He didn't look away.

Slowly, he brought up his hands and, cupping her face gently, brushed her lips with his. They barely touched, but she felt them burn into her. He pulled away,

143

ever so slightly, then kissed her again, softly, lightly. She felt as though she was writhing deep inside, wanting more. The tip of his tongue traced the shape of her lips, until she thought she would explode, or faint. He kissed her again, gently, but there was a promise of urgency.

'I won't sleep with you' she whispered.

'I know' he murmured between soft kisses.

'I won't leave my husband.'

'I know' he breathed against her mouth.

And then they were kissing as she had never kissed, never been kissed. His tongue found hers, touching the very tip, darting, teasing, tantalizing. She could taste his lips, his mouth, his tongue with hers. His fingers were in her hair, her arms around him, feeling the strength of his body beneath the soft leather of his jacket, her hands moving, exploring his neck, his hair. They were one, fused together, hearts beating in time, pulses throbbing through their bodies, his hardness pressed against her, pounding, until she thought she would burst, feeling the wetness between her legs …

The footsteps were heavy and loud, and gave them a fraction of a second to pull apart before the door flew open.

'Alright everyone, time's up!' The caretaker came in with a jangle of keys. 'I've given you as long as I can – the rest of the college is all locked up, so it's time for you to go!'

The two of them busied themselves with picking up their papers, heads down, she trying to slow her breathing, calm the thudding of her heart.

'Thanks mate' said Byron, as they followed the caretaker out of the room. It was clear he was going to escort them from the building, and they walked sedately in front of him. He stood at the door while they opened their cars.

'I'll lock the gates after you' he shouted.

'Can I call you?' Byron muttered as they parted. After only a split second hesitation, Anya gave the slightest of nods as she got into her driving seat, and she knew that her life was about to change.

CHAPTER 10

SORROW AND LOSS

1973

She knew what it was. The pain. She knew the ropes. It was familiar. Dreaded, but familiar. She walked, doubled over, towards the open front door of the bungalow, and lowered herself onto the step, where she sat, arms around her hunched knees, waiting for him. She turned her wedding ring round and round, pressing it into her finger till it hurt, trying to deflect the pain that was racking her body. She stared at the gold band, thinking back. Back to 1967.

What a day that had been! They knew what the whisperers were saying. And they didn't care. Nineteen years old, ambitions thrown to the wind, unconventional matrimonial garb their last rebellious act, grown-ups now, as they stood outside the narrow façade of the registry office, and grinned for the camera.

The flowing multi-coloured dress on her tiny frame, the floppy-brimmed hat perched on the blond urchin cut, she could have stepped out of a fashion magazine. She looked delightedly at him, self-conscious in his bell-bottomed suit and kipper tie, his brown hair falling in waves onto his flowered shirt collar. She put her arm around him, loving the feel of him, his narrow waist, his slim hips. She patted him.

146

'Nice arse!' she whispered.

His smile was perfect for the photograph.

Her hat had blown off, his carnation drooped and fell, and still they didn't care. They had a secret, which wasn't a secret at all. But none of the handful of well-wishers standing around them, some sombre with stony disapproving faces, some with eyes LSD-bright, knew how their secret was changing their lives.

She had never thought of herself as maternal. She had her future mapped out, and an exciting one it was to be. Science, of course. Maybe medicine. Excelling at her girls' grammar school, even the most reticent of her teachers had forecast top results for her. And they weren't disappointed. The university place was secured. She could have gone anywhere. They had even mentioned Oxford. But she would not leave him, couldn't be so far away. He still had three more years as an apprentice. So Swansea Uni it was.

Although apart during the week, they were inseparable at weekends. She would take the bus back home on a Friday afternoon, jumping into his arms as he met her at the stop, laughing. Or he would join her in the Students Union and stay with her in her cramped hostel room, listening to *Sounds of Silence*, turning up the music to drown out their laughter and their love-making, lest the warden suspect a man on the premises.

Two terms in, everything changed.

'I'm late' she told him.

'How late?'

'A week.'

'That's not much, is it?'

'For me it is.'

Two weeks later, still nothing. Then a second period missed.

'I think that's it, love' she said. 'I think I must be pregnant.'

And as if a switch had been pressed, they became two new people. Not the schoolkids they had been, basking in the glow of first love, nor the teenagers holding hands, seeking out places where they could be alone, or even the young adults furthering their careers, but budding parents. Never any question of denying that, never any consideration of an alternative. Legal abortion was not yet an option, though it was coming, but thoughts of that, or God forbid, an illegal procedure, never entered their heads. A light-bulb moment told her that this is what she wanted. This is what she was made for. All the careers advice in the world couldn't have prepared her for the feelings she had right now.

They revelled in their news. Parents were horrified, of course. Hers, because she was giving up a career, to be tied down with children, this the first of many they were sure. How could she? How could she have been so stupid? So irresponsible? She listened quietly, secretly yearning for the child inside her, wanting to hug herself with joy. How could she not? Wasn't this the best thing ever? Their own little one? But she listened and looked suitably remorseful, as was expected of her. Until her father had said she was throwing herself away on "that little grease monkey". Then she walked away.

His parents no better. Tying himself down with a baby at his age! What had he been thinking? Didn't he know how to take precautions? And her - a girl no better than she should be … At this he had to speak up, defend her. He loved her, he said. They loved each other, he said. And he, too, had walked away.

So the hurried wedding was planned, and she didn't care about the guests, the wedding breakfast in the back room of the local pub, the flowers, all the things that brides are supposed to care about. She only cared for him, and their unborn child. They rode away on his James 250cc bike, a pair of lovers with all before them.

For three months they played house in the caravan they rented on a camp site outside the village. They loved it. It was to be only temporary, of course. While they waited for a council house, or looked for a flat. But it was perfect. Their own little love nest. He rode home from work each evening to be engulfed in her sweet-smelling arms as she pulled him onto the bed, kissing him as he did her, asking about his day, telling him about her walks and the women she had met in the little site shop. He told her stories of his workmates, his boss, the latest jobs he'd been assigned. She experimented with foreign recipes she could barely pronounce, and he pretended to enjoy them. They slept dreamlessly in each other's arms, and woke looking forward to each day.

The pains had started suddenly, and they frightened her. Was this labour? Surely not. Surely not yet. It was night time, and she had woken with a start, frightening him too. He had tried to reassure her, everything would be fine, he said. But we'll go to the hospital, just in case. Quickly. No time to get to the phone box, to call an ambulance. The pains were stronger, more

149

regular. So she rode pillion on his bike, and they flew through the night. But she knew what was happening. Their baby was coming.

Rushed to the labour ward, her mind was in turmoil, impatient to meet her baby, terrified it was too soon. Babies survived at six months, didn't they? He was ordered out. This was no place for the father, they said. So she did what they told her, pushed when they told her, panted when they told her. Every pain worthwhile, every contraction helping to push this little mite into the world it wasn't ready for. And there he was, a tiny son, taken away to be worked on, at last rewarding the midwives with a weak cry. She saw the look they exchanged, the slight shake of the heads. The crying stopped.

She had held him. Warm, perfect. Her hot tears fell on him, as if to revive him. But they were no phoenix tears. He lay limp in her arms, little eyes closed, miniature hands not clutching her finger as they should. She devoured every inch of him with her eyes, memorising, storing every detail. And his father was there, holding her, holding his son, devastation written on his face, not knowing what to say, what to do.

That was the start. The despair, the anguish, the tears, the grief, all greater than they could ever be again. But there she was wrong. The next time, she never even reached a birth. She lost her child at ten weeks. What a soulless term for the death of a baby. Lost it? Her baby had died. Another baby had died. And the word miscarriage seemed to imply, at least to her, that she had made a mistake, done something wrong. And that's how she felt. Grief didn't seem to be expected of her this time.

She was supposed to carry on as if her second baby had never existed. But the loss was as bad. And the next. And now she sat, staring at that gold band, willing him to come home, knowing there was nothing he could do, hoping there was.

He found her there, dry eyed, all cried out over the past six years. He didn't have to ask, but he did.

'Again?'

'Again.'

He raised her gently to her feet, and walked her to the car. A family car. Made to carry the brood of children they should have had. Everywhere she looked, there were reminders, the hope that next time, next time … The swing he'd built in the garden, empty, squeaking in the breeze; the washing line starkly still, no nappies to fill it. And the outline of a pram, seen through the shed window, stored away lest it upset her. Tempting fate, her mother had called it. Tempting fate to buy a pram so soon. That was for – what – baby number two? Or was it three? How could she possibly not know, she thought, shocked at her callousness.

They all had names. Their first, the one she had held, the one whose little face invaded her dreams, making her wish she would never wake, was James. The others had silly ones to start with, and, not knowing whether boy or girl, they had carried on doing that, but the humour shrank along with their hopes. Munchkin first, then Fluff-Bunny. Babykins. And now this one. Cariad. Just Cariad. Boy or girl, it didn't matter. A word that means Love couldn't be wrong, could it? And she had dared to hope. They didn't talk about it. Couldn't be seen

151

to "tempt fate" yet again. And the time went on, longer than last time. She reached that elusive twelve week watershed, passed it, hardly dared to breathe. And then this. He helped her into the car.

The nurses were kind, as ever. The doctor too. But there was nothing to be done. She was told to go home and wait. Keep anything she passed.

'Keep anything?' she said. 'If you mean my baby, please say it'.

There was bitterness in every syllable.

'If you mean I must catch my baby as it comes away, in a bowl, or a bucket, so that a nice friendly midwife can come along tomorrow, straight from delivering a nice bouncing one, a screaming one, a live one, and examine the mess that's all I can manage, just say so.'

The nurses looked embarrassed, helpless. She wasn't crying. She didn't do that any more.

'It's ok love' he said, 'they're only doing what they have to. Come on, let's get you home.'

And he did. She lay on the caravan sofa all night, he holding her hand, until she pulled away, turning her face from him. Then, writhing with pain, she walked calmly to the bathroom and let her baby, her little one, her Cariad, drop into the clean plastic bowl. She covered it with a towel and left it there, returning to the sofa and him, not saying a word. Then Claire reached for the whiskey bottle.

CHAPTER 11

ONE HOT SUMMER

1983: June

Anya drove without noticing where she was. Her breathing was still fast, her pulse too rapid. She had never experienced any feeling like the one she had just shared with him. A purely physical feeling, deep inside her, throbbing even now as she remembered it. She felt dizzy at the memory of his touch, and had to concentrate hard to ensure she drove safely. She was in a turmoil. She had nodded her head, told him he could call her. She had had no time to think, to consider, and she knew that in that small action, she had acknowledged that she wanted this again, wanted more.

The flat was in darkness when she arrived home. She was grateful that the children were with her mother, and surprised but relieved that David wasn't in. She couldn't settle, couldn't eat, couldn't sit. She stared out of the window, not knowing what she saw.

David arrived home after nine o'clock, quite sober. His re-acquaintance with some old allies and his friendship with new workmates over recent weeks seemed to have made a difference, ostensibly a positive one, although a perverse part of Anya's mind resented it, needing as she did to cling to all the reasons she had not to stay with him. They spoke little, apart from the pleasantries that meant nothing - *...how are you? ... have* *a good day? ... have you eaten?* and were barely listened to by either.

Anya lay awake next to her husband, and they might as well have been in different countries. He was soon snoring gently, but she could not sleep. She wanted to pace around, go for a walk, watch TV, but she didn't want to risk waking David by disturbing the squeaking bedsprings. A few times lately he had moved towards her while they lay there, put his arm around her, kissed her, started to fondle her breasts.

In the past he had become surly when she had occasionally said, truthfully, that she was too tired for sex. He had taken it as an affront, a personal slight, and for days had made spiteful remarks, not quite under his breath, but audible only to her. So when, on the first night in their new home, he had wanted to make love to her, she had let him. No more than that. After all the weeks living with her mother, she guessed that he must have been frustrated, not wishing to chance the thin walls to give them the privacy they would need.

On that first night in the plain wooden bed in the dingy bedroom, when he had lifted her nightdress, groped for her, climbed onto her, already erect and panting, she had made some attempt at being responsive, had said the right things, had tried to move in the way she always had. And she had felt nothing. And he didn't seem to notice. It was enough. Each time he had wanted her over the past few weeks, she had tried, and failed, to participate as she knew she should, until she began to dread his approach. He hadn't made any move towards her for a week or more

154

though, and she was afraid to wake him now. She wouldn't be able to pretend, not tonight.

All the next day, Anya couldn't settle to anything. Her mother asked her if she was well, said she looked as if she had a fever. She couldn't concentrate, and went through the day, cleaning, cooking, answering her daughters' chatter, with her mind racing, asking herself questions she couldn't answer, analysing every minute of the previous day. Did he think she had encouraged him? Had she sent out those inexplicable signals, saying she was interested in him? She didn't think so. She had known she was attracted to him, had known that long before he had kissed her at the bottom of the stairs. But so were other women on the staff, from what they said. She had never flirted with him, never "given him the eye", as her mother would call it. Or was she just another notch on his proverbial bedpost? The latest in a long line of conquests, the next to be chosen? And so her mind raced. And still he didn't call.

Sunday. Another day of anxiety and unanswered questions. And now she felt angry – angry with him, but mainly angry with herself. How could she have been so stupid? Did he know what it had cost her, to give that nod? She may only have had a fraction of a second to consider, but in that time, she knew that she was opening a door that wouldn't be shut. And it clearly meant nothing to him.

When, after lunch, the phone rang, she jumped as David answered it. A workmate arranging tomorrow's lift. It rang again at teatime. Again, David answered it, while she sat, her heart beating so loudly she thought the others were bound to hear it. Wrong number.

155

By the time the girls were bathed, hair washed and asleep, Anya was emotionally drained and just wanted to sleep. She made no objection when David said he was popping out for a quick one. She set up the ironing board, dragging herself to the laundry basket for clean school and work clothes to press for the coming week, piling up the dresses and cardigans, hanging up shirts and skirts, taking too long over everything. The phone rang.

'Anya?'

She sat down, hard, on the tapestry-covered seat in the tiny hallway.

'Yes' she whispered, all her anger gone now, all her energy returned, fizzing through her.

'Thank God. Can you talk?'

'Yes' she said again.

'I'm so sorry, Anya. I didn't have your number, did I?'

Of course he didn't. Why hadn't she thought of that?

'I rang Elaine, left a message, told her you'd left something in the printing room, and I needed to let you know. She's only just called me back.'

She was as light as air.

'I phoned earlier – I think your husband answered.'

The wrong number.

'Anya? Are you ok?'

'Yes, I'm ok. I'm glad you rang.'

'I can't stop long though. I'm in a phone box.'

He stopped. Then,

'Anya, about what happened. I just wanted you to know – I don't make a habit of behaving like that…'

So he was regretting it. She should have known. She should have …'

'…but there's something going on here, isn't there? Something with us. Something …'

She held her breath.

'Look, I know I'll see you tomorrow, but we won't be able to talk, will we? Not properly. Can I see you next weekend? Saturday? In the afternoon? Can we meet?'

She didn't have to think about it.

'Yes.'

'You're sure? I don't want to …'

'I'll sort something for the girls.'

'Ok. I'll let you know where, when. Is that alright?'

'Yes' she said. Then,

'Byron …'

'What?'

'Nothing. See you tomorrow.'

And he was gone.

Anya lay on her bed. David would be home soon, and she would be asleep. Her eyes would be closed, her breathing deep and steady, she would make sure of it. But sleep? Her mind was racing, her body aching, betraying her. She knew she should feel guilty, but her heart was singing.

The following week was endless. She looked at Saturday as if down the wrong end of a telescope. The exams were in full swing for most of Anya's classes, each set of papers needing to be marked, and this should have made the time fly, but instead it stood still. The times when she saw Byron were beacons in her day, making her heart beat faster, her face flush. She found herself surreptitiously glancing out of the staffroom window at the engineering workshop whenever she could, occasionally catching a glimpse of him, and sometimes he her, when he would raise his hand briefly, then, head down, continue on his way.

And so the week wore on. Anya told her mother she had been invited to Georgia's, one of the hairdressing staff, for a pre-end-of-term get-together. She felt a pang of guilt as she said this. She had never worried about leaving her daughters when she had been at college, or at work, because it was out of necessity, and because they loved being with her mum anyway. But this – this was pure selfishness. She was meeting Byron because she wanted to. No other reason. She questioned her morality. She had been indignant at Hugo Larsson's advances. Was Byron so different? Had he just taken a different approach, taken his time? Was her reaction, her acquiescence, simply because she found Byron more attractive? Was she so shallow? And so her mind raced, even if time didn't.

She woke early on Saturday to a glorious, sunny morning. In truth she had slept little, but felt awake as never before. She had prepared breakfast, cleaned and tidied, and put the first two loads of washing in the old

158

twin-tub machine before the rest of the household appeared. The girls were chatty as always, looking forward to spending the afternoon with their granny, and although it was a Saturday, David was soon on his way to work.

'Overtime is always handy' he told her as he left. 'I may be a bit late back – some of the boys are playing in a darts match, and …'

'Yes of course' she said. 'Have a good day.'

He shouted goodbye to Em, Fran and Lucy as he clumped down the clanging stairs, and Anya breathed a sigh of relief. She wouldn't have to worry about his being home when she returned. Somehow that was important. The phone rang, and Jessie was asking if the children would like to stay over again. She didn't need an answer: she could hear them cheering when Anya put it to them.

'I think that's a yes, Mum!' she said, laughing.

'Lovely' said Jessie. 'Drop them off whenever you like – I'm in all day.'

Somewhere in the back of her mind, Anya wondered briefly if her mother was lonely. She dismissed the thought, knowing as she did how much her mum relished her independence, and her own company.

She busied herself with gathering up sleepwear and toothbrushes, piled the girls into the car, and set off for the short journey to the other end of the town. It occurred to her that David hadn't suggested he use the car that day, which he could have, and which would have made her arrangements very difficult. Briefly, she wondered why, especially as she hadn't heard the works van, but soon put the thought out of her head, grateful that the issue had not arisen.

With the girls making themselves at home in her mother's living room, Anya took her leave.

'Thanks Mum' she said, giving her mother a hug, 'You know how grateful I am.'

'Nonsense!' Jessie said with a smile. 'I love having them. And anyway, you deserve to have a little fun. Enjoy yourself. Now off you go!'

Anya's guilt only lasted until she reached the end of the road.

They had arranged to meet in the carpark of an out-of-town supermarket, where her car wouldn't seem out of place, sitting unattended for – who knew how long? She parked, and waited, and then there he was, in his two-tone Ford Cortina, parking next to her. He leaned over and opened the passenger door and patted the seat. Anya felt a split second of panic. He's done this before, she thought suddenly. And I haven't.

Getting into his car, sitting so close to him while he drove through country roads, listening to him talking, quietly, pleasantly, made this extraordinary afternoon feel as normal and ordinary as any other, and yet as different as it could be. The car pulled off into a tree-lined lane which, after half a mile, disappeared and opened instead into a small clearing surrounded by sycamore, hazel and hawthorn.

'We shouldn't be disturbed here' Byron said, looking at her for the first time. 'Are you ok? We can go back if you want to.'

'No, no, I'm ok, really. Just a bit nervous, if I'm honest. I don't really know what I'm doing here.'

He turned to her, smiled his beautiful smile, and took her hand in his.

'We're here to talk. Maybe listen to some music.' He turned the ignition switch and pushed a cassette into the player.

'Anything else is up to you.'

The beautiful sounds of Beethoven's Pastorale symphony washed over her as he spoke. She smiled.

'Thank you' she said.

They sat, listening, talking about music, their likes and dislikes, for an hour, and it seemed the most natural thing in the world to get out and sit together on the soft dry grass surrounded by cowslips and bluebells. He pulled off his jacket, and she teased him about his Walter Raleigh act as he lay it down for her. He sat, his arms around his bent knees, chewing a piece of grass, his long hair flopping over his eyes, while he spoke about his love of classical music, his passion for teaching, for fair play. She watched him, and thought him the most beautiful man she had ever seen. Her throat constricted with an emotion she had only ever felt for her children. But she wasn't thinking of her children now.

He turned to her, and gently drew her to him. There was no resistance. She looked at him, no fear now. They kissed, softly at first, then with a growing urgency. His hands in her hair and hers on the nape of his neck, he lay her down. Their tongues exploring, darting, tasting, their lips burning. He raised his head and looked at her, her face, her body. He lay his hand on her flat stomach

161

and she gasped as she felt his warmth through the thin cotton of her dress. Her heart was pounding. He slowly slid his hand down, down, to the hem, and stopped.

'Do you want to do this, Cariad?' he whispered.

'Yes' she breathed. And she knew she did. She had never felt so alive, every nerve tingling, her whole body aching for him.

His hand moved along her bare leg, hardly touching her, but setting off electric tremors she could not control. She lay, eyes closed, breathing fast, savouring every touch, experiencing sensations new to her. His fingers reached the top of her leg, and, gently pulling aside the crotch of her panties, entered her. She gasped again, out loud. She was wet, so wet, as he slowly moved inside her. She writhed under his hand. Never, ever had she felt anything like this.

'Please!' she moaned.

And he was on her, in her, urgent, thrusting, his every move matched by hers, her cries escaping through her bitten lips, until she was overcome by a tingling, breath-taking, glorious numbness that crept through her body, gushing out of her, taking her to a place she wanted to stay forever, while his deep moans grew louder, faster, as he emptied himself, lying at last on her chest. Their breathing slowed. She felt him inside her still, his body on hers, as if he were part of her. She felt whole, for the first time. She touched his hair with her lips. She was content.

Such was the start of the most memorable, wonderful, exciting summer of Anya's life. Their times together were few and precious. Anya became adept at inventing new events with colleagues as excuses for her

162

mother, whom she relied on for child-minding. So it also became the most guilt-ridden and confusing summer too. She and Byron couldn't meet more than a couple of times each week, sometimes not even that, and while she suffered remorse and shame in the subterfuge and lies she was constantly telling her children, her mother and her husband, the thought of not seeing him made her feel frantic, and when she was with him, everything and everyone else went out of her mind. She remembered telling him that she wouldn't leave her husband. And yet she secretly considered it, even though Byron never gave the slightest hint that he wanted her to. She fantasized about a life together, ignoring the realities of the problems that might bring. And in the meantime, she revelled in their being together, gloried in every conversation, exulted in every kiss and every touch.

She treasured their intimate moments, when they would share their thoughts and wishes and fears, when he would allow her to know him as no-one else did. And she came to understand some part of him that seemed so contradictory, so paradoxical. He talked, at last, about his wife. And like constantly touching a painful tooth with a probing tongue, she wanted to hear it all.

He told her how he had married Claire when they were both nineteen, he an apprentice, she a student and three months pregnant. Claire was beautiful and clever, an entrancing socialite, a popular and articulate companion. They were young, in love, nothing could touch them. But the baby, the reason for their precipitous marriage, had been born prematurely and had not survived. Their marriage had continued, but that, too, had not really survived. He told her how one miscarriage had followed another, each one taking its sad toll on them both, driving them apart instead of drawing them closer. And now? Claire was an alcoholic. A functioning alcoholic, to use the correct term. Not sitting in a shop doorway, bottle in hand. Not drinking all day, every day, permanently inebriated, as depicted in the films.

She had been able to hold down her job as a pharmacist's assistant for a long time, succumbing to the inevitable pull of the whiskey bottle or the wine only in the evenings and weekends, lashing out at her husband, verbally, physically, all behind closed doors. Then had come the interludes of all day, all night drinking; not eating, not moving, not leaving her bed; interludes that may last for a week or more, and resulted in her being hospitalized for a different ailment – vomiting blood, kidney malfunction, dangerously high blood pressure - before she would stop. Had to stop. A short course of lorazepam, or diazepam, or whichever was the current "mother's little helper" on offer, would allow her to return home.

She would continue to drink, but for some weeks, or occasionally months, she would control it again, limiting her consumption to the evenings, when she would take a glass – a large glass – before dinner. Always before dinner. More effect then. After eating a morsel or two, she would continue drinking until she passed out. And so it went on, until something, or nothing, triggered the bingeing, and the cycle started again, with days or weeks consumed by her constant craving for alcohol.

'I can never leave her.' Byron looked into Anya's eyes, as they sat, surrounded by the sight and scent of summer meadow blossoms, incongruous somehow as a backdrop to the grey and wretched story he had shared.

'Do you love her?' Anya dared to ask it.

He was silent. Then,

'I don't know. I really don't know. I think I do. I did love her, I know that. I loved her very much. But now – I care what happens to her; I don't want her to be hurt. And I don't want her to be alone. Does that mean I love her? I don't know.'

As the long summer holiday drew to an end, Anya made a decision. She would put thoughts of a future with Byron in the box in her head labelled "impossible" and determined to enjoy the times they had together. She didn't know whether his certainty that his wife would not cope on her own was fact, or a cowardice, an excuse for him not to rock the boat. She knew how she felt about him, and on some level it didn't really matter to her whether he was weak, or just committed to his long-term partner. It didn't change her feelings. She knew that what she felt now was so much more than the overwhelming physical feelings that exploded each time she saw him. She loved him. And she knew that, whatever happened to her relationship with him, whether it lasted or not, she could no longer live with David as man and wife.

The annual trip to Swansea to buy school clothes for the new term was more fun than usual. Anya watched the excitement on her daughters' faces as she told them that, yes, they could have the coats, the shoes, the jumpers that they really wanted. She had yet to receive her first pay as a permanent member of staff, but she would give them this little reward for foregoing so many things over the past few years. C&A was their playground for a couple of hours, and tea and cakes in Debenhams' cafeteria topped the day off in style. They returned home, tired and happy, and having paraded around the flat in their new outfits after dinner, they were soon ready for bed, and fast asleep by the time David arrived home.

She put his dinner on the table, feeling edgy as she did so, and pottered around, tidying things that didn't need tidying, plumping up already-plumped cushions.

'Have you eaten, then?' He asked, between mouthfuls.

'Yes, I had my dinner with the girls.' She kept an eye on his slow and steady progress through his meal, until she was able to sit opposite him and say, as he pushed his plate to one side,

'David, we need to talk.'

He looked up.

'What about?'

'About us.'

'Us? What about us? We're ok.' It was a statement.

Anya drew a breath.

'Well that's just it, Davey. I don't think we are.'

He said nothing. He looked at her enquiringly, clearly waiting for her to elaborate.

'We don't talk, David. We don't do anything together. We don't have anything in common. Not any more.'

166

She could have said so much more. She could have told him she couldn't trust him, not after he lost them their house. She could have told him she found him stubborn, boring, that he refused to discuss her work or his, her opinions or his, her thoughts or his. Heaven knows she had tried to show an interest in anything he was involved with, but no, he brushed her attempts aside. She could have told him she hated the way he took no interest in their children, that she didn't need him, that her skin crawled at the thought of him touching her. She could have told him how she felt about Byron. But she didn't.

'So – what do you want to do?' He spoke calmly at first, and she was relieved. 'Or should I say – what do you want *me* to do? Because I'm guessing you think it's my fault.' His voice was harder now.

'No, David, no. It's no-one's fault. We've just grown apart, that's all. We've changed.'

He thought about that for a while.

'*I* haven't changed' he said.

It was Anya's turn to take a moment.

'You're right, Davey. You haven't changed.'

And she suddenly saw the truth in this. He was exactly the same person she had met all those years ago. She saw that he behaved in whatever way he deemed appropriate to the occasion. He had courted her, and had been lively and chatty, flattering her, complimenting her. They had married, and there had been no need to woo her any more. So he didn't. He had worked hard, and knew how to act with his workmates, and with his bosses. Then everything had come crashing around his ears when he lost his job. He hadn't known how to act. He wasn't the breadwinner any more, and started to behave in the surly, selfish way he seemed to equate with being unemployed. But lately, he was working, they had their own place again, and he reverted to what he had been years before. No, he hadn't really changed.

'You're right' Anya said again. 'It's me. I'm the one who's changed.' And she knew this to be true.

'So what do you want to do?' he repeated.

Anya took a deep breath.

'I think we should separate.'

He didn't react. She wasn't sure quite what she had expected from him, but she had expected something.

'I don't mean living apart, not just yet.' she went on in a rush, 'We couldn't afford that. But we should separate as – um – husband and wife.'

'You mean we won't sleep together? You mean we won't have sex?' His voice was rising now. 'Well not much change there, then, because there's been precious little of that going on for quite some time.'

'No, I know. So I thought I would bunk in with the girls …'

'Is there someone else?'

'No' she lied.

Thinking about it later, lying next to Lucy and Fran in the double bed they shared, she felt a huge sense of relief. It had gone better than she could have hoped. He had been shocked, she knew, and angry at times; in a half-hearted way had asked her if they could try again, but he had eventually agreed to live separate lives under the same roof, until the time came when they would make it more formal. Neither mentioned divorce, although she

168

knew they were both thinking it. She wondered if she should get in touch with Esther, now a fully-qualified solicitor. But she felt free, and saw the start of the new term, just one weekend away, as a new start in many ways.

CHAPTER 12
CHANGES AND A FAREWELL

1983: September

Enrolment week was something new to Anya. Schools – infant, junior, comprehensive – all knew what numbers they could expect at the beginning of the academic year. Even universities. But for FE colleges, it was jumping into the unknown each September, not knowing what classes would recruit enough students to be viable, how many staff were needed, and who would be teaching what. She saw now the advantage of employing part-time and temporary staff. They allowed some give in the system, some flexibility. Their contracts could be terminated at short notice. The realisation that she was now a permanent member of staff made Anya doubly relieved.

But all practicalities, all administrative tasks, paled into insignificance compared with the news that greeted them on the first day of term. A large poster had been placed in the entrance hall notifying staff of a meeting in the staffroom at nine o'clock. Instead of Hugo standing at the front of the room, Anya was surprised to see Cllr Geraldine Mainwaring sitting, looking relaxed, flanked on either side by Paul Falder and Elaine. She didn't need to ask for quiet. The room was silent as Geraldine rose and introduced herself to those many staff who had yet to meet her.

She gave her announcements in a matter-of-fact tone that nevertheless allowed no invitation for questions. The facts were these: Hugo Larsson had resigned – no reasons were given, and none asked for; Paul had been appointed principal, causing a murmur of approval around the room; and the greatest surprise – Elaine was now vice principal. The first female senior manager in the history of the college. The murmur increased to a steady hum, threatening to become a dozen whispered conversations. Geraldine headed that off with a subtle raising of her voice as she continued.

'There will be some other changes of structure, and you will see notices about these during the week. I'm sure you will support the principal and vice principal in their new roles, and they will be addressing you directly very soon. But for now, I'll let you get on – it's going to be a busy week.'

Her prediction of a busy week proved to be an understatement. All day and every evening, staff were on a rota to sit at tables in the big hall, peddling the college's wares to youngsters who had found their exam results weren't enough to stay at school or get the job they wanted, or who hadn't achieved the entry criteria for the courses they had applied for. Either way, a course would be found for them. Staff were expected to advise and enrol students onto courses other than their own, if necessary, well out of their comfort zones, and Anya was astonished at the knowledge they demonstrated for courses across the college.

'It's practice, dearie, just practice' Ethan told her when she talked to him about this. 'You hear the crap from the next table often enough, you could recite it in your sleep!'

171

But Anya heard him give information about secretarial, tourism, and nursing as well as engineering courses, and didn't believe he was simply repeating facts verbatim. She knew him well enough now to know that he rarely took credit for the extra effort he put in. And the same seemed to apply to the rest of the staff. She admired them more than she could say.

By the end of the week, Anya knew she had full classes for all the courses she taught on, and she had learned a lot about the admin work behind the teaching, the courses across the other departments, and her colleagues. She had worked two evenings, and was on the rota to do the same the following week, when the focus would be on enrolling adults for part-time evening classes. She and Byron had had no chance to see each other alone, and had no choice but to content themselves with a look, a smile, a hidden meaning in an ordinary conversation over a hurried lunch. It wasn't possible to arrange anything for the weekend either. Anya couldn't in all conscience leave the children with her mother again so soon in the term. Anyway, she had missed seeing the girls, and wanted to spend time with them, even though her mind often strayed, unbidden, to the special place in the clearing where she and Byron had spent so many hours over the summer.

Week two threatened to be busier, if anything, than the preceding week. Meeting new students, introducing them to her subject and its place in their course, helping them to find their way around, laying down ground rules, all filled the days, and then there would be enrolment sessions on the two evenings she was booked on duty.

Except she wasn't.

Wednesday morning saw another poster advertising another staff meeting, this one led by Paul and Elaine. Anya was thrilled for Elaine and had taken the first opportunity she could find to congratulate her on her promotion. She sat now, along with Jean, Marjorie and others, and listened to Paul giving a short talk before announcing some changes.

'As you'll be aware, with Elaine in her new role, there is a vacancy for a Sociology lecturer. We will be interviewing candidates this week. Also – we have put in some new levels of management. We feel it's important that managers are working closely with teaching staff, and to that end, we have created four new roles – course co-ordinators - at senior lecturer level.'

This announcement was greeted with considerable interest. Anya had become aware, over the past year, of the difficulty that staff found in "climbing the ladder" in such a static management structure, and appreciated that many were disgruntled, so there was a palpable attentiveness within the room at the principal's words.

'So.' Paul paused, then continued, interspersing his announcement with further pauses, allowing his audience time to absorb what he was saying.

'Ethan will be the course co-ordinator for Electrical Engineering; Dan for Mechanical Engineering; Ruby for Office Practice & Tourism, and Jean for Caring and Personal Care – that is, Nursing & Hairdressing'

'Wow!' breathed Marjorie. 'Well done Jean love!'

Jean allowed herself to look pleased at last.

'Geraldine has certainly made some changes!' whispered Marjorie. 'She said she would, but this is bigger and faster than any of us expected. And what about Ethan! Good on him!'

'The key to it all was Hugo going' said Anya. 'I have a feeling it wasn't entirely by choice …'

'Sshhh!' hissed Jean. 'There's more!'

'Ok, ok!' Paul was smiling. 'You've had your little gossip! I'm not going to ask you if you approve of our decisions, but I will ask you to support them. Now – back to business. Full time enrolment numbers are up…'

'Hooray!' shouted one wag, and everyone laughed.

'Yes, thank you!' He smiled. 'And so far, part time enrolments are looking quite encouraging. I want to thank you all for your fantastic efforts, and for the number of people who volunteered to take an extra session this week. The good news is – you don't need to do a second evening, so if you've already done one, we won't need you again this week. Take an evening off. Go and introduce yourselves to your long-suffering families!'

The meeting ended. And a glance between Byron and Anya was all it took. An evening together – a couple of hours at most, but an unexpected gift, with childcare already sorted, alibis in place – this was not to be forfeited. So at the end of their busy day they drove to the nearby country park and sat in his car, hers parked nearby, and they talked. They listened to music, their favourite pieces, his arm around her, each knowing that opportunities for meeting each other in the next few weeks and months would be few and far between. But their relationship had developed to the point where the physical act of love-making wasn't always necessary, and this was enough for now.

So the term raced on, Anya balancing the pressures of teaching with the discomfort at home and her efforts to assure her children that all was well. At work, her glimpses of Byron as they both went about their daily duties were rays of light in her day, and the quickening of her heart, the delicious tingling throughout her whole body, and the lump in her throat that the sight of him gave her didn't diminish no matter how many times she saw him. They found very few, and only the briefest, occasions to talk alone in the working day. Their conversations and discussions over the lunch table were now even more valuable to them both, and while the topic of debate would invariably be that of politics and the plight of the miners, the sheer act of speaking together was something to relish.

The half-term break at the end of October came and went; Anya had managed to snatch a precious few hours to spend with Byron mid-week, although their evening together was not as she would have wished. The clocks had gone back by then, and it was too dark and wet to leave his car, parked as it was near their quiet clearing. She cherished their closeness, the smell of him and the feel of him, but making love in that cramped setting was reminiscent of her early days with David, making her feel uneasy, and she was unnerved when she thought she heard a car engine close by.

Life at home was like walking on a tightrope. Little was said about their current living arrangements, but the atmosphere was taut. As always, Anya strove to keep a steady background to her daughters' lives, and she thought she largely succeeded, although now and then, she would see Emily looking at her with a surprisingly knowing expression, before smiling, or laughing, or hugging her.

Christmas plans were the most important topic for the three girls, and they made it quite clear that they wanted to spend the festive period with their grandmother. Jessie was only too happy to oblige; David said it would be difficult for him to join them, as he would be working right up until Christmas eve, and back again two days later, so he would stay at the flat, but he made no objection to their going. This was a bonus for Anya, and took it that it was all part of his acceptance that their marriage was, in effect, over. He was spending more and more evenings out, sometimes not returning home until two or three in the morning. She knew that she no longer had any right to ask him where he had been, and she really didn't care, but she occasionally wondered if he were having an affair. And she hoped and prayed that he was. It would assuage her guilt somewhat if it seemed that it was not only her unfaithfulness that was causing the breakdown of their marriage.

As the term drew to a close just a few days before Christmas, Anya was aware it was unlikely that she and Byron would be able to meet before the holiday started, and a rendezvous during the two-week vacation was going to be difficult. They swapped the numbers of their nearest public phone boxes, and agreed some times when they could call each other. There was nothing more they could do. Much as Anya loved spending time with her family, it was going to be a dismal Christmas in other ways.

It was the evening before Christmas Eve – or Christmas Eve Eve as Lucy liked to call it. Bags were packed with two days' worth of clothes and carefully wrapped gifts, ready to go to Granny's the following day, and the children were uncharacteristically eager to go to bed, convinced as they were that the morning would come that much sooner. It didn't look as if David was going out that night, and Anya was surprised to see Jessie at the door.

'Hello Mum!' she said, giving her a hug. 'Can't stay away, can you? I'd have thought you'd seen enough of us!'

'Well, it was David who asked me to call, love' she said. 'I have no idea why.'

They both turned to look at David, who was smiling as he walked in from his bedroom.

'Hello Jessie. Thanks for coming over. Why don't you sit down? You too Annie.'

They both did so, looking at each other, eyebrows raised.

'What's this about, David?' asked Anya.

'Well now, there's something I thought your mother would want to hear. Ought to hear. About her precious little girl.'

'David, have you been drinking? Because ...'

'Oh yes, Annie. I've been drinking. I've been drinking quite a lot as a matter of fact. And I've been doing a lot of thinking, too. I was thinking all over the summer holidays. And then you told me our marriage was over. Oh!' he said, seeing the surprise on Jessie's face at this, 'she didn't tell you about that, did she?' His voice was rising. 'She didn't tell you she sleeps in with the girls these days, did she? That we're as good as separated while living under one roof?' He paused, visibly controlling himself and lowering his voice again.

'Well, something else she didn't tell you about. The man she's been fucking. Meeting him while you were babysitting, taking you for as much a mug as me.'

Anya felt the blood drain from her face. She didn't look at her mother. She said nothing. She waited.

'Anyway' he said conversationally, 'I thought I'd do some checking. And I followed you, Annie. I followed you, half term, in the rain, to a romantic little place in the woods, where you got out of your car and into his.'

Anya couldn't believe it. Not like this. Not in front of her mother.

'And I parked, and I waited. I saw someone throw something out of the car window. I waited till you'd both gone. And I picked it up.'

With that, he held out a clear plastic bag for them to see. It took her a moment, then Anya gasped, drew back, hands over her mouth. She thought she would be sick. The bag contained a condom. A used one.

'So,' went on David, standing over them, still smiling, 'that's your little girl for you. She's fucked us both too, hasn't she? She's nothing but a whore, she's...'

He reeled back under the force of Jessie's slap across his face.

'You bastard' she whispered as she stood in front of him, looking up into his face. 'You think you can come between my daughter and me with your little plans and your filth? Well think again. And hear this: we will not be broken. Understand? UNDERSTAND? Now go and put away your little memento. It didn't work.'

He stood stock still.

'Mum...' Anya whispered. 'I'm so sorry ...'

'I know. We'll talk about it later. First we need to get you out of here. The girls won't mind being woken ...'

'His wife was none too happy about it either' David said.

It took a moment for that to sink in.

'But I forgive you' he was saying. 'If you promise not to see him again, I'll forgive you. We can start again...'

Anya was incredulous. Surely not. Surely he can't think ...? And what did he mean...?

The ringing of the telephone broke through, sounding normal amid this nightmare. Anya walked to the tiny hallway and lifted the receiver while trying to absorb what her husband had just said. Before she could speak, she heard Byron's voice.

'Anya! It's Claire – she's .... They don't know if she'll make it. She tried to kill herself … She …'

'Where are you Byron?' Anya cut across. 'Which hospital?' then, 'I'm on my way.'

She only had to look at her mother, who nodded. She grabbed her keys and ran down the clanking steps.

She saw him at once. She had told the reception staff that she was his sister, and they had let her through to the inner part of the emergency department. He sat, his head in his hands, and she stopped for a moment, steadying her involuntary intake of breath, loving him still. Then she sat by him.

'How is she?' she asked.

He looked up, shook his head, and grasped her hands.

'I don't know. I don't know yet.'

'Was it pills? With drink? Was it an accident, d'you think?'

He shook his head again.

'No. It was no accident. She cut her wrists. It was only by chance that I came back for some tools. Blood everywhere.' He buried his head again.

'Did she say anything?' asked Anya.

He shook his head. Anya took a long breath.

'She knew, Byron. About us. David told her.'

She didn't want to see that look in his eyes. She turned away.

'Mr. Jones?' A doctor came towards them. 'Your wife's out of surgery. The immediate danger is over, but

180

she will need to be seen by the psychiatric team before she's discharged. You can go in to see her now, but she's very groggy and may not know you're there. The main thing is to keep her calm, and not to question her.'

Anya watched through the glass partition as he sat next to his wife, as he held her hand very gently. She knew he hadn't been exaggerating about her vulnerability. She knew that this love, the love he had for this fragile woman, was born of worry, of responsibility, of a shared past. It was not the love of passion, of hope, of shared minds that he felt for her, Anya. And as she looked at the ravaged face and body, denied the one thing she had wanted, denied that most natural of all desires, Anya knew she could not take away the one person who cared for her.

She had managed to find a payphone and call her mother, who had told her not to worry, to stay with her friend as long as she needed to. Thirty minutes later, Byron came out and sat next to Anya. Neither spoke.

Anya put her arms around him, not knowing how he would react. He stiffened, then relaxed into her. Leaning against her. And in that moment, she felt the power shift. She had never acknowledged that she had been the acquiescent one, the compliant one, in this affair, he the one taking the lead. But now she knew that the power was with her. She had to use it. She had to let him go. She spoke to him now as she would to one of her children.

'Sweetheart' she said softly. 'We can't do this any more. We can't do this to her. We've hurt her. So you and I, we're going to say goodbye …'

He nodded, his head lowered.

'I know, Annie. I know.'

'We'll still see each other, still talk, still be good friends, the very best of friends …' she broke off as her voice cracked.

'I'm going now, before we have to give explanations and tell any more lies.'

He clasped her hand as she rose to leave.

'You know I love you, don't you?' he said.

She closed her eyes, kissed him gently.

'I know' she said, and left him.

Twelve hours later, Anya, Jessie and the girls were sitting around the table in the small council-house kitchen, peeling sprouts and cutting up swede. This very ordinary seasonal activity allowed the adults to hide their concerns while the children laughed excitedly and looked forward to the next day.

'I'm going to stay awake all night!' declared Lucy.

'Well, he won't come then, will he?' scoffed Emily.

'I tried it last year' said Fran. 'I heard him on the stairs.' She paused, waiting for Lucy to show a fitting response. She obligingly gasped loudly.

'I closed my eyes very tight so he would think I was asleep. He took ages! He took so long that I must have fallen asleep, because next thing I knew, I could feel something heavy on my feet.'

Lucy was staring wide-eyed at her sister now.

'I put out my hand very slowly to the side of my bed, and I could feel my stocking, and it was all bumpy, and full of paper crackling. I knew he'd been – but I wasn't sure if he was still around. So I kept my eyes closed. Next thing, it was morning!'

Lucy had been entranced; even Emily looked impressed.

'Well, there you are, Lucy' said her grandmother. 'You might as well go to sleep tonight!'

It had been two in the morning when Jessie had met her daughter as she returned from the hospital. She took one look at her face, pale and drained, gave her a quick hug, and said,

'We can talk later. Have a cup of tea while I pack some more things for you. You can't stay with that man. You're moving back with me.'

By the time the children were awake, the car was packed with all they would need for a week or so. David hadn't surfaced. Anya had let her mother take control, while she moved around like a sleepwalker, smiling vacantly when spoken to, doing what she was told. The girls were thrilled to be going on this adventure so early on Christmas Eve, and took Jessie's explanation that their mum was very tired at face value.

Anya didn't know how she would have got through the next few days without her mother. Christmas for her children was made as wonderful and magical as ever, just as Jessie had always made it for her. In the evenings, when the girls were in bed, they talked. About

Byron, about David, about how she felt. Her mother didn't criticise or judge. She accepted the facts, and though Anya was sure she must have been hurt by the lies she had told, Jessie was firmly on her side. David's attempt to alienate the two of them had backfired. He had not taken into account the fact that a mother will defend her child against any attacker, no matter what the story behind it.

On New Year's Eve, while Anya was taking the girls for a walk along the beach, Jessie answered the door to a gaunt, handsome man who looked as though he hadn't slept for days.

'Byron?' she asked.

'Yes. Hello Mrs Hughes.' He sounded weary.

'Anya's not here I'm afraid, but she won't be long. Do you want to wait?'

'No, no. I don't want to see her. I mean ...' his voice drifted off. Then, 'Could you give her this, please? From me?' He handed her a small package. 'It's not much, just ...' He turned to go, then turned back.

'Thank you' he said, his eyes meeting hers, and she knew he meant more than gratitude for taking a parcel.

Anya didn't open the gift all that day. They did the usual things – the children wrote down their new year's resolutions, mainly comprising renewed determination to keep their room tidy, put their dirty socks in the wash, and making sure they cleaned their teeth properly each day. They tried to stay awake to see in the new year, and failed; Jessie threw some coins out of the back door, to be picked up the following day, ensuring a prosperous year ahead. All was as it always was. And yet it was like no other time. The church bells chimed at midnight, agreeing with the TV that it was in fact the start of a new year; Anya and Jessie toasted each other with some sweet sherry, which was all the alcohol they had in the house, and fireworks started banging and crashing from half a mile away, as this new form of celebration made its mark.

'Would you mind if I popped out for a little while, Mum?' Anya asked. 'Just for a run in the car. Just to clear my head.'

Jessie looked doubtful.

'Don't worry, I'm not going far. I promise. Just to the prom. Back in half an hour.'

So she sat, looking out over the dark sea as the waves rumbled in, breaking around the rocks; seeing the reflection of the intermittent flashing from the lighthouse, the looming shape of the breakwater wall. And she took out the small package from her pocket. It was a cassette. A home-made one, with the only marking a capital B and an x. She turned the ignition and pushed the little present into the player, and heard an old song. It was one she knew, but she had never really listened to the words before. Leo Sayer. *When I need you.* And she thought her heart would break. The song died away, to be replaced by the uplifting strains of Beethoven's Pastorale. As the music swelled around her, the tears came at last, her sobs drowned by the celebrations in the night sky.

CHAPTER 13

A HOUSE ON A HILL

1984

The first day of the new year dawned bright and clear. The timeless optimism of children was infectious, and Anya was determined to look forward, not back. She tried, unsuccessfully, to put Byron from her mind, and the memory of Claire's face haunted her. But she put on a good show for her girls.

The morning started well, with the girls finding the not-very-well-hidden coins outside the back door, and took this as a sign that this would be a great year. The five of them went for a walk across the fields and returned via the sea front, running from the spray and shrieking as the floating foam reached them. They made it home just in time to avoid the drizzling rain that came sweeping in. Lunch over, the girls settled down to play with their presents from Santa – Lucy putting her pair of My Little Ponies through their paces, Fran dressing and undressing her Cabbage Patch doll, and Emily singing along to her Sony Walkman. Anya didn't regret spending a little too much this time round – there had been precious few occasions when she could spoil them over the past few years.

'Come on, let's do our own resolutions' said Jessie as she handed Anya a sheet of paper and a pen, and settled down at the kitchen table.

Anya stared at the blank paper for a few moments, then seemed to come to a decision.

'Ok' she said. 'Number one. I want to move away. Away from Port Haven.'

Jessie looked taken aback.

'Well! I wasn't expecting that!' she laughed. 'Quite a drastic one to start with!'

'I know what you're thinking, Mum. You think it's because of Byron.'

He mother said nothing, but raised an eyebrow.

'It's not. Not entirely, anyway. It's just - it's time to take stock. I've been thinking about it since Christmas Eve, and I really think it would be a good move. Starting again somewhere new, somewhere with a garden, where the girls can play, somewhere with none of my history. I could afford something bigger if we moved into one of the valleys, maybe closer to work – houses are much cheaper there, and I think I might get a mortgage now I have a regular income.' She paused.

'You've thought about this then, love' said Jessie quietly.

'Yes I have. And I'd like you to come with us.'

Anya knew this was a big ask. Her mother had spent most of her life here, had been excited to move back here as a young wife, had never mentioned any wish to leave this little up-market town. She waited for her mother to respond. It took a few moments.

'I've lived here for a long time, Annie. I know lots of people, I know their families and their secrets. I managed to join the WI and the choir, once the scandal of your dad's death had died down. I've fitted in, made a life here.'

'I know, Mum. I know. And I'll understand if you can't come with us. We won't be that far away. I'll miss you, God knows, and the children … but I completely understand. I just want you to know …'

'…but life won't be anything without you and the girls' Jessie continued. 'Not the house, or the town, or the people, they won't make up for losing you.'

'Oh Mum, I don't want to …'

'No, you don't understand. I'm saying that I want to come with you. I'm ready for a new adventure! And I'm touched that you want me to. You may be all grown up now, but a part of me still thinks you wouldn't be able to cope without me.' She paused, cleared her throat. 'Now, where do we start?'

Having a house move on her mind made it easier for Anya to return to work at the start of the new term. She wasn't sure how she would react when she saw Byron, or indeed how he would. But she needn't have worried. His smile was warm and welcoming, his eyes sought hers and told her all she needed to know, and although her stomach flipped in its usual way at the sight of him, her voice remained steady, as did his, as they wished each other a happy new year.

'How's your wife?' Anya tried to keep her voice light, just a normal, friendly enquiry about his family. Nothing strange there. Nothing to cause gossip.

'She's better, thanks' he said. 'Getting lots of help, you know.'

Their first encounter over, she didn't need to try too hard to avoid seeing him, as he seemed to have the same idea himself, and she was grateful. She missed him desperately and wasn't sure she could have hidden her feelings if she saw him too often. She managed to get through the weeks partly by looking forward to the house-hunting expeditions at weekends.

By the end of February, Anya and Jessie had seen quite a few houses. From the tall house in Cwmtwrch, perched on the side of a mountain and threatening to slide onto the road below, to the cottage in Shwt that sat in a damp field so waterlogged it looked like a moat, to the one-roomed shack at the end of a track in Pont Nedd Fechan, they spent every weekend searching. And each time their natural enthusiasm had almost taken them further. Almost.

'Well, it hasn't slipped down yet, has it?'

'I'm sure we could sort out some sort of drainage…'

'We could always build on. Maybe we could get a grant?'

But common sense had prevailed, and they had, regularly and sometimes reluctantly, pulled back from a disastrous brink. They had suggested to the girls not bringing them house-hunting with them after the first few visits, having seen how excited – and then disappointed - they became at each viewing, but the children were having none of it.

'It's the best fun, Mum!' declared Emily. And Anya had to admit that, as frustrating as the process was, there was a part of her that was enjoying it.

189

On March 6th, something happened nationally that would have consequences for the college, the local community, and indirectly, Anya and her family. The National Coal Board announced plans to cut coal output by huge amounts, and the mining union declared this would mean that twenty collieries would close. Many communities across the country, including in south Wales, would lose their main source of employment.

The lunchtime discussion that day was intense, and Anya joined colleagues in the canteen for the first time that term. Byron wasn't surprised at the news.

'This has been brewing for a while' he told the other diners. 'Scargill has told us the government wants to close more than seventy pits. This is just the start.'

'But the government's denying that' said Dan, although he sounded worried. 'They say that Scargill is lying, and there aren't any plans to close any more pits. Only those they've announced.'

'And you believe MacGregor, do you? The government's well-paid puppet? He would say that, wouldn't he?'

'So what do you think will happen, Byron?' They all looked to him now.

'They'll strike. I'll bet on it. But Thatcher will be ready for them this time – last time around, the miners had the government over a barrel. Brought it down, in fact. But Maggie will have prepared for this.'

.

And all of Byron's predictions came true. Six days later, industrial action spread across the country. Scargill declared his union's support for the regional strikes that were already taking place in the north of England, and called for action from miners across Great Britain. While his decision not to hold a nationwide vote was causing concern among the public and some other unions, the miners, including those of south Wales, and those of the Nanllai Valley, held firm.

Byron had been right about the government preparations too. Enough coal had been stock-piled this time to allow steel to be produced and electricity to be generated. But the miners were determined, and were backed by wives and mothers, even as money ran out and food became scarce. The men earned no money and as the strike was classed as illegal, they weren't entitled to any benefits; they and their families had to rely on scrimping, using up savings, and handouts.

Men who were used to spending their days underground were now standing on picket lines, around the colliery and at the gates of the steelworks ten miles away. Tempers were high, and the taunting by some of the police, handsomely rewarded for their overtime, often proved too much for men who had to watch their children go hungry. Fights broke out, more severe than scuffles, and arrests made.

The college continued to function as normal, but there was an undercurrent of tension that would not be diminished. No-one knew what their future would hold, or indeed whether the college had any future at all.

There was one more effect that Anya had not expected. House prices in the valley tumbled. She felt uncomfortable, even guilty, seeming to take advantage of the dire state of the local community, but she could not ignore it.

The lane was narrow, steep and pot-holed, bordered on either side by over-hanging branches of brambles which, Anya was certain, would be even more luxuriant – and more hazardous – in a few months' time. The sign on the main road had said "passing places only" but she was yet to see another car– or indeed any places to pass it if she did. She honked the horn at regular intervals, to warn any oncoming traffic that she was speeding up the hill towards them at a juddering fifteen miles an hour, the most her ancient Vauxhall could manage on this incline, but no vehicle came hurtling towards her. She changed down another gear and glanced to her left. Her mother sat, cool and elegant even in the warmth of the day and the dust of the road, grey hair immaculate, linen suit seemingly uncreased. A sharp contrast, Anya felt, to her own flushed and freckled face, slightly damp red curls and rumpled dress. She sighed and drove on.

Her mum had been wonderful. Never a word of criticism, not a single "I told you so". There was plenty of advice from others for her to ponder though. Ever since she'd mentioned to friends in her home town that she was thinking of moving, and crucially, where she was looking, the comments came rolling in, including a few that must have seemed hilarious in their cosy little circle.

'But that's the back of beyond!'

192

'You must be mad!'

'Isn't that where tumbleweed comes from?'

'I think gingham is new there...',

and from Veronica, concerned and genuinely puzzled:

'Surely you're going in the wrong direction, Anya? Now a move to Cowbridge, that's the place! And what about your mother? Jessie's not getting any younger is she? It'll be a big challenge for her ...'

Yes, everyone thought she was making a mistake, she knew. Moving west was not the fashionable thing to do; at least, moving to the valleys she was looking at. Not the done thing at all. And moving there from the self-proclaimed up-market seaside town she had called home throughout her life, full though it was, it now seemed to Anya, of complacent pensioners and in-comers who had made it big - well, she must be crazy. She answered the questions and the jibes in terms of the benefits of fresh air, space for the children to play, getting back to nature, a simpler life. She didn't add that she hoped the people may be kinder. May accept her recent past - and her planned future – more readily. Or not know about it. Nor did she add that the houses were more affordable there. How else was she to start again, on her own? It was 1984 and houses in her home town weren't cheap.

She also knew that moving so close to where she worked could have its disadvantages as well as the benefit of less travelling. The turmoil she felt had been surrounding her and her family for the past few months had, as far as she was aware, not reached the ears of her colleagues, although she guessed it would only be a matter of time, and living on the college's doorstep would not make that any less likely.

The state of the road didn't auger well for what they would find around the next bend – or maybe the one after that. She wouldn't have blamed her mother if she were less than enthusiastic about viewing yet another house in yet another valley.

And now they were here, in the Nantllai Valley, driving up a lane opposite the now-silent colliery, to view a house that the estate agent had clearly considered so bad that he had just handed them a printed sheet and an enormous old-fashioned key, and left them to it.

'Shouldn't be far now. Maybe this will be the one. Fingers crossed!' Anya said with an anxious smile that didn't fool her mother.

'I'm sure it will be lovely, Annie.' Her daughter raised her eyebrows at her mother's words, but she appreciated the attempt at optimism.

The opening came into view quite suddenly on their left. They didn't say a word as Anya stopped the car and they got out. They walked the short distance to look over the big five-bar gate and stared. From the narrow and darkened lane, the landscape opened up, like an oriental fan, in a thousand shades of green. A wide gravel driveway, a hundred yards long or more, led away from them. Flowers and weeds had forced their way through the rough stone carpet, impatient to be where they belonged. This broad untidy path was flanked on either side by grass verges and low hedges, giving onto an endless view to the left, over fields that dropped to the road below and rose again over the mountain opposite, while to the right, more fields climbed upwards to who knew where, not so steep now, matching the softening gradient of the lane that lay behind them.

The drive ended at another large wooden gate, an entrance to fields beyond. And on its right, snuggled against the mountain, lay the house. Sturdy and square, with symmetrically-placed windows both up and down, it had what looked like small outbuildings jutting on either side, giving it the look of a crouching cat basking in the sunshine, paws outstretched. Specks of marble in its white walls glinted in the sun, its windows in their green frames blinking at this group of strangers. It was called Ty Clyd - 'Cosy House' – and as they stood there it seemed to live up to its name.

'Now that's more like it!' breathed her mother.

The opening of the gate didn't break the spell. Anya drove through and parked just inside. The children jumped out first, ready to run, to explore. The silence that had struck them at first started to disappear. Unseen sheep calling to their invisible young, birdsong tumbling from above and around them, a bark of a distant dog, and the low rumble of traffic in the valley below them, all slowly made themselves heard to ears unaccustomed to the sounds.

The hedges were coming alive. Tiny hawthorn buds promising the white May blossom to come; delicate catkins letting loose their pollen amid soft downy hazel leaves; pink wild-rose buds already giving off their distinctive fragrance; glossy dark green prickly holly, patiently waiting for its season to come.

Anya held her breath. She had talked about going "back to nature" but hadn't expected this. She remembered watching episodes of *The Good Life* on TV of course, and like others had laughed at the attempts of Tom and Barbara to bring the countryside into their front lawn. But this – this was something different. The sounds and the sights and the smells – of grass, of earth, of animals – were real here. And she was scared. She had been scared for weeks now. Scared that she couldn't make it on her own. Scared that she would let her children down, disrupt their lives too much, prove to be too weak to cope. But now she was scared of something else – that the house wouldn't live up to its enticing introduction. She knew it was unlikely to be habitable, let alone in reasonable condition, whatever the estate agent's blurb might say. As they walked closer to the house, Anya and her mother looked again at the information sheet he had given them,

'*In need of modernization* ... that could mean anything' said Anya. Having seen some of the most unsuitable properties over the past months, she had come to know how little this sort of information meant. She had also learned what to look for, with "damp" featuring high on the list: damp smells; damp patches - both visible and those hastily covered by recently-applied wallpaper; fungi growing in corners and inside cupboards – she had encountered all of these. The type of plug sockets were often a giveaway as to the state of the wiring, if indeed there were any wiring at all. So she had known what questions to ask, and the agent had helpfully scribbled

196

down some useful little embellishments on the type-written sheets.

She took from her bag the huge key with a cardboard label on it. *Maes Ty Clyd* it read. The name sounded as if it should have been a farmhouse. And perhaps it had been, once. Now it was just a house, the sort of house that children learn to draw when they first put pencil to paper. A proper stone house with a porch over the front door.

'Girls, we're going in. Coming?' she called. She didn't have to ask twice – they were at her side, jumping with excitement.

'Can we buy this one, Mum?' Fran asked. Anya laughed.

'We'll see.' She put the key in the big wooden door, took a deep breath, and opened it, praying she was prepared for anything. And there it was. A tiny hall with stairs leading straight up, and a door each to right and left. No piles of masonry, no decaying smell, no rodents scuttling about, none of the disaster or ruin she had dreaded. Anya let out the breath she hadn't realized she'd been holding.

While the girls ran ahead, Jessie opened both doors off the hall. 'Nice lounge for you here, love' she said looking through the door to their left. 'And this will do me nicely!' as she walked through the opposite door into a small, square room. 'Needs decorating of course, but that won't bother me.'

As if a decision had been made from standing on that square metre of quarry- tiled floor, they started their inspection. The lounge, with the large sash window overlooking the drive and the mountain opposite, was as large as she could want, the ceiling higher than she had expected. An unlit coal fire set into a tiled surround was flanked by cupboards fitted into the recesses. Through to the living room, with its Rayburn range and overhead clothes airer - so far so good. So far too good to be true! Anya looked around. Ok, so no radiators. But the stone flagged floors and the walls with their drab and peeling floral wallpaper looked dry. A well-worn chintz armchair stood at one side of the clinker-strewn hearth, which bore the rings of a hundred cups of tea.

The small room to the right had stone walls that had once been whitewashed; an old electric cooker, its thick cable hanging loosely at its side, hinted that this was the kitchen. Under a tiny window sat a huge fireclay sink. Anya turned its single tap and yes, some water trickled out. She studied the information sheet. '*Mains water supply*' said the typed sheet. '*Only one tap brings water from the mains*' added the helpful scribble. '*Tap in the kitchen brings water from an outside rain trough.*' She handed the sheet to her mother as they peered through the dirty window. She could see the trough below – wooden, with a slatted cover allowing rain to drip through. She wondered what else may have dripped through. Her gaze was drawn to the garden at the back – even through the grime she could see it was steep and grassed and appeared unending, the children running its length. She and her mother looked wordlessly first at the tap, then the trough.

'Not impossible' said her mother.

Wondering where the elusive mains water supply might be, they walked across the living room to the door opposite.

'The bathroom?' suggested Jessie.

'Can't be, Mum' said Anya. 'Look, there's a back door here. And the small detail that there's no bath!'

'Well, it's got a handbasin.' Jessie turned the tap. 'And water!' Anya referred again to the printed sheet. *'The mains water supply is in the bathroom'.*

'Ah! Right. Ok. So this is the bathroom.'

'The supply tends to get cut off on Sunday mornings' continued the scribble, as helpful as ever *'because there's only one pipe for this mountain and the next and everyone will be cooking dinner.'* They started to laugh.

'And there is a bath here. Look' said Anya, still laughing, pointing to an oval steel one hanging on a hook on the wall.

The staircase leading upstairs was narrow and the walls either side painted a shade of orange that had once been bright. Perhaps it was the bedrooms that would be the disaster Anya had been dreading. But no. Three decent sized bedrooms, four if you counted the box room, and stunning views out of every window. They retraced their steps and went outside through the back door.

A small outhouse stood, adjoining what they now knew was the bathroom and it was here that they found that vital missing element – a toilet. But no ordinary toilet. *'A chemical toilet is located conveniently close to the bathroom'* said the information sheet's typing, and scrawled across it was handwritten *'Maybe a septic tank in the future???'* Anya carefully lifted the toilet lid. A blue liquid swirled darkly, giving off a not-unpleasant disinfectant smell.

'How do you use it?' asked Anya in a hushed voice.

'I've seen one of these in a friend's caravan.' Jessie was inspecting some squares of carefully cut newspaper pinned to the wall on a rusted nail. 'You need to empty it regularly, then it's ok. Not bad at least. Fairly hygienic.'

'But where, Mum? Where would we empty it?'

'Presumably we would dig a hole in the garden and bury it' said her mother in a matter-of-fact tone. 'I imagine that would account for the wonderful show of rhubarb up there.' She turned and pointed to a large patch of land further away, where a mass of young curling leaves and pink shoots were showing.

Anya had glimpsed the back garden from the little kitchen window, but was taken aback at the full scale of it. It stretched away to a hedge at the top. It was a full hockey-pitch long, and almost as wide. Low dry-stone walls stood on either side, separating it from the fields beyond, where they could now see the sheep they had heard earlier; their offspring, tiny woolly creatures, jumping with all four legs off the ground, were eliciting cooing noises from Lucy. The grass in the field didn't look smooth and soft, but rough and uneven, with gorse bushes and small boulders sprouting here and there. Anya and her mother walked up the stone path that lay between the rhubarb patch and the rest of the overgrown grassed area, passing a small wooden shed on their way.

200

When they reached the top, they sat on a surprisingly firm garden seat they found there. They looked down, and saw that they were level with the roof of the house. They looked further and saw fields stretching away up the valley and down, across the mountain opposite, surrounding occasional small shapes that were houses, or farms, or outbuildings. Toy cars moved along the road below, silenced now by distance. Anya saw that Fran had found an old oven built into a stone wall; Emily had discovered an ornamental wishing-well hidden behind a mound of fern fronds, and Lucy was sitting astride a metal rocking horse half buried under the long grass.

'Well, what do you think, Mum? Honestly?'

'OK, let's see' Jessie replied. 'No water supply in the kitchen unless you want to drink flies and frogspawn. No hot water, or radiators, and only a range to cook on. A tin bath, an outside toilet that needs to be emptied, and a house that's miles from anywhere.' She paused. 'I think it's perfect.'

CHAPTER 14

NEW LIFE, NEW FRIENDS

1984: May

The move. Further away than she'd gone before. And Anya learnt a new skill – driving a Ford Transit van along busy roads and through as-yet unfamiliar country lanes. The children had a good view of their new surroundings from the passenger seat of this exotic transport, taking turns on each of the three journeys. Her mother remained in her house, and helped by her neighbours, stood ready to feed the ever-diminishing pile of boxes and furniture into the van as it returned, depositing one child and picking up another.

How she managed to maintain her energy throughout the day, Anya didn't know. While there was some help to load up the van, there was none when she arrived at their new home. Sheer determination and stubbornness got the heavier items from the vehicle, as she dragged cupboards and chairs, bed frames and a table, onto the drive, walking the larger items in, moving them slowly into the house in what must have looked to any observer like a comic dance, step by step, corner by corner, all the while chatting, albeit breathlessly, to whichever daughter accompanied her on that particular trip. Although of course there was no observer.

The only items needing to be taken up the stairs were the parts which made up the bedframes, and the mattresses. Who knew mattresses could be so heavy, so lively, so unhelpful? By comparison, the boxes of bedding and clothes were a cinch. The two single wardrobes – flimsier and therefore lighter than they looked – she left in the lounge. They could wait. So she pulled and dragged and swore under her breath until everything was, at last, under her new roof.

The hired Transit returned to the garage, she drove thankfully back to her mother's house, where Jessie and the children were standing on the pavement, waiting for her. A quick look around the stripped, spotlessly clean, now abandoned house, then all five of them piled into her car, along with the last-minute bits and pieces that had seemed to scatter the place once the larger items were gone. A cushion, a plastic toy, a long-lost but much-loved teddy, some knitting – everything was squeezed into the boot or balanced on laps. They said a fond farewell to the home they had all known for varying lengths of time. There seemed to be none of the sadness Anya had feared her mother must be feeling at this point. Was she hiding her feelings for the sake of her family? It wouldn't be the first time. They drove away, bowling along in high spirits in the growing darkness.

In Pontarafon, they stopped at a fish and chip shop and bought their supper, the tantalizing smell seeping through the newspaper, reminding them just how hungry they were, and how anxious they were to reach their new home.

No meal had ever tasted better. Those who couldn't find a chair sat on boxes and cushions, and they ate silently, apart from an occasional moan of appreciation. But as exhausted at they were, Anya and

Jessie couldn't allow themselves to rest. The children, now replete, were sleepy, and beds needed to be put together. Upstairs, they set to with spanners, fitting the metal bars and spring bases, headboards and mattresses. The children fell gratefully into bed, the three cwtched together for tonight, and were asleep before the adults had left the room.

Anya and her mother sat in the living room with cups of tea poured from a thermos, looking around at the chaos, and seeing through it.

'It's going to be ok, you know' said Jessie.

Anya smiled.

'I know. I know it is. It's just – strange. But exciting!'

'How was David? Did he cause any trouble?'

'He was surprisingly helpful, actually' said Anya.

She had spoken to her husband very little since she had taken their children and left him on that Christmas Eve. Her mother had dutifully dropped the girls off at the flat every Saturday morning, picking them up a few hours later, speaking the bare minimum to her son-in-law and only out of respect for her grandchildren. Anya knew she could never forgive him, and although she knew she was the one who had been unfaithful, try though she might, she could not feel remorse. She didn't try to justify her affair to herself, and she could not regret it. She could still remember how Byron had made her feel, his touch, his voice. She told herself she tried not to think about him, but in truth the memory of that summer was sometimes the only thing that kept her going. She hoped that this new home, this new start, would signal a new life for her in many ways.

'I say we leave all this till tomorrow' said Jessie, startling Anya out of the daydream she felt she shouldn't have had. 'What do you think?'

'Oh, yes, of course' she said quickly. 'Thank heavens it's half term next week. We'll be able to sort everything out, and the girls can start to enjoy it all.' Then,

'Thank you Mum. For everything. You know what I mean. I ...'

Her mother stood up, and kissed the top of her head.

'I'm your Mum. Now get to bed – you must be dead on your feet!"

'Come in, come in! So nice to meet you all!'

The headmaster greeted Anya and the girls with a huge smile and a warm shake of their hands.

'We've only spoken over the phone, Mrs Gethin,' he went on, 'but I know you've completed all the forms. Now,' he said bending down to speak to the children, 'shall we go and find your classrooms – and your new friends?'

By the time she left the school, Anya was satisfied that it was the right place for her daughters. She knew what a massive thing changing schools was for them, leaving their friends and the teachers they knew. It was something she had tried to warn them about, to prepare them for, before they had agreed to move, but she also knew that their minds had been firmly on lambs and flowers and playing in the garden. The classes here were small, the teachers and children seemed as friendly as the headmaster. A minibus would collect the girls each morning, along with other pupils from remote farms and houses, and deliver them to the school, bringing them home again in the afternoon. Everything was in place, and it was with a huge feeling of relief that she drove away.

She had been given the day off work to settle the children in to their new school. Now with the day ahead of her, she decided to call into the village for some groceries before she went home to join her mother in the seemingly unending tasks of unpacking and sorting. The little community of Cwmdawel was quite close to the college, and she had shopped there a few times in the past, but as she parked outside the general stores, she was aware of a very different atmosphere to the one she remembered. The single street of shops was empty of people, and a number of shop-fronts were boarded up. Large posters were everywhere, and she stopped to read the nearest one.

Support the Miners!
Can you help?
We need people to pack and sort food boxes,
make phone calls and write letters.
Call into the Community Centre (next to the Seren)

The poster was handwritten, as were, she saw, all the others on view. She glanced up the road and noticed the pub for the first time, proudly announcing itself on a hanging sign as "Yr Hen Seren", reinforcing its name with a large faded star beneath. On impulse, she left her car and walked to the community centre. She knocked on the huge double door, and hearing no reply, turned the heavy doorknob and walked in. She was in an enormous echoing room, chairs stacked against two walls, folded tables against a third, and an impressive stage, decorated with worn velvet curtains held back by gold braid and tassels, filling the space to her left. Directly ahead, between the neatly piled seating, she could see an open door and could hear voices issuing from the room beyond. In for a penny, she thought, and walked purposefully towards it, knocked, and entered what could only be a kitchen.

Stainless steel and spotless china were the first things she registered, followed quickly by the sight of a pretty, plump, dark-haired young woman with folded arms, talking to another, taller woman standing at a sink, who, though she had her back to Anya, looked somehow familiar. She turned, soapsuds up to her elbows, and smiled.

'Anya! How nice!'

'Geraldine! What on earth are you doing here?!'

'Well, I could ask you the same thing. But let's start again, shall we? Sian, this is Anya, one of the lecturers up at the college. Anya, this is Sian, a mainstay of the community and one of that heroic breed – a miner's wife.'

Anya, hiding her confusion at seeing the chair of governors wearing a flowery apron and washing dishes, greeted Sian politely. She felt that some sort of explanation were needed as to her presence, but Geraldine continued.

'And as to what I'm doing here – well, I live in the village, and this is the ward I represent on the council. Didn't I mention that? And I may not be a miner's wife, but I am a miner's widow. And a miner's daughter. I like to do my bit for this wonderful community. And now your turn!'

Anya smiled.

'I'm sorry. That was rude of me – not a very polite entrance at all. I've just moved near to the village, and I saw the posters, and I wondered if I could help …'

Her voice faded away as she heard herself, and wondered if she sounded like Lady Muck, moving to the backwaters and offering to do her bit for the natives.

'Oh yes' Sian's interruption was a kindness, and Anya was grateful for it.

'You've moved into Ty Clyd, haven't you? I've always loved that house. I used to go up there to fetch eggs on a Saturday when it was still a farm…' and the ice was broken.

They sat drinking strong tea from clean china cups, while the two women explained to Anya the reality of living on the little money they received from the Union during the strike. The fast-dwindling savings, the limited diet, the cost of washing powder and electricity, school uniforms for the ones going to the comp in September, the worry about the children missing out on school trips and parties … The list went on, facts, not complaints.

'Though the school's been really good' continued Sian. 'They put on little local trips to the woods, or to the park, and make it good fun. The kids love it.'

Anya listened, occasionally asking questions, as Sian and Geraldine told her about the effect that not working was having on the men of the village.

'They're an old-fashioned lot' Sian said matter-of-factly. 'My Bryn feels less of a man because he's not working, and the others feel the same. Doesn't know what to do with himself. Angry most of the time, depressed the rest. But they'll not give up' she added proudly. 'If we think this is bad, imagine what it would be like if they closed the mine? There's no other work around here. This village would die.'

By the time Anya left, she had learned a lot. She had offered to come along at evenings and weekends whenever she could, and had been immediately roped in to help with a birthday party for one of the local children the following Saturday, which she was happy to agree to. But their conversation had left her thinking. All the safe lunch-time discussions she had joined in at work, all the theories she had heard put forward about the miners – this is what it had meant. This was the reality. And only Byron had seemed to understand the devastating effect that the strike would have on the community that sat on their doorstep.

Returning to work the next day was like a homecoming. She had worried about moving so close to the college – so close to Byron – but once she walked through the gates, it was all fine. Although it had only been just over a week since she had seen her colleagues, it seemed much longer, and a lot had happened. She realised she had missed the morning coffee-break chats. These were her friends, as well as her work-mates, and even though the little group had changed over the past year, she still looked forward to catching up with them and the latest college gossip.

Only rarely did Elaine join them these days, having confided to Anya that she felt she may make some in the staffroom feel uncomfortable. Even though Paul, when he had been VP, had sat with them, Elaine had additional issues she was aware of, including the fact that a woman had been promoted over some longer-serving male members of staff, and that didn't go down well with everyone. Her replacement as sociology lecturer, Rob, now sat with them, as did Ethan, and Georgia. This change to the group dynamic took some getting used to, particularly by Marjorie, who had clearly resented the presence of two men in their little circle, but even she had soon found that her solitary breaks sitting in her lab were not much fun, and surprised herself by eventually accepting the new make-up of the group, saying no more about her previous reservations.

'So!' began Ethan as soon as their coffee cups were ranged in front of them. 'Anya is now officially a local, a valley girl!'

They all laughed.

'Well, very much a newcomer, Ethan' Anya replied. 'But I'm working on it!'

'How have your girls settled in?' asked Marjorie. 'And your mother?'

Anya gave them a quick resumé of the very brief time they had been living in the area.

'But what else has been happening here? I feel as if I've been out of the loop these past few months!' She saw a look, ever so slight, pass between her friends. Were they more aware of what had been happening in her life than they were letting on?

'The big news is - well – they've done it' said Georgia. 'Jean and Paul – they're together!'

Anya's gasp of surprise was all they could have hoped for.

'Yes!' Georgia went on, settling down to her story. 'Jean won't mind me telling you this. So - Paul left his wife, Jean left Bruno, and they're settled in a flat together!'

The details of the drama were enthusiastically filled in by all, taking turns.

'Well, I can't say I approve of this sort of thing' said Marjorie, 'but they really do seem to love each other. Both of them were in unhappy marriages. I suppose it's a matter of four people being unhappy, or two being happy and the other two not. I'm glad I don't have to make that sort of choice.'

Anya silently considered Marjorie's words.

'Oh, and talking about unhappy marriages' Georgia began, warming to the theme, 'what about Byron?'

'Byron?' Anya asked, a little too quickly. She felt her face suddenly becoming warm and hoped no-one else noticed. 'What about him?'

'Looks as if you've joined the ranks of lovelorn women staff swooning over him, Anya!' laughed Georgia, before continuing, 'Well, you know how there have always been rumours? About him and other women? Nothing proved of course. But we were all pretty sure he and his wife didn't exactly have a loving relationship, and weren't ever seen together. But since Christmas, she's been with him, at restaurants, shopping, you name it. Mind you, she looks terrible. She used to be a stunner, but now – well, haggard, painfully thin, sort of grey colour to her face. Something must have happened …'

Mercifully for Anya, the buzzer ended the conversation, and they went their separate ways, leaving Anya with much to think about.

Saturday afternoon found Anya in the kitchen of the community centre alongside a dozen other women, slicing and buttering bread, grating cheese, piling plates high with sandwiches, while her mother produced fairy cakes in the industrial-sized oven, and the girls played with the other children in the hall, running up and down, enjoying the echoing sound of their feet on the wooden floor, the boys sliding on their knees, oblivious to the risks of torn trousers and splinters.

Despite the basic fayre and second-hand gifts, the party was a huge success, and Anya thought her family hadn't had so much fun in a long time. Emily confirmed this by suggesting that she and her sisters held their joint birthday parties – which was now the accepted way to celebrate – in the community centre too. Anya warned them that they would be expected to have the same sort of sandwiches, cakes and jelly as they had just enjoyed – nothing more fancy. The last thing she would do is to set themselves apart by providing the food she could now afford, but the girls were happy to accept this, and her new friends welcomed the idea.

If she had needed any confirmation that she had done the right thing by moving, this was it. The women seemed to accept her, teasing her good-naturedly about her anglicised accent and her lack of knowledge of the area. She, in turn, vowed to them she would catch up on local geography very soon, and made some good attempts at the local dialect, which had them in fits of laughter, herself included. There were hardly any men to be seen, but apparently this was the norm.

'They don't see kids' parties as a place for them, see' said Jen, a tall blond mother-of three, as she deftly guided her boys into their seats. 'That's not just since the strike – they've always thought that. But now it's worse, because they don't have an excuse.'

'An excuse?' Anya asked.

'Well, before, they would say they were tired. Working hard, doing men's things. But now – well, they don't have the excuse. It's their pride, see. You can say it's stupid, but it hurts them. You can see it. They get angry, hardly talk, and when they do, they jump down your throat. We've all had it.'

'It's easier for us' said Sian. 'We talk to each other. About how we feel, what's worrying us, anything. But they won't. They're all going through the same thing, but I don't think they talk about how they feel inside. They talk about the strike, about Thatcher, Scargill, MacGregor. They'll talk about meetings and pickets and voting and what's happening up north. But feelings? No! Never!'

Throughout June, Anya spent most Saturdays and a couple of evenings each week at the community centre, often with her daughters, writing begging letters disguised as fund-raising requests as the children played. She had felt guilty at first, leaving so much of the work at home to her mother, but Jessie was adamant – she was more than capable of cleaning, painting and papering, and she was delighted that Anya seemed to be coping with the ending of her affair with Byron. In that she was wrong. It was true that the work she was doing with the miners' wives was a welcome distraction, and she was pleased to be able to do something practical that helped them, but her feelings for Byron hadn't changed. She was getting better at hiding them, pushing them beneath the surface, but they were there just the same.

The term came to an end, with exam papers written, printed, sat and marked. Another year over, and a painful reminder to Anya, as if she needed one, of the contrast with last summer. She worked alongside Byron, saw him most days, and sometimes they spoke, but gone were the lively debates, the loving looks, the intimate laughter. He looked thinner, his face drawn, always serious now but without the passion he had always shown. And she accepted that she, too, was sad. And that there was nothing to be done about it.

The last week of July and the first week of August had always been "Miners' fortnight". She had known this all her life, as Port Haven, with its nearby caravan park, was one of the natural holiday destinations for the colliers and their families. Not so this year. Money was scarce, and getting scarcer, and holidays for striking miners were out of the question. Instead there would be a shindig in the Miners Welfare Hall. Anya was assured that all the village would attend, and that the children could come too.

'If we couldn't take the kids with us, we'd never get out!' explained Sian as they cleared away crockery and cutlery at the end of an evening session of letter-writing and planning.

'And maybe you could introduce yourself to everyone' added Geraldine, who joined the women at the centre as often as she could. 'Give you a chance to meet the husbands, the actual miners. They'll be there. Mainly because there's a bar, but still, they'll be there.'

'Introduce myself?' Anya asked, frowning. 'How do you mean, Geraldine?'

'Say a few words. From the stage. Nothing to worry about.'

Nothing to worry about. Of course not. Easy for Geraldine to say.

'It's fine for her, Mum' Anya fretted. 'She's used to standing up in council meetings, making speeches, and goodness knows what!'

'She probably thinks it's no big deal for you, either' her mother reasoned, as they walked home, children running ahead, challenging each other to reach the next gate, the next tree. The walk was a long one, but they all took it in their stride nowadays.

'After all' Jessie went on, 'you stand up in your classroom and talk all day!'

'It's not the same though, is it? I stand up and talk about a subject I know, and I've prepared for. This is different.'

'Well, there's your answer then. She wants you to introduce yourself, doesn't she? So talk about the subject you know better than anyone else. You!'

Anya sighed.

'Who am I kidding. Mum?' she said, unusually despondent. 'Who am I to presume to help these people? They have real problems. My life is a cushy number compared to theirs. Any problems I've had, I've brought on myself. Yes, I have' she said quickly as her mother opened her mouth to disagree. 'I could have behaved differently. I could have been more patient with David, more understanding. When he lost his job, he must have felt just as emasculated, just as helpless and hopeless as the men on strike. And what did I do? I made him feel worse. I put him down. I betrayed him.'

They were silent for a moment.

'That's just not true, Anya' said Jessie at last. 'Yes, he probably did feel as bad as you say. But you never put him down. I watched you, day by day, treading on eggshells in case you hurt his pride. I watched you work, day and night, to keep your family. And you did. And …' she stopped. 'You're tired, love. Let's talk about this tomorrow.'

They walked on in silence. It was as they reached the turning to the lane that they heard Emily, who had won the race and reached the gate, calling.

'Mum! There's a car! A car in the drive!'

216

Anya and her mother exchanged glances in surprise. Visitors?

'I hope the loo doesn't need emptying!' said Anya as they both hurried up the hill.

Neither of them recognized the dark blue car parked outside their house. As they drew level with it, the driver's door opened and a man got out.

'Daddy!' shouted Lucy and ran to her father.

The other girls were quick to follow. Anya stared at David as if she had conjured him from her thoughts a moment ago.

'Hello Anya. Jessie.'

Jessie nodded.

'David.'

The girls finished greeting him and turned to the front door, readiness for supper overtaking their pleasure at seeing him.

'I'll start the meal, Anya' said Jessie stiffly, walking past him and leading the children into the house.

'See you Saturday!' shouted David, and Emily waved goodbye, disappearing with her sisters through the heavy front door before it was firmly shut by her grandmother.

'David, what are you doing here?' Anya's question seemed unnecessary, superfluous even to her own ears.

'It's good to see you, Anya. It's been a while.'

The conversation so far could have come from any cheap book or second-rate film.

'Do you want to …?' Anya gestured vaguely towards the house.

217

'No, no, I'll leave them to get on with their supper. I just wanted to have a chat. Out here will be fine.'

David glanced around at the little house he'd never seen before, the fields, the drive. He pointed to a makeshift stone bench that Fran had de-mossed earlier that week, but Anya shook her head, preferring to stand. Conversation was stilted and slow, polite, not saying anything.

'So, this is where you all live.'

'Yes.'

'It looks nice. I mean – plenty of space.'

She nodded.

'You're settled here, then? For good? You're not thinking of moving back? To Port Haven, I mean.'

'No David. This is our home now.'

Then,

'Anya, I'm sorry. I was a bastard. A complete bastard. For a long time. I should never have treated you the way I did. I'm sorry.'

She heard the words, but they didn't penetrate. He repeated how sorry he was. How much he still loved her. And still they meant little to her. She was so tired. She was tired of being strong, of fighting to stay in control, of convincing herself she could make everything ok. Tired of being a woman on her own.

David was talking, softly now, gently, and she was looking at him, trying to see the man she had met all those years ago. They had been happy, hadn't they? She had felt safe, loved. She knew she hadn't loved him back then, even if she had tried to convince herself she did, but she had been a loving wife. Could she wipe out those

218

years in between? Could she fall back into a comfortable life with the father of her children, both now older and wiser, each forgiving the other?

Anya closed her eyes and she felt his hands gently, firmly grip her arms, pulling her to him. And she did not resist. She rested her face against his shoulder, feeling the roughness of his jacket, smelling the familiar mixture of his aftershave and the mints he always carried in his pocket. She felt him hold his breath, felt him stroke her hair softly, her eyes still closed.

Pictures swam before her, as the proverbial drowning man, pictures of him, and her life, passing in quick succession but as clear, as vibrant as the day they were formed. David, in his unaccustomed collar and tie at the wedding where they met; David, walking on his hands along the island beach just for her amusement; holding Emily as a newborn, then Fran; David, his face full of pride as they moved into the house she grew to love.

Then – David, silent and surly; David suspicious and resentful. She stiffened in his arms. David – sitting, brooding, in the living room as Lucy was born. David dropping the first bombshell at Christmas, drinking, laughing as she learned they would have no home. And David – holding up that mortifying evidence, his face triumphant, jeering, shocking her mother, spreading his own humiliation as far and as painfully as he could. She saw Claire lying on her hospital bed, betrayed, lost, hopeless. And she saw Byron …

She pushed him away, not roughly, but firmly.

'I'm sorry David. I can't. I'm sorry.'

And he got into his car and drove away.

219

CHAPTER 15

ISLANDS & ICEBERGS

1984: July

The hall was full. Jessie and the girls were sitting around a table at the back with Sian and some other wives, some other children, enjoying the luxuries of crisps and pop, courtesy of Ethan and a group of his gay friends from London who were visiting nearby Onllwyn in the Neath valley. Geraldine had explained that she wouldn't be able to be there, as she had a council meeting that evening, and Anya wasn't sorry. She didn't relish making a fool of herself in front of the chairman of the college governors, even though she now counted her as a friend. She had agonized over her little speech, and wasn't sure why it should matter so much to her. Was it just personal pride? Or could it be that she valued the friendship and the opinions of the people in this community more than she could have thought possible?

Her confidence in herself had been shaken by her encounter with David just a week ago. She had thought she was sorted, strong, independent, but now she saw herself for what she was – weak and vulnerable. It would have been so easy. To be looked after, to be someone's wife again, to be loved. And she had almost let herself fall into that soft and welcoming place. But she hadn't, had she? She had known what it was to love someone, really love them. She knew how much it hurt, and although she wanted the pain to go away, she couldn't pretend that her feelings had gone away too. She straightened her shoulders and raised her head, stubborn, determined.

Entering the large room by the impressive side door with its carved wooden shutters, Anya placed herself in the front row as instructed by the steward, ready to be called, as he mounted the stage. At last, after much 'Thank you, comrades!' and 'Settle down, ladies and gents!' the hall was eventually quiet, save for the inevitable hum of whispered comments and continued discussions.

'Well, here we are comrades. Not quite a trip to the seaside…' pause for laughter which didn't come … 'but we're going to have a good night. We all know it's not a good time for us …'

'You can say that again!' shouted a heckler.

'…but we're not going to let that woman in number ten stop us from having a bloody good time!' Weak cheers this time. This was a tough audience, thought Anya. The steward went on,

'Now, before we start, there's a young lady here who'd like to say a few words to you. She's just moved to the village, and I hope you'll give her a big welcome. Mrs Gethin.' He looked down and beckoned her up. The room was silent. Her heart beating fast, she climbed the steps at the side of the stage, and, smiling, took the proffered microphone from him as she stood behind the lectern.

'Thank you, ladies and gentlemen. My name's Anya Gethin and I'd like to introduce myself to you.' She saw a sea of unsmiling faces, looking at her with vague curiosity or complete disinterest, and, perhaps, some resentment. She glanced down at her notes. 'I have

222

worked at the college here for two years, and I moved to live just outside the village in May. I have ...'

Anya could sense, rather than see or hear, the restlessness, the shuffling in the seats. She stopped. She put down her notes on the lectern in front of her, and walked around it to stand centre stage. She left the microphone on the lectern too. She didn't need it. She knew how to project her voice.

'This may not be an AA meeting – but my name is Anya and I'm a "wedi-dod". She had their attention. 'I'm an in-comer, a newby. And I know my place.' Some smiles now, some laughter.

'You don't want to know my history, do you? You don't want to know where I've lived or what I've done. Not yet, at least. But you may want to know what I've learned since I've been here.'

And she talked to them. She told them how she had learned about the colliery and its history, about the libraries set up in this and many other villages throughout Wales, by miners who were desperate to learn. She told them how she had seen the strike, and the picket lines, portrayed on the TV and in newspapers, and how she had heard and seen a different story for herself, and from the women she now called friends, a story of intimidation, provocation and humiliation that never made the news. And they were listening to her.

'I'm not telling you anything you don't already know. But there are plenty of people out there who really don't know, who need to know. They need to know because we need to change this government. Thatcher, MacGregor, and all the others who have forced this upon

223

you - upon us - they're done with listening, if they ever did such a thing. But the people who really need to know are all those millions who will be voting in the next election. Yes, it's a long way off. And yes, it's not going to solve your problems today, or tomorrow, or next week – but a new government, a different government – they can make sure that your children, and your grandchildren, won't ever be where you are now. But they will learn from you, as I have. And they will be proud of you. As I am, a wedi-dod or not. I'm proud to know you, and I would be proud to help, in whatever small way I can. Thank you for listening to me – and have a great evening.'

She walked off the stage. And as she did so, she was aware of some clapping, then more, then all-out applause, and some stamping of feet. Feeling ten feet tall, Anya started to make her way to her family and friends at the other end of the room, when she stopped abruptly at the door she'd entered earlier.

'Geraldine! I thought you couldn't make it!' But Anya heard little of her friend's reply. Byron was standing there too, half hidden by the shutters.

'Anyway' Geraldine was saying, 'I'm glad I was able to pop in, just in time to hear your "few words". And I thought you might need this.' She held out a folded sheet.

Anya was glad to have a reason to lower her eyes from him. His sudden appearance had flustered her, and she knew she must be blushing. She read the title of the leaflet she had been handed. "Application to join the Labour Party of Great Britain." She looked up.

'Fill it in and bring it to the meeting a week Friday, back of the library in Pontarafon' said Geraldine over her shoulder as she walked away. 'Sorry – have to dash.'

Byron turned to go too, then stopped, glancing down at the application in Anya's hand.

'About bloody time too!' he growled, his smile, so rare these days, belying his rough words. Then he was gone.

Anya made her way to the back of the hall, covered in a confusion that had nothing to do with her performance on the stage, but willing her family and friends to interpret it that way. She joined in the chat and gossip, listened to the music now issuing from the loudspeakers placed around the room, but her mind was elsewhere. She had thought she was moving on, starting to get her life back in some sort of order, but tonight showed her, yet again, how wrong she was.

She was aware of someone at her elbow, putting down a glass in front of her.

'Anya. Anya!' Sian was calling her, laughing. 'You really are miles away, aren't you! This is Bryn. He's bought you a drink. She's not usually like this, love' she added to her husband.

With many apologies, all readily accepted, Anya greeted Bryn, and introduced her family.

'Nice to meet you all' he said. 'Siani's been telling me you've moved into the old Ty Clyd house. Haven't been there myself for years, but it must need a bit of work by now – it was a bit run-down even then!'

'Well, yes, it could do with a few improvements …' started Anya, but Lucy was keen to elaborate.

'We don't have a proper toilet, not inside like we used to. It's outside, but quite fun.'

'And we have to bath in the living room, in front of the range' added Fran. 'It's very cosy. Except for Em – she can hardly fit in it …'

Anya interrupted before Emily's hand could reach her sister for an intended slap, although she was half hiding a smile, and the others laughed at the innocent honesty of the children.

'It is still a bit primitive, yes' she said. 'But we're managing'

'We love it' added Jessie, defensively. 'It's really starting to look like home.'

Bryn nodded.

'I'm sure it is' he said. 'But maybe some of the boys and I could help a bit. We've got nothing to do all day. We'd be glad of the work.'

Sian and her friends looked sceptical, but didn't disagree. Anya guessed that there were probably many jobs their husbands could be getting on with in their own homes, but that wouldn't be seen as work, so they said nothing.

'That's really nice of you Bryn, and when we can afford it, we'd love you to do the work, but we can't quite manage it just yet …'

'We won't want paying!' He sat up straight and his voice was indignant. 'I told you, we'll be glad of the work. And anyway, with the classes you're giving to the girls…'

'Classes?' interrupted Anya. 'What classes?'

Her friends were looking a little awkward. Sian looked daggers at her husband and kicked his shin under the table.

'Ah, well, we were going to ask you' she said apologetically. 'We wondered if you could help us with some maths. Ready for when the kids go back to school. They'll be having lots of homework and we want to help them.'

'Only our maths is rubbish' piped up Jen. 'Never listened in school, did we? Too busy eyeing up the boys.'

'But I'll be damned if anyone is going to look down on our kids' said Sian, angry now at an anticipated slur. 'They may have hand-me-down clothes at the minute, but they're not thick.'

'No-one's going to say they're thick, love. Of course they're not.' Bryn turned to Anya. 'But the girls would feel a bit better about themselves if they could understand the kids' homework. And I didn't mean to jump the gun – I thought it was a done deal, the way they talked about it – and about you. They think you're the bees' knees! Sorry, Anya.'

The lump Anya felt in her throat surprised her. Too many emotions in one evening, she suspected.

'I'd be delighted to do some maths with you!' she said, and she meant it.

'And if you need someone to look after all your young ones while you're doing that, I'd be happy to help' added Jessie.

All in all, the evening was turning out very well indeed, but she couldn't stop herself from glancing at the door now and then.

Bryn was as good as his word. Three of them arrived first thing on Monday morning with bags of tools, measuring implements, and friendly greetings.

'We'll do a quick reccy first if you don't mind, Anya' said Bryn. 'Oh and I'd better introduce you, so you'll know who's rummaging around in your house.'

They were a mixed-looking bunch of men. All were tanned and their rolled up sleeves showed the strength in their arms.

'And here comes grandad!'

The men laughed good-naturedly as Bryn called out to a newcomer who was walking unhurriedly up the drive.

'Meet Geraint, known as Tarzan. He's getting on a bit, but he's not bad with a shifting spanner!'

Tarzan was indeed older than the other men, and took their ribbing with good grace. He was a powerfully built man, weather-beaten rather than tanned, with rugged features, an impressive beard and long copper-coloured hair.

Anya, in turn, effected the introductions from her side, while Jessie offered them tea.

'Not just yet love, ta' said Bryn. 'We'd better do a bit of work first!'

It was over an hour later that the four men arrived back in the living room, having inspected pipes, windows, walls and the range.

'Wouldn't mind that cup of tea now, please love' said Bryn, as he and the others sat around the room.

Their assessment was much as Anya had expected, but it was the cost of their solutions that she was dreading.

'First off – you'll need a proper water supply' started Bryn. 'And it would be better if we swapped your kitchen and bathroom over.'

Anya looked alarmed.

'But why?' she asked.

'You're going to need a septic tank at some point' explained Tarzan. 'You've got a nice little piece of land at the side of the kitchen – that would suit nicely. But you've only got the field outside your bathroom, and it doesn't belong to you. And it's not really a bathroom, is it? Just a room with a tap. And a tin bath.'

It transpired that the cooking range in the living room had a space for a back boiler that could heat the water, and that the men weren't at all daunted by the thought of installing radiators throughout the house.

'And your windows aren't bad, but the lintel's gone over the back door' added Bryn.

Anya and Jessie shared a worried glance. How were they going to afford to do all this work? Their look didn't go unnoticed.

'Now, we can get a lot of the big stuff from the reclamation yard in Pontarafon' Bryn went on. 'You'll need to get new screws and nuts and bolts of course, and waste pipes, but they shouldn't cost too much.'

'You'll need a bathroom suite' said Tarzan. 'A mate of mine in Swansea's putting in a new one – I reckon

I could get his old one off him cheap. Don't know what colour it is, mind. Are you fussy?'

Anya laughed and assured him she wasn't.

'Your biggest cost will be the septic tank' he said. 'But you could leave that for now – we could put the pipework in ready, then just carry on using the chemical loo for a while.'

Anya's head was swimming, as she added up in her head the money she would need. But Bryn was speaking now, reassuring her.

'Don't worry, Anya. We'll do it bit by bit, as you can afford the stuff. We'll start with the water supply and heating though – can't have you trying to thaw icicles to drink or freezing to death in the winter.'

'Don't worry about paying for labour either' said Tarzan. 'cups of tea and the odd biscuit will do us. And this cake's a bit tasty too, Jessie!' He winked at her mother.

When the men had left, Anya and her mother sat down over their own cups of coffee.

'Nice men' observed Jessie as she sipped her drink.

'Mmm' agreed Anya. Then,

'That Tarzan fancied you, Mum!'

Her mother's eyebrows shot up, but she blushed nevertheless.

'Don't be ridiculous' she said, laughing now.

Anya continued to tease her mother for a few more minutes, then became serious.

'Didn't you ever think of re-marrying, Mum? After Dad died?'

Jessie was silent, staring unseeing over the edge of her coffee cup. At last she put her drink down.

'No love, I never considered it. It sounds corny, but your dad was the love of my life.'

'But you were so young Mum. Twenty two. You must have been lonely sometimes.'

Jessie smiled.

'I had too much to do, too much to think about, to be lonely. I had you, a two-year-old. I had nowhere to live, no cash in the bank, no insurance money, no income.' She shook her head. 'Sorry love, this is sounding like a sob-story' and she started to get up.

Anya put a hand on her mother's arm.

'No, don't go. Please tell me. We've always talked about everything, but you've never told me about those first days, months, years. Please.'

Jessie resumed her seat.

'Not so much to tell really' she began. 'I didn't have any friends in the town any more – I'd moved away at sixteen and only just moved back with your dad. I had no-one. Except for Peggy. You remember Auntie Peggy? She was amazing.'

'What about Dad's parents? Couldn't they have helped?'

'No love, no. His mother had died when he was a youngster, and his father passed away just before I met him. Anyway, they didn't get on. So – Peggy helped me find rooms with a woman in the town – just a bedsit as you'd call it now. To start with, I helped out in her B&B instead of paying rent. Cleaning, doing the laundry, you know. Then bit by bit, things got better. I found a job in a children's nursery. You didn't need any qualifications back then, and it meant I could take you with me. I was on the council's waiting list for a house, but I couldn't believe it when I was given one. It was wonderful. I had you, I had a house with a garden, I had my little job. I didn't need anything else. Re-marry? Never. I loved your father then and I love him now. I didn't believe he killed himself, Anya. And I still don't. Looking back, over the years, I've sometimes thought - maybe he had been depressed. But such things weren't talked about then. Only women were supposed to suffer with "nerves". He loved me. He loved us. He wouldn't have gone without saying goodbye.' She cleared her throat. 'But enough of this!' she said briskly. 'Come on, we have work to do.'

'But Mum ...' started Anya.

'No, that's enough for now. Another instalment another time!' she laughed. 'And anyway, what about you?'

'Me?'

'Yes, you. You're a young woman, not bad looking ...'

'Gee, thanks!' Anya mocked, while her mother laughed again.

'Ok, you're beautiful. Are you going to tell me what happened with David the other week? Or what Byron said to you on Saturday ...?'

'Ok, ok, I get it. When I've got something to tell you I will, and I suppose you will too.'

They both rose, each heading in a different direction, and as Anya left the room she said,

'But for now, I can tell you that David wanted us to try again. And I said no.' She knew she was simplifying a fairly short conversation and a torrent of emotions into a few words, but they would do for now.

'And Byron just said I should join the Labour party.'

The summer flew by in a sea of activity, broken here and there by the occasional tropical island and the odd iceberg. The four men from the village walked the two miles to the house every day, in between their duties on the picket line. The banging and clanking, and quite a lot of singing, livened the place, and no-one minded the mess. Jessie called a halt to her decorating, and concentrated instead on keeping the family, and the workforce, fed. She was also spending many mornings at the community centre where she supervised an ever-growing crowd of children of varying ages as they played, while Anya sat with a small group of the local mums in the kitchen, teaching them the sums they hadn't understood at school.

A few days stood out for her. Her first Labour party meeting was one. She was welcomed like an old friend, even though she knew very few of the couple of dozen people there. It struck her that half of them were women – and that all but one of those were making tea for everyone else. The one exception was, not surprisingly, Geraldine. Then there was Byron. She'd guessed – knew – that he would be there, but his presence still sent shock waves through her. She steeled herself to concentrate on what he was saying as she listened to his reading of the minutes of the last meeting. She found that the discussions mirrored, although on a far greater scale, the lunchtime debates that now seemed to be things of the past.

The topics were all there. The fight for fairness, for equality, for employment. And of course the strike. Forceful interruptions interfered with the order of business, but this seemed to be expected, with only mild admonishments from the chairman. It was a fiery meeting; although all present were on the same side as far as the strike was concerned, the range of views as to exactly where on that side they stood, and what actions should be taken, varied hugely. They differed widely as to whether a national vote should have been taken, should be taken. Assessments of Scargill himself, his handling of the strike and of the media, his intentions, his ambitions, were aired every few minutes, and shot down in flames just as quickly. The ranting against the government was there too of course – expressed far more vociferously than she had heard previously, but the points put across were cogent and reasoned.

The meeting ended, but no-one left. Tea and Welsh cakes were shared and enjoyed, and it seemed that this informal, now friendly get-together was as important to the evening as the previous two hours had been. Geraldine made her way to Anya's side.

'Well, what did you think of it? We haven't put you off I hope!'

Before Anya could reply, they were joined by a large, red-faced man dressed, unlike most others present, in a three-piece suit complete with watch and chain.

'What's this, what's this, Gerry?' he said jovially, clearly unaware of the wince his use of the diminutive had evinced in his target. 'Not trying to groom her to take your place on the council, eh?' and he laughed loudly, although his eyes were shrewd and not at all amused.

'No indeed,' she said coolly. 'I'm sure Anya has much greater aspirations than that. Anya, let me introduce you to Maldwyn Rees …'

'Councillor Maldwyn Rees, Gerry!' he corrected her.

'As I was saying, Maldwyn Rees. Mal is the councillor for our neighbouring ward.'

Turning back to him, she added, 'and we don't use titles at our meetings, as you well know, Mal. We are all Labour members – no hierarchy here. But if you're trying to find out whether I'll be standing down at the next council election you needn't worry. If I have the support of my fellow Labour members, I'll go on till I drop.' And she swept away, her arm around Anya.

Eventually Anya found herself almost alone with Byron, separate from the others in a corner of the room. She couldn't pretend to herself that she hadn't manoeuvred it, although she hoped it hadn't been obvious to him.

'You made it then' he said. His voice was natural, even cool. But his eyes were saying something different. They made smalltalk for a few minutes, neither able to ignore the undercurrent of their conversation, but neither voicing it. Then,

'We'll be knocking doors on Saturday morning, if you're interested. Just in Cwmdawel. That's our branch.

We try to put out leaflets when we can – but it's too pricey to print them at the moment, so we'll be talking to people instead. Better in the long-run, of course, but it takes longer. I know you have the girls …'

'They're usually with David on a Saturday morning' she answered, a little too quickly.

And there were her tropical islands. Saturdays with Byron and half a dozen other men. Each week, the girls had continued to be dropped off by her mother, who spent some time catching up with old friends and their gossip before picking the children up again, so Anya need feel no guilt – not on that score anyway. They walked for miles, knocking doors, talking to people, spreading the word about the local Labour party and its hopes for a new government at the next election. Anya was learning a great deal and was keen to learn more.

'But isn't the next election ages away?' she asked Byron as the little group trudged up yet another hill. 'And surely everyone here would vote Labour anyway?'

'It's three, maybe four years away, yes. But that's nothing. We've got our work cut out here. You'd think that this was a Labour place, wouldn't you? You know what they say – "you can put a donkey up for Labour in Wales and it would win". But not here. Here, it's Plaid. Plaid Cymru. Nationalists. Always has been. And it's going to be hard to turn that around – especially with our new Labour leader. Neil Kinnock's got a lot going for him – but he's set himself against Scargill, and most of the men here see that as setting himself against the miners. So – we campaign all year round, every year. Plaid have got no chance of winning a majority in parliament, but Labour

236

could do it. And that's our only hope of getting any fair policies into government.'

The spark that had dimmed in Byron since last Christmas returned momentarily as he spoke, and Anya too felt a thrill that wasn't only to do with her feelings for him. A quiver of excitement ran through her as she saw a different future for her, for her children, for the people she now called friends in this village.

Occasionally, their Labour candidate, Emrys Locke, joined them. Anya didn't find him inspiring. He had fought, and lost, the last three general elections, and however enthusiastic he may have been to start with, there was little evidence of it to Anya's eyes. But the weekly events, full as they were of hard slog up hills and across fields, were becoming an important part of her life, getting to know other members and their views, getting to understand the intricacies and complexities of party policies and party figures, getting to meet more of her neighbours.

And then there was coffee time. Every session ended in the small café opposite Yr Hen Seren. Squeezed in as they were onto benches that surrounded their usual corner table near the window, Anya sat next to Byron as Gino kept them supplied with his best brew. Neither had agreed this, both contrived it. Through the chat and easy conversation, every glancing, accidental touch was a caress filled with electricity. She wanted this to go on, never stop; like playing with a bad tooth, wanting those tiny pleasures, that exquisite pain, going back for more, knowing it was never enough.

At night she would writhe in her bed alone, aching, remembering the way he had made her feel that summer, re-living every moment, every word, every caress. And she touched herself, back arched, her rapid breaths hushed, the sweeping all-consuming pleasure flowing through her like a tidal wave, to be quickly overcome by shame and sadness and loss, until she cried into her pillow, stifling her sobs.

Meanwhile things were going well in the house. The men had worked like Trojans, not only in the physical, back-breaking jobs of lifting and bending, fixing and building, but in getting hold of the things they needed to bring the little house into modern-day living. A second-hand bright pink bathroom suite, some unwanted kitchen units that only needed a coat of paint, a couple of radiators – they each knew someone who knew someone who wanted rid.

The kitchen and bathroom had been swapped and pipes run from the solitary inlet; she now had water, clean water, fresh water, in both rooms, even though it still sometimes disappeared on a Sunday. The outlet pipes from the newly installed but as yet unusable loo, sat patiently waiting for a container to receive them, like sprouting overgrown roots pushing their way into the deep hole the men had dug in readiness for that elusive final part of the jigsaw – the septic tank. The boiler was connected, hot water was hers at a turn of the taps, and the radiators were set to take the chill off the house come winter. Yes all was going well. Until she hit the iceberg.

It wasn't a huge iceberg. Not enough to sink her. But enough to push her off course. It reared up in front of her in the form of an official-looking letter, arriving by special delivery, needing to be signed for. It was a notice that her husband had petitioned for divorce, on the grounds of her adultery. But that wasn't what shook her. He was also applying for custody of the girls.

'He hasn't got a hope in hell!' raged her mother. 'How dare he? How dare he do this? The bastard!'

'I don't care about the divorce' Anya told her. 'I really don't. I'm glad it's happening at last. But custody? Over my dead body!'

'Oh don't kid yourself this is about the children' stormed Jessie, pacing the living room. 'He doesn't care about them. He doesn't want custody of them! He just wants to hurt you. Because you knocked him back. He wants to scare you!'

'Well he's not bloody going to!' Anya, too, was incensed by his threat. 'I'll fight this. He can cite me as the guilty party all he wants …'

'Oh yes! And that's another thing!' Jessie stopped her pacing and faced her daughter. 'He can cite you – but you can do the same. He's been carrying on with some woman since well before that little episode last Christmas.'

Anya was silent. Then,

'What? Who? How do you know?'

'Someone called Gwyneth. An "old friend" apparently.' Jessie made the quote marks in the air. 'Veronica had heard about it – she and Peggy and I meet up now and then on a Saturday morning after I've dropped

239

the girls off. It made sense of some of the things Lucy had said lately – about a lady being at the flat, keeping Daddy company. I'm not sure if he'd told the other two not to say anything, and I didn't want to question them. It's not nice, asking them to break a trust. But I asked Veronica, and yes, she and everyone else knew he was carrying on with her – has been for over a year. She and her husband split up a while ago. And it looks as if she's moving in with him.'

And now the late nights, the weekend overtime that hadn't seemed to bring in extra money, now it made sense.

'Oh is she now? Well she's welcome to him. But I think it's time I stopped feeling guilty. Stopped feeling sorry for him. And started to ask for some maintenance for the children. His children. Let's see what the court thinks about that!'

And now, she decided, was the time to take up Esther's offer, given so many years ago, of legal advice. It was freely given. By the end of the summer holidays, Anya had counter-petitioned for divorce, citing his adultery, and had formally applied for payment of alimony. And she had successfully navigated around the iceberg.

The last week of the holidays saw Anya at the college, waiting with staff and students for the announcement of the exam results. Although she had been pleased with the marks her students had achieved the previous year, now was the real test – the first full year of her teaching her own groups of nurses as well as the hairdressers. She wasn't disappointed. In fact she was thrilled, as were her students, many of whom made a beeline for her, waving their result slips, smiling broadly. The experience put her in an excellent frame of mind to return to work in September, spending the last few days of August shopping in Swansea with her daughters for school clothes, school bags and an endless supply of stationery.

CHAPTER 16

GIRLPOWER

1984: September

The hectic round of greetings and enrolments started as soon as she walked through the doors. This same entrance hall she had entered just two years previously had remained the same, and yet her life had changed in so many ways. She was part of this place now, as she was part of the village, and part of its politics.

First meeting of the new term over, she joined her workmates in the hall, where Paul was giving his welcome speech to the new intake. She soon had her little flock of youngsters to steer to her base room – now that she had been made a course tutor, she had a few more roles than a mere lecturer, being responsible for the welfare, as well as the academic progress, of one group of students on the nursing course. She would still teach the other groups of course, both first and second years, and some of the hairdressing groups, although student numbers had grown considerably, and new staff had been taken on.

The mid-morning break came and went in a whirl, with hardly more than a 'Hi!' shared between the staff, as coffee cups were grabbed, filled and drunk, before another round of inductions and enrolments took them away to their respective corners of the college. At lunch time Anya did make time to sit with her colleagues in the canteen, exchanging class numbers and anecdotes concerning the new entrants. She glanced at Byron across the table, as he looked up.

'You ok?' she asked, her voice light, non-committal. 'Classes full? I don't suppose you have any difficulty filling the engineering courses ...'

'Not usually, no' he answered in the same manner, taking his cue from her. 'But this year it's different. People aren't sure whether there's going to be a coalmine here in the future, or any engineering jobs at all. So too many are hedging their bets. But we have enough for all the classes to run.'

The conversation moved from enrolments to the strike, with every possible view being expressed around the table. Anya found she could now argue, debate and disagree with a degree of confidence, having spent a few Saturday mornings honing these skills on doorsteps, at farm gates and over cups of tea in people's front rooms. As she warmed to her subject, she made a conscious effort not to preach at the other diners. She knew, from her short but intensive experience, that such a tactic was counter-productive. So she listened, nodded, showed she had taken a point on board – then convincingly dismantled it. She was enjoying herself.

'We'll make a politician out of you yet' said Byron quietly as they left the canteen and prepared to enter the fray once more.

As Anya went to take her seat in the hall on the second week, ready for the adult part-time course enrolments, she was pleased to see several women from the village that she knew, most of whom she had taught over the summer. She stopped briefly to chat to them, before she was engulfed in bodies, all eager to involve themselves in some form of second-chance education. After two hours, she left her seat for a well-earned break, but was waylaid as she reached the door by the women she'd spoken to earlier. It was clear that they were not happy.

'I tell you what' Anya said, speaking over the growing volume of their worries, 'why don't you come with me to the canteen? It's open late this evening – and I'm gasping for a cuppa!'

Over tea and slices of buttered toast, Anya was able to find out what was troubling them. Sian started first.

'We've just signed up for a sewing class. Learning to make Christmas toys and cushions and whatnot' she said. 'But that's not what we wanted!'

Anya was confused.

'So – why did you sign up for it?'

'Because there wasn't any other bloody choice!' exploded Jen. 'Sorry Annie, I know it's not your fault, but - well, you made us think we could do something. Really learn something. When all we can do is sewing, or cooking, or pottery.'

'We want to improve ourselves!' added Sian, slamming down her cup. 'We want to show our kids that it's worth working hard at school, that it's something that'll help us. And who knows where we'll be this time next year?'

Others joined in.

'What if we lose this strike? What if the mine closes? And the men have no jobs? It'll be up to us to keep our families.'

'And making bloody cushions isn't going to help!'

'When we asked some bloke if we could do maths, he laughed at us.'

'And all the things we asked about – they're only for the youngsters. Only full-time.'

'Ok, ok' said Anya. 'I hear you. I had no idea the courses you want would be so limited. I've always enrolled adults on the plumbing, or the car maintenance, or the welding courses.'

'All men, I suppose' sniffed one of the women.

Anya thought for a moment. They were right. This wasn't fair.

'Right. Tell me what you wanted' she said, taking a pen from her pocket and grabbing an out-of-date notice from the wall nearby to write on. 'Tell me what you'd hoped for. Tell me what you want to do next, next year, the year after. Let's see what we can do.'

It only took ten minutes. Anya had a list of subjects, qualifications, hopes and barely acknowledged ambitions down on her list. From O levels to degrees, from shorthand to computers, child care to medicine, these women wanted so much more than they'd ever dreamed of asking for. By the time she returned to the hall she had formulated the beginnings of a plan.

The next morning, Anya tapped on Elaine's door, and a voice told her to enter.

'Well, you're an early one!' said Elaine. She was seated at her desk, sipping coffee, and surveying the mounds of papers in front of her.

Paul stood in a corner with his cup in hand, and he smiled at Anya.

'It's barely eight o'clock!' he said. 'Either you're asking for a promotion, or you're handing in your notice' he laughed. 'So which is it?'

'You'll be pleased to know it's neither' Anya replied, unfazed. 'And it's really good that you're both here – it'll save me from putting my proposition twice.'

So she told them her plan. She didn't ask them – not yet. She just put it out there. As an idea. And they listened.

'So, what do you think?' Now she was asking. She held her breath, crossed her fingers, then started to breathe again. This would take some time.

'Let me get this straight.' Paul was now sitting, as was she, facing Elaine across the desk. 'You want to start a course, a part-time course, for women. For them to learn maths, English, some science, maybe sociology, to O level standard, in the day, and perhaps in the evening, and you don't want them to have to pay for this?'

Anya took a breath.

'For adults' she corrected him. 'Yes. That's right. Though they would be mostly women, at least to start with.'

She had given her two bosses twenty minutes of reasoned argument, described the lives of actual people, shown that this could be financially viable. All she would need is for the principal to support the concept, get the governors to approve it, and the county council education committee to give it the go-ahead. That was all.

'So what do you think?'

246

They hadn't laughed at her. They said they would give it some thought – and when, two weeks later, Elaine called her in to give her an update, Anya knew they had been as good as their word. She arranged to meet the group of women – "her ladies" as she called them – on Saturday morning at the community centre, and before she headed home on Friday, she explained to Byron why she wouldn't be campaigning the following day. She made a point of speaking to him in the staffroom, in front of several other staff, so that she would not be tempted to linger.

'Ok, I'll let the others know. Maybe you'll be able to make it for our usual coffee later? Shall I keep your seat warm?'

It was an innocent enough question but his eyes were laughing. Anya felt herself blushing as he looked straight into hers.

'I hope your ladies appreciate you, Anya, I really do' he said. Then, as he left, he called 'Get them to join the party!'

She had talked to her mother about her plan. She had talked to the girls. She was aware that she could be away from them for a few more hours each week if it came to fruition, and she felt a little guilty. But exhilarated. And they were fine. Emily, in her last year at primary school, had plenty to keep her occupied in the evenings, as, indeed, did the others. Between homework, reading, playing games and just generally running about, they were happy children, and knew they were safe and loved. Jessie was keen that her daughter's time and attention was being taken up by her career and not by worrying about her soon-to-be-ex-husband. So when Anya met her ladies that Saturday morning, she had quite a lot to tell them.

She talked to them about her idea – to set up a course specifically for women in their position, having to balance family, school runs, and home-making with the learning they were so hungry for. A course that would fit around school times in the day and offer alternative sessions in the evenings. A course that would give them qualifications, and could lead on to other things – more or higher qualifications, well-paid jobs. It would be called an Access course, and apparently wasn't a completely unknown phenomenon. Far from feeling deflated by the fact that she hadn't got there first, she was elated. She had come up with a suggestion that had already proved successful elsewhere, although not in Wales. She felt sure that the offer of this sort of provision would one day be the norm for women like these – but they couldn't wait for the rest of the educational world to catch up. They needed it now.

The women were delighted. But then she had to tell them that it would take time. Months, at least. She understood the various stages her proposal had to go through but the women didn't. There would be no short cut. It would be the following academic year before it could start.

They were disappointed at having to wait so long, now that their expectations had been raised higher than they had ever thought possible. But Anya had a solution to fill the gap.

'How would you feel about me teaching you? Not here, informally, with the kids running around; I mean at the college, properly enrolled, say one or two evenings a week?' She tried to read their various expressions, but went on,

'One evening: maths; another evening: human biology. You could do one or both. Starting next week.' She paused again.

'So? What do you think? It would keep you occupied till next year, and prepare you for some more formal study ...'

She needn't have worried. They were all for it. The questions started and they talked over each other.

'How much will it cost us?'

'What do we need to bring?'

'Will there be other people in the class?'

'Will there be youngsters?'

'Can we sit an exam?'

Anya was able to reassure them on all counts. They would be the only people in the class, unless others in the same position came forward, which was unlikely at this fairly late stage in the term. And it wouldn't cost them anything.

She had offered to teach without payment, but that wasn't possible. So she would be paid for her extra hours as overtime, as well as covering some other classes that were currently waiting for a part-time lecturer to be found. She would have hardly any free hours for her preparation and marking, but she was willing to do that in her own time, at home, in order to get this idea off the ground. None of this background she shared with her group of ladies.

So Anya began one of the busiest periods of her life. She had put her credibility on the line for these women, and none of them quite realised how much work was going to be involved. But they were up for it. They were the most attentive and interested students she had taught, soaking up facts like sponges, asking questions, and asking again if they didn't understand. More and more, she was able to give them work to do at home or in the college library, and their efforts effectively doubled their tuition time.

Christmas came with a welcome break, and Anya didn't argue with her mother when she insisted that she would be doing the cooking for Christmas day.

'Mum, I'm so grateful' said Anya as she flopped into an armchair as she arrived home on the last day of term. She looked around the lounge, decorated with holly and berries, tinsel and crepe paper garlands, and an impressive tree laden with painted fir cones, cardboard stars covered in silver foil, and a knitted angel on the top. Her mother had done all this, with enthusiastic help from the children.

'Here, drink your tea' said Jessie with a smile, handing her a mug.

'I mean it, Mum. Looking after the girls, and the house, cooking, cleaning, decorating …'

'I've enjoyed it. You know that.'

'…and taking the nursery group on a Saturday afternoon …'

'Oh yes, about that ...' Jessie sat opposite her, her own mug in hand.

Anya waited. This sounded ominous. She wasn't sure how she would replace her mother. Although the core of the women were now coming to her evening classes, they relied on the informal meetings at the weekend as another opportunity to confirm their understanding and bolster their confidence. And other people came along too, including a couple of men, which Anya saw as a real breakthrough. But one of the things that made this all possible was the creche that Jessie had set up.

'I've decided I want to get a qualification' Jessie said now.

'A ...what?' This wasn't what Anya was expecting.

'A Nursery Nurse qualification' her mother went on. 'I spent years working as one, only too grateful to have found a job where I could take you with me. But I've never had any proper training for it – only the 'sit-by-Nellie' method! And now I think I'd like to do it. I've applied to the community centre in Pontarafon – they do it there - and I can start after Christmas.'

Anya was flabbergasted, but delighted.

'Mum! You never said!'

'Well, I know how busy you've been. I wanted to get it all sorted before I said anything. It's only a bus ride away, and ten till two, three days a week ...'

'It sounds brilliant! Good for you!' Anya put down her mug and hugged her mother, who returned her embrace happily.

'There's one more thing' Jessie said as she returned to her seat, and Anya was surprised to see a faint blush on her mother's cheeks.

'Oh yes? Got a guilty secret, Mum?'

'Don't be silly! Nothing of the sort!' Jessie retorted sharply, but her colour was growing. 'I just wondered ... he's on his own you see ... I wondered whether ... I mean, Christmas can be lonely for some people, can't it? ... so I wondered ...'

'Mum! You're gabbling! I've never heard you gabble! Do you want to invite someone for Christmas? Who ...' light was dawning on Anya's face 'Tarzan? You want to invite Tarzan? Oh of course! That's wonderful!' and she jumped up and clapped her hands like a child.

Jessie's face was now a deep shade of pink.

'Anya, don't be silly!' she said again. 'Sit down for heaven's sake! And his name is Geraint.'

Christmas 1984 was the most peaceful and pleasant one they had known for a few years. Stocking-fillers had been sewn, knitted, crocheted or glued, along with the secret presents known as "hush-hushes" the girls made for their mother, father and grandmother; polite letters had been written to Santa and sent up an accommodating chimney, and they had clearly reached him, as he had obliged by filling the stockings hanging by their beds.

Christmas lunch – always referred to as Christmas dinner – was a triumph of every sort of seasonal vegetable cooked in every possible way, barely allowing room on the plates for the perfectly cooked chicken and stuffing. There was much chatter and laughter, and it didn't seem at all strange that Geraint had joined them. He was good company and a most appreciative guest. After the Christmas pudding and custard, the children were excused and went to play with their new toys and games, while the three adults, having hurriedly cleared the table, sat, replete, with coffee cups in front of them.

'So, Geraint ...' began Anya

'Oh-oh! Here it comes" Geraint said good naturedly, and laughed. Anya laughed too, but her mother was looking apprehensive.

'Mum, I'm winding you up. Geraint is very welcome here – and no inquisition, I promise.'

'Thanks for that Anya. And thank you for using my name – up till today, your mother's the only one who has called me Geraint for a very long time.'

His brief glance at Jessie couldn't have been clearer, no matter how much he – and she – tried to hide it, and it didn't go unnoticed by Anya.

'So – where did the Tarzan thing come from?' asked Anya. 'Not that you don't look perfectly capable of swinging through trees ...'

'Well, it was more to do with my late wife really' he said. 'Her name was Jane, and she was beautiful. Just beautiful. Long blond hair, gorgeous figure, the lot. Way out of my league. And I was not the Tarzan type at all! Scrawny, gangly, wouldn't say "boo" to a goose. Our friends made a joke of it, started calling us Jane and her Tarzan – and it stuck.'

'I don't know you well, Geraint,' said Anya, 'but I wouldn't exactly call you scrawny now. So what happened?'

'I decided to call the joke back on them. I got fit - took up rugby, got a job on a building site, then in the mine. I grew a beard, grew my hair long, and learned to answer back. So there we were – Tarzan and Jane!'

He stopped. Then,

'She died. Giving birth to our son. He died too.'

'Oh Geraint, I'm so sorry. I shouldn't have …' started Anya.

'No, don't be. It's good to talk about them. Sometimes it feels as if they never existed. But they did. And she was …' he hesitated.

'The love of your life' Jessie said quietly.

He looked at her.

'Yes, she was.'

CHAPTER 17

WORRIES AND WOES

1985: January

The year started badly for the miners and their families. And it got worse. Even after nine months, the south Wales coalfields had the highest number of striking miners of anywhere in the country, still retaining their pride and determination. But in areas which depended almost wholly on this single industry, south Wales was suffering hugely with deprivation and often the breakdown of communities.

In Cwmdawel, too, strains and stresses were felt. They saw television news reports of others - broken, defeated - returning to work, worn down by the poverty they now experienced, the tensions within their families, the sight of their children in too-small clothes, with empty bellies. Personal relationships were often close to breaking point, and many feared they would rupture completely as they had elsewhere, as some men decided they had no choice but to work through the strike, calling upon themselves the derisive term of "scab". This hadn't happened in Cwmdawel – yet. They saw these returning miners being attacked by their former friends, their workmates, on the picket lines; miners were clashing with the massed ranks of police repeatedly and with increasing ferocity all over the country. Many families – too many families - were finding it impossible to sustain themselves. Union funds were running too low even to pay for transport to the picket lines.

In March, a vote was passed to return to work. There was no new agreement with management. The strike was over, and the miners had lost.

By contrast, Anya's life wasn't going too badly. She felt desperately sorry for her neighbours, as they tried to come to terms with a humiliating defeat and an unknown future. She did all she could, simply by doing what she had been doing: ferrying people and food parcels around, helping in the community centre, working with those few adults who still had the will to turn up on a Saturday afternoon, and trying her damnedest to make sure her little band of evening class women made a success of their efforts. A few had dropped out, despondency and depression winning over hope and enthusiasm, but the majority were clinging to their studies as a single positive in their frightening and uncertain futures.

But at home, things were looking up. While heavy snow in January and February brought much to a halt and proved more than a nuisance to most adults, the children loved it: sliding down the lane on tin-tray toboggans, trudging to the village in snow-walled tunnels that used to be a road, laughing through snow-ball fights until gloves and mittens were soaked through, and thawing out in front of the open cooking range, getting as close to the leaping flames as they dare. With the college's boilers out of action, the term didn't properly start until March, coinciding with the demoralising news of the end of the strike. Anya and her mother, with a little help from the girls, used the enforced home-time to continue their work on the interior of the house, and news that David's alimony was being back-dated, arriving on Anya's thirtieth birthday, meant that they could afford to buy the septic tank at last.

'Not yet though, Mum' Anya had said when the cheque arrived in the post. 'We'll wait till the summer. There'll be a lot more digging to be done to get that in the ground!'

She was relieved to get back to work when the college was deemed fit to re-open, although the atmosphere there was grim. Her colleagues, like her neighbours, were fearful of what might be in store for them. Jean and Marjorie now joined her and others in the canteen at lunchtime, the long trestle table becoming the same boat they were all in. Conversation was subdued in volume, but passionate in tone. They were worried. About their jobs, about the college, about the community they served. Would the colliery survive? Would there be any need for apprentices to be trained to work in the mines? Would there be any mines? Could the college summon up a new raft of courses, a new cohort of students, enough to justify the employment of the staff currently in place? The arguments and ideas went round in circles, as they must, given that no-one knew the answers.

And all the while these discussions went on, all the while she listened, nodded, agreed or disagreed, gave her considered opinion, she was only really aware of one person. Byron sat opposite her as usual; they spoke little, but a glance and a smile was enough to know that he had missed her as much as she had him. Thanks to the weather, there had been no Saturday morning campaigning sessions, with the reward of sitting in the cramped little café afterwards, since before Christmas, and she looked forward to the end of the week with the eagerness of a child awaiting its birthday.

But she was to be disappointed. Turnout by Labour members was poor that Saturday, and those few who did turn up felt that, with the village in the grip of depression following the end of the strike, it wouldn't be right to knock on doors that weekend. Byron was astounded.

'What? Not right? Now of all days we should be talking about a change of government, a Labour alternative …bloody hell, boys, this isn't a game!'

But he was out-voted, and the handful of activists that had turned up soon drifted away.

'Well, fuck them! Sorry Annie. Still I suppose we could have a coffee anyway' he said.

So they sat, nestled close together even though there was no need, sipping coffee and eventually, giving in at last, holding hands under the table like a couple of lovesick teenagers.

'This isn't what we should be doing on a Saturday morning' said Anya comfortably, making no attempt to move.

'No?'

'No. When we're not knocking on doors, Saturday morning is for shopping or cleaning – I can feel my old twin-tub calling me from here!' she laughed.

'Or for some form of political discussion of course!' answered Byron with mock severity. 'And talking of which …'

He turned in his seat to face her.

'Some news. First – we have some new members. Your ladies. They all joined.'

'Really? Oh bless them! I only asked them once – didn't want to nag, or turn our lessons into some sort of rally.'

'And that could be important' went on Byron, sitting back now, running his fingers through his hair, which momentarily was a distraction for Anya. She forced herself to concentrate.

'… because our candidate is not looking well. He's worn out, and looks downright ill. I can't see him lasting the course for another two years.'

'Is it definite that's when the next election will be?' she asked.

'Well, not definite, no. She could call it any time. It's usually after four years, can't be more than five. But she'll call it when she thinks she's got the best chance of winning.'

They sat quietly for some minutes, before Byron faced Anya again.

'I think you need to think about standing. For election. Parliamentary.'

The idea had never occurred to Anya. She had briefly considered standing for the council elections, but had dismissed the idea. She didn't have the experience, and anyway, as she was technically employed by the council, she wouldn't be allowed to stand. Not in this area

259

anyway. Now here was Byron, suggesting she stands as an MP. She laughed at him, rejecting his suggestion out of hand, but he was not to be so easily put off. As he told her what she would need to do, and why she should do it, she found herself becoming annoyed.

'You're not listening to me, Byron!' she said forcefully. 'I'm not ready for this. It's not me. I can't just...' She tailed off.

'Ok. Sorry. Forget I said anything. You're right – I get carried away sometimes.'

'Oh really?' she said, raising an eyebrow.

Smiling, he stood.

'Come on, Annie-May,' he said. 'I'll give you a lift home. Save you the walk.'

It was only when they drove up to the house that she realised her mother and the girls wouldn't be there. Of course, the children were still at David's, Jessie having coffee with her friends while she waited for them. Byron stopped the car on the drive.

'Er – do you want to come in?' Anya asked tentatively. And after a long pause, Byron nodded.

'Ok. Just for a minute or two.'

They stood in the lounge. She realised he had never been inside her house before.

'Er ... do you want some coffee?'

He smiled.

'No thanks, just had one. And so did you,'

It was inevitable. She must have realised that. He pulled her to him and she clung to him. Their kisses were passionate from the first, no gentle build-up now, no tentative exploring. This was urgent, hungry. Their tongues darted and pushed, their hands ran over familiar frames, every touch eliciting a gasp. She felt his fingers in her hair as she ran her hands inside his shirt, feeling his warm flesh, his heart pounding in time to her own. She felt him hard against her, pressing at her. She gasped again.

He pushed away from her, suddenly, still holding her.

'I don't have anything. A Durex.' His voice was hoarse, breathless. 'I wasn't expecting ...'

She moaned.

'Please Byron!'

'Ok' he whispered as he kissed her neck. 'It'll be ok. I'll pull out ...'

Then they were on the sofa, bodies burning, demanding, aching for the release they had longed for, for so long, so long.

And he was in her, every thrust met by hers, moving rhythmically, together, building to that crescendo, all too soon, until suddenly he pulled back, lay on her, bursting, shooting onto her belly, while she gasped, touching herself, moving her fingers until she, too, reached the climax she had been longing for. They lay together, the only sound their breathing and the pounding of their hearts..

Spring unfolded before them. The opening of buds and greening of the hedges and trees, the sight of new-born lambs always bringing that extra helping of delight to Anya, Jessie and the girls, who never tired of this wondrous celebration of new life. Their lives were moving on: Jessie's course had started, albeit later than expected; Emily's days in the junior school were coming to an end, as she prepared for the big move to the comprehensive school. Fran was excited at the thought of being the oldest Gethin girl in Cwmdawel Primary, and Lucy would be moving up from the infants.

And Anya, while continuing with her heavy load of teaching and weekend campaigning, was giving more and more thought to the seed of an idea that Byron had planted. She made no mention of this to him, or to anyone else, but the questions going round in her head were moving from "I couldn't!" to "How on earth could I?" and then to "Could I? One day?" She found herself listening even more closely to political discussions on TV, and reading sections of newspapers she had previously only skimmed. The little research she was able to do showed her that MPs were ordinary people, with no particular qualifications, indeed often with no qualifications at all. She started to see it as a possibility, some day, and it excited her.

But other thoughts were in her head too. A worry that was growing, waking her at night with a start, until, by early May, she knew. She was pregnant.

She also knew, before she told him, that she couldn't have this baby. His baby. And that was the point. She was carrying his baby. When his wife couldn't, when this may be the only chance he had of having a child of his own. Her natural instincts, hormonal or simply maternal, railed against the only option she could see. There were too many practicalities, too many things that just wouldn't work. Her job for one. How could she ask her mother to look after yet another child? Just as the girls were growing up? Equally, she couldn't give up her job. And then there was Claire, always on the brink, fragile as ever, ready to break. How could she ask Byron to do that to the girl he'd once loved?

And so, on a sunny May Day morning, in the little café where they had felt so close, she told him her news, and her decision. In the same instant, the promise of a new life, shattered by news of its impending loss. He didn't argue with her, although he tried to put forward alternatives.

'It's your decision love, but ...'

There was no alternative, she said. She'd seen her GP, who, after some preaching at her and severe frowns, had referred her to a second doctor as he must, and reluctantly booked her into Honour House Hospital in Swansea. They specialised in this sort of thing, he said ...

She had to stay strong. She would not show Byron that this was breaking her heart. But after she left him that morning, she cried as she drove home. And she cried over the sink as she washed up, and she cried as she swept the yard. She could not have kept this from her mother now even if she'd tried, and when Jessie arrived home, weighed down with shopping bags, Anya dissolved once more into tears.

Relieved that the girls were at a Mayday play event, Anya sat with her mother and told her everything. Jessie comforted her daughter with hugs and kisses, but said little. There was little she could say. The deed was done, the decision made.

263

It would be three weeks before Anya would have the procedure, thankfully during the spring bank holiday, but she would need to go to a pre-operation consultation first. She gratefully accepted her mother's offer to accompany her, and, having taken a day from work, they drove to the little hospital. It was off the main road running out of Swansea, hidden away behind trees, as if aware of the shame that was deep-rooted in the building and its occupants. The consultation was as bad as Anya had feared it would be. She felt wicked twice over, for having become pregnant, and then for deciding to kill an innocent child. She would need to deliver her tiny baby, to suffer the pains of labour, in an attempt to make her appreciate and regret her misdeeds.

These were not the words that were spoken, of course. The nursing sister who sat in front of them was kind and used anodyne phrases, non-judgemental instructions and information, but what Anya heard was rebuke, reprimand, scolding, admonishment. She was silent, travelling home, as her mother fought back her own tears.

Two weeks later, Anya was packed and, on the face of it, ready. She knew that Byron had accepted the reality of her decision, and they spoke little about it, but it was always there, unsaid, colouring their every conversation, their every glance. She just wanted it to be over, to put it behind her, to forget it. If she could. She tried to stop herself from playing the "what if" scenarios in her head, with varying degrees of success. There were just twenty-four hours to go before she would leave for this unwelcome trip to the hospital when Jessie, seeing her

264

daughter's pacing and fidgeting, made her sit with her at the living room table.

Anya stared out of the window, focusing on the little rockery she and the children had made just a few days ago, as they had pushed tiny alpine plants into cracks and crevices till they disappeared.

'Drink your tea, love' Jessie said. Then, 'Annie, I can't bear to see you like this.'

Her daughter smiled at her, but with such sadness in her eyes that her mother winced.

'It'll be ok Mum. I've just got to get over the next couple of days. Then I'll be back to normal.'

'No love, you won't.' Jessie's voice was gentle but firm. 'So, what are we going to do?'

'Do? What do you mean?' Anya's eyes were back on the rockery. When would those little plants flower, she wondered. Would they thrive? In such hostile ground?

'Anya, listen to me. Maybe there's some way we can do this.'

She had never felt happier. A huge weight, even greater than she had admitted to herself that she was carrying, had been lifted from her shoulders. They could do this! How could she ever have considered an abortion? She touched her stomach. Was there a swelling there yet? Was she imagining it? She laughed. It didn't matter. Her baby was inside her. Their baby. She had to tell Byron. She knew there were still huge obstacles to overcome, but now she knew they could do it. Her mother's words had made her see that. On impulse, she took a risk and phoned his

265

number, crossing her fingers, hoping and praying that it would be he who answered. He did.

'It's me. Can you meet me in the café? Now? Or – in ten minutes? I've something to tell you!'

She put the phone down and ran to the car, calling to her mother that she wouldn't be long. She looked around her as she pulled out of the drive and into the lane, thinking that her little piece of home had never looked lovelier. She couldn't wait to tell Byron. Down the lane, turn right at the bottom ...

The world spun around as she felt the sideways thud and crash, heard the sickening crunch of metal. She didn't feel it. Not yet. Then all seemed silent. She couldn't move, couldn't breathe. Pinned to her seat, she realised that the engine was still running. Time froze, or speeded up. She didn't know. Then there were faces, talking to her through the space where the windscreen should have been. A man telling her he was sorry, he hadn't seen her, heard her car. People at the side, where she couldn't see them, machines cutting away the car door which had rammed into her, people gently unfastening the seatbelt that had saved her life, lifting her out on the car seat where she still sat. Then her mother, in slippers and pinny, white and terrified, assuring her that everything would be ok, not to worry about anything.

The journey in the ambulance took minutes or hours, she didn't know. She lay there, trusting these strangers as they checked her, took readings, talked to her in voices she did not hear. Then the hospital. She saw lights above her, flashing at intervals, as she was wheeled along corridors. When they started to lift her from the

266

trolley onto the bed she felt as if everything inside was broken. She felt like a bag of shattered bones that had been shaken up with only the casing intact. Surely she would fall apart? But they were gentle, and the jarring she expected, dreaded, did not come.

'What's your name, sweetheart?' A female voice.

It took a moment, then,

'Anya' she gasped.

'Ok Anya, that's good. Can you tell me where it hurts?'

She thought about that. She hurt everywhere, but had hardly registered the pain, masked as it was with the shock.

'Where does it hurt the most, Anya?' Someone else was speaking to her now. A man.

She pointed to her chest.

'And my leg' she said breathlessly.

'Ok Anya' the female voice said again. We'll sort you out. Just leave everything to us.'

Jessie sat, still as a statue, arms around her three grandchildren. Her face was streaked with tears, but she wasn't crying any more. The girls patted her hands, rubbed her back, taking comfort in comforting this rock of a woman. She looked up as Byron came bursting into the relatives' room. He, too, was as white as a sheet.

'Mrs Hughes ...'

"Jessie' she said automatically.

'... I just heard. What happened? Is she alright? Are you alright? What ...'

His stream of questions was cut short as a young doctor entered the room. She smiled reassuringly.

'Anya's going to be ok' she told them, and they visibly exhaled, seeming to shrink down in relief.

'She's broken a number of bones, including several ribs, one of which has punctured her lung. Don't worry' she said quickly as she saw renewed alarm on their faces. 'That's all in hand. She will also need an operation on her leg, and we'll be keeping her in for a few weeks. But she'll be fine.'

The girls, cheered now and quick to accept the doctor's reassurance at face value, broke away to examine the dog-eared children's books piled in the opposite corner.

'And the baby?' Jessie asked quietly.

Byron stared at her.

'I'm afraid Anya has lost her baby, Mrs Hughes.'

After the doctor had left them, Byron sat down.

'You knew?' he whispered.

'Yes I knew. And I knew what she had decided to do. That she was on her way to tell you that she'd changed her mind.'

And then Jessie was crying as if her heart would break, crying for her daughter, for the little mite that was no more, crying for the three bemused children looking at her, and, she realised though her tears, for this man, whom Anya loved and who loved her, who looked stricken with horror and guilt. And he, too was crying, taking Jessie in his arms as they each mourned what might have been, shedding tears of joy and relief for the deliverance of the woman they both loved, and of grief for the life lost.

It was six weeks before Anya left hospital. The college term had finished and the school term was nearing its end. She needed to use a wheelchair, occasionally walking with the aid of a stick around the house, and she had a series of appointments with the physios to look forward to, but she was home. However, she found that she did not feel as ecstatic as she had expected. She was frightened. She had spent weeks leaving everything to others, knowing there would always be someone close by if she fell, or felt ill, or was in pain. Now she felt completely alone, even though her family was around her.

She discovered that, in her absence, the septic tank had been bought and installed by the men from the village, and at last they had a toilet that flushed, but she could raise no enthusiasm for this project that once would have been the cause for much celebration. She spent a great deal of time sitting at the table in the living room, looking out of the window at the little rockery, which was now a blaze of colour. It calmed her, and sometimes gave her a kind of hope, but she was gripped by a depression that, she was told, often happens after a long hospital stay. Her mother and the girls were wonderful, and she tried hard to put on a cheerful face, but a huge guilt was engulfing her. Jessie was worried about her, and did the only thing she could.

When Byron walked in, Anya thought she had conjured him up from her imagination.

'Hi, you!' he said, smiling his beautiful smile.

She broke down then. He held her as sobs racked her body. When they had subsided, she sat up.

'Sorry' she said, as she wiped her eyes. 'I'm sorry.' More tears threatened to overtake her again, but she controlled them.

'There's nothing to be …'

'You don't know, Byron, you don't know!' she shouted as she interrupted him. 'But I need to tell you. I need to tell someone.' She paused. 'When I lost the baby, I was relieved.'

His expression was unreadable.

'I was relieved' she went on in a jumbled rush, 'and I know that's wicked, I so wanted your baby, and then after I'd decided to get rid of it, then changed my mind, and when I lost it, it was my punishment for planning an abortion in the first place, for getting pregnant in the first place, and then I didn't need to make that decision any more …' her words were tumbling over each other, becoming incoherent as she became more distressed, tears flowing once again.

He put his finger over her lips. Very gently.

'Shh' he said quietly.

She fell silent then, with only the occasional hiccup to remind them both of her fretfulness.

'It was an accident, Anya. You didn't have any say in it. That's what accidents are.'

'But … afterwards … I kept thinking how much easier it would make everything' she whispered. 'How you wouldn't have to tell Claire, how she wouldn't have to be so …so…'

She started to cry again. He opened his mouth to speak but she continued.

'... and then ... and then ... I was thinking about that little baby, that I wanted so much, who never had a chance, who ...'

'Anya. Listen to me. It was terrible that you lost the baby - that we lost our baby in that way. But who or what do you think is punishing you? You can think of this as fate, as God's will, as some unexplained event of the universe, but it's certainly not your fault. You made a decision not to have the baby. That wasn't wicked. To some, yes, but not to me. You were thinking of other people and it was the only one you felt you could make. But then you decided to keep it, didn't you? Your Mum told me. So don't you think you've been through enough, without carrying this great burden of guilt as well? Be a bit gentler with yourself, Cariad.'

Anya let out a huge sigh then, and rested against his shoulder, exhausted. When Jessie popped her head around the door, she saw Byron kiss the top of her daughter's head, and she knew she'd done the right thing in calling him.

CHAPTER 18

NEXT STEPS, NEW STEPS

1985

The world gradually righted itself. The summer was wet and windy, with little sunshine, but the flowers and the newly-planted vegetables in the sloping garden flourished. Geraldine became a regular visitor at Ty Clyd, enquiring about Anya's health, bringing her tonics and health supplements and fussing over her, and Anya was surprised to see her mother's hackles rise, as she viewed, with distaste, this woman who seemed to take a proprietary interest in her daughter. She's jealous! thought Anya, and while she didn't enjoy seeing her mother's discomfiture, she couldn't help but be amused. But as the weeks went on, the two women developed a grudging respect for each other, until Geraldine's visits were as much to chat to Jessie as to check on Anya.

The children found plenty to do, particularly as Jessie was happy to act as their personal taxi driver with trips to the swimming pool in Pontarafon, visits to friends' houses and events in the community centre. The village, too, was recovering in some small way. The mine was still open, at least for now, which meant that money was coming into the homes, helping families to get back on track, masking some of the humiliation and anger they felt.

Exam results day at the end of the holidays was heartening for Anya. She had discarded her wheelchair and only occasionally used her stick, determined to be fit and well for the new term. Once again, the young people in her classes had done well, and she was especially delighted at the achievements of her group of women from the village. They had exceeded all expectations, surprising themselves into the bargain, and proving to Paul and Elaine that they had been right to back Anya's idea.

September arrived with warmer weather, and Anya waved her eldest daughter off as she walked proudly down the lane, blazer and tie in place, to catch the school bus.

The college term started much as it always had, with a few new faces in the staff room and a few empty chairs, as some colleagues became ex-colleagues and were, on the whole, quickly forgotten. The small group with whom Anya had forged such strong friendships remained close, with promotions and movements across departments rarely threatening to displace the relationships. Fears about low student numbers were, so far, not realised, although all were aware that changes to the mining industry could take a while to work their way through to their community, and the college. The new Access course was well subscribed, and not only by the group of Anya's friends. Word had spread, and women were coming from further afield than Cwmdawel. She had to admit that she was relieved not to be taking two evening classes this year, and although she felt an absurd pang at the thought of other staff teaching them, she knew that this was what they needed, and that her colleagues would teach them well.

She and Byron knew that any overt relationship between them was not possible, and they met only at work, chatting as normally as possible over lunch, and sharing an occasional cup of coffee in the staffroom. Their Saturday morning campaign sessions were becoming more important to Anya, not only for the pleasant and secretly intimate finales in the café, but for the actual politics. She couldn't pretend that she hadn't started to think, again, about Byron's suggestion, made all those months ago. He had not mentioned the subject again, leaving Anya to mull over the idea in her own time. But too much had happened since then, and she needed to focus on the future.

It was Geraldine who raised the issue, in a roundabout way, as she was leaving their house one Saturday afternoon, having spent a pleasant hour with Jessie discussing the opportunities for childcare work in the valley. Anya walked her to her car, parked in the drive, and was surprised when Geraldine halted and said, in her direct way,

'Be careful, Anya. I know Byron's a good-looking man, but take care.'

Anya looked flustered.

'What? I don't know what you mean!'

'Oh come now, dear. You don't honestly think you can live in a community like this and keep an affair quiet?'

Anya blushed furiously, but tried to argue.

'Geraldine, there's nothing …'

She was stopped short by Geraldine's raised hand.

'Anya, please don't insult my intelligence. I'm not judging you, girl! I'm just concerned about you. He won't leave Claire – I expect you know the background?' She went on, without waiting for confirmation. 'But something like this could spoil your chances of any political ambitions you may have. And you do have ambitions, I can tell. An affair won't necessarily ruin your chances, but breaking up a marriage, damaging an already-damaged woman like Claire – that won't go down well locally.'

Anya didn't speak.

'So,' Geraldine went on, 'be careful. Be discreet. From what I hear, it's all gone pretty quiet at the moment. I know there was a – shall we say, an event, back in early summer...'

'What?! What have you ...'

'Best to put that behind you, dear' she said more gently. 'It's not common knowledge and I certainly won't be broadcasting it, but I wouldn't recommend repeating it. I'm sure you wouldn't want to either.'

She patted Anya on the hand.

'Just thought I should mention it.'

And Anya watched, stunned, as Geraldine drove away.

Christmas came round, quicker than ever. As always, the girls were happy to break up for the school holidays, and spent a great deal of time getting scratched and pricked by the holly they were determined to pick and to decorate the house with. Once again, Anya listened to Jessie's

275

uncharacteristically awkward request for Geraint to spend Christmas day with them, and once again she laughed and teased her mother as she happily agreed.

A further addition to the Christmas table this year was Geraldine. Anya knew very little about her friend's personal life, but had always assumed she had a family or friends she would spend her time with. It was Jessie who had broached the idea of her joining them for lunch, and she, too, was surprised but delighted when Geraldine accepted the invitation, albeit in her cool and somewhat off-hand way. Anya wondered what her daughters would make of this seemingly austere and forbidding character, but she needn't have worried. Seven-year-old Lucy had her own very direct way of eliciting information from their guest, who answered as she would to an adult. Emily and Fran soon joined in the conversation, which Geraldine ensured never became a one-way interrogation.

The no-man's-land between Christmas and New Year was a quiet and peaceful one, in contrast to some in the past. Anya fretted quietly to herself about the fact that she would not see Byron on Saturday, as campaigning was not considered appropriate during these holiday periods.

'You'll just wind people up' explained Ethan when she'd queried the decision to cancel. 'They don't think much of politics and politicians anyway, and to have us disturbing their holiday will turn them off even more.'

However, politics reared its head sooner in 1986 than Anya had expected. The phone rang early on January 1st.

'Anya? Geraldine. Emrys Locke has died.'

"Emrys …? Oh, our candidate!'

'Parliamentary candidate, yes. Dropped dead last night, poor lamb. Massive heart attack, so I've heard. Anyway, we need to talk. Can we meet today?'

'Um, I expect so. Yes. Here?' Anya was a little flustered by the urgency in Geraldine's voice.

'Best not. Byron will need to join us. Secretary of the CLP, after all. So – café? Ten o'clock? Or maybe eleven. Yes, eleven. See you then.'

And she was gone.

'Why the rush, Geraldine?'

Anya sat herself down opposite her friend, pulling the ready-ordered coffee cup towards her. She brushed her hair back from her face which was pink with hurrying from home, to say nothing of the thought of seeing Byron.

'Well maybe not a rush exactly – but time is of the essence!'

Anya laughed.

'I'm serious Annie. We never know when an election may be called. It probably won't be till next year. Or the year after. But we don't know, and we have to be prepared. Could be next month! Ah, here's our secretary now.'

He sat down next to Anya, who glanced at Geraldine surreptitiously, looking for a reaction from her, but there was none. There had been no further mention of the concern the older woman had expressed weeks ago, but this was the first time since she had dropped her bombshell that she would have seen Anya and Byron together. However, she didn't bat an eyelid.

277

New year greetings and niceties over quickly, they got down to business.

'Ok, so we need the selection process to start straight away' said Byron, clearly agreeing with Geraldine on this. 'We don't know when an election may be called, and we need to be ready"

'We will need to select a new candidate who could win an election this time' continued Geraldine. 'We'll need to get the name known, and that will take time – which we may not have.'

'But surely it will be Maldwyn Rees?' said Anya. 'I thought he was next in line …'

To her surprise, both Byron and Geraldine laughed aloud at this.

'It doesn't quite work like that' said Byron. 'Part of your political education I've clearly overlooked! No. It's the Labour members who will select someone to stand as their candidate in the next election. Selection is a damned sight harder than the election if someone's looking to become an MP in Wales. Once he – or she - gets selected as a candidate, it can be a foregone conclusion that they'll be elected. Well, in most places anyway. And it has to be open to any member to put themselves forward, as long as they have some people to nominate and back them. I'm sure Maldwyn will be one to throw his hat into the ring, but he won't be alone. And I'd be surprised if he got the support from members that he'd need.'

'We will need important backers' added Geraldine. 'Influential ones. Influential within the party, that is. So we need to select a good candidate. And we have one. Sitting here, in front of me.'

For a moment she thought Geraldine meant Byron. But as she saw them both looking at her, she realised that they meant her.'

'Hey, wait a minute …' she started.

'Come on Annie, don't say you haven't thought about it, because I know you have.'

She was silent. Then,

'Yes, I've thought about it!' Anya replied slowly, 'and I know I'm not ready for this. Maybe in the future, sometime. But not now!'

They were smiling at her.

'I'm new to all this, and there are people far better prepared, far better qualified, far more eager to do this than I am. I have a family. I have children. And a job.' She wasn't shouting but her voice was firm. And they continued to smile.

'What do I know about the great and the good in London? In Parliament?' She was getting into her stride now, and they were annoying her. She realised her hands were shaking and she put down her cup.

'What do I know about debating and public speaking and fighting for causes? I'm just a mother, a teacher, a neighbour, and a very small local cog in a big political machine. No, I'm not ready for this.' She stopped to draw breath.

She expected them to look irritated, exasperated, impatient with her. Instead they were still smiling. Smugly, she thought.

And she saw those smiling faces, and she was suddenly angry that they should presume, should treat her as their puppet, expect her to fall in line with their scheming plans.

'And don't look at me like that!' she was shouting now. 'Don't patronise me. I'm not your toy, good little Anya, we'll mould her ...'

'Hey, hey!' Byron was frowning, concerned.. He put his hand on her arm.

She stopped shouting. Gino carried on about his work. He had heard enough arguments in his little coffee house not to be bothered by them. Neither Byron nor Geraldine was smiling now.

'But don't you see?' he said. 'That's what we mean. We think you are ready. Not because we're trying to do some Svengali act on you, but because you're bloody good.'

'It's precisely because you ARE a mother. "Just" a mother' said Geraldine. 'And a teacher, and a neighbour. Who do you think you'd be representing as an MP, eh? Not lords and ladies, powerful businessmen, the great and the good. You'd be representing people like you – mothers and teachers and neighbours. Men who've lost their jobs, women who have had to become breadwinners. And you know about them. Because you are one of them.'

'And as for debating and public speaking and fighting for causes' went on Byron, 'what do you think you've been doing every lunch time, at every Labour meeting, every union meeting, every time you knock on someone's door on a Saturday morning? Every time you argue with me and put me in my place? Oh yes you do!'

he said quickly, seeing she was about to disagree. 'On more occasions that I'd care to admit!'

'And what do you think you were doing when you made that speech to the miners, or when you set up the courses for their wives?' said Geraldine. 'You're not such a small cog as you might think.'

Anya was quiet now. She felt a little embarrassed at her outburst – but she was stirred by what they were saying. Could she? Could she possibly? Little Annie-May?

'I'll need to talk to the girls' she said calmly.

She hadn't realised how mature they were. Even Lucy. They asked her how long she would be away each week, if they'd have to move house, move schools. They wanted to know if she'd be home for Christmas, birthdays, school plays. And she answered them honestly, insofar as she knew what the answers were. She told them that this was just a possibility, maybe far into the future, and that it may not happen at all. And she told them that if they didn't want her to do this, she wouldn't. And she meant it.

'So I could be eleven. Or twelve.' said Fran.'

'Yes. Or you could be ten – if it happened this year.'

'I'd probably be a teenager, Mum' said Emily. 'I'll be growing up. I'll be more independent by then.'

Anya swallowed hard.

'Yes love, you will.'

'If we said no, you wouldn't do it?' asked Lucy.

'No love, I wouldn't.'

281

'But would that make you sad?' the little girl said. 'If you said I couldn't go to Llangranog with the school, I'd do what you said, but I'd be quite sad.'

Anya laughed and hugged her.

'No, I wouldn't be sad. Because I'd have you three monsters! And Granny!'

She had of course talked to her mother about her possible, vague, unlikely plans. She wouldn't be able to even consider the idea without her. But her mother had been as supportive as she had always been.

'You'd be taking on a lot, Annie. From what I hear, long hours, hard graft, and time away from your kids. But I think you'd be good at this. Really good. So go for it if you can!'

'There are so many ifs and buts' Anya said, over coffee one evening. 'If I got nominated. If I got selected. And the big one – if I got elected. Did you know that there's only one woman MP in the whole of Wales? That there have only ever been four? Just four? The odds aren't with me!'

'Put like that, yes, it sounds unlikely, doesn't it?' said Jessie. 'But if you don't give it a try, you definitely won't do it, will you?'

'Would it cause any problems with your – er – friendship with Geraint?' Anya asked.

Her mother sighed and put down her cup.

'Ok, let's talk about Geraint. He's a friend, yes. A good friend. He may want to be more than that – in fact I'm pretty sure he does. But – oh, I don't know, Annie. I've thought of myself as your dad's wife for so long, I'd feel unfaithful. Yes, I know that's silly. But that's how I'd feel. I think. I don't know…'

'I've never known you to be indecisive, Mum' said Anya. 'Remember when we first looked at this place?' she motioned around the room and through the window. 'You saw how ridiculous the thought of living here was, but you also saw through all that. It was you who made the decision. Well, helped me to decide. So why not give it a try? Just dip your toe in the water. At the moment you're both tip-toeing around each other, both afraid to make the first move. Just let him know that you might, you just might, give it some thought.'

The next few weeks were frantic and secretive. The tight little circle of people who were aware of their plan grew larger, as first some branch members, then constituency, and finally union members were brought in, consulted, petitioned for support, their backing being crucial to secure Anya's nomination. They knew that the role would be hotly contested.

A political career was like no other. No formal qualifications were needed, but potential parliamentary candidates were expected to have "earned their stripes", "done their time", all of which credentials were highly subjective and difficult to evidence outside the people who already knew them. To be known and respected in branch meetings and in one's home village was one thing. To take that further, across all the other branches in the South Powys constituency, that was something else.

Vacancies didn't come up very often, and when they did it was usually as a result of a failed election campaign, or death. Emrys had been fortunate to have remained as the Labour candidate for three consecutive elections, losing them all. Anywhere else, and he'd have been pushed to one side, de-selected well before the following election was looming. But this was Plaid territory, and there was no long queue waiting in the wings to suffer yet another humiliating defeat. So he'd ploughed on, unchallenged. But things were changing. A Labour victory here was within touching distance now. So there would be a lot of interest in this seat.

Anya was thankful that she didn't need to do the glad-handing all by herself. Self-promotion was not one of her strengths, although she knew she'd have to work on this. It was Geraldine and Byron who threw the first pebbles into the pond, knowing those ripples would spread as the prospect of an early election gained hold.

So the protracted process swung slowly into life, gaining momentum, then sweeping them along, meeting after meeting, step after step, until they were here, at the selection meeting. Anya felt battered and bruised from the fight so far, a fight amongst those who should have been friends, fellow Labour members, all hoping and praying for a Labour win here, a Labour government in Westminster. But a woman? Never! She'd had no idea that here, now, in the late twentieth century, people could be so anti-women. And it wasn't just the men. Far from it. She heard her fellow women members declaring that this was a man's job. She could hardly believe it. Then came the cry for the choice to be made on merit. What did that even mean? That being a woman meant she warranted no merit at all? But far from frightening her off, these arguments made her want this even more. And if she caught Geraldine or Byron, or others of her growing number of supporters, smiling when she spoke passionately at local meetings, she didn't get angry at them any more. She smiled back at them.

The selection meeting wasn't taking place on what Anya felt was home turf, but in **Pontarafon**. She could laugh at herself now, at the way she'd been unnerved to realise she wouldn't just be aiming to represent little Cwmdawel but the whole constituency of South Powys with all its many small villages and towns, including the one in which she now stood, waiting. She'd almost balked at the realisation – not because she didn't think she could do it, but because she had been so naïve as not to realise it. Once again, Byron and Geraldine had been there to hold her up, steer her forward, and she'd realised that there were quite a few others, a small team growing bigger every day, all positive, enthused, willing to talk to other members, making her believe she could do this.

The chamber of the town hall was full, but there were few faces she knew. Five other people had been shortlisted for selection, all men, Anya noted with no surprise. She had come across them all, of course, on the bumpy road that had led to this evening's gathering. They had, over the weeks, all smiled at her while their eyes were steely, resenting her for bringing this unnecessary feminine element into their masculine world.

They stood apart now, scanning pieces of paper, or muttering to themselves, practising their speeches. Then officials were on the raised dais, speaking, setting out the programme for the evening, laying down the rules, assuring everyone that all present had been verified as fully paid-up members. The chairman called the nominees up, and Anya joined the other five. Looking out at the tiered rows of party members, she was dismayed to find hardly anyone from her local branch. Then, just as the chairman was about to order the doors to be locked, there was the sound of a scuffle at the entrance, raised voices, angry exchanges.

'Mr Chairman, this is out of order!' shouted the man in charge of the entrance. 'These members are too late! They can't be allowed in!'

And there was Bryn.

'Yes, something is out of order, Mr Chairman' he was saying from the doorway. 'The notices we were sent gave the wrong time of this meeting. I'll be charitable, and say it was an accident, a typing cock-up. But it seems it only happened in Cwmdawel.'

The room was hushed now.

'So either we have our membership checked now,' he went on, 'and be allowed to take part in the selection, or I'll be on the phone to report to Labour party headquarters that the result of this meeting must be declared null and void, due to some questionable tactics that have been used here.'

The chairman turned to his colleagues, then spoke to the nominees, asking their opinions. Anya could see one of her fellow hopefuls looking slightly pink in the face, though whether this was due to a guilty conscience or over-exertion she wasn't sure. But all agreed, including a thankful Anya, that there was nothing to be done but to allow the new arrivals to join the crowd below them.

It took a further fifteen minutes before all were checked in as bona fide members, then in they came. Bryn, Geraint, and most of the other men from the village. Anya smiled with relief. And then – Sian, and Jen, along with the Access course women, other wives, some daughters. Anya was overwhelmed. So they had all come! She knew, in her heart, that she stood little chance of being selected, but their support was all the affirmation she needed just then.

They had drawn lots as to the order in which they would speak. Was she pleased she was drawn last? She didn't know. But as she listened to her rivals speaking and answering the follow-up questions from the assembled members, she became more anxious. These men clearly knew all the local problems, and had suggestions as to how they should be addressed, although Anya privately wondered how much influence a single MP could have in bringing in the wish-lists of laws and regulations that these prospective candidates were promising. But the members were being told what they wanted to hear, and were applauding enthusiastically. Should she be doing the same? Play the political game? And was she being unduly cynical, or did some of the challenges from the floor sound a little less natural than they might? A little rehearsed? The responses a little too well prepared? She dared a glance down at her team. Was it her imagination, or did Geraldine look suspicious too? Is this how it always went?

And it was her turn. She looked at the script in her hand. Conscientiously written. Hours of research and painstaking preparation. She had been proud of it. But now? Having heard the pitches of the others, she saw it for what it was. Lacklustre, bland. Sanitised, unlikely to offend, using all the right words, the familiar phrases, toeing the party line, promising the undeliverable, and castigating the current government on dogma only, not on their actions, the effects of their policies on the people like those in front of her now. She saw Byron's face as he watched her tear the papers up and place the pieces carefully on the lectern. Geraldine too. She smiled, he nodded, and Anya started to speak.

She was back on the stage at the Cwmdawel Community Centre, back nearly two years ago. Only two years? Surely not! Surely a lifetime ago! Then, she had said *"You don't want to know my history, do you? You don't want to know where I've lived or what I've done"*. But now they needed to know. They needed to know that she, too, had felt the blow that unemployment can bring, not only to the men laid off, but to their wives, their children. That she had been one of those wives, her daughters just three of those children. That these crippling policies were not just a philosophy of the ruling party, but the reality, the practicality. She had seen, and understood, and felt the impact of the government's pit closure programme, the strike, the marching back to work with hearts in their boots and heads held high. So she told them what the Labour party would do for them. Not she, one individual, but she, as part of an army of individuals who could form the next government, if they, the people in this

288

chamber, worked with her to win the next election. If they gave her a chance.

'And finally' she said, as she saw her fifteen minutes was drawing to a close, 'you may have noticed I'm a woman.' Some laughter. 'But don't be fooled into thinking that means I don't have the guts to do this. I ask all the women here – don't you think you have it in you to hold a family together, to balance work and home, and in between, to give birth to the next generation? You know you do. You're doing it every day. As I am. And to all the men - just ask your wives, your sisters, your mothers, your daughters, the same. I think you'll find we're up to the task.'

Her speech was met by more applause than she was expecting. As much as her rivals had got, anyway. Then came the questions. She was relieved to find she could answer most of them. And those she didn't know the answer to, she told them just that. She told them she would not lie to them, or pretend she knew more than she did. But she promised them that, if they selected her, she would find out the answers; she would ask her own questions, and learn from others.

Then it was over. A steady stream of members trickled out into the vestibule to cast their votes, and returned, some munching on sandwiches and sausage rolls supplied by the women members. She and her fellow nominees were to remain in their places until the votes were counted, which seemed to take an inordinate amount of time. At last, the tellers approached the chairman with a slip of paper. As if a silent whistle had been blown, a hush fell over the room, and everyone took their seats. The

289

chairman stood before them, seeming to revel in his short-lived importance. He cleared his throat and made his brief announcement.

'The person you have chosen as your parliamentary candidate for the South Powys constituency is – Anya Gethin.'

The room clapped, some enthusiastically, some politely. Her supporters were cheering, others were not, some were frowning, muttering, some nodding as if at least resigned to the outcome. Her little team seemed overjoyed, and, it must be said, surprised, by this result. Anya was stunned. The chairman signalled for her to join him, and stepped back from the lectern for her to take his place. She realised that she would have to make a thank-you speech, something for which she was completely unprepared. But she collected herself, even though still in a state of shock, and thanked members, the chairman, other nominees. She reiterated her promise to listen to them and to learn from them, to start campaigning right away, and hoped they would all stay for the buffet, half of which had already been eaten. She kept it short, which was appreciated by everyone, then stepped down to stand with her friends.

After a lot of back-patting and congratulations, amid a buzz of newly energised enthusiasm, she found herself a seat in an ante-room with Geraldine and Byron.

'You did good, my girl!' Geraldine said. 'And now the work starts. First – you need an agent. And if I might suggest – with many reservations, I must say - this young man is probably the best you'll find, although your past relationship may make that difficult.'

Anya blushed to the roots of her auburn hair. How could she say that? In front of him? But Byron seemed not to be embarrassed at all.

'Why Byron?' asked Anya, playing for time.

'Because he's done it before, Annie. He was Emrys' agent in the last two elections. He knows the ropes.'

'Not exactly a glowing recommendation, mind you. We lost. Both of them.' Byron smiled.

'Oh, right,' Anya said. 'So – would you? I mean – could you? What do you think?' She was struggling to make sense of her thoughts.

'I don't mind doing it Annie. But I'd have to ask Claire. It would mean you and I working together, spending hours together. And she – well, you know.'

'Oh, of course' Anya replied a little too quickly. 'Of course you must ask her.'

'Ok, I'll do that now' and he turned to leave the little room.

'What?' Anya spoke sharply. 'Now? Here? Claire is here?'

'Of course' he said calmly. 'She wanted to vote for you.' and he walked into the packed chamber, visible though the open door.

'Come on.' Geraldine took her arm and steered her out into the jostling crowd. 'Better to be surrounded by people for this.'

'You don't think she'll want to meet me?' The prospect was too terrible to contemplate. And yet here she was.

Tiny, almost skeletal, but still beautiful in an ethereal way, Claire stood before her, upright, head held high, unsmiling. Anya had only ever seen her once, lying unconscious on a hospital bed, bandaged wrists lying limply on the covering sheet. Byron now stood behind her, his expression unreadable. Anya smiled and held out her hand.

'Hi. I'm …'

'I know who you are' she said shortly, although she took the proffered hand in her fragile one. 'Byron says you'd like him to be your agent. Yes, alright. He'll do a good job. This is something that's important to him. And he's made me a promise. But …' she stood on tip toes, and, leaning forward, whispered in Anya's ear 'keep your fucking hands off my husband.'

CHAPTER 19

AN END AND A BEGINNING

1986 / 1987

It was more hectic than she could ever have imagined. Every waking hour, when she wasn't working at the college, it seemed they were knocking on doors, dropping leaflets through letterboxes, attending concerts, shaking hands, presenting prizes, all events cleverly arranged by Byron. They were getting her name known. Anya got into the habit of recording her thoughts on a little dictaphone that Geraldine had given her, to save precious moments in writing them down. Often, Jessie and the girls joined the campaigning team that had grown into a force majeure. And increasingly they were being joined by Geraint.

The months passed, each week bringing rumours of an early election, raising the intensity of expectation, to be discarded briefly before another upsurge of mild hysteria among the politically-aware. To the rest of the world, this activity went largely unnoticed, apart from an unwanted knock on the door or an unread leaflet to be put out with the rubbish.

At work, her colleagues were backing her all the way. Covering her classes when necessary, sorting her printing, making sure that all she had to do was teach. And she loved them for it. She insisted on finding time to enjoy the coffee breaks and the gossip in the staffroom as often as she could, and she enjoyed the brief respite from

293

campaigning as she laughed and ooh'd and ah'd at some juicy titbit that Georgia was guaranteed to bring.

Lunchtimes felt very different now. Suddenly she was no longer the new girl, asking questions and listening; she was the Labour parliamentary candidate – or she would be, officially, once an election was called. She was the one they were listening to now, asking questions of, and she would sometimes catch Byron, sitting silently, watching, her proud mentor.

Christmas gave a welcome break from campaigning – a whole week set aside for her team to enjoy family, celebrations, worship – but even then, conversations centred around the forthcoming general election, even though it could be eighteen months away. The new year was greeted with a renewed energy. This would be the year. Probably. Possibly. The weather during the first few months was kind to them as they trudged along roads and lanes, determined not to leave out a single farm, isolated cottage or hidden terrace. Their reception on the doorstep was, on the whole, positive, although the challenges were there. Too many people said "I'm not interested in politics"; too many women said "I leave all that to my husband", both responses eliciting from Anya lengthy enlightenments that were too often greeted with blank stares and stony faces.

It was April when the announcement came. A general election would be held on June 11th. It was a relief for Anya to have some certainty, and far from being panicked, she felt calm now. She had kept her colleagues at the college in the loop throughout the months, so when she approached Paul and Elaine to formally discuss her position, they weren't surprised, and agreed to hold the post for her till after the election, although by election rules she did have to resign. It was a big step for her. No income for the best part of two months. But she had known this would have to happen, and was prepared for it.

Now she was officially a parliamentary candidate. Her nomination papers had been submitted and accepted, and she was grateful to Byron, who took on the arduous task of officialdom that being a candidate's agent required. And everything was speeding up.

When she received the invitation to a meeting in Westminster with some of the senior Labour figures, alongside other candidates, she wasn't sure she could, or should, attend. But Byron was adamant.

'It's a chance to meet people who can help you, Annie. People who are well known, whose opinions are trusted. I've got a list here, look. These are the MPs you can talk to, listen to, learn from, have your photograph taken with. John Smith, Robin Cook, Gordon Brown, Tony Blair – all in the shadow cabinet. Some not well known yet, but with a great future. And Neil Kinnock. It's one day, Annie. On the train. The constituency will pay – we've hardly spent anything yet. You really need to do this.'

Hearing those names, she suddenly felt she was kidding herself and everyone else. Punching well above her weight. Here she was, trying to get elected to parliament! What was she thinking? She could never do this! She'd never even been to London, let alone to the House of Commons. All she heard about the capital these days was to do with IRA bombings. This was all getting a bit too real.

As if he'd read her mind, Byron smiled as he took her by her shoulders.

'This is normal. This is how you should feel. If you didn't feel nervous, I'd be worried. I'd wonder why I'd been backing someone either so arrogant, or so unaware. But I'm not worried. I believe in you Anya. You can do this.'

'Will you be there?' she said in a small voice.

He laughed aloud.

'You don't think I'd trust you to go on your own, do you? Of course I'll be there!'

'And Claire?'

'Claire will understand. We understand each other.'

How could she have considered missing this? she asked herself. The grandeur, the history that oozed out of every wall, every corridor. As she walked into the vast Westminster Hall and up the wide stone steps, along St Stephen's hall with its magnificent paintings, to the central lobby, she felt a tingle, and a humility she'd never experienced before. It wasn't the opulence that impressed her, as wonderful as it was, but the knowledge of what had been achieved in this place, both good and bad, but always moving forward, inch by inch, over the centuries, to where they were today. The chamber itself, smaller than it appeared on TV, was the showpiece; the committee rooms were the work places. She soaked it all in, as Byron quietly pointed out the features of particular interest. He watched her, and smiled.

The meetings with the powerful men – all men, she noted silently – were far less daunting than she had feared. They were mostly warm and friendly, some pre-occupied, some downright distracted. Byron pointed out that their futures were on the line more than hers was, so a little inattention now and then was not surprising. They too had seats to fight, each a personal election to win, as well as a government to topple. Neil Kinnock, leader of the Labour party, their hope for the future, their hoped-for next Prime Minister, was more friendly than most.

'Ah, our little Welsh girl! I've heard of you, Anya – making a name for yourself in the homeland, I hear!' he greeted her jovially. 'Our valleys aren't too far apart, are they? I intend to visit yours very soon!'

Byron had warned her not to mention the miners' strike – there was still a lot of bad feeling back home about what they saw as their leader's lack of support, but now was not the time to raise it. She liked him. He was down-to-earth and quite normal, and she knew his famous speeches off by heart. From the words he'd spoken on the eve of another election four years ago, at a rally just a few miles from her home town, warning of what was to come under a Thatcher government, to the powerful conference speech he had made two years later, she knew he was a formidable orator. And their future was in his hands. As he sat with her in the beautiful Pugin room where he had led them, drinking coffee and talking in his educated-Welsh accent, she thrilled at the thought that this man

297

could change so many lives. And she wanted to be part of that. She wanted it so badly.

'Well, glad you came?' Byron asked, quite unnecessarily, as they made their way to Paddington station at the end of the day.

Her face was radiant. She beamed at him.

'I want this, Byron. And I can do this.'

He nodded. He knew.

Paddington station was heaving. Anya didn't know it, but it was nothing unusual to see vast crowds swarming in the concourse, passengers glancing up at two-minute intervals to check on the electronic notice boards as to the status of their trains. Then the rush as if a starting gun had been fired, as hundreds made their way in ungainly and usually unnecessary haste to a platform suddenly identified in glowing neon.

They were there in plenty of time to catch the 6.15 Swansea train. They sat on a bench, munching burgers, Anya still animated, still full of the excitement of the day, Byron looking content, pleased that the visit had gone as he had hoped. They talked, planning the next few weeks, hardly daring to voice the hope, the possibility, that she could win.

The voice boomed out of the tannoy system. Louder by far than the tinny announcements of trains arriving and departing.

'Warning! Warning! This is a bomb alert! Please evacuate the station immediately!'

For a second, everyone looked at each other. Then pandemonium broke out. People were screaming, running, jamming the exits, running down motionless escalators, banging on closed lift doors. Anya and Byron seemed to be in the centre of this surging mass of humanity, not knowing which way to turn. Slowly the crowd was thinning, an exit in sight, escape within reach, when steel gates clanged into place, metallic diamond shapes expanding before their eyes, blocking their way. At the same time a voice, a different voice, calmer now, but full of authority, was talking over the loudspeaker. The hush that fell on the remaining crowd was instant.

'There has been a coded bomb warning received by the police. We do not know if this is a hoax, but there is no possibility of taking any chances. The suspect packages are situated outside the main concourse. I repeat, outside the main concourse.'

Panicked glances flew between couples, groups, strangers.

'All those people now on the concourse or on the platforms' the voice went on 'will remain within the boundaries of the station until such time as it is deemed safe for them to leave. All buildings leading directly off the station may be accessed, but will not, I repeat not, allow exit from the station. No trains will run into or out of the station while these precautionary measures are in place.'

A click told them that the message had ended. The small crowd was silent, still. Then it started to move, breaking up, heading for porters, station masters, anyone wearing a uniform, asking questions that no-one could answer.

'I guess we'll just have to wait for an update' said Byron.

Anya wasn't afraid. Maybe she was a little stunned, but not afraid. Perhaps she was just foolhardy, inexperienced. But the warning felt unreal. And she trusted Byron.

'I wonder how long we'll have to wait?' she asked to the air around her, not expecting an answer.

'I think we'd better telephone home, just in case. In case they worry.'

Anya looked at him sharply.

'Oh, of course. This may be on the TV. Yes, let's find a phone box.'

They found one, but had to wait in the long queue for half an hour before they could use it. Anya phoned her mother, who seemed relieved to hear her voice.

'Yes, it's been on the news' she said, her voice trembling slightly. 'You take care. Don't worry about us, just be careful, and do as they tell you.'

Then it was Byron's turn. He rang his home number but got no reply. He rang again.

'Looks as if Claire's asleep' he told Anya. 'Or …' He didn't need to finish the sentence. 'I'll phone Geraldine.'

Geraldine promised to drive to his home and let Claire know what was happening.

'I don't expect you'll be able to leave much before the morning' Geraldine told him. 'In my experience, it'll take hours before they let you go. Better make yourselves comfy. Look after Anya. And ...' she hesitated. 'Just be careful, that's all. I'll go and see Claire now.' She hung up.

They sat back down on the bench they had used just an hour ago. Everything looked so different – or was it her imagination? All around them people were looking stunned. Most of the huge crowd that had filled the area earlier had managed to leave before the gates closed, and the place looked unusually sparse.

'I think we should check into the hotel' said Byron suddenly, an hour later.

'What? But we can't leave the station!'

'There's a hotel here. The Hilton. There's an entrance up those stairs. I'm guessing that's one of the buildings leading off the station he was talking about.'

'The Hilton? But that will be so expensive!' protested Anya.

'I know. But what choice do we have? We could be here all night – probably will be according to that last announcement. We can't sleep here and we can't leave. I've got a cheque book.'

They made their way up to the next floor, to the entrance of the hotel. They weren't alone – several others were standing at the reception desk. When it was their turn, Byron asked for two single rooms.

'Sorry sir, no single rooms available. Doubles only. And only two of those left.'

Byron looked at Anya. She knew it would make sense for them to share a room in these unusual circumstances. Surely no-one would question it. Well, maybe one. She felt a thrill of dread as well as excitement at the thought.

'Then we'll take the two doubles, please' Byron was saying.

Their rooms were on the same floor, but a little distance apart along the corridor. They bade each other an awkward goodnight before withdrawing behind their respective doors.

She certainly couldn't complain about her accommodation: large and spacious, with a king-sized bed, and an enormous bath in the ensuite bathroom. Her mind was racing. The excitement of the day, the alarm of the earlier evening, and the unbidden anticipation she had felt in the foyer, all contrived to make her feel dizzy, confused, and guilty. She ran a bath, adding salts and foam from the plentiful supply on the neat little glass shelf at the side. She stripped off her clothes, less than fresh now after a long day in London, and sank into the hot, deep water. This was what she needed. She lay, soaking herself, for a long time, while she calmed her thoughts. Logic and sense took over. There was so much at stake. The election, of course. But Claire too. Byron's marriage, his promise to her.

She sat up, washing herself briskly. It was only when she had stepped out of the bath that she realised she had no clean clothes to put on. Wrapping herself in the over-large towelling bathrobe that had hung behind the door, she quickly washed her underwear in the hand-basin, thinking to herself that never before had her clothes been lathered in such extravagant soap. They should be dry by the morning, she thought, as she draped them over the radiators.

She heard the tap on the door as she walked back into the bedroom. And she knew. She opened the door and he stood there, no tie, no jacket, shirt collar open. She stepped back as he entered, but made no pretence at surprise. Closing the door behind him, he reached for her, holding her gently by her shoulders.

He pulled her to him, and then they were kissing. Not hurriedly, not urgently, but slowly, savouring every second, tasting each other, marvelling in the glory of it all. He held her close, her lips searched his. One hand in the small of her back, gently pulling her to him, the other caressing her neck, his fingers pushing up into her still-wet hair. Her hands moving gently, deliberately, down his back, feeling the heat of his body through his damp shirt, wondering at his strength, until she was halted by a leather belt. Her hands moved around then, slowly, ever so slowly, towards the front, till she reached those inviting hollows that led down, down. She felt him gasp. He held her a little way away from him then, while the bathrobe fell to the ground, and he looked at her.

He kissed her breasts, kissed her nipples as they hardened to his touch, making her shiver, giving her spasms of excitement below, and she felt the sudden wetness there. He pushed back a damp auburn tendril from her shoulder, a small curl from her cheek. She unbuttoned his shirt until it hung loosely on him. She undid the buckle of his belt and the zip beneath it, as it strained against his swelling erection. She loosed it then, embraced it, wondering at its power. She bent, knelt

303

before him, touching it with her lips, her tongue. She drew him into her mouth, feeling it pulsate. With a groan, he raised her to her feet, drew her to the bed, casting off the few clothes he wore. They clung together. Limbs intertwined, bodies moist, no hurry now, they explored every inch of each other as they never had before, with their hands, their lips, their tongues. They whispered sweet nonsense to each other, every disjointed phrase cut short by a kiss. Until they could delay no longer, until the need to consummate that aching desire was too great, and at last they were joined, her body receiving his in a crescendo of passion that ended all thoughts.

The journey home early next morning was relaxed, companiable, comfortable. No awkwardness or embarrassment. They were past that. Without discussing it, they knew that they couldn't be together, not in the way they wanted to, and they had accepted it. They had stopped trying to guess their future, for now at least. So they talked quietly about their families and their pasts, the campaign plans for next week and the weeks after that, about the chances of actually winning the election, about work and how she would fit back in if she didn't. She asked him why he had never thought of standing for election himself, though she knew the answer before he gave it. Claire. They held hands under the table and snuggled close when no-one was looking. They knew they wouldn't have a chance to do this again for quite a while.

They were surprised to see Geraldine waiting on the platform when the train pulled in to Swansea station.

They walked towards her, smiling, until she noticed them. Striding up to them, they heard her say 'Thank God!' then

'Byron, it's Claire. Come on, I'll drive you. You too, Anya.'

As she drove, Geraldine described how she'd found Claire, collapsed, at their home.

'Had she taken something?' Byron's voice was hoarse. 'Was it because I'd gone ...'

'No, no nothing like that' Geraldine said. 'They believe she's had a heart attack. They're checking her bloods to be sure, but it certainly looks like it. There may be other problems too though. The doctors will tell you.'

As they sped to the hospital, Anya wondered why Geraldine had insisted she join them. Surely she should keep well away? Her car was at the station where they'd left it the previous day, and she could easily have driven herself home. Most of the journey was spent in silence, and it wasn't until they got out of the car in the hospital grounds that Geraldine pulled Anya to one side as they all walked towards the entrance.

'He'll need you, Anya. One way or another, he's going to need you.'

Once again she saw him sitting at his wife's bedside, as she watched through a glass panel. Once again she saw him hold her hand, ever so tenderly, but this time Claire knew he was there. She had smiled at him as he walked in, and Anya heard her whisper:

'I knew you'd come.'

A machine started beeping and a nurse walked briskly into the room, followed by a doctor, who seemed to ask Byron to go with him to where they were waiting.

As he did so, Anya and Geraldine started to leave, but Byron insisted they stay.

'They're my friends' he said simply.

'Well Byron, there's no easy way to say this. Claire's body is shutting down. Yes, she has had a heart attack, but it was anyone's guess as to which organ would fail first. I'm sorry. She doesn't have much time left.'

Byron nodded. He walked back to his wife and continued to hold her hand. Anya watched them as he sat for hours, morning melding into afternoon, evening, night, his head bowed, sometimes talking to her, sometimes wiping her forehead. Claire looked peaceful, as if she were sleeping. Tubes and some wires had been removed from her now, the only ones remaining were monitoring her heart.

The machines suddenly burst into life and medical staff came running, checking readings on the monitor, which was making a flat humming sound. But they did not ask Byron to stand back, didn't try to resuscitate her. She slept on, her hand in his, while he looked down at her, dry eyed.

The election campaign had a life of its own, and ploughed on. Thank God, thought Anya. She had wanted to stop it, pull out, end the whole thing, but she knew he would have wanted her to carry on. So she went about the work they had planned, visiting, making speeches, attending hustings, all on auto-pilot. Alone now, without Byron by her side. Alone despite the team of people helping her. She felt the life had been knocked out of her. Not in the way it had done for Claire - so completely, so finally. Or for Byron. But her soul seemed to have lost something. She felt diminished, a lesser person. She thought little of the words she was speaking, the promises she was making. Even with her children, she was going through the motions of routine, sure she would feel no normality ever again.

Her mother watched from the sidelines, a rock, an essential part of Anya's life she could not live without, yet unwilling to let her in to the grief she had no right to, to the selfishness and anger she felt. Until Jessie could stand it no more. The children had returned to school after their half-term holiday and Anya was heading out of the door.

'Annie, we need to talk.'

'Not now Mum, I really must ...'

'Yes, now' her mother said firmly. 'I need to talk to you. Now. And I think you may need to talk to me.'

Anya held herself stiffly, and Jessie felt more distant from her daughter than she had ever done. But she continued.

'I don't pretend to know what you're feeling. What you're going through. I don't know because you won't tell me. But whatever it is, I want to help you if I can. I'm sure you feel upset for Byron ...'

'Upset?' Anya turned and whispered the word with such vehemence, with such rage contorting her face, that Jessie took a step back. 'Upset? You don't have a clue! You don't ...'

'Then tell me!' her mother shouted. 'Tell me! How can I know? You don't talk to me, you behave as if you hate me ...' and to Anya's horror she found that her mother was crying, shouting through her tears. 'Do you think I don't care? That I won't understand? That I haven't had feelings as strong as yours? That I haven't loved? It's you who doesn't have a clue...'

She was crying in earnest now, and the sight of her strong, calm mother reduced to tears like this was too much for Anya to bear.

'Oh Mum, don't, please don't!'

And they were sobbing on each other's shoulders, shaking, holding each other. With a shuddering sigh, Jessie pulled herself upright and smoothed her daughter's hair.

'Well, what a pair we are!' she said shakily, wiping her eyes.

Anya gave a little laugh that ended in a sob. She too wiped her eyes.

'Maybe we'll have that talk now' she said in a small voice.

They sat then, and Anya talked. The words came pouring out, unstoppable. She told her mother that she felt alone, bereft, without Byron, without any hope of any future with him, now that she had witnessed his wife, his beautiful, ravaged, broken wife, dying in his arms. She told her that she felt so guilty, that they had been making untroubled love while Claire had been lying, ill, waiting for her husband to come home. And she told her that she felt so angry with Claire for doing that, for being the wronged one, the weak one, the one who needed protection, and that in turn gave her more guilt, until she was suffused with bitterness and self-loathing. She paused as racking sobs made it impossible for her to speak.

308

Jessie said nothing, but took her daughter in her arms.

'I don't pretend to know exactly how you feel right now' she said again, as she stroked the auburn curls, 'but I do know about grief, and anger, and guilt. I lost your father in the most horrible way imaginable. I'd lost him, and I grieved for him – I'm grieving still. But I was angry with him for choosing to leave me, to leave us. Angry and so hurt that he hadn't even said goodbye. And I felt guilty that I'd never seen he might have been feeling so low, suicidal, and then guilty for being so angry with him, when all I wanted was to have him back.' She too was crying now.

So they sat for a long time, holding each other, until with a final sob and a huge sigh Anya sat up.

'I'll be ok now' she said.

Byron called the next day. Anya hadn't seen him since Claire's funeral two weeks before, when she had been too full of remorse and sadness to do anything but hold his hand briefly as she filed past him with other mourners. Jessie welcomed him in, offered her condolences, gave him tea, then made a discreet withdrawal. Anya sat opposite him across the table, suddenly tired.

'I'm so sorry, Byron. I don't know what else I can say.'

But he smiled at her.

'I know Annie. I know. It's hard to talk about, isn't it?' He drank his tea, and they sat in silence. He looked at her.

309

'We were married for a long time you know, but for most of that, she needed a carer, not a husband. She would fly at me, rage at me, then collapse and cry like a child. I didn't know how to handle it. So I looked for some comfort elsewhere now and then, in the early days. And that hurt her, I know it did. We were no good for each other, but there was no way out for either of us. Until she became really ill. Then I knew I would take care of her. Out of duty maybe at first, but then, out of love. A different kind of love I think, deeper than we'd had when we were younger. Purer. Does that make sense? I knew she needed me, and she couldn't give me any of the things I thought I needed from our marriage. But she gave me a purpose, and I could live with that.

'Until I met you, Anya. You know how I feel about you, I think. You know I love you. In every sense of the word, I love you. But I can't promise you anything. Not yet. I'm sorry. I need ...'

She put her hand on his.

'It's ok' she said gently. 'It's really ok. Maybe sometime, maybe never, but it's ok. I love you too, and that's enough.' And she smiled.

The final week of campaigning. Election day was very close, becoming very real. Over the weeks, Anya and her team had knocked on more doors, and delivered more leaflets, than she could possibly count. Up and down hills, up and down steps, fingers caught in unforgiving letterboxes or grabbed by silent dogs lying in wait behind doors; smiling in the face of indifference or verbal abuse.

310

And now, the last lap. No letting up. She allowed Byron to set the pace, knowing that he needed to do this. And the pace was fast, almost feverish. No sitting in cafes now. No time for that. No risk of simple intimacies around cups of coffee. The finale was in sight.

And then - Thursday June 11th. Election day. Anya was up before dawn, dressed and ready to go. Jessie too, although the children were sleeping soundly.

'Well love, this is it' Jessie said. 'Win or lose, you couldn't have worked harder.'

'I know. I won't pretend I won't be glad to have a bit of a rest. But I think I'm running on adrenaline at the moment – I just hope it lasts me through the day!'

Anya cast her vote in the community centre where she had spent so much time over the past few years, and where she had learned such a lot, and gained so much inspiration. She was moved to see people applauding her as she did so, and she was overcome with affection for them. She wanted to do right by them. And she would. Maybe not as their MP, but she knew there were many other ways she could help.

From one polling station to another, she did the rounds that day, Byron by her side, as her agent and her friend. Their only conversation revolved around the election – by silent but mutual consent, they avoided any topic more personal, more painful. This was work, and they both threw themselves into it, as they had done for the past weeks.

And then it was ten o'clock. The General Election of 1987 was over. Nothing more they could do. Polls were closed, her team making their way to the count in

Pontarafon, tired but exhilarated, knowing they had done all they could, quietly hoping against hope that it had been enough.

Friday June 12th. 2am. All votes cast and counted. Anya stood on the raised platform at the front of the huge sports hall, its nets pulled back and its pitch markings covered with rows of trestle tables, each in turn covered with piles of boxes, stacks of papers, surrounded by sleepy officials who had been counting voting slips for nearly four hours. She wasn't alone. Her opponents, candidates from other parties, stood alongside her, sporting their variously coloured rosettes, her red one proudly pinned to the smart jacket bought especially for the occasion. The evening had been long and tiring, and had followed a gruelling last day of campaigning, shaking hands and smiling. The past weeks, and months, had all led to this.

She looked down and saw the waiting crowd, made up now of the hardy few who had made it till this late in the night, this early in the morning. She saw her mother, standing with an arm around each of Emily and Fran, while Lucy stood in front, hugging her grandmother's waist while trying to keep her eyes open. And behind her, Geraint, steady as an oak. She saw Elaine, Jean, even Marjorie, who was sitting on a stool, irresolute, determined to stay awake. There were Paul and Jean, together now, and Dan, and lovely Ethan. Sian, Jen, their husbands - all were there still. Even Esther, her schoolgirl ally who had helped her from afar whenever Anya had asked. And Auntie Peggy, her mother's

312

companion and help over so many years. Geraldine, upright, stern, her mentor and her friend. All looking anxiously up at her, wishing her well, willing her to win.

The microphone buzzed and crackled.

'I, Carwyn Lewis, being the Returning Officer at the election held on Thursday, 11th of June 1987…'

As she looked at all these people she loved, she knew that she didn't need to win an election. She was strong now. There was no end to what she could achieve. She was blessed. She had made it.

'…do hereby give notice that the number of votes cast for each candidate is as follows…'

She knew that she had a future. That she and her family had a future. She wasn't sure what it would be or where it would take them, but she couldn't wait to find out.

'And I do hereby declare that Anya May Gethin is duly elected for the parliamentary seat of …'

She looked at them all as they cheered loud enough to take the roof off. And there was Byron, smiling broadly now, a hand raised in greeting, a nod that was just for her. And she knew that they, too, would have a future. One day.

She stepped up to the lectern and took the microphone in her hand.

END OF BOOK ONE

BOOK TWO

Secrets to be told ...

1930 – 1997

CHAPTER 20

A FAMILY BROKEN

1930

'Lift it boy! Lift it!'

The sweat poured down Meic's face. He felt it trickle down his back, soaking his thin shirt, staining it a darker blue. But he wouldn't give up. Not now. Not in front of him. The bastard. He heaved the huge machine once more, muscles taut, sinews straining, and it was on the trailer.

'About bloody time too' grumbled his father. 'Proper little weakling we've got haven't we? Sort yourself out, boy.' And Thomas Bowen Hughes cuffed his son about the head.

Michael stood his ground. He didn't move. At fifteen years old he had learned how to survive his father's taunts, if not his punches. He said nothing. Hatred burned in his eyes. His father was in his face again, so close he could feel the tobacco-stained saliva spitting from his mouth as he spoke.

'You can think yourself lucky to have work, Mikey boy. Lucky you can pay your board and lodge. Not many jobs around, are there Danny? Eh?'

His foreman, for want of a better term, grunted agreement.

'He's pulling his weight though, TB' he said, uncomfortable at the treatment the boss's son always received. 'He's a good little worker.'

TB turned away, not willing to argue with his only other employee. He couldn't do without Danny Morgan and he knew it.

But Thomas Bowen Hughes was right. There weren't many jobs around in south Wales in 1930. The collapse of the post-war economic boom in 1921, increased competition from abroad, the disaster of the General Strike of 1926 and the decline in the mining and steel industries all combined to cripple the British economy. So the crisis of 1929 that led to the slump that turned into the great depression simply made an already bad situation worse. And the worst hit areas in Britain were those still dependent on the old heavy industries - south Wales being one. The depression would leave its legacy. They were told that things were starting to pick up elsewhere. In England maybe. The south east. But not here. Not in the Nantllai Valley. So yes, Michael Hughes was lucky to have work. Any work. His father told him so, often and forcefully, regularly accompanied by a clip around the ear, or a punch in the ribs.

TB Hughes and Son, Builders. TB, who would turn his hand to most things, and turn a blind eye to the legal niceties if it suited him. So Michael, at fifteen, could build a decent wall, fit a window, and fix a leaking roof with the best of them. He hated his father. Simple as that. And one day he would move away, he told himself. He would go to Cardiff, or even London. He'd get away from his pig of a father and start a life somewhere else, somewhere clean and new. But in his heart, he knew it would be a long time, if ever, before he could leave this run-down stone cottage with its gloomy cluttered rooms full of the tick, ticking of the myriad clocks, and its piles of rusting machinery in what should have been a garden. This house that was called a farm but had not a single fur or feather to justify the name. Maes Ty Clyd. Field of the Cosy House. Nothing cosy here.

But he couldn't leave. His mother needed him. Hannah-May Hughes had never been strong. She had been a beauty, slender and pale. She had brought the property of her late parents to the marriage, a lovely farmhouse set on the side of the mountain, with fields all around. Then slowly she had watched it as it crumbled and perished of neglect, as she herself did. TB had filled the place with tools and old gear, all to be repaired and sold on, he said. And in truth some had gone that way. But never enough to keep up with the never-ending input of old scrap and rubbish, filling the garden and the fields around.

She had done her best to keep house, as a wife should, but a combination of her husband's loud, hurtful criticisms of her, and her naturally frail body, resulted in her complete inability to achieve anything when he was near. And Meic saw this. He had tried to stand up to his father, to protect her, but to no avail, succeeding only in alienating him from the older man. Thomas Hughes was a big, powerful man, and he thought nothing of striking his only son across the face with his large, calloused hand, should he dare to question him in his own house.

On one occasion the blow to the side of Meic's head was so severe that his ear bled and continued to bleed for some days. But still Meic stood his ground, never flinching, although his head was humming. Never complaining even when he realised that he could no longer hear in his left ear. When they were alone, Meic would sit with his mother, and she would stroke his hair, tell him she loved him, calling him 'Mihangel bach'. And he knew he could never leave her here with that man.

But two weeks – just two weeks – that would be alright, wouldn't it? Meic hardly dared to hope that Danny's request would be granted.

'He'd be a bit of company for me, TB' he heard Danny saying to his father. 'I've got the time owing to me, you know that. And I've got the offer of this tent, big one, down near the beach, in Port Haven.'

A rare chink of light in a bleak existence for Meic. But he knew his father was not likely to agree to anything that his son might enjoy. However, Danny was fond of the boy. He saw the stubborn, set face of his boss, and sought to head off his arguments before they started.

'He'll be more trouble than the worth of it if he stays here without me to keep an eye on him, to check his handiwork. You'll need to keep on his back morning noon and night. No fun for you, TB.'

And it worked. So the young Michael Hughes bade goodbye to his beloved Mam, assuring her that he would be back in two weeks.

'And you take care' he told her. 'No more fiddling around in the back garden, not till I'm back, alright? You've already scratched yourself once. There's too much rubbish out there, too many rusty tools and buckets and God knows what. Look after yourself!'

319

She kissed him, told him to enjoy himself, happy for him to be having some fun.

The holiday was a revelation. Despite living less than thirty miles from the coast, Meic had never seen the sea. The expanse of white sand seemed endless, leading down to the rolling waves and tiny ripples, and decorated with the dense tufts of spiky marram grass as it spread back to the downs further inland. Danny laughed at the amazed expression on the youngster's face.

'Come on, Bach, we need to put this tent up. It looks like a bloody big one.' And he opened the back of the battered van to reveal a mass of canvass and wooden poles.

Between the two of them, they managed to pitch the borrowed tent far enough from the beach to prevent it being washed away by the tide, but close enough to enable them to enjoy the wondrous view at all times.

Danny was fifteen years Meic's senior, and that made all the difference. He had been the only man in his family since his own father had been killed in a mining accident when he was nine years old, and he had worked at anything he could in order to keep his mother and sister in their home. The job with TB Hughes had come up when Danny was only thirteen years of age, but he had proved himself to be indispensable to the cantankerous builder.

Meic was fascinated by everything.

'What's that over there, Danny?' he asked now, pointing to a huge skeletal structure about a mile away.

'Ah! That's your surprise!' Danny laughed. 'Come on!' And he led Michael away, towards the town, towards the mysterious construction that stood silhouetted against the sky. A short walk further on, they stood before it.

'The Roller-Coaster. Just been built. Well, moved here. It's supposed to be the scariest ride you'll ever have!'

Michael stared at it, mouth open.

'Can I have a go?' he whispered.

And so their holiday began. Nights spent in the cosy tent with talk and laughter, food cooked on a Primus stove and eaten on makeshift cushions on the sand, days exploring the beach, the town, the funfair – and the girls. They were everywhere. Selling ice-creams from the little kiosks along the sea front, leading donkeys down to the beach each morning, walking sedately through the town, running into the sea wearing their revealing bathing suits.

Meic had never seen girls in such attire or such surroundings. There were girls at the elementary school, of course, but they were dressed in the drab garb thought suitable for such a serious but pointless enterprise as education for girls. And he had seen very little of most of them for the past couple of years. While officially he should have stayed at school until he was fourteen, his father had kept him at home, working, for much of the time since he was twelve. School inspectors had meant nothing to TB Hughes; their explanations regarding the law, and his son's future, their pleas turning to threats, brushed aside as wholly unimportant, irrelevant.

Meic had had an occasional encounter with a girl from the farm at the top of the hill, had been excited when she allowed him to fondle and kiss her large breasts, had been shocked, delighted, frustrated all at once, to find how his body had reacted, had burst into life, only to be slapped down and pushed away as she laughed and ran. It happened on more than one occasion, and each time he would find a quiet piece of land where he could relieve himself, discovering the age-old method of release that was as natural as the guilty pleasure he experienced. And now here were these girls, smiling at him, some winking at him, making him blush.

'You be careful now, Meic bach' warned Danny. 'You don't want to go home with a little more than you came with.'

Michael looked blankly at him.

'VD. The French disease. Syphilis.' he expanded.

But the girl who took Meic's eye looked to him to be wholesome, clean, rather shy. And Danny agreed. Her name was Margaret, and she lived in the nearby town of Port Haven, which Danny said was a good thing. A local girl would have her family to answer to, maybe the whole community, if she went off the rails. Even better, she had made friends with another girl, Elizabeth, who was visiting an aunt in the town. And Elizabeth took a shine to Danny, despite his greater age. Elizabeth was seventeen, as was Margaret, and Danny didn't correct him when Meic said he was seventeen too. He looked it – he was tall and strong for his age, with muscles built from hard graft.

So Michael discovered the delights of lovemaking, of lying under the stars while he kissed and caressed this young girl who had consented to his explorations, his penetrations, and his satisfaction. He had no thought of her needs of course. Girls didn't feel the same way as boys about sex, did they? But he felt tenderness and gratitude towards her, and when, on the last night they lay together, she asked him if he loved her, he said he did. It was the least he could do.

The fortnight came to an end, as he knew it must. He saw Danny and Elizabeth exchanging addresses, so he did the same with Margaret. They were silent for much of their journey home, Meic revelling in the knowledge that he was now a man, reliving those exciting moments on the sand, until the remembered thrill threated to become too apparent and he forced himself to take an interest in the roadside trees.

'Thanks Danny' he said suddenly.

Danny seemed to have been woken from a dream-world of his own.

'Thanks? What for, Bach?'

'For this. For the holiday. For getting my father to let me go. Thanks.'

Danny laughed.

'No need to thank me. I had a good time too. And I might ask you for a favour in return, one of these days.'

'Anything Dan, anything.'

The cars were pulling away as the van turned into the lane. Not unusual. Though they weren't normally cars like this

– big and shiny and black. They were usually dust-covered, dirt-spattered, rusted. But not today. These were different.

'OK if I drop you here, Meic?'

Danny had stopped the van.

'I need to get back to Mam and Cerys.'

' 'course Danny. See you tomorrow.'

Michael walked up the lane, his paces getting longer, faster, his heart thumping. Something was wrong. He knew it.

His father stood in the porch, the door open behind him. Did he look smaller than before? His face was set.

'Where's Mam?' said Michael as he pushed past him into the tiny hall.

'She's gone.'

Michael went cold.

'Gone? What do you mean – gone? Gone where?'

Meic stepped back outside, facing his father.

'She's gone Michael. She died. Nothing anyone could do.'

Michael dimly registered the fact that his father had used his full name. He'd never done that before.

'Died? Died?' he whispered. 'Died? How? When? Where is she?'

'Couple of days after you went. Took a turn for the worse. Blood poisoning the doctor said. Seems she'd cut herself in the garden. Just a scratch.'

Just a scratch. Just a scratch. Michael's mind was a fog. His father went on.

'Just had the funeral.'

'What? You – what?'

'Just had the funeral. Today.'

Silence. Then, a whisper again.

'Without me? You couldn't wait for me? You couldn't …'

'No point, Boy. Nothing you could do. A funeral's not the place for a kid. Not much of a turn-out anyway …'

That's when Michael hit him. All the anger, all the hurt, all the hatred built up over so many years went into that blow. The force knocked his father off his feet, lifting him up, only for him to come crashing down across the porch, his head landing on the quarry-tiled floor of the little hall. And he was still.

Michael saw the pool of dark red blood beginning to ooze from under his father's head. And he ran. Terror welled up in him, replacing some of his anger. No grief. No pain. Not yet. It was too soon for that. He ran till his lungs were bursting, his muscles screaming, not knowing that he was crying, sobbing, gasping, until he reached Danny's door.

'I killed him Danny' he shouted, his face wet with tears. 'I killed him. And I'm glad I killed him. But I'll be locked up.' And only then,

'My mam … my mam …' and he collapsed into his friend's arms.

CHAPTER 21

WELCOME TO THE PALACE

1987: June

'I, Carwyn Lewis, being the Returning Officer at the election held on Thursday, 11th of June 1987...'

'... do hereby declare that Anya May Gethin is duly elected for the parliamentary seat of South Powys'

She sat upright on the train, hair pulled back, hands folded on her lap, as it sped her towards her new life. She was still reeling from the events of Thursday – no, Friday morning, she thought. Just three days ago. Just one weekend ago. A weekend made up of congratulations, phone calls, visitors, all wishing her well. Those who felt differently didn't bother to call, so it would have been easy to think that the whole world was pleased for her. But she knew better than that. And anyway, the most important thing that Friday, that Saturday, that Sunday, was to talk to her daughters, and her mother. They were part of this, but their lives must go on, uninterrupted by affairs of state, by the prospect of her weekly journeys two hundred miles away, to the Palace of Westminster.

Her life had been changed immeasurably over the past five years. Nine years really, she thought, ever since David was made redundant and she found herself the sole breadwinner. But surely this would be the biggest change of all! She stared out of the window, only faintly aware of the scenery flashing past, of the stations zooming up, and zooming away again.

She had discovered the world of politics – or rather, the world of politics had discovered her – just a few short years ago. She hadn't thought of it as politics at first. When her ex-husband had lost his job, when their house was repossessed, that wasn't anything to do with politics, was it? The door to promotion firmly closed at the college where she found work, the acceptance of groping and intimidation from the men at the top – politics? And then – the miners' strike. Seen first-hand in the valley community she had adopted and she now called home. The hardship, the picket lines. That was politics. The support her new neighbours needed, the help she could give them and that they gave her – that turned out to be politics too. It was everywhere. Coloured every aspect of her life, her family's lives, everyone's lives. And now here she was – a Member of Parliament, travelling up to Westminster to take her seat. She glanced across to Byron, sitting opposite, scouring documents. Byron. Her agent, her mentor, her friend, her some-time lover. She smiled, sat back, and at last enjoyed the scenery.

She walked up to the police officer at the entrance. St Stephen's Gate.

'Anya Gethin' she said, sounding more confident than she felt. 'New Member.'

'Yes Ma'am. South Powys, Ma'am?'

How did he know? She marvelled at the communication system that had clearly been at work for the past days. With that, a vision appeared from inside the huge now-open wooden door. He was dressed for all the world in what appeared to be a full morning suit, but with the addition of an enormous gold-coloured medallion hanging low on his chest.

'Doorkeeper' Byron whispered in her ear.

Then began the tour. It reminded her vividly of the day she entered the college which had been her second home for five years – the route march that Elaine had taken her to her best ever, most welcoming interview, and the slightly more leisurely and instructive walk back with Ethan. Except that this time she was being led by a stylishly dressed guide who addressed her deferentially as "Madam", and being followed, just a pace behind, by Byron, today in the role of agent, adviser. Her brief mental comparison of the Houses of Parliament with the little college made her want to chuckle. She resisted.

They were walked along some corridors and spaces she had seen for the first time just a few weeks ago. But then – more stairs, back stairs this time; more corridors, more doors. Behind each one that was opened, a different department, where she was given information, and sometimes paperwork. Information about the workings of The House as it was referred to. Its rules and regulations and her role in it. Her office accommodation, the staff she may employ and how she would pay them. How she would be paid, her pension. What expenses she could claim and what she couldn't. Who she could call on for help. Information about where she could find information. Her head was buzzing.

And all the while, as they were led quickly from one department to another, she was aware that she and Byron were just two people in a very long line of others, a discreet distance being kept between each new MP and his or her entourage, each little grouping headed by an impressive Doorman. Or Doorwoman, she thought, as she noticed several women in the same uniform. Of course, she thought. All the new MPs who arrived this morning would be taken on the same circuit as she was.

It was two hours later that she found herself sitting, with Byron, in the Terrace café.

'Wow!' was all she could say, and he laughed.

'Quite a lot to take in' he said, setting down two coffee cups on the table between them.

'The art of understatement, Cariad – I mean ...'

She blushed. In this aftermath of the past days' excitement, the lack of sleep, and now the whistle-stop tour of one of the most famous buildings in the world, she had at last relaxed, and reverted to that term of endearment they had both used not so very long ago, but now mutually, silently banished.

'It's ok, you know. I get it.'

He smiled.

'Admittedly it's not the usual form of address for an agent here...' he went on, putting her at her ease again.

'...although I very much doubt that anyone around us at the moment would have a clue what the word means!'

She started to relax again, when he looked over her shoulder and greeted someone he clearly knew.

329

'Phil!' he said warmly, then under his breath to Anya, 'I take it back; here's someone who might understand the language of heaven!'

Byron stood as he shook the hand of a tall young man Anya didn't know.

'Congratulations Phil! Great to see our numbers growing! Anya' he said, turning to her, 'this is Philip Christopher, newly elected MP for the Trefni Vale constituency. Phil, meet Anya Gethin, newly elected MP for your neighbouring constituency, South Powys. You may have a lot in common, being two new MPs from Wales!'

Introductions and handshakes over, Byron excused the two of them, Philip promising Anya that he would keep in touch, Anya assuring him she would look forward to it. As they made their way through Westminster Hall towards the exit, Anya wondered why they had to leave so soon.

'A small matter of seeing where you will be living, Annie! During the week at least.'

She had forgotten. How could she have forgotten? This wasn't a day trip, a fleeting visit. This would now be her second home. Not the cosy, friendly FE college she had come to know, but this edifice, this city. She felt exhilarated and terrified in equal measure. This was it!

'The flat I've sorted for you is on a short lease' Byron was saying as he led her along the pavement.

Crowds of people were here, peering through the railings, cameras much in view. Ordinary people, from all over the country, all over the world. Ordinary people like her. But now she had an extraordinary job. And an extraordinary privilege.

'...it's not very grand, and not very big. A glorified bedsit really. But the main thing is that it's in walking distance.'

She was listening now.

'And is that so important?' she asked, walking quickly at his side. 'With the underground, all the buses, is it important to be able to walk here?'

'It could be. Think of rail strikes. Roadworks, road closures. Underground stations closed. Or – heaven forbid – bomb scares. You need to be able to get here, do your job, make your voice heard. That's what you're here for, right?'

'Right.' She was emphatic. That's what she was here for.

They were out in force to meet her. The toot-toots from her car had been a clue, a hint as to her imminent arrival, but hadn't been needed, as her family stood, waiting in the middle of the lane, waving, smiling, cheering, as the car rounded the last bend before home.

They hadn't had a chance to do this, give her a proper welcome home when she had returned after the election result had been called. They had all returned together, the girls almost asleep before they climbed into their beds, Anya and her mother too tired to talk. But now, she would get the greeting they felt she deserved.

Byron stopped the car as the small army opened the gate for him to drive through. But Anya opened the

331

passenger door and got out, stooping to say something to him, before she turned and ran to her welcoming committee. He turned the car around, waved through the window, and drove back down the lane.

'Anything wrong, Annie?' Her mother, though smiling, looked worried.

'Wrong? No of course not! Why would there be?'

'Well, I was just wondering why Byron drove off like that …'

Anya laughed.

'He just wanted to give me some time with all of you, that's all. I haven't seen much of you lately, have I?'

Jessie looked relieved.

'He's a thoughtful boy, isn't he?' she said, half to herself.

It was good to be home, even though she had only been gone since early that morning. Even if it were only for a few days. And even if most of that would be spent packing up the essentials she would need for her flat in Kennington. Her mother let her settle in, have a cup of tea and supper with the girls and tuck them in. Anya was smiling as she came back downstairs.

'Emily's not too old for a cuddle and a kiss goodnight even at the grand age of thirteen' she said to her mother as she sank into her favourite chair at the side of the hearth.

'No, thank goodness! But she'll need a room of her own soon. She's been happy sharing with Fran all these years, but she's growing up now. And only Lucy is small enough to sleep in the box room.'

'I know' said Anya. 'We'll have to think of something.'

'Well, while we're thinking about that, there's something else we'll need to think about. Sorry Annie, but you can't sit down yet!'

And Jessie led Anya to her own little sitting room. She opened the door and Anya gasped.

'Mum! Where did all that come from?'

The normally tidy, organised room was cluttered now with cardboard boxes and shopping bags all full of envelopes. Large envelopes. Some official-looking envelopes.

Jessie laughed.

'From the postman, love. All for you. Ms Anya Gethin MP. I think you've got your work cut out here!'

Anya opened a few. All from one charity or another, one lobby group or another, all congratulating her. Wishing her well. Then … asking her to plead their case. Some inviting her to a launch, to join a group, to support their aims, to speak at an event. She put a bundle down.

'This will take weeks to sort out, Mum. I'll never do it! And look at the space it all takes up!'

'Maybe I shouldn't have bombarded you with this right now, almost as soon as you've come through the door. …'

'No Mum, I need to know. Otherwise how am I going to deal with it?'

She sighed then, and ran her fingers through her hair.

'Come on, let's have our supper and talk about something else for now. Tell me about the girls' school news. Tell me about Geraint. Tell me about you!'

Byron joined them early the next morning. Anya had slept little, her mind racing, full of the experiences of the day and the worries of carrying out her new role, but she brightened as she prepared breakfast, revelling in those ordinary things that she knew would, in future, be restricted to weekends and recess times. The chat around the table was loud, disjointed, argumentative and full of laughter. Just as at every meal time. Just as it should be, she thought. She would miss this.

Children dispatched to their various schools, Anya and Byron settled themselves at the living room table, notebooks at the ready. Jessie brought them cups of coffee as they both glanced through the window at the little rockery, flowering beautifully, both remembering a very different meeting here, two years ago. Jessie made to leave, but Anya called her back.

'Stay. Mum. If you can. Some of this will affect you.'

'Yes Jessie' said Byron. 'Anya's shown me the state of your sitting room! Now, let's start with all the letters, all the mail that's been arriving. And will continue to arrive.'

'What we've agreed so far, Mum, is that Byron's going to run things from this end, only part-time though. I won't be able to pay him enough for him to give up his job completely, but he can work part-time at the college for a while. Elaine's ok with that.'

'Yeah, that's the plan. And to be honest, I'm protecting my interests too. A career as an MP is a precarious one, Anya, you know that. You've put your teaching career on hold and that's always a risk – but fingers crossed! But it doesn't make sense for me to do the same. I need to keep a foot in the door.'

Jessie nodded. She understood what they were saying.

'We have to work out where he'll be based though' went on Anya. 'Maybe we can use the community centre in Cwmdawel. Or the leisure centre in Pontarafon. That must have a room or two we could use.'

'Seems a sensible plan' he said. 'But a postal address at the leisure centre isn't ideal, so you're still likely to have stuff arriving here. And that's going to give us a few problems. Where to keep it in the short term, how to get it to a make-shift office at the centre, and who can sift through it all to decide what's urgent, what needs a response, what needs filing and what can be binned?'

They both looked at Jessie.

'If I can help to wade through the batch that's here, I'm happy to. Just to put them into piles, etc. If I'm allowed to. There may be sensitive stuff there.'

A loud knock on the front door made them all look up.

"I'll go' said Anya.

She returned with another large bag full of envelopes.

'Bloody hell! So – this is how it's going to be, ladies. You up for this?'

They stared at the growing pile of post.

'I'll take your silence as a *Yes* then. And I have a suggestion – Anya, why don't you take your mother on as one of your staff? You can do that you know. Not much of a salary, especially as it would be part-time, but it would solve the problem of security. You'd be on the books, Jessie! And maybe you could bring the urgent ones over to me each day – wherever I may be based.'

And so it was agreed.

'I have another suggestion' Jessie said then. 'It's partly a family issue, partly an MP one.'

'Go on Mum. We can send Byron out of the room if it gets too personal!'

He grinned.

'Well, here it is.'

She took a deep breath.

'You need an office here. Emily needs a room of her own. So – how about if I move out ...'

'No! No Mum! Please ...'

'Wait to hear what I have to say, Annie. Now, Emily could have my bedroom, and you could use my sitting room for your office...'

'No! I ...'

'Wait!' Jessie looked at Anya with one of the *I'll speak to you later!* looks she hadn't used since her daughter was a child.

'Geraint and I have been thinking. Yes, Anya, there is a "Geraint and I". If you were willing, he would build me a small bungalow on your land, at the side. Not an extension, we couldn't do that because there's something in the way ...'

'Something?' asked Byron.

Anya laughed.

'She means the septic tank. You can't see it, it's buried ...' She saw her mother's face.

'Sorry. Go on, Mum.'

'As I was saying – he could build a little bungalow there. For me. Maybe – for us. We'll see how that goes. But it would free up some rooms here, in the house. Not straight away, I know, but eventually.'

She stopped.

'Ok, you can speak now!'

The next few weeks, months, were crazy. Anya had little time to think about what was happening at home – she spent her weekends dividing her attention between her daughters and the constituents who needed her help, interspersed with meetings and events. During the week she sat on the famous green benches, listening intently, resolved to know and follow all the rules. She was allocated to, rather than volunteered to join, various sub-committees and working groups, and realised just how much she had to learn. But she also became aware that she was not alone in this, although the fact didn't seem to bother some as much as it did her. And she found that there really was an abundance of help available.

She was to share an office with her fellow Welsh MP, Philip Christopher, who although a new MP like her, seemed to know a great deal about every other member, when they were first elected, the size of their majority, and a great deal more. She started to feel a little intimidated by him, even though he seemed pleasant enough. When she told Byron this during one of their Friday afternoon briefings, he chuckled.

'Don't worry about Phil. He's ok. Yes, he knows a lot about many things. He's been swotting for years, he collects information like a magpie. You could do worse than work with him, Annie. And he can learn a lot from you.'

Anya missed having Byron around during the week. She would have loved to have him work with her in her office full-time, but she knew that wasn't possible. Or even a good idea. Their relationship had shifted a few times over the years, and she wasn't sure it could survive a move like that. So she contented herself with his occasional mid-week visits, when they would relax in her little flat, cooking dinner together, drinking a glass of wine or two, making love. As if they were a couple. Just for a while.

She knew she would have to employ someone to work in her office soon. There was no shortage of possible candidates, and eventually she settled on a young woman who had previously worked for an MP and who knew the ropes – and, just as importantly, knew the constituency. Philip, too, chose an assistant and the four of them work in the cramped joint office.

Anya was determined not to wait too long before she made her maiden speech. She wrote it and re-wrote it, making sure it wasn't controversial, that she thanked her predecessor, and that it spoke warmly about the area she represented. That last was easily done, not so the first. She was thankful that there was no televising of what went on in the chamber, although she had been told that it soon would be. And then it was done. Byron had sat in the Strangers' Gallery, giving her unspoken support as always. He assured her later as they sat in St Stephens Tavern amid her barrage of questions bordering on an inquisition, that she had done well, and that everyone else would think so too.

'How many times, Annie?' he said patiently. 'You're a good speaker. You shouldn't need me to tell you that. You're the boss now. You're the top dog!'

She glanced at him sharply. Was he being sarcastic? Was he bitter? Did he resent her success? Did he envy her? Did he feel ...but he was smiling his beautiful smile, melting her heart as always, and she knew he was proud of her achievements.

'So' he went on, 'you're a fully-fledged MP now. There'll be no holding you. Up on your feet at the drop of a hat ...'

She kicked him under the table, and he laughed.

'And what crusades are you going on, Annie? Whose battles are you going to fight? Anything in mind?'

'Well' she began, 'there is something ...'

She realised he was teasing her. She went on anyway, her chin raised in a now-familiar stubborn expression.

'Phil tells me he's had quite a few enquiries about illnesses, birth defects, even some cancer cases on a council estate in Trefni Vale. The people there are convinced it's to do with the land the houses are built on. Used to be a chemical plant, but none of the residents seem to have known that when they moved into their houses.'

339

The waitress brought their food, and they started to eat.

'Apparently most people have moved out, the houses were so badly built,' went on Anya. 'But some are still there, don't have anywhere else to go. The council won't re-house them, they don't accept any responsibility for the illnesses. So they're trapped, and frightened.'

'Mmm. Interesting. But Idon't you have your own issues, in your own constituency? Don't get me wrong, I can see that it's something that needs to be looked at – but how does that affect you?'

'That's just it, Byron.' She was warming to the subject.

'The housing estate is in Port Haven, my old home. It was built nearly thirty years ago, so my mum may remember something about it. He wants to talk to her, ask her about what was going on at the time. He's trying to get involved in looking at an environmental bill that's on the cards – hoping to make it much stronger …'

He listened and watched her as she spoke, as passionate as ever, willing to give her time to another's campaign because it seemed the right thing to do.

'What?' Her voice was confrontational, accusatory. 'Why are you looking at me like that?'

'I love you, Annie-May' he said.

CHATER 22

AN ARROW STRUCK

1950

August. First time in Port Haven since that holiday, his first holiday, forever tainted with the memory of its aftermath. He saw the place differently now though, twenty years on. Now it was an up-and-coming residential town on the coast, as well as a bucket-and-spade holiday resort. Now it boasted a huge caravan park in place of the makeshift tents on the sand. And now he was here for his father's funeral, twenty years later than it should have taken place.

Danny met him at the door.

'Well, Meic' he said.

'Dan. My good friend.'

They embraced, neither embarrassed at this less-than-masculine display of affection and emotion.

'Come in, Bach' Danny said. He was shorter than Michael remembered, but just as thin and wiry, his red hair thinner now, speckled with white.

'You remember Beth, don't you? Or Elizabeth as she was known back then.'

Beth nodded stiffly, a hard expression on her pretty plump face. Michael had not changed so much since she had met him all those years ago. He seemed taller, and had filled out, his dark hair was thick and cut fashionably short, and he sported a pencil-thin moustache. But he was as handsome as she remembered.

'I'm sorry for your loss' she said formally.

Michael glanced at Danny. Surely he would have told his wife about the circumstances of his friend's departure? Or at least of the relationship – or lack of one – between him and his father?

'Come and sit down, Meic, have a cupppa. You must be parched. It's a long drive down from Croydon!' Danny started towards the little scullery, but Beth put a hand on his arm.

'What are you thinking, Dan? Meic will want to see his dad.' She nodded towards the closed door of the front room.

'No, you're alright Beth. Thank you, but no.'

Beth looked astonished.

'But he's your father! And his coffin is lying in there, in the parlour, just a few feet away! Surely ...'

'It's ok Beth' Danny interrupted, 'Maybe later. Meic must be tired.'

'Well we're all tired, aren't we?' No disguising her antagonism now. 'I'm tired too. But it was ok for us to keep an eye on the old man for twenty years, was it? Ok for me to run back and forth to that God-forsaken place, to take him his meals, do his washing, cleaning ...'

'I'm sorry Beth.' Michael saw, suddenly, why she was so angry. 'I didn't know. I really didn't. I had no idea you'd been left with the job of looking after him. I'm truly sorry.'

She looked slightly mollified, but wasn't going to thaw out just yet.

'Perhaps you can show me his coffin now?' Michael said.

She opened the door.

'It's an open casket' she said, unnecessarily, in a softer voice.

Michael looked down at his father. The father he'd thought he had killed all those years ago. Nothing intimidating now, not glowering or scowling. Just a dead old man, yellowing skin stretched over his cheekbones, wisps of hair lying across his forehead, hands folded meekly on his chest. He had expected to feel nothing, but he was wrong. Emotions washed over him in a tidal fury. Anger, hatred, bitterness. And guilt. A conviction that his mother would not have died had he been there, had he not left her that time. But a great sadness too. Sorrow that he hadn't been allowed to say goodbye to his mother, that she had already been laid in the earth by the time he knew she had died. Sorrow that their small family had ended like this. What a waste. He turned.

'Thank you Beth' he said. And then, politely if not truthfully, 'I'm grateful.'

Michael and Danny at last sat at the tiny table in the scullery, a brown china teapot and a small plate of Welsh cakes between them. It didn't take long for each man to report on twenty years of living; the information exchanged between them in their occasional correspondence over the years had been sparse to say the least, but both were men of few words.

Danny knew that Michael had fled to Surrey, thinking he had killed his father. It was Danny who had given him the introductory letter to a friend in the building

343

trade, Danny who had asked this friend to give him somewhere to stay. Michael had worked like a Trojan, showing his willingness to do all the unpleasant and difficult jobs, acquiring skills as he did so. He had wanted to join up in 1939, as the war started, but the legacy from his father of one too many punches made this impossible. His eardrum was punctured, and he was pronounced medically unfit to serve as a soldier. So he stayed on, working for his builder boss, one of the few strong young men still around. Slowly he gained a reputation as a good worker, slowly he saved enough money to set up on his own, and slowly he had built up a good business. He was settled now, no intention of ever returning to Wales, where the bad memories outweighed the good ones.

Danny had married the girl he had met on that fateful holiday and they lived as a couple in the home in the Nantllai Valley he shared with his mother and sister. When both of those two much-loved women had contracted tuberculosis, Beth had needed no persuasion to move the family to the coastal town where her holiday memories were all happy ones, where it was always summer. All the doctors seemed to agree that the sea air would be beneficial for this crippling illness that was taking its toll in the valleys, in the industrial towns, in the poor areas of south Wales, and the four of them managed to rent the little house in Port Haven where they still lived, a two-up-two-down terraced house in Highland Place, a back street behind the single road of shops that comprised the town. Sadly the woman and the girl that Danny had devoted so much of his life to did not improve as he had hoped, and within two years, they had died.

344

Michael put his hand on his friend's arm.

'I was so sorry to hear about your Mam, Dan. And Carys. I know how much they meant to you.'

'Thanks Meic. But I have a consolation, you know. My little Jessie.'

And right on cue, in walked the most beautiful girl Michael had ever seen. Her strawberry-blonde hair was long and loose and tumbled in waves over her shoulders. Her blue eyes were clear and pure and heartbreakingly innocent. Her shape was that of a girl not yet used to being a woman, her young breasts straining at the gingham top of the simple sun-suit she wore. Michael felt his breath catch in his throat.

'This is Jessie, Meic.' Danny's voice was full of pride. 'Jess, this is my old friend Meic – Uncle Michael to you!'

Michael regained his composure.

'Hello Jessie' he said, smiling. 'Very nice to meet you. And no need to call me Uncle – Michael will do very nicely thank you!'

Jessie smiled impishly.

'Hello Michael. No, I can't call you Uncle – that makes you sound as old as Dad!'

The funeral went as funerals go. People attended out of respect for Danny and his family, rather than for the old man. No-one in Port Haven knew him, and there were no mourners from the Nantllai Valley. He had stayed in the old house as it continued to crumble around him, and Danny had kept an eye on him as best he could.

345

'But we couldn't hold the funeral up there' Danny told his friend as they sat over two bottles of beer in the parlour that evening.

'So we had the coffin brought down here. Just for the funeral. Couldn't have anyone seeing what had become of the place.'

They each took a pull of beer as their thoughts went their separate ways. Then,

'He changed, Meic. After you went. After your Mam …you know. He was still a nasty piece of work, mind. But he lost all interest in his work, lost all interest in anything. Never a kind word to Beth, mind, after all she did for him. Never a kind word to anyone. Sat all day, reading the papers, making spills for his pipe. Didn't talk much. Never mentioned you to me Meic, not once. Sorry Bach.'

Michael shrugged.

'I didn't expect him to, Dan. Unless it was to curse me. So what will happen to the farm? To the house?'

'Well that's up to you. There's a family interested in buying it. Want to run it as a small-holding, hens, ducks, you know. They'd expect to get it for a bargain though, just because it's in such a state.'

'They can have it. I never want to see the place again.'

'Ok. I'll sort it if you want me to. Least I can do for the old man. And for you.'

Michael put his hand on Danny's.

'He never knew what a good friend he had in you, Dan. A good friend to me too.'

Danny cleared his throat.

'Well, you'd do the same for me, I know you would.'

'So, tell me about Jessie' said Michael, changing the subject to avoid his friend's discomfiture.

It worked. Danny beamed.

'Just fifteen, and bright as a button she is. I missed out on some of her growing-up though. She was only four when I got called up. But we've made up for it since. Apple of my eye. Clever enough to do her exams too, her School Certificate. Or that new GCE that's coming in next year. Clever enough to go to college. She wants to leave school of course, like most of her friends, earn some money, but we're hoping she'll change her mind. At least we haven't had the worry of boyfriends yet – she doesn't seem to fancy any of the young bucks around here!'

Michael stayed on. He knew his firm was in good hands back in Croydon, and in his regular phone calls his loyal and trustworthy staff assured him that they could manage, especially as this was the first holiday they had known their boss to take. So he stayed longer than he had planned, longer that Danny had expected, although he was delighted to have his friend from his home village back in his company again.

Despite Danny's protests, Michael had insisted on staying at one of the many hotels that had sprung up, knowing that there was precious little space in the Morgan's house. But he visited every day, helping Danny with his work, not afraid to roll up his sleeves and do the heavy work he'd been brought up with.

Danny had worked for a small local builder for nearly two decades, and he practically ran the business now that Ray, his boss, was getting older and stiffer. Michael enjoyed the time on the construction site with his friend and his co-workers. He realised that, now he spent much of his day in one office or another, he had missed the camaraderie that was evident whenever a group of hard-working men got together. In the evenings, he accepted Beth's offer of a meal with them, and for the first time in his life, experienced a family that talked and laughed and argued good-naturedly. He rarely contributed to the conversation himself, preferring instead to listen, to watch, to soak up this atmosphere he envied. And to look at Jessie.

He was mesmerised by her. He kept reminding himself that she was a child, that she was Danny's daughter. But he wanted to bathe in that glow she seemed to exude, he wanted to wrap her up, protect her. He wanted to touch her.

She was smart and witty, quick with a comeback to her father's comments, which clearly delighted him. He would talk about her future, maybe as a secretary, or a teacher, and her mother would talk about her finding a nice young man and starting a family. But she would tell them, in no uncertain words, that she wanted to earn her own money, to buy clothes, to live in a big house, maybe in London. The future was here, now. She couldn't look ahead any further than that.

And she seemed to like Michael. She would smile at him, not coquettishly, not provocatively, but innocently, melting his heart and taking his breath away. She showed him around the town, around the caravan site, the beaches and the countryside behind. She would pack a picnic and sit with him on an old woollen rug while they ate, talked, laughed. He was more confused than he'd ever been. He knew he shouldn't have these feelings. He was twenty years her senior, her father's friend. He fought against it every day, but by the end of the month he knew. He loved her.

'Dan, I need to talk to you' Michael said one evening as they walked, hot and sweaty, back to the little house.

'Me too, Meic, me too.'

Michael glanced at his friend. Danny's face looked pinched, worried, and Michael realised that he had been so wrapped up in his feelings for Jessie that he had failed to notice that her father had become quieter over the weeks.

'What's wrong Dan? Can I help?'

Danny gave a crooked smile.

'Well yes, maybe you can. That's what I want to talk to you about.'

And it came pouring out. His boss was retiring. The business was closing and Danny would be out of work. Simple as that.

'But can't he sell the business Dan? Surely …'

'Yes, he can. And he will. He'll sell it to Evans & McAndrew, the biggest firm around. They'll take all Ray's contracts and his contacts, all his plant, everything except for the people. They don't need us. We're expendable. And I'm too old. Seems that fifty is too old for building work. For them at least. The two youngsters will find work easily enough, but me, I'll be out. Looking for something new. At my age.'

Michael listened in silence. Then,

'What can I do, Dan?'

'I don't like to ask you, Meic. I really don't …'

'I told you once, didn't I? Anything. And I meant it. Anything.'

Danny took a breath.

'I could buy Ray out, Meic. Keep the business going. I know it inside out. And there's plenty of work out there – new houses being built everywhere. But I'd need the money to buy him out. A bit more that Evans & McAndrew are offering. I'll need to convince him that mine's a better deal. And then I'd need some to get it started in my own name. It's a lot, Meic.'

'It's yours. Whatever you need. Of course it is. We'll go down to the bank tomorrow. I'm sure Ray will let you leave early if he knows the reason.'

They walked without speaking for a full five minutes.

'I don't know what to say Meic.'

'Nothing. There's nothing to be said. I told you – anything. Any time. Now let's see what Beth has cooked for us today.'

August ended on a high note. Danny's buy-out was going through nicely, and Michael had agreed to stay on a little longer to help with the legal stuff that he was used to and Danny wasn't. Jessie agreed to return to school, at least for the term, as she wasn't sure exactly what she did want to do. And Michael, at long last, had the talk with Danny he knew he must have.

At Michael's request, they went for a walk along the beach one evening after dinner, away from Beth's acute hearing. Michael knew that this concerned her too, but he wanted to talk to his old friend first. He knew he may need to be packing his bags before the end of the night.

Danny was silent as Michael talked, stumbling uncharacteristically over his words. As they walked over the dunes where they had shared their first holiday together, Michael told him how he felt about Jessie, that he thought he loved her, that she knew nothing of his feelings. He told Danny that he knew she may be horrified at the thought of his interest. And he asked his permission to approach her, to find out how she felt, to court her. To marry her.

Danny remained silent as they walked, head down, hands in his trouser pockets. When he spoke, his voice was quiet, measured.

'She's a clever girl, Meic. She could go to college. Have a career. She's not even sixteen yet.' He looked up. 'Are you really asking to take her away? To make her a wife, a mother, while she's still a child?'

Meic knew that this was exactly what he was asking.

'But she could do anything she wanted, Dan. If she married me. She could go to college – married women do that sometimes. And we wouldn't have to have children – not right away.'

Both men stopped, as if by mutual agreement, facing each other, as the marram grass blew around their feet and the sound of the waves creeping up the beach grew louder.

'Jessie doesn't know what she wants to do with her life, Meic. She's young, wants nice things, wants to see the world.'

'I know. I would take care of her Dan. I'd give her anything, everything she wants. I'd make her happy. I'd love her.'

'Find out what she wants then, Meic. Do that. Then we'll talk again.'

And they retraced their steps, in silence this time.

Michael didn't find it easy to start the conversation with Jessie. They continued to talk, to walk, she pointing out her favourite places around the town, he waiting for the right time, the right place, to tell her how he felt without scaring her off. But time was moving on, and he knew he would have to return to his business soon.

It happened quite naturally one Saturday, as they walked up the hill leading out of the town.

'There!' she said. 'The big house. That's the house I want to live in!'

She stood looking up at the impressive white house with its low red roofs, set at the top of a wide, winding drive on the side of the shallow hill, half hidden by trees and shrubs. Hill House.

'You ought to see it in the spring!' she said as she stood, eyes wide, transfixed. 'There are daffodils all around, and huge patches of bluebells under the trees. Can you imagine living in a place like that? Wouldn't it be – well – just the living end?'

Michael laughed at her exuberance, and at her youth.

'Yes, it would be "the living end" Jess!' he said. Then,

'I could build a house like that. Or buy it. For my wife, if I had one. For a family.'

'Lucky lady!'

'Do you think so, Jess? Really?'

She saw that he was looking into her eyes now, serious, waiting for an answer. She looked back at him, squarely, appraisingly, as if seeing him for the first time.

'Yes I do, Michael' she said quietly after a moment. 'I really do.'

It was much easier after that. As they walked, retracing their steps, he told her, gently, how much she had come to mean to him over these past weeks. And she, in turn, let him know that she liked him, felt at ease with him. And that she found him attractive, exciting. She blushed as she told him this, but it was as if she knew they needed to be honest with each other. By the time they had reached her home, she had agreed to go to dinner with him the following evening, saying how grown-up that sounded, then giggling at the thought. Michael was enchanted, but he knew his mind. He wasn't a kid any more. He knew what he felt, and he knew it was real.

Beth was surprised, to say the least, when her daughter announced that she was going out for the evening with this older man, a man Beth herself had met when she was barely older than Jessie was now.

'Oh please Mum! He's going back to London soon' the girl pleaded. 'He's really nice and kind, and clever and funny. And I've never been out to a proper restaurant before!'

Beth glanced at her husband, looking for his support.

'It will be nice for her, Beth' he said. 'Meic's a good bloke. He's been good to us. Let him have a good send-off.'

And so the cautious courtship began. It was made up of dinners, lunches, teas and coffees over the weekends when Michael drove down to Wales. An occasional lift to school on a Monday started many tongues wagging among the pupils, and some of the staff, but Jess seemed unfazed by it. There was little physical contact between them. Now and then, on one of their walks, they held hands, she smiling shyly, he very aware of their age difference but quietly exultant. By the time they got to Christmas, they were more at ease with each other, although Michael was still unsure about her feelings for him. Was he an uncle figure? An older man in whom she could confide? Someone to be seen with, to shock her friends?

On Christmas Eve, after their late evening meal, Jessie surprised him by catching his hand and, dragging him towards the door, and pleaded with him to walk with her up to Hill House. And so they walked along in the cold, arm in arm this time, until they reached the little wood that surrounded Jessie's dream house. She stopped, and turned to him.

'Do you think I'm still a child, Michael?'

He was taken aback.

'What?'

'Because I'm not, you know. I'll be sixteen in two months' time.'

'Yes, I know.'

'When you talked, a few months ago, about building a house like this for your wife, I thought you meant me' she said simply. 'But now I don't know what to think. We talk and laugh and we understand each other; I love being with you and I think you like being with me too. But ... you've never kissed me, Michael. Never tried.'

Michael was afraid to speak. He looked at her lovely young face, turned up to him, at her full lips and clear blue eyes.

'I did mean you, Jessie. Of course I meant you. I love you.'

'Well then ...' and she stood on her tip toes, reached up to him, and gently kissed him on the mouth, letting herself linger there, until he put his arms around her, holding her to him. And then they kissed, and it was on equal terms.

The two people who reached the house were not the same as those who had left it just a few hours earlier. They walked comfortably, closely, arms entwined, leaning into each other, laughing, planning.

'Dad will go Ape!' Jessie giggled. 'Mum will be ok – all she wants is for me to get married, have kids, be like her. Though I don't think she had someone quite like you in mind...'

But her father surprised her. Although he looked solemn, he said he was happy for them. Beth got over her initial shock once she realised there was a wedding to plan for.

'Plenty of time to sort it all out, anyway' she said, lists already lining up in her head. 'A three-year engagement will be nice – or longer if you want it. But not too long. You don't want to be far into your twenties before you start a family ...' and she continued to make the future arrangements, talking more to herself than to the others.

Michael and Jessie exchanged a glance.

'We were thinking of something sooner than that, Beth' he said.

'Much sooner' added Jessie.

'Oh?' Beth looked surprised. 'How soon?'

'March!' declared Jessie.

Even Michael looked surprised at this.

'March?' said Danny. 'That's just three months away! Why the great rush?'

The colour drained from Beth's face.

'You're not ...'

'No, no, nothing like that!' Michael quickly assured them both.

'You really think I could be pregnant?' Jessie was indignant. 'How stupid do you think I am? No. I'll be sixteen in February, and why wait?'

The discussion went on for some hours, all thoughts of Christmas gone. By the time Danny saw

Michael to the door, the church bells were ringing to welcome in the special day.

'Seriously Meic – why the rush?' he asked, a frown on his face. 'I know I said you could find out how she felt, but this …?'

"I know Dan. I wasn't expecting Jess to come up with that! But she's right – why wait? We'd just be treading water, waiting for the sake of waiting, me travelling back and forth every weekend. And I can't see her staying in school if she's planning to get married, can you? Please don't worry Dan. I'll look after her. I promise.'

The weeks passed quickly. Beth was in her element, despite the rush, which her neighbours assumed was down to it being a shot-gun marriage. But Beth held her head high. She knew her daughter would have a good life. Michael had money, didn't he? Jessie wouldn't have to struggle as she had, as they had. She would have all the good things of life, even if she would be living such a long way away. That had come as a shock at first. She had assumed that they would be settling down locally, maybe in one of the new houses being built along the seafront. But Jessie had other ideas.

'I want to live in London, Mum!' she insisted. 'It will be so exciting! And anyway, Michael's business is up there. But you and Daddy will be able to come and visit us!'

'It's Croydon, Jess, not London' her father corrected her.

'Oh, close enough!' she retorted.

And so it was done.

Two things happened on the day before their wedding, both to have longer-lasting effects that anyone could have predicted. Michael was, at last, looking through the piles of documents that had been left in his father's house. They needed to be sorted, to be kept, or disposed of, before the new owners took possession. Michael had insisted he would have no interest in relics of another life, and had wanted to throw them out, as he had with everything else that had belonged to his father. But Danny had insisted.

'You must look through them Meic' Danny had said. 'You're about to start a new life – with my daughter. Start it fresh and clean, nothing hanging over you. You can throw them away once you've looked at them. But look at them you must.'

So Michael had retraced the steps he had taken so many years ago, his heart beating fast, dreading seeing the place, not knowing how he would feel when he did.

He had barely recognised it. At first. The overgrown driveway, the dilapidated outhouses, the greenery covering the walls of the house. Then, in a blink of an eye, he was home, and he saw it as he had known it. Still cluttered and chaotic and shabby, but home. He had felt an unwelcome lump in his throat. The last time he had left here, his mother waved him off. No, he was wrong. The last time he left, he was running for his life, running never to return. The memory hardened him, and he walked in through the door.

Danny had been right. He must do this. The yellowing papers sat in crates, carefully piled there by his friend. Sitting on a small stool in the dismal kitchen, the only light coming in through the tattered half opened curtains at the window, Michael placed empty boxes on either side of him. To his right, he would place documents to be discarded. After two hours, those boxes were filling fast. Bills, final demands, receipts, undecipherable scribblings, in they went. To his left, those he wished to keep. This single box was empty. And then – he stopped, staring at the image in front of him. His mother. As she had been as a girl. Beautiful, confident, draped in flimsy layers, a lacy headdress low on her brow, her fair hair coiled on either side of her smiling face. As he'd never seen her. And on the back, a message, written in her careful hand,

To Tommy
You said you wanted a picture of me and here it is.
From your Hannah
xxx
June 1912

He slowly, carefully, placed it to his left. Then another photograph. Faded sepia, as the first, but this time two individuals, standing outside a church. He recognised that church. So this was where his parents had married. He looked harder. His mother had been happy once then. She was beaming. He was not. Grim, unsmiling, clearly uncomfortable in his Sunday best. And yet – proud. Yes, proud. Another one for the box on his left. And then birth certificates, a marriage certificate. Two boxes later – a death certificate. So his father had told him the truth then. His mother had died from blood poisoning.

One by one he scanned the pieces of paper. One by one he discarded them. Until – an unopened envelope. And then two more. Addressed to him. Addressed to Mr Michael Hughes, at Maes Ty Clyd. Never opened. Until now.

4, Heol Gadlys
Port Haven
October 12th 1930

Dear Mike
I think I'm having a baby. I don't know what to do. My mam will throw me out. Please help.
Love Margaret xxx

Then another.

4, Heol Gadlys
Port Haven
December 15th 1930

Dear Mike
My mam has found out about the baby. She says I must go somewhere else to have it, that it will be the death of her. I am very frightened. Please write to me.
Love
Margaret

And a third.

Salvation Army Home,
21-22 Moira Terrace
Cardiff
May 12th 1931

Dear Mike
I'm staying in a place for unmarried mothers.
There are 16 of us here. Some of the other girls
are quite nice but I would rather go home.
I've had a baby girl. I call her Margaret, after
me. My mam says I must have her adopted.
from
Margaret (Daniels)

Michael put his head in his hands and wept.

And then the second thing. Danny and Beth kept their voices low, but their tempers were rising.

'You promised me, Danny, you promised me' she was saying.

'I never promised anything Beth. You know that.'

'You did! You promised me that one day, when you had your own business, we'd have a new house, a house of our own, up by Blue Cove. And now you've got your own business, and we're still stuck here, still renting this pokey little house, while our daughter, barely sixteen, will be living in a mansion in some swanky part of London ...'

'Ah, so that's it! You're jealous! Jealous of your own daughter! Well I'm sorry Beth.' His voice was rising now. 'I'm sorry I've let you down so badly! I'm sorry that I haven't been able to make a fortune after six months – just six months – of running my own business! And I'm sorry that I haven't been able to match up to your future son-in-law.'

'Yes, he's done alright out of it hasn't he?' Beth shouted. 'He's got a pretty young bride, and all it cost him was a couple of thousand pounds to bail you out!'

They both turned at the sound of Jessie's gasp. She was standing in the doorway, horror written on her face.

'Jess, it's not like that …' Danny started to say, moving towards her, but she cut him off, pushing him away.

'You sold me?' she whispered. 'That's how much I mean to you? Bought and sold? I hate you.'

And she walked out, closing the door behind her.

CHAPTER 23

HILL HOUSE

1954: September

Life was good for Michael and Jessie. Married over three years, and deeply in love. They were part of the social set in the smart little suburban town of Walton-on-Thames, living in a lovely rented riverside cottage, lunching at the Swan, dining out at the Weir Hotel with friends. They made an eye-catching couple, and were popular guests at house-parties and local events. True, now and then Jessie would think back to her childhood home, fondly, but her memories were tinged with bitterness at the way she had said farewell to her parents.

She could not forgive her father for agreeing to her marriage purely because her husband had given him money. It made her sick to think of it and she had not spoken to her father or her mother, nor replied to their letters, since. She had never told Michael of the snatch of conversation she had heard that day. It had not made her doubt that she wanted to marry him, or that he loved her, and she would not taint their marriage with such a memory. But now and then, she would hear a Welsh accent, or catch a glimpse of a wiry man with greying red hair in a crowd, and she would have to hold back her tears. Especially now.

When she told Michael she was pregnant, his reaction was all she could have hoped for. And after the kisses and the careful hugs and the sheer delight on his face, he said.

'And I've a surprise for you too. It can't quite match up to yours of course!' and he took her by the hand, and led her to the shed at the bottom of the garden.

He covered her eyes as he led her inside. She stood, laughing.

'What have you done, Michael? Have you ...'

'You can look now' he said, as he lowered his hands.

There, on a sturdy table in the centre of the little building, stood a dollshouse. But not just any dollshouse. This was a magnificent structure, not a toy, but a work of art. Every part of it was to scale, every detail exactly as he remembered the house on the hill, back in her home town.

She gasped.

'Oh my!' she whispered. 'Oh Michael! It's Hill House! You did this for me? Just for me?' and she burst into tears.

And as he held her, he knew that these were tears of happiness, of longing, of hiraeth.

'Would you like to move back, Jess? We can do that if you want to. I know there's something wrong between you and your dad, and I don't know what it is, but maybe it's time to sort it out. And with a baby on the way, well...'

She was nodding, her head against his chest. And then she told him, haltingly, about the reason for the rift. And at last he was able to put it right, to tell her the truth about what had happened, about the gift to her father, about the halting request to be able to court her, and he was able to assure her that the two things were not linked, not in any way, that he had been happy to give her father any help he could, that he owed him, big time.

They sat then, on a wooden bench in that dingy shed, light from the dusty window slanting across the scaled-down mansion he had made for her, and he told her the things he had kept secret for so many years. He told her how he had thought he'd killed his own father, and that he had been glad at the thought. He told her about the guilt he still felt, at leaving his mother alone that time, a time when she needed him most. And finally, he told her what he had discovered on the day before their wedding.

'I have a daughter, Jess. She'd be older than you. I never knew, on my honour, I never knew.'

He told her about that fateful holiday, how he had been so overcome on his return by his mother's death, and what he'd thought he'd done, that he had never given that young girl a second thought.

'She wrote to me, but I'd left home, and my father never even opened the letters. All I know about her is that her mother gave her a name, but she was adopted, so she's probably not called that any more. I've tried to trace her but no luck. I'm sorry sweetheart. I should have told you. I was so ashamed when I found out. And it was too late then. Too late to do anything.'

'No more secrets now then, not any more' Jessie said, laying her head on his shoulder. 'I'm glad you've been trying to find her.'

'And what about you and your dad, Jess? Will you get in touch? You know he loves you. He wanted you to go to college, have a career, but he knew how stubborn you were, that you didn't want to stay on at school. And I'm sure he only gave us his blessing because he didn't think for one moment that you'd listen to him anyway!'

She laughed.

'Yes, I'd have threatened to elope with you, go to Gretna Green, whatever it took!' Jessie sighed. 'I'll write to him. Tell him and Mum about the baby. Say that we'll visit soon.'

'And tell them we'll move back, as soon as I have some work sorted out down there!'

Little Anya May Hughes was born on St David's Day, March the first, the following year, just as the daffodils in Jessie's window boxes were flowering. She was loved from the start, both parents doting on her, hardly able to believe that they had produced a creature so exquisite. For Jessie, Anya's birth was a line in the sand, a division between her as a child and as an adult, and she relished this new role. For Michael though, deeper, sometimes darker feelings. Contrasts between his own childhood, and what he promised himself would be in store for this precious bundle, filled his mind when he looked at her. In Jessie he saw feelings that he knew his mother had had for him. He wondered if he could measure up to the task of being a dad, that huge but welcome task he wanted so badly, having never known the love of his own father. But his determination to do so grew with every day, with every tiny wave of a hand, every grasp of his finger. The smiles that were priceless, the gurgling and chuckling that made him laugh as he never had before. He loved his little daughter, and loved his wife more than ever, so thankful was he to be given this chance, this double chance, of happiness. He called this little scrap his Annie-May.

November 1955

'Hello? Is that Meic Hughes? Meic Hughes of Maes Ty Clyd?'

Like a blast from his childhood, the voice, with that unmistakeable accent, came booming down the 'phone line. Michael stared at the mouthpiece, unsure what to think, unsure whether to slam the handset down on its base, or to reply. He chose to reply.

'This is Michael Hughes, yes' he said. 'Who's calling?'

'Meic! Meic my boy! Long time no see! Well, no hear, anyway!' and the caller guffawed delightedly.

Michael cast his mind back, back to his school days.

'Steff? Steffan Evans?' Michael said incredulously. 'It can't be! Good God, it's – it must be over twenty five years!'

'Spot on, Bach! I knew you'd never forget a voice like mine!' and he roared with laughter again.

Michael was both surprised and delighted to hear from his old school friend. Well, perhaps not so much a friend. A classmate. For a while. Steffan – the only boy in Michael's year to go to the grammar school, to go to university. He had no idea what he had gone on to do after that, but Steff was quick to bring him up to date.

'So, here I am, Chairman of Trefni Bridge Council! Who'd have thought it, eh? Wasn't sure we

367

Independents would win May's elections, mind you. Plaid are snapping at Labour's heels but we're doing ok here. We're having to throw them the odd morsel, you know!' He laughed loudly again, then lowered his voice.

'Seriously though Meic, I have it on good authority that you have a pretty good building firm. And that you're thinking of moving back to the land of song.'

'Where on earth did you hear that? We've barely decided ourselves!'

Steff laughed.

'Ah well, seems we have a mutual friend. Danny Morgan. He was doing some work in the town here, and I bumped into him - found we had a lot of history in common – including you. Nice that he seemed to remember me from all those years ago. We were just kids, weren't we? And he seemed so old!'

'Oh, of course, Danny. He's a good friend. And now my father-in-law.'

'Yes, I heard. But enough reminiscing! I'd like to meet up with you, Meic. There's a lot of building work coming up around here, a lot of council work. We'll be putting out some big tenders. But I have a very particular proposal for you.'

'Oh yes?'

'Not over the phone, Meic. Can you get down here? To meet up? It's quite – sensitive.'

'You don't mean crooked? Because I won't ...'

'No, no, I'm not asking you to do anything like that. I wouldn't. Just – shall we say – mutually beneficial.'

'I'm intrigued. Yes, ok. I'll talk to Jess and we'll try to come down next weekend. She'll be glad to see her parents anyway – we both will. I'll give you a call.'

Jessie was thrilled, if a little apprehensive, at the thought of seeing her Mum and Dad for the first time in over four years. She spent the week choosing just the right outfits to take, for herself and for little Anya, then discarding her choices and starting again.

'It's just two days, sweetheart!' Michael laughed.

'I know, I know' she said. 'But it's been a long time. I know we've been writing for a few months, but …I'm a different person now. I want them to see …'

He hugged her.

'They'll see. They'll know.'

Friday morning came. They piled the luggage – far more than was necessary for one weekend - into the roomy two-tone Ford Zodiac, climbed onto the leather-trimmed bench seat, Anya snuggled between them, and they set off. It could take them up to eight hours to reach Port Haven – longer if they stopped for too many breaks. The weather was cold but it was bright and sunny. They chatted and laughed as they followed the main road out of Surrey, occasionally reverting to B roads to avoid traffic hold-ups.

They made Worcester in good time, and stopped at a roadside café for some lunch. Anya had slept for most of the morning, so was wide awake enough to entertain the other customers there, the antics of an eight-month-old guaranteed to raise a smile on even the grumpiest of lorry drivers.

They joined the A48 now, and with it the feeling that they really were heading home. The route was unfamiliar to Jessie, as she had travelled it just once, following their wedding, but Michael knew it well, and gave her regular updates as to where they were and when they were likely to arrive. Malvern, Ross-on-Wye, Monmouth – as they drew closer to her home town, Jessie became more and more quiet. She didn't know what sort of reception she could expect.

They drew up outside the little house in Highland Place. Then the front door flew open, and Beth was wrenching at the car door, dragging Jessie and Anya into her arms, and Danny was hugging his old friend, and everyone was laughing and crying, and little Annie-May was gurgling happily. What on earth had she been worried about, Jessie asked herself. Then her Dad came round the car and hugged her gently, as if she were a fragile piece of porcelain, and she could feel the tears on his cheeks, mingling with her own. No need for explanations, no apologies. No need for words.

Saturday was again a clear bright day, and Jessie and her parents went walking along the sea front, pushing Anya in a borrowed pram, showing her off. Jessie wished she had been able to bring the beautiful Silver Cross baby carriage they had at home, but lovely as it was, it was far too big to be transported.

Meanwhile Michael headed into Trefni Bridge for his meeting with Steffan. As he drove up the hill out of Port Haven, he passed Hill House. The house Jessie loved so much. And there it was – For Sale. The sign shouted down to him as he stopped the car to take a better

look. Yes, it really was on the market. But this would be way, way out of his range. This would take all he had and more. It would mean a big mortgage. And even then …
He was thoughtful as he continued his journey.

Trefni Bridge was not a place he knew, but he couldn't miss the imposing town hall, a Palladian-styled building that housed the council offices in this, the county town. He climbed the steps, reached the enormous wooden door, and as he opened it, was greeted by a larger-than-life character that he would have been hard-pressed to recognise had it not been for the familiar booming voice.

'Meic bach! Glad you could make it! My word, you're looking good! Better than me, eh?' and Steff chuckled loudly.

Michael smiled, inwardly agreeing. His friend must be at least twenty stone, with a huge beer-belly and several chins. Nevertheless he had to recognise, albeit reluctantly, that he was somewhat in awe of the success Steffan had become. The badly-educated farm boy in Michael had never gone away, despite the good life he had built for himself and Jessie back in Surrey.

'Come on' his friend was saying. 'We'll go to the café round the corner. Prying eyes, you know' and he tapped the side of his nose.

The café was a good deal further way than the nearest corner. It was seedy to say the least, tables greasy, and the woman serving them seemingly annoyed at being disturbed from reading her magazine.

'Not the greatest place, Meic, I know, but what I have to say to you is pretty private. Very private in fact.

Can't afford to be overheard – and there's no chance of anyone I know coming in here!' and he laughed again.

'So what's this all about, Steff?'

'All in good time, all in good time!' Steffan smiled. 'What about you and your good lady-wife? Are you serious about settling back in Wales? You've been away a long time.'

'Perfectly serious, yes. I never thought I'd move back – but that was before I met Jess. I'd do anything for her. And although she doesn't say it, she'd like to have her family around her. Especially now we have little Annie-May.'

Michael's face lit up when he talked about his wife and daughter, and this wasn't missed on Steffan.

'Well, I expect you'll be looking for somewhere to live, if you do come back. I might be able to help you there ...

'Woah! Slow down Steff – let's get the work situation sorted out first. I'd be leaving behind a business I've taken years to build. It's not something I can just transport down the A48, is it? My men won't want to move down here, I know. And I have a lot of plant invested there. I can't just "sell" my business. Not up in Surrey. Small firms like mine are ten-a-penny. I'd have to wind down all the work I have, pass on some contracts, and then start all over again down here, get the men, the machines, the supplies, and most important, the contacts – all that will take time.'

Steffan smiled again.

'As I said, I can help you. Contacts? You have me! We have a lot of big building contracts coming up.

Council houses, whole estates, being built everywhere. And I have some private contacts too, big houses being built, lots of them. They don't call them estates when they're that expensive, but that's what they are. You could take your pick, Meic. Enough work to last you for ten years. At least. And I can get you the men, the machines, the supplies – timber, bricks, blocks, sand, cement – the lot. All at good prices.'

'So what's the catch, Steff? And how could you be sure I'd get the contracts? Isn't there such a thing as a tendering process down here?'

'Of course there is. But that's where I can help. I'm in a position to do that.'

'Hold on – you're talking about cheating the system? Bid-rigging?'

'No Meic, no. Not rigging. Just a little peak at some of the bids as they come in. Look, the system we've got is out-dated, archaic. The lowest bid always gets the contract, even if it's a firm with no standing, or no history. A firm that won't be able to do the work for the cost they've bid, not in a million years. But we've got no choice. It's the law. It will be changed in time, sure. It will have to look at some sort of quality standard, so that the lowest bid won't be enough, on its own, to get the job. But that's way off yet.'

Michael thought about what he was hearing, and it made sense. He knew how the system worked – he'd submitted tenders in the past, with realistic costs, but had sometimes lost out to a firm that couldn't finish the work for the amount they'd bid, or in the time they'd promised. Occasionally the firm went bust. More often, if it were a big contract, the extra money was found. Which made the whole tender process a farce.

'So – what are you suggesting?'

The process was this: Steffan would tell Michael what tenders were coming up. Michael would work out the costings, but hold off submitting a bid. Meanwhile, Steffan would wait until the deadline for bids was reached, find out the lowest bid amount put forward, and tell Michael by how much he needed to reduce his costs. Michael would be able to undercut the lowest bidder, and submit his amended bid, pre-dated to comply with the tender process. Steffan would make sure that it would find its way into the batch of "unopened" tenders.

'After all" he boasted, 'I am the Chairman of the Council!'

After a few minutes, when Michael was taking this in, he smiled and sat back in his chair.

'One problem, Steff. How am I expected to carry out the work for less than the actual costs? Winning a contract is no good to me if I can't deliver!'

'Ah, and this is the beauty of it!' Steffan looked around him. No-one was near them but he lowered his voice.

'I can arrange for you to have all the machinery and supplies you need at cost price. The money you save will more than cover any short-fall, I'll make sure of that. You'll be quids in. And if it comes to it, if you go a little over-budget, well ...' he spread his hands 'so what? The council will cover it. Not in their interests to halt the building of houses, is it? Not when so many families are crying out for them, living in slums. No-one will think anything of it. But no-one must know about our little arrangement.' That's important, Meic.

His face was serious for a moment.

'Or everyone will want a slice of the pie!' and he laughed loudly at his own cleverness, waking the waitress behind the counter out of her reverie.

On the drive back to Port Haven Michael thought long and hard about Steff's proposal. It didn't feel right. He knew it wasn't right. But he also knew that, should he not accept, Steff would not be happy, and Michael would be hard-pressed to find any big contracts in the area if he crossed him.

Jessie was glowing, a mixture of the sea air and exhilaration at the thought of coming home. There was no doubt, this was home for Jessie. Although she was happy in Walton, this would always be her home. Michael decided not to tell her any details of the meeting, not wanting to either raise her hopes of moving back to Wales, or to dash them. He knew that she would not approve of anything underhand, and although he had more or less decided not to take up Steff's offer, he was still not entirely certain.

The remainder of the weekend was a pleasant one, and before they left, Danny and Beth had promised to spend Christmas with their daughter's family. They hugged and kissed and waved as they drove away, and it was as the car climbed the hill out of the town that Jessie gasped.

'It's for sale! Oh Michael, Hill House is up for sale!'

He pulled in to the bottom of the drive, wide enough to feel like a layby, as he had done on the previous morning. Jessie just gazed at the house she had always loved.

'I don't suppose we could ever afford this, could we?'

Michael thought of the words he'd said to her, just a few years ago: *I could build a house like that. Or buy it. For my wife, if I had one. For a family.* And he remembered the promise he'd made to her father, to his friend: *I'd give her anything, everything she wants. I'd make her happy.*

'We might, sweetheart. We might.'

1956/1957

It was the news on the radio in July that decided Michael. President Nasser of Egypt had taken over the running of the Suez Canal, and supplies of fuel from the Middle East had been blocked. Petrol would be in short supply, and the rumours of rationing were growing by the day. He knew that if this happened, it would affect his business dramatically, not only because of the petrol-hungry machines he relied on, but because of the anxiety, alarm and fear of an unknown future that would be triggered in his customers and clients. Work would slow down, he knew. Would it dry up? He couldn't risk it. He phoned Steffan.

By November they had moved back to Wales, and Michael knew he'd made the right decision. It was confirmed that petrol would be rationed. Many people had thought that the Suez crisis, as it was known, would fizzle out by the end of the summer, but no. The rationing period was expected to last for four months, from December to April the following year, and would be controlled through books of coupons. Businesses would be allowed an extra hundred miles a month in petrol, over and above what was issued to normal car users. Not generous enough to have saved Michael's business. Farmers, vicars, and essential local authority workers will be allowed more, and Michael had no doubt that Steffan would manage to get himself classified as one of the latter. Doctors, and a few others would be allowed whatever petrol they needed, and all petrol stations were already being asked to restrict sales between now and the start of rationing.

He, Jessie and Anya moved in with her parents in Highland Place, and though crowded, the family were happy to be together. Michael was going along with Steffan's plan and the contracts were coming in, albeit small ones. He had a team of men working for him, courtesy of Steff of course, and true to the council chair's word, supplies had been provided at a reduced price. But his profits were reduced too. His bids had been lowered to such an extent that he was barely breaking even, but Steff assured him that the big contracts would be coming soon. He also reminded Michael that he could help him with buying a house. When Michael confided to him that Jessie wanted to buy Hill House, which was still on the market, Steffan wasn't fazed.

'Leave it to me' he said confidently.

And sure enough, he delivered. He bargained with the seller and got the price down quite substantially; he put Michael on the payroll of a builder friend – temporarily, he promised - and provided him with documentation which showed that his income was considerably higher, and considerably more regular, than was the truth. And Michael was so eager to give Jessie the house of her dreams, he went along with it. He stifled his qualms, he smothered the fears and anxieties that rose in the night, waking him, threatening to overwhelm him. He got the mortgage he needed. He knew it would cost far more than he could really afford just yet, but surely that contract for the new council estate would materialise soon? He pushed all his reservations, all his worries, to the back of his mind, focusing instead on the delight he would see on Jessie's face.

It was the birthday present he had wanted to give her. He took her by the hand as he helped her from the car, eyes tightly closed as he had instructed.

'Where are we Michael? I want to see …'

For a moment he stood. Just stood, looking at her. She was twenty two years old, still so young but with the glow, the maturity, that motherhood had given her, and more beautiful than ever. He loved her more than he would ever have thought possible. He would do anything to make her happy. Had he sold his soul to the devil? Maybe. He hoped not, but maybe. Would he do it again? Time would tell.

'You can open your eyes now' he said.

She did. She looked up, at the big wooden gates, at the wide gravel drive snaking its way up the little hill, at the budding daffodils nodding on either side, and at the house. That huge, white-painted, gabled red-roofed house. Then he handed her a bunch of keys.

'Happy birthday my darling.'

CHAPTER 24

FACING TRUTHS

1957: May

Jessie was in her element. Making lunch for her parents in their new home, her husband at her side, their daughter toddling happily through the beautiful rooms, across the elegant hallway, into the drawing room, her grandmother following close behind. Her newly-acquired housekeeper was quietly sorting out the china and cutlery. Danny looked over Michael's shoulder at the carrots he was trying manfully to slice.

'C'mon Meic bach, when are you going to show me this games room you've been talking about?'

Michael was happy to oblige, and Jessie happy to release him from the vegetable preparation to which was so unaccustomed.

'Yes, take him away Dad' she said, laughing. 'He's more trouble than he's worth in the kitchen!'

Although his father-in-law made all the right noises and comments about the dark wood, the leather, the green baize pool table, it became clear to Michael that it wasn't the games room that he was interested in. They sat together on the brown chesterfield.

'So what's the trouble, Meic bach?'

Michael stared ahead.

'Don't know what you mean, Dan.'

'Come off it, boy. I've known you for too long. Ok, with a twenty year gap, but I think I know you as well

380

as anyone does. And I know when there's something wrong. You look terrible for a start. What's going on, Meic?'

Michael didn't tell him everything. He couldn't. But he told him about the long wait for the big contract, and the fact that he was struggling to keep up the mortgage payments.

'Mind you' he said, perhaps defensively, 'Steffan's been great. I wouldn't have got the jobs I've had, or this house, without him. He ...'

'Steffan?' interrupted Danny. 'Not Steffan Evans?'

'Yes that's right. You know him, don't you? He's the Chairman of the Council, and ...'

'Oh yes I know him!' Danny's voice was bitter. 'Only too well. He's not to be trusted, Meic, never was. Even as a boy he was a slippery customer, getting others to do his dirty work for him, taking all the credit and none of the blame. He's shifty, Meic. Dodgy. Don't have anything to do with him!'

Michael looked astonished.

'But he's got me contracts, Dan. He's got me supplies at cost price. He's even got me the men I needed.'

Danny laughed but there was no humour in the sound.

'I bet he did. Don't tell me – they were council contracts, yes? Contracts he couldn't have got himself if he'd applied in his firm's name? A little matter of conflict of interest perhaps?'

'I don't understand, Dan.'

Danny looked at Michael earnestly.

381

'You don't know? You really don't know? Steffan Evans is the Evans of Evans & McAndrew. The same Evans & McAndrew that wanted to buy out my old boss. The ones you helped to outbid. And there is no McAndrew. That was added to make the name stand out. Jesus, Meic, he's not a character to mess with.' Danny ran his hand through his thinning hair.

Michael was trying to take it all in.

'But he's not a builder, Dan! He went to university! He's a councillor! He's ...'

'You don't have to carry a hod or mix cement to own a building firm Meic. He owns it. Gets others to do the work. Skims off the profits.'

'So you're saying – I was getting those jobs for him? That he was pulling all the strings? Is that why ...' Michael stopped.

Danny looked up. Sharply.

'Is that why what? What else has he done, Meic?'

Michael put his head in his hands. Then he told his friend about undercutting the tenders, rigging the bids. Danny looked shocked.

'He put me on the payroll of a "builder friend", he said. To help me get the mortgage for this place. It was temporary. But now – I'm not sure, I never checked, I was so wrapped up in the house and Jessie, and ... ' He looked up.

'I think I'm working for him, Dan. I think he's taken away my business, and I've let him. I was so impressed by his position, so keen to move back down here, to get Jessie this house ... Oh God, I've been so stupid.' and he dropped his head once more.

'Don't tell Jessie any of this, please Danny. Not till I sort it out. And I will, I promise you. Steffan's away just now, but as soon as he's back, I'll have it out with him. I promise. Just don't tell Jessie. She thinks the business is doing well. I didn't have the heart to tell her any different. Let her enjoy this while she can – I have a feeling we'll lose it all.'

'Ok. I won't. Just don't let him threaten you, Meic. Don't let him try to blackmail you. Remember, he has more to lose than you have. His business, his seat on the council, his status …he has to make this right. He must. Oh, and a word of advice – write all this down. Somewhere. Anywhere. Don't let it be just me that knows about this. Write it down. Keep a diary – and keep it safe. I may not always be around.'

Danny's words rang in Michael's ears as he stood, upright, white faced, at his graveside just three weeks later. Michael held Jessie, who stood rigid, dry-eyed, all cried out, at his side. Both of her parents. Gone in a matter of a fortnight, two of the early victims of the deadly Asian 'flu.

Since April, it had been known that the epidemic was affecting thousands of people in Hong Kong, then India. As an entirely new strain there was no immunity in the population and no vaccines were available abroad or in Britain, where the first cases were now being reported. Even the medical profession was amazed at the extraordinary rate of infection of the disease, and the suddenness of its onset. Jessie and her family had little warning that her parents were unwell, and no inkling of what was to come.

She was thankful that she had little Annie, who was too young to understand the huge blow that her mother had been dealt, and who needed her as much as ever. But at night, when their daughter was sleeping, she would alternately cry and rage at Michael, railing at life's injustice, bitterly regretting the years she had wasted, blaming her parents for something they had not done. Having no-one to blame now, she blamed herself. Even as she saw other families suffering the same fate over the coming weeks, her feeling of unfairness, of unfinished business, remained.

Michael was determined to do as he had promised Danny. He would confront Steffan, no matter what the consequences. He would have to tell Jessie about their finances, and prepare her for what could be a big change in their circumstances, but now was not the time. How could he burden her with his mistakes when she was grieving like this? And anyway, he thought to himself, maybe Steffan would put it all right. Deep down he knew he was deluding himself, but he tried to keep a flicker of hope gong in these dark times. Meanwhile he took Danny's advice, and started to keep a diary. More of a journal really. He wrote down all of the details of every bid, every contract and every transaction. He found that putting Steffan's scheme in writing helped him to see the pattern, see how the scam had been working. It was so clear now.

He carried on as before, waiting to hear back from Steffan, phoning him every day. Then one day in early August, he at last heard a voice on the other end of the phone.

'Meet up? Sure, any time Meic. I'm free at the end of next week – any good?'

'Yes that's ok. Listen Steff, I need to talk to you about our arrangement. I'm not happy with it. There doesn't seem to be any sign of that big development you promised me …'

'Any day, Meic, any day …'

'It's not going to happen though, is it? Why didn't you tell me about your building firm? About Evans & McAndrew? You've taken me for a sucker, haven't you? And I'm not having it any more.'

'Now now Meic, no need to get upset. We'll sort all this out. And I've got some good news about that big contract, the new estate – it's ready to go. So no need to panic. How about we meet up next week? Friday? At the site office in Port Haven – say nine sharp?

As Michael put the phone down, he wondered if he had said too much. He hadn't meant to. He had intended to confront Steffan face to face, but his anger at the way he had been treated, and the consequences of his own stupid actions, had got the better of him. He made a note of the conversation and hid his diary in its usual place. And for some reason, he took an extra precaution.

He withdrew all but twenty pounds from his bank account, hiding that too. You never know, he said to himself.

CHAPTER 25

END OF THE LINE

1957: August

'Do you want a lift into town, Peggy? Or is it too early for you?'

Michael finished putting papers onto the kitchen table, emptying his brief case. He sipped his coffee and looked enquiringly, and somewhat cautiously, at the housekeeper. He never knew what mood she would be in.

'Oh, yes please Mr Hughes. I want to help Jess with the jumble later, so I'll be able to get a bus back earlier than I thought I could.'

'That's fine then. And Peggy, remember, it's Michael, ok?' He left the room, papers in one hand, a distracted frown on his face.

Thirty minutes later he returned to the kitchen, Anya toddling after him. He swept her up and hugged her.

'Look after your mummy, Annie-May' and he put her down again, watching as she ran off to play.

'I'm off, Jess. Have fun, take care, enjoy your dollshouse.' He kissed her on the cheek, then pulled her close. 'I love you sweetheart, you know that don't you? And remember - things aren't always what they seem.'

She kissed him.

'What's that supposed to mean, Michael?' she laughed.

'See you later' he smiled. 'Peggy, you ready?' and he was gone.

The journey to the centre of the little town was quite a short one, so making conversation with Peggy was not going to be as difficult as it could sometimes be. However, she was in a chatty mood today.

'I'm not going to be long today, mind. Just some paperwork in the bank to sort out. They won't be open yet, but I can pop in to see my mother first, instead of coming back this afternoon. My mother ... my mother's in a home, see. The Cliff Tops home. Has been for years. She doesn't know what's going on most of the time. She took a shine to you though, Mr Hughes! I mean – Michael.' She seemed uncomfortable, using his first name, as she always did.

'She saw a picture of you in the Weekly Record' she went on 'when you and Jess moved back here – that big piece, remember? About how you'd bought the old house? She kept jabbing at your picture, pointing, getting quite agitated she was. She's kept it in her room ever since, bless her. Got one of the helpers to put it in a little frame. Anyway, they need me to sign some stuff. And because it's the bank, it's got to be in my full name, my real name.'

Michael nodded, hardly listening, just relieved that she seemed happy to share her thoughts and plans without needing a reply. She took a sheet of paper out of her bag, and smoothed it out.

'...So I'm Margaret Daniels today, just ...'

Her head went forward, only just missing the windscreen, as Michael slammed on the brakes.

'What? What did you say?'

She looked taken aback, and not a little annoyed at the car's sudden halt and his direct questioning.

'I said I'm Margaret Daniels today ... why?'

'Margaret Daniels? But your name is Peggy. Peggy Morris!'

'Peggy – short for Margaret, Mr Hughes!' she said, speaking to him slowly as if talking to a backward child.

'But Daniels? Daniels?' Michael made a conscious effort to speak calmly as he re-started the car.

'Oh, yes, that's my real name. Morris is just the name my mother used. Pretended she was married, see. When I was born. My father died before they could get married, so she said anyway. She moved away to have me, and when she came back, she said they'd been married. To stop the gossips, you know. Not sure if his name was Morris, mind. Might have been just made up. You can drop me here.'

'What?'

'You can drop me here, please. I can cut through to Cliff Tops.'

'Peggy ... Peggy, I need to talk to you.'

'Yes, ok Mr Hughes. I can stay on a bit this evening if you like. But I have to go now.' She opened the door and lowered herself out of the car.

'Thanks for the lift.'

He was in a stupor as he drove to the builders' yard. Surely it couldn't be. His daughter? Seeing her every day these past months and not knowing? He thought about the

389

letter he had read, just a few years ago. *I've had a baby girl. I call her Margaret, after me.* He thought about the words Peggy had spoken. *She kept jabbing at your picture ... Got one of the helpers to put it in a little frame.* Oh God. He had to put this right.

He skidded his car to a halt outside the glorified shed that acted as his site office, then saw that someone was waiting for him. This was not a face he knew.

'Mr Hughes? I'm Neville. I've just started with the council, working for Councillor Evans. There's something I think you should see.'

Not now, Michael thought. Not now.

Neville was clutching a large buff envelope. He glanced around, looking nervous.

'You need to see this, Mr Hughes. But you didn't get it from me, ok?'

Michael's natural civility took over.

'Thanks Neville. What is it?'

'Just take a look Mr Hughes. He told me to dispose of it, incinerate it. But I think it's important.'

Michael looked at the envelope. Despite the whirl his mind was in, he was curious.

'Why would he ask you to do that, Neville? If it's important? Does he trust you that much?'

Neville snorted.

'Trust me? He doesn't know I exist! I'm just a lacky who turns up to do what I'm told. I don't think he even knows my name. I don't suppose it occurred to him that I might keep it, might read it, might give it to you ...'

He handed it over.

390

'Please Mr Hughes, please don't say where you got it. He's not a nice man, Mr Hughes. Not nice at all.'

Head down, the young man walked quickly out of sight.

Sitting alone at his desk, his mind was reeling. He'd found his daughter! Was it possible? What were the chances? But – this was Margaret's home town. Not so unlikely that she would bring up her daughter – their daughter – in the place she knew best. And a fake husband, a fake father – all believable. So she had raised her. No adoption. No wonder he hadn't been able to trace her through the agencies. How she must have struggled! She had loved him, and he had abandoned her. Not given her a second thought. He could never make this right. But he was going to try.

He glanced down at the envelope still in his hand. He opened it. It was the report they had been waiting for. The report on the land designated for the new council estate. Clearly, it had been read – dog-eared pages, thumb prints.

Words jumped out at him. *Contaminated land .... contains substances in and under the land that are hazardous to health ... oils and tars, chemical substances, preparations and solvents ... heavy metals ... a long history of industrial production ...*

'Jesus Christ' he whispered under his breath.

He folded the document and put it into his case. Then he picked up the phone.

'Steffan? I need to see you today. Now.'

'Well Meic, that's not possible I'm afraid. We've arranged a meeting for Friday, haven't we? I ...'

'I've seen the report, Steff' he said quietly.

Silence on the other end of the phone. Then,

'I'll call you back. Are you at the office?'

Michael waited. Ten minutes, twenty. He was about to call again when the shrill ringing made him jump.

'Ok, I can meet you at twelve.' No laughter now. Steffan's voice was low.

'I have to be somewhere first, so I'll meet you on my way back. On the coast road, behind the old roadside café. You know it?'

Michael scribbled the details on the nearest thing he could find. A piece of blotting paper.

'I know it.'

Michael picked up his case, locked the door behind him, walked to his car and drove away. He'd left the note of his destination on his desk, but he knew where he was going. He would be early. He would wait. He was not going to be part of this.

CHAPTER 26

JESSIE'S STORY REVISITED

1957: August

Sorting through the bags of clothes had become monotonous work, even with the small-talk.

'Part of being Lady of the Manor, eh?' Peggy's tone was light, but today Jessie resented it nonetheless. She was very aware of how she was perceived in this little seaside town, despite its being her childhood home. She smiled.

'It's nice to be able to give something back, you know?

'Yes' said Peggy, arms outstretched in the process of folding a vast jumper. 'It's great that so many people have given us their cast-offs for the Jumble. I'm sure that all the poor people will love them.'

This time there was no mistaking Peggy's tone.

When the doorbell rang it was a welcome distraction for Jessie. Peggy opened the door to two police officers, a man and a woman.

'Mrs Hughes?'

'No, I'm Peggy Morris, the housekeeper. I'll fetch Mrs Hughes.'

She turned, started towards the drawing room and saw her young employer walking across the hall.

'Jessie, it's …' she began.

'It's ok Peggy, I heard.' Jessie turned to their two visitors. 'How can I help you?'

'Mrs Hughes? Mrs Jessie Hughes? Sergeant John Dodds, Constable Pam Groves.'

Their ID badges were flashed briefly.

'May we come in?'

'You'll have to excuse the mess – we're sorting some donations for tomorrow's charity sale.'

Jessie led the officers into the spacious drawing room, where several boxes stood, carefully stacked. A neat pile of folded clothes lay on a large polished table, and the sunlight streamed through the two tall casement windows. A magnificent dollshouse stood on an impressive stand in a corner, and a toddler was playing, very gently, with its contents. Jessie noticed their glances around the room, and became aware that this was not the sort of "mess" they may be used to. She sat on one large sofa and motioned them to another.

'How can I help you?' she repeated.

'Do you want me to stay, Jess?' asked Peggy.

'Yes please Peggy - can you keep an eye on Anya for me? She's due for her nap soon.'

'Mrs Hughes' Constable Groves began. She cleared her throat. 'I'm afraid we have some bad news about your husband, Michael Hughes.'

She hesitated. Then,

'I'm sorry to tell you that he's been found dead in his car'.

Jessie was silent for what seemed a long time. Doris Day was singing *Que Sera, Sera ... Whatever will be, will be* on the radio.

'What?'

'I'm afraid ...'

'Dead? Michael? Dead?'

'I'm sorry, yes.'

Then,

'Would you like a glass of water?'

Did she look as numb as she felt?

'Dead?'

The officer looked at Peggy, standing near the door, now covering her mouth with both hands, horrified.

'Could you fetch Mrs Hughes some water, please, Mrs …?

'It's Miss. Morris. Peggy Morris' she whispered.

'Yes of course.'

Jessie heard her daughter, oblivious to the earthquake around her, offering tiny pieces of china to the mannequins seated in the dollshouse.

'Cuppa tea?' she was saying.

'Do you feel up to answering some questions Mrs Hughes? Or can I call you Jessie?'

Jessie nodded.

'When did you last see your husband, Jessie?

' … um … this morning, early. About eight.'

'Did he say where he was going?'

'No, not really. He was going to the office I expect, or to one of the building sites. He was dropping Peggy off first.' Her voice was quiet, almost a whisper.

'And did he do or say anything unusual?'

The door opened again, and the officer waited while Peggy handed over the glass of water with shaking hands.

395

'Um - he said his usual goodbye stuff – have fun, take care, enjoy your dollshouse … love you …' Jessie swallowed. She took a sip of water.

'Enjoy your dollshouse?'

'Yes. Family joke. He called this…' she waved an arm around the room '… my dollshouse.'

"Ah, I see.'

'I'm afraid I must ask you to come with us to identify your husband's body, Mrs Hughes.' Now it was the sergeant – Dodds? Did he say Dodds? - who spoke, reverting to the more formal mode of address.

She nodded.

'Is there anyone we can call for you? Your parents? A friend?'

She shook her head.

'My parents died. A few weeks ago. There's no-one else.'

'I'm sorry, Mrs Hughes.'

Then,

'He said *things aren't always what they seem*'.

Sergeant Dodds stopped writing in his notebook and looked up sharply.

'He said that? This morning? What did he mean?'

Jessie shook her head.

'I have no idea' she whispered.

In a quiet but steady voice, she asked Peggy to finish folding the clothes.

'And can you look after Anya for me please?'

As Jessie was leaving the room, Little Annie-May ran to her, holding out a scrap of paper.

'There y'go Mummy!' she said, beaming.

Jessie bent to kiss her, hug her, willing herself not to fall apart.

'See you later Sweetheart' she said, putting the fragment in her pocket. 'Be good for Auntie Peggy.'

She allowed herself to be escorted to the black police car waiting at the top of the long drive. She had never been inside a police car. She stared ahead. The journey wasn't a long one – to the nearby market town of Trefni Bridge – but it seemed endless.

'Where was he when he died?'

'His car was parked on the coast road. By what used to be the roadside café.'

'And how did he die? Was it a heart attack?'

The constable paused.

'We're waiting for the post mortem. Everything will be clearer then.'

This was not something she'd been prepared for. Michael always prepared her for everything, protected her, warned her. As if she were a child. And she knew that in some ways she would always be a child to him – a child he'd fallen in love with. He had worshipped her, put her on a pedestal and made sure she never toppled. She smiled to herself, thinking of him – then remembered where she was, where they were going, and why.

Jessie didn't know what she had been expecting. She followed the police officers into the hospital. Into a part of the hospital she'd never visited before. A number of people spoke to her – were they doctors? Police? All very kind, very gentle.

'You can look through this window if you prefer' someone said 'or you can go into the room. You don't have to say anything, apart from confirming that the body is that of your husband. You can say "yes" or simply nod your head. Are you sure you wouldn't like someone with you, Mrs Hughes? A family member? Mother? Father?'

She shook her head.

'I'll go in.'

Jessie looked down at her husband. She felt strangely distant, removed. This wasn't really happening. This couldn't really be her Michael. She'd kissed him this morning. Said goodbye, went about her day. And now this. No, this wasn't happening.

'Why is he so pink?'

'Can you confirm that this is the body of your husband, Michael Hughes?'

She swallowed. Hard.

'Yes.'

Then

'Why is he so pink?'

'If you follow me to my office Mrs Hughes, we can talk there.'

She walked after him, stiffly, conscious of putting one foot after the other. His office was dark, full of laden bookshelves and filing cabinets, the one small window did little to relieve the gloomy feel. She sat on the hard wooden chair in front of his desk. Who was he?

'I'm Ben Turner, from the Coroner's Office, Mrs Hughes.'

As if he'd heard her. Had she said it aloud?

'I will try to answer any questions you have.'

They were joined by the two police officers that had come to her house this morning. This morning, she thought? Really? Only a couple of hours ago? How can so much happen in one morning?

'Why is he so pink?' she asked again.

Ben Turner took a deep breath.

'We'll need to wait for the result of a post-mortem before we can be certain about the cause of death, Mrs Hughes. A death has to be reported to the Coroner if it's believed that the cause was sudden, violent or unnatural such as an accident, or suicide. To answer your question - Michael was found alone in his car in circumstances that would indicate he died of carbon monoxide poisoning. Which would account for the pink colouring you saw. The Coroner will ask the police to gather the information about his death. I'm so sorry Mrs Hughes.'

Jessie sat, hands folded in her lap. She tried to take in what he was saying, but her mind was numb, foggy, full of cotton wool. This was harder to grasp than being told he was dead. Eventually she spoke.

'He committed suicide. Is that what you're saying?'

'As I said Mrs Hughes, we will need to wait for a post-mortem before we can be certain ...'

"No. No. He wouldn't do that. He couldn't. He wouldn't choose to leave us. He wouldn't ...'

She bent her head, but not before she saw the glances between Ben Turner and the police officers. Even in her state of utter disbelief, of shock, of horror, she knew what they meant. She guessed that all the wives said what she had said. They all thought their husbands loved them too much to do this terrible thing. The fog cleared.

399

'My husband didn't kill himself. And your post mortem will prove it.'

'Mrs Hughes.'

A new voice. She looked up.

'Mrs Hughes, I'm Inspector Daly. Would you like to come with me? The station is just across the road – don't be alarmed. There are a few questions I'd like to ask you – and you may have some for me.'

Another name. Too many names. She'd never remember them all. She rose dutifully and followed him from the room, out of the building and across the quiet back road, in as dignified a manner as she could muster. She sat in his office, accompanied by the three police officers. Comfortable chairs this time – sofas. A bigger window, plants on the sill, fewer books.

Rob Daly looked across at her, not unsympathetically. Pretty woman, he noted mentally, storing away his observations for another day. She wasn't looking her best, naturally – no tears yet, but her eyes were reddening and her strawberry-blonde hair looked dishevelled. Quite a bit younger than her husband, he guessed. An affair? Maybe. Jealousy? Too hard to live with? Or corruption? Bribery? Time would tell.

'Mrs Hughes, can you tell us something about your husband? About Michael?'

She nodded.

'OK. When did you see him last?'

'This morning. When he left for the office. About eight.'

'Did he have any money worries? Work worries?

'No. He had a big contract coming up. It was a lot of work; he was a bit distracted, waiting to hear whether he'd got the job.'

'And what job was that, Mrs Hughes?'

'A big contract with the council. Building the new development over on Melin Fach. He's waiting to hear if he's got the contract. But he has other jobs on – smaller ones. He's a building contractor you see, my husband' she said proudly, lifting her head.

'I mean – he was …' Her head dropped again.

'And did he have any problems with colleagues that you know of? Or with neighbours? Friends?'

She shook her head, not raising it.

After a pause, Inspector Daly stood up.

'That's all for now, Mrs Hughes. Thank you for being so helpful. We may need to be in touch again. Is there a relative or friend we can contact for you?'

Jessie realized she had no relatives. Not any more. No friends. Not here, not in her home town. She shook her head again.

She left the office and the building, sat in the waiting car, was barely aware of the drive back home. Home? Not now, she thought. Not ever again.

The next few days, weeks, were a whirl of activity and nothingness. Jessie found herself doing only the things she had to. At two years old, Anya wasn't yet aware of any change in her routine. Michael had often worked long hours and sometimes went for days without seeing his little daughter. His precious Annie-May.

Jessie knew she needed to organize a funeral, contact Michael's staff, the council, insurance companies, the bank ... but she couldn't bring herself to do any of these. She would have to say the words "Michael's dead". And that would make it real.

Peggy stepped up and helped. She changed from being the often critical, wordlessly disapproving and sometimes downright sarcastic creature she had been since she had started working for the couple. Michael had sometimes wondered why his wife had given her the position, but had accepted her decision without question. She didn't know why, but Anya had felt an attachment to this woman, despite the permanent frown and the brusque tone. She trusted her. And now Peggy took over the arrangements for her widowed employer, making phone calls and answering them, contacting the funeral director, protecting Jessie from curious journalists. She came into her own.

Then on day three, the nothingness stopped, to be replaced by a series of small explosions. Explosion one - the police had carried out their routine checks and found that Michael had made a large withdrawal of cash a few days before his death, and had virtually no money in his account. Explosion two - he was suspected of bribing council officers. Or colluding with them. Fraud of some sort, anyway.

And so it went on. He had taken out a much larger mortgage on their house than she knew about. The news that the insurance company wouldn't pay out if the cause of death were confirmed as suicide.

The post mortem concluded that Michael had died from carbon monoxide poisoning. Ben Turner called to see her when the result was known.

'There will be an inquest, Mrs Hughes. But given the result of the post mortem, there is little doubt that the cause of death will be that of suicide.'

And he was proved right. Even though there was no suicide note. But there had been the pipe leading from the exhaust. She'd seen it in the films, there was always a pipe. So had he planned this? Taken that pipe with him? Had he known, when he kissed her goodbye, when he laughed and waived to little Annie-May, had he known they would never see him again? She would never believe it.

Inspector Daly called to see her. Sitting on her sofa now, on her turf.

'I understand you have some questions for me, Mrs Hughes' he said.

'Yes. Thank you for coming. The pipe, Inspector. How did he get it? Where did he get it? He must have planned this then. Must have known. And yet...'

Her voice died away.

He nodded, and smiled sadly.

'I know. It's hard to accept. We believe – and more importantly, the Coroner believed – that Michael had taken a pipe with him, with the intention of killing himself. It wouldn't have been hard for him to get hold of such a thing. He was seen leaving his office in the builders' yard that morning. He could easily have picked one up from the site. That, and his precarious financial status, the possibility of corrupt practices in gaining contracts with the council, all these things add up to only one conclusion. Michael committed suicide. So we won't be investigating his death as suspicious. I'm so sorry.'

Where was she to go? Jessie was determined to leave her home before the building society forced her to. She had nothing left but her pride. And her daughter. But panic was starting to replace the numbness she had felt since Michael's death. Since the death of her parents in fact.

Peggy knew a woman in the town who ran a Bed and Breakfast business, and let a couple of rooms. Single rooms, each with a bed and a table-top stove. She was also looking for casual staff to do some cleaning, some laundry, some cooking. So Jessie swallowed her pride, moved in, and helped out in the B&B in lieu of rent. Six months on, and she saw a vacancy in a private children's nursery. She applied, and got the job, first making sure she could take Anya with her. Some of her numbness was starting to wear off, being replaced by an increased fear for the future, and anger towards her late husband. But she was grieving still. It was Peggy who helped her apply for a council house, got her on the waiting list, pestered the officers until at last she was given a house. Three bedrooms. And a garden.

This was her life now, she told herself. Her daughter, a home, a job. Michael was a photograph on the sideboard and a visitor in her dreams. She willed herself to be happy.

CHAPTER 27

A VOICE FROM THE PAST

1988

It was a long time before Philip had a chance to visit Anya and her mother in Cwmdawel. A whole year since the election. He drove over from his home, not so far away, on a bright Saturday morning, and Anya was proud to welcome him, knowing that her little piece of Wales was looking its best. Despite the evidence of building work at the side of the house, the cement mixer, the piles of bricks, slates and window frames, the house and the garden looked wonderful.

'Welcome to Ty Clyd, Phil. We're not usually such a building site – my mother's having a bungalow built here. Some friends are building it, so they can only work on it in their spare time. Come in. Coffee? Tea?'

She led him inside where she introduced him to her mother.

'I'm not sure how much I can help, Philip' Jessie said as she sat with them. 'I know you said the houses were built in the late 1950s, but I wasn't really in the know when it came to what was being built where, even though my husband was in the business.'

'Anything you can remember may help, Mrs Hughes. More and more of my constituents are coming to me now, more and more illnesses, and yet the authorities don't seem to take it seriously. It's coincidence, apparently. No link to where the houses were built.'

'So where is this estate?'

'Melin Fach. North of the town.'

Jessie's face drained of colour. She seemed to sag in her seat.

'Melin Fach?' Her voice was quiet as she turned to her daughter.

'That's ... that's the contract your Dad was supposed to get, Annie.'

No-one spoke for a minute.

'But he didn't build it?' asked Philip.

'No. He ... he died.'

'I'm sorry, Mrs Hughes. I didn't know.'

'That's ok' Jessie said, sitting upright again. 'How could you? Yes, he was waiting to get the go-ahead on the development, when he ...'

She raised her head.

'When he took his life.'

Silence again.

'Are you ok, Mum? I'm so sorry, I didn't know the connection. I wouldn't have ...'

'It's fine, Annie. It's fine.' She turned back to Philip.

'The work was taken over by another local firm. Evans & McAndrew. They went on to build it.'

'And do you know anything about them, Mrs Hughes?'

'Call me Jessie, please. Only that my father didn't rate them. He was in the building trade too, but on a much smaller scale. Other than that, I'm afraid I don't know.'

'Did your husband ever mention an environmental report? On the land? Maybe it wasn't called that then – it was a long time ago.'

'I know they were waiting for some report or other. That's what was holding up the start of the work, holding up the contract.'

'Things were done very differently back in the fifties, I know. Some changes have happened since then, but even with the new environmental bill coming forward, decisions about where houses can be built will still be in the hands of the local councils. I think it was pretty much the same back then – although they would have had to take account of reports they received on any land they had an application for.'

'I'm sorry I can't be of any more help, Philip.'

'You have been a great help. Thank you, Jessie. And I'm sorry if I've raked up some of the past you'd rather not be reminded of.'

It was as he was leaving that he turned back.

'I don't suppose you remember anything about Trefni Bridge Council at that time, do you? Any names?'

'The only one I remember is the chairman. He went to school with Michael. His name was Steffan Evans.'

The work went on. In the chamber of the House of Commons, in the committee rooms, her office, and often during informal chats with others over lunch, coffee, sometimes dinner. The work continued at weekends, in the community centres up and down the valley, where she met up with Byron, met with her neighbours – now called constituents – in Pontarafon, Cwmdawel, other villages. And the work on Jessie's bungalow went on too.

Each weekend, each recess, Anya could see the little building grow, until at last it was finished. Painted and decorated, furnished, all ready for her mother to move in. It was a time for celebration. Jessie was moving just a matter of yards away, but it marked a subtle change in the family relationships. The girls were getting older and welcomed the privacy, the independence that each having a room of her own would bring. Anya would have a home office at last, free to put up shelves, install filing cabinets, her computer, restoring her lounge from the store-room it had become. And Jessie – well, Jessie would have her own place for the first time in five years. And then there was Geraint. He had helped to build her house. More than helped. He led the way. His friends were wonderful too, and between them they had all the skills needed to make sure this was a proper, safe, sturdy little building. It would be up to her to turn it into a home.

As she packed up her belongings, she stopped, dawdled, over every item, each one holding a memory. Finally, only two things left to move. A box of documents, and her dollshouse. She went through the documents carefully. Birth certificates, Anya's school reports and exam results. Letters. From her father. From Michael. She read them once more, smiling now, not crying as she had once done. Savouring the memories they brought back. Then more documents. From that awful, horrible time of over thirty years ago. The post mortem result. The inquest verdict. Michael's death certificate. A folded piece of blotting paper. A scrap of paper handed to her that morning, given to her by a beaming Anya. *'Here y'go Mummy!'*. She opened it up, smiling, looking at the words, now barely legible. Looking at Michael's handwriting. She'd know it anywhere.

'Check the attic' it said. It must have been a note he had written to himself, a reminder, something Annie had picked up as she toddled around. But later, Jessie had done as the note commanded. Before she moved out of what had been her dream home, she had checked the attic, hoping against hope that she would find something that would make sense of the senseless horror that was her world. Nothing. The attic, like every part of Michael's life, had been ordered, tidy, uncluttered. Nothing to see there. Nothing to find.

Jessie sighed as she carefully returned the crumpled piece of paper to the box. She was ready now. Geraint would be over soon, helping her to take these last two items to her new home. Maybe to *their* new home? Time would tell.

The bungalow was laughingly referred to as 'The Lodge' by the family. Jessie followed Geraint as he carried the heavy box through the hallway and into her new living room. A pretty room, she thought, and smiled. All her favourite bits and pieces were here, the ones she had brought with her from Port Haven, the ones she had added over recent years, the few – the very few – that she had kept from her life in Surrey, and in Hill House. They were all here. Except one.

409

'Right!' announced Geraint. 'Now for your dollshouse. I expect you'll want to supervise that?'

Jessie laughed.

'Too right I will!' she said, and they made their way back to the house.

They carefully lifted her precious possession onto the new table he had made for her, a table with hidden, lockable castors so she could move it wherever she wanted. She stood back, admiring it.

'Thank you' she said quietly.

'It's quite a piece of work, isn't it!' he said as he gently wheeled it from its corner. 'A work of art! All made to scale, beautifully finished too. The way those balustrades are turned, the finish on the spindles ...'

And before she knew it, she was showing him all the beautifully decorated rooms, the furniture, the hidden hiding places, trap doors and secret passages. She hadn't looked inside it properly for all these years. She hadn't been able to face it. The children had played with it of course, moved the dolls around, changed the seating arrangements in the lounge, put different pans on the miniature cooker, just as Anya had liked to do as a toddler, despite being told not to. But she hadn't been able to bring herself to look too closely. The memory of Michael's last words to her – *enjoy your dollshouse* – seemed to mock her then, and had haunted her ever since. But now she found she could open it up, show Geraint with pride the wonderful craftsmanship her husband had demonstrated when he had made her this gift. He had made it as a promise to her, that he would take her back to her home

410

town, and that she would live in a house like this. And he had, and she did. For a while.

Slowly they managed to get it through the doors, and position it just where she wanted it, in its new home. Just where Geraint, thoughtful Geraint, had planned for it to go, when he drew the layout of the rooms. They stood back.

'I'd have thought there'd be an attic, you know' he said. 'A place this size. Seems there must be quite a bit of space under that roof.'

'Mmm, yes, you're right. You'd think …'

She gripped his arm.

'An attic' she whispered. 'Of course there'd be an attic!'

He looked down at her, bemused. She ran to the box of documents he'd brought in earlier, and started to rummage through it, her hands shaking.

'An Attic! *Check the attic*!' and she held up a scrap of paper.

Geraint stared at her.

'Are you ok, love?'

'There is an attic! I know there is! Please Geraint, please find it, find the attic, find out how it opens! Please!'

He asked no more questions, but set to, examining, touching, feeling, and then …

Click

He swung the gable up, up, on its hidden hinge, released now by the pressing of a tiny button, unnoticed in the decoration on a miniature bedroom wall. The rooftop rested, fully open, stopped from falling by

411

cleverly-placed stays, exposing its contents, hidden away safely for a generation. Jessie stared.

Papers. Some neatly bound with ribbon, some with string. Letters. A diary. And on the top, a roll of bank notes, and …

'What's this, Jess?'

Geraint was holding a small rectangular object.

Jessie had gone white.

'We used those in our answering machine' she whispered. 'Our telephone answering machine. They were prototypes – nobody had them in Wales. Michael had a contact …'

She took it in her hands, turning it over and over.

'Can you get Anya's dictaphone?' she said quietly.

She sat down. Waited till he returned. Then, at last, she heard her husband's voice, from so long ago. It made her heart constrict.

'Jessie, sweetheart. I'm leaving this in your dollshouse, in the attic, and I only hope that Annie-May doesn't find my hidden note before you do. I've messed up love, really messed up. I got greedy and stupid. I believed Steffan. He made big promises, Jess, but he's a crook. I know that now. Your Dad warned me, just before he died, and I promised him I would sort this out, and I will. I'm meeting Steffan next week, I'll tell him I'm finished with his schemes. But I don't trust him. Your Dad told me to write everything down too, so I have. It's all here. Just in case anything happens to me. It's a sort of insurance. I've lost nearly all our money. I'm sorry. That'll mean the house too. I'm so sorry, I know how much it means to you.

412

*And I may end up in jail. But I have to do the right thing.
I hope you understand. I've put a bit of cash in here. I love
you Jess. Don't ever doubt that. And our Annie-May of
course. I hope you'll never need to hear this tape, I'll get
rid of it once this is all over, but ...'*

Michael's voice died away as the tape finished,
whirring and spinning to a stop.

They were all laid out before them. Well, almost all. The
papers, the letters, the diary, the tape. She had asked Anya
to bring Philip with her, and Byron. She needed them to
see what she had discovered, each with their own interest,
each able to provide an insight, an answer. She hoped.

Anya was the first to arrive. Home earlier than
usual on a Friday. She hugged her mother.

'You ok?' she asked, looking at Jessie anxiously.

'Yes, I'm ok. A bit shaken, if I'm honest.'

'I'm not surprised. Look, I hope you don't mind,
but I've asked Esther to come too. I though a bit of legal
advice ...'

'Esther! How lovely! Is she with you?'

'No, she'll be here soon.'

They heard a car coming up the lane, slowing
down at the gate which Anya had left open, and Jessie
squinted to see who the first visitor was. Byron jumped
out, smiled at Jessie, and planted a gentle kiss on Anya's
cheek. His car was followed, over the next half hour, by
Philip's and Esther's. Warm greetings over, they walked
into Ty Clyd.

The table was strewn with the memories of so long ago. Jessie took the lead. No preamble now. She had prepared for this over the days since her first sight of them, the days she had sat and stared, racked her brains for signs she may have missed, summarised the information she had seen written there. She wouldn't let their minds stray, wouldn't let herself meander into nostalgia. She wouldn't let the flood of emotions she had felt, both remembered and new, get in the way now. She wouldn't let them miss a thing. She would just give them the facts.

'Michael – my husband – left a diary. A journal. It's been hidden till now. It tells, in great detail, about a fraud he was involved in, a way of securing council contracts. It had been set up by the council chairman, Steffan Evans. Michael clearly had no idea how serious a racket it was until shortly before he died. He had arranged to meet with Evans, to confront him, the week he – the week he was found dead.'

She paused, took a breath.

'He had found that Evans owned a building firm. The same building firm that built the housing estate you were asking about, Philip. Evans and McAndrew. He was putting tenders, planning applications, everything, through the council without declaring he would profit by it. He was using Michael. The report they were waiting for – it was about the condition of the land. But it hadn't arrived.'

She stopped. No-one spoke.

'I don't know if Michael met Evans. And if he did, I don't know what he said, or did. All I know is that the last entry in his diary was on the day he died, and that he'd arranged to meet him two days later.'

When the others started speaking it was like an avalanche, a rush of questions, of suggestions, of theories. Jessie let out a sigh of relief. They had heard her. They believed her. Why wouldn't they? She didn't know, but it was important to her that they did. She understood why Philip and his constituents needed to know, but she wasn't sure why it should be so important to her that this truth should come out. Even though it showed that Michael had, in fact, been involved in the corruption that was hinted at all those years ago. But maybe – just maybe – some other truths may come out of this. And would explain his parting words – *things aren't always what they seem.*

They all scoured the documents on the table, and by the time Philip left - having drunk tea, eaten cake - he had Michaels' diary in his possession. He promised Jessie he would take great care of it, and that he would find out what had happened to Steffan Evans.

Esther raised the question of evidence. All they had at the moment was one man's writings, a man who was a self-confessed fraudster. Jessie winced at that.

'I'm sorry Jessie. I have to say it, because that's what he'll be called if we can't find any corroborative evidence. I'll make it my business to try to find someone else who was at the council at the time, someone who may have seen something, who may know something. I'll be honest though, it's a long shot.'

Esther, too, left soon after, as did Byron. Anya and her mother waved them off as they drove down the lane, then turned back to the house.

'Are you ok, Mum?'

'Yes, I'm ok. But there's something else I need to show you. Just you.'

Jessie's table this time. In Jessie's little home. More papers, more letters.

'Before I show you these, Annie, I need you to know that your dad had a daughter before I met him. Long before. And he hadn't known – not until just before we were married. He told me a little while later. He tried to trace her, but never managed it.'

Anya stared at her mother.

'A daughter? Dad had a daughter? I mean – another daughter? I have a sister?'

It took several minutes for this to sink in. Then Jessie spoke.

'Now, I want you to look at these letters.'

She handed Anya the three letters, written by that abandoned young girl so long ago, telling the boy she loved that she was pregnant, that she needed his help, that she – that they – had a daughter.

'Oh Mum, that's so sad! Did he ever …'

'Look at the envelopes, Anya. Look at the address.'

Anya read it aloud.

'Mr Michael Hughes, Maes Ty Clyd, Cwmdawel.'

She looked up.

'What? Maes Ty Clyd? Here? He lived here?'

Her mother nodded.

'I've checked out the deeds, Annie. The house – this house, the land – was transferred to Thomas Bowen Hughes in 1913. It seems it was a gift on his marriage, from his bride's parents. This was where your Dad grew up, Annie. We came home.'

The news that they had made their home in what had been his was incredible, wonderful, and powerfully emotional. That they had stumbled across this house, hidden away on a hillside miles from anywhere; that they should have fallen in love with it, worked on it, made it their own, was somehow mystical. It was some time before they could settle to continue their conversation.

'I love this place more than ever now Mum!' Annie said.

But Jessie wasn't finished.

'More to come, sweetheart. Look at the name. The name at the bottom of the last letter.'

'Margaret Daniels' read Anya, looking puzzled.

'And the words above ...'

'I call her Margaret, after me. My mam says I must have her adopted.'

'So?'

'But she didn't have her adopted. Anya, I knew that name. I'd never seen these letters till the other day, but I knew that name. Margaret Daniels. When you employ someone, there's paperwork to be done, isn't there? Even thirty years ago. Even when you're only employing a housekeeper. And you need their full name,

417

the name on their birth certificate. Not a shortened name, or a changed name. Margaret Daniels. Not Peggy Morris …'

Anya gasped.

'Your Auntie Peggy isn't your Auntie at all, Anya. She's your sister.'

CHAPTER 28

PIECING THE JIGSAW

1989

Anya awaited their visit to Peggy's with mixed emotions, but not, she guessed, as mixed as her mother's. It had been quite a while since she had visited her home town, and she looked forward to seeing her childhood haunts and familiar landmarks. But this was no ordinary visit. This was to tell an old family friend that she was in fact the older sister to the little girl she had taken care of; that her own mother had died never knowing that the father she'd never seen had been oblivious to her very existence. What sort of conversation would that be?

Jessie was quiet during the drive, but the girls made up for her lack of chat. They still saw David each Saturday as they had for so long, and this was a good time to combine their weekly visit with the unenviable task of breaking the news to Peggy. They were dropped off at their father's new flat, a distinct improvement on the previous one, and stood with him as they waved goodbye for the few hours they would spend there.

Peggy welcomed them into her bungalow. She had lived there since she was a small child, a council property her mother had managed to procure by dint of sitting doggedly outside the council offices day after day, her pregnancy becoming more and more apparent, until they gave in, and handed her a key. Anya sat now, feeling anxious, willing the next half hour to be over. Jessie appeared calm, but her fingers fidgeted.

'Well, you're out in force today! I don't often see you here Anya – a busy lady like you!'

As always, Jessie wasn't sure if her friend were mocking her. If she was, she ignored it, as always.

'Peg, I've come across some papers. Some quite important papers.' She swallowed. 'Papers that concern you.'

'Have I come into some money, Jess? Come into a fortune?' Peggy laughed.

Jess laughed too, though a tad nervously.

'It's like this, Peg.'

She stumbled through her rehearsed speech, too fast at times, mixing up time frames, prompted by her daughter to get back on track. She stopped at last, panting. She had run a race. She clasped and unclasped her hands, waiting for Peggy to speak. She waited. Peggy was staring down at the letters in her hands, letters written by her mother, before her birth, after her birth.

'I wasn't adopted then?' she said at last, still quiet, still looking down. 'Because it says here ...'

'No, no, you weren't' Jessie said quickly.

They sat for a long time then, saying no more.

Peggy looked up.

'It makes sense now' she said. 'He knew, you know. Michael. He knew he was my father.'

'What?' Mother and daughter were in chorus.

'Only that day, Jess. Only then. He gave me a lift, remember? For some reason I mentioned my name. My full name, you know. And he went very odd – slammed

420

the brakes on, went a funny colour. I nearly banged my head. He said he had to talk to me, but I wanted to see my mother. And I was cross – I could have hurt my head! So I said I'd stay on that evening, he could talk to me then.'

'How do you remember all that now, so clearly, Auntie Peg?' asked Anya. 'It was such a long time ago.'

'I was annoyed, Annie. No-one ever asked me if I had anything to say, if I knew anything, if he'd said anything to me. And I got very cross. I did in those days, didn't I Jess? I was cross a lot of the time. I thought – why don't they ask me? Because I'm just the housekeeper. A servant. What would I know? But I know one thing – he didn't sound like a man who was going off to kill himself.'

Much was happening during 1990. The introduction of the Poll Tax across the country triggered widespread unrest, and riots in some areas. All the pent-up frustrations felt towards the government spilled over, and many felt they would soon get their wish, that Margaret Thatcher's time was up. It was a turbulent time. But Anya had other things on her mind, both in Westminster and at home. Her postbag continued to be full, her committee work took up a great deal of her time, and she relied more and more on her staff. She appointed a second assistant, at the same time managing to secure an office of her own, and giving Phil the space he needed.

He, in turn, was ploughing on with his investigation into the illnesses in Port Haven, which, to no-one's surprise, was taking longer than anyone would have wished. Months. A year. And more. Then – a breakthrough.

'I've found it, Annie' whispered Esther

They sat at a table on the terrace of the House of Commons. Three huddled together against the October wind.

'I found a list of councillors and officers at Trefni Bridge Council when that development was going through. I never thought I'd appreciate the painstaking record-keeping of every meeting since the year dot! I found the minutes of the planning meetings around that time. Councillor Evans chaired all the meetings, never declared any interest. Which of course he should have – it was his company who would do the building on a lot of the contracts. And from what your dad wrote in his diary, it was actually his company that submitted the winning bid for the Melin Fach estate, even though it was in your father's name. And – I found a name. Someone who signed for receipt of a report. A report from the organisation that checked on environmental issues in planning applications. There's no mention of such a report in any of the planning documents.'

'So where now?' Byron lowered his voice too.

'I think we should get together again. I know that's difficult. We need Phil as part of this, Annie. And your Mum – I think there may be bits she's forgotten, doesn't even realise she knows. And it was her documents that started this. It's only right she should be involved.'

The meeting this time took place in Anya's flat. Geraldine had offered to see to the girls so that Jessie could travel to London. There was an air of expectation in the room. Esther started their discussion.

'Right. What do we know? We know that Evans was using his position to get planning consent. We know that Michael was part of the fiddle to tender for the contract. And we know that a report on the land was sent to the chairman's office. What we don't know is what the report said, or whether Evans saw it. There don't seem to be any copies, and that organisation has been re-invented several times since then, so .... we also don't know if Michael saw it either, and if he did, what he did about it. If anything.'

'We know a bit more than that' said Philip. 'Steffan Evans is living in Spain, still owns the business, and has put his son in charge of it. If we can get the evidence that he saw the report, and ignored it, I think we've got him. Prosecution. Compensation for the families. Rehousing of the poor bastards stuck in those crumbling tombs.'

'What's the name of the guy who signed for the report, Esther? asked Byron. 'Any chance he could tell us more about it? Another long shot I know!'

Esther looked through her notes.

'Neville' she said. 'Neville Passmore.'

'Well, I suppose it wouldn't hurt to ... What's wrong Mum?' Anya looked at her mother, who had started at the name.

'Neville ... Neville ... I'm sure I've seen that name' she said. 'I can't think where, though. No, wait ... Annie, can I use your phone?'

The little group looked bemused, but Jessie calmly stood up, went to the sideboard, and dialled her home number.

'Geraldine? Can you check something for me? In my bedroom, in the wardrobe, there's a box of papers. Can you go and fetch the file on top of it, please? I'll hold on.'

No-one spoke while Jessie stood, phone in hand. Then,

'Ok. Now can you look for a piece of blotting paper? A folded piece of blotting paper? It should be near the top.'

She stood waiting again.

'Annie, give me a pen, quick. And some paper.'

Back to the phone.

'Please read out everything that's written there. Yes, everything. Yes, the numbers too.'

She scribbled on the paper before thanking her friend and ringing off. She returned to her seat at the table.

'There was nothing in Michael's briefcase. They found it in his car, but it was completely empty. And there was very little of Michael's left in his office that day. The day he ... he died. Too little, I always thought, but no-one seemed interested. No papers, no files. Just a couple of sheets of blotting paper, and that's all I found when I went there. But one of them was folded over, and inside was some writing. Michael's writing. These are the words written there..'

She cleared her throat.

'Neville... SE ... roadside café, coast road ... noon'

It was easier than they thought it might be to contact Neville Passmore, now a senior officer in a council in Kent. And he was surprisingly amenable to the request for a meeting. He sat now, in a quiet café in Tunbridge Wells, with Anya, Byron, Philip and Esther.

'I've been waiting for this for thirty years. Over thirty years. It's a relief. It really is.'

They waited. Then he told them. He told them he had received the report, signed for it, passed it to Evans, watched while he read it, and was told to destroy it. That he'd kept it, read it, passed it to Michael Hughes.

'Why did you do that, Mr Passmore?' Esther asked.

'I'm not stupid, Madam. I saw what it said and it frightened the hell out of me. And I didn't trust Councillor Evans. Nasty man. And a dangerous one. I knew it was a risk, taking it to Mr Hughes that day. But I couldn't just do nothing, could I? Not when I knew what that report said. Then, when I found out what had happened, that Mr Hughes was dead, found dead just a few hours later …'

'Wait, Neville' Anya interrupted. 'a few hours later? When exactly did you take the report to my father?'

'On the Wednesday. Wednesday morning. The day he died. I assumed he went to see Councillor Evans after I left.'

They sat in silence, each pondering their own thoughts.

'How come you remember all this so clearly, Neville?' Byron asked.

425

'Because I've felt guilty ever since. It's prayed on my mind. If I hadn't given him that report, maybe he wouldn't have died.'

'You think he took his life because of it, Mr Passmore? Because he was implicated in building on this land?' Esther's questioning was gentle.

'Good God, no! I never believed for a minute that he killed himself!'

The four looked stunned.

'So what did you thank had happened?'

'I think Councillor Evans killed him. Why do you think I was frightened? I was scared when I handed over the report, but after Mr Hughes ... well ...'

He rose from his seat, prepared to leave. Turned at the door.

'Do you want a copy? Of the report?'

And he drew a large manila envelope from his brief case.

Things moved quickly then. Esther believed they had the evidence they needed to show that the land at Melin Fach had, in fact, been contaminated. That Evans had known about it, hidden the fact, and abused his position to ensure that planning permission was given. All for his personal profit. The legal wheels turned, and there seemed little doubt that Steffan Evans would have his comeuppance. But Anya had other things to think about now.

'D'you think it's possible that Evans really did kill my father?'

They lay, staring at the ceiling, hands clasped together, heads close on the pillows. Byron didn't answer immediately, but the silence was a comfortable one.

'It's possible, of course. I don't know how, though. I don't know much about the details of your Dad's death.'

'I don't either, to tell the truth. I know that my Mum never really believed he killed himself, despite the inquest verdict. And now – now I'm wondering too.'

Anya turned in the bed to face him.

'There are too many coincidences, Byron. Too many flukes. The tender scam, the report, Neville's account of what happened that day …'

'I know. But some unanswered questions too. According to his diary, your Dad was going to meet Evans on the Friday, not Wednesday. So we don't know if he ever got round to confronting him.'

'But we don't know what happened to the original report either. It wasn't in the office, or in his car. What did he do with it?'

She sighed.

'Just too many questions, aren't there?'

'Why don't we have a chat with your Mum this weekend about it all?

She nodded.

'And in the meantime, my Cariad, come here.'

And he pulled her close.

CHAPTER 29

COLD CASE

1991

Rob Daly remembered Jessie. When Pam Groves had asked him to be her second-in-command in this investigation – what could be an investigation, what may turn out to be nothing - he had looked at all of the paperwork, from back then and now, as keenly as ever he had done as a serving police inspector. He sat with Jessie now, in her neat bungalow, drinking her tea and eating her cake. He had no office of his own. A shared space with his two colleagues, in a run-down part of the station that no-one visited. Or rarely. A far cry from the room he had once called his own, complete with sofas and potted plants. He was on her territory now.

Small-talk over, he went through every detail of what she had discovered about her husband's death. He scribbled and nodded, while she watched him. Then,

'One more question, Jessie' he said, putting his pen down. 'Michael died on the Wednesday. Neville Passmore gave him the report on the Wednesday. And yet in his diary, he has an appointment with Steffan Evans on the Friday. Do you have any idea if he may have changed his plans? Re-arranged their meeting? Anything at all?'

'He didn't tell me about any meeting.' She sighed. 'No, I'm afraid I don't know what his plans were or if he changed them. Only that, if he'd seen that report,

I can't imagine him sitting on it for two days. I'd have thought he'd have gone to see Evans straight away.'

'We've checked Evans' whereabouts that day, and the old diaries put him at a meeting in Bury Port. It's difficult to be any more definite than that. We don't know what time he went or returned.'

Jessie started to clear away the teacups.

'Well that's that then' she said briskly. 'There's no more … Hang on …'

Once more she went to her box of documents. When she came back, she laid the torn piece of blotting paper in front of him. *Neville… SE … roadside café, coast road … noon.*

'SE – that must be Steffan Evans, mustn't it?' she said. 'Roadside Café. That's where Michael … where he was found. And it's on the coast road. Evans could have come back from Bury Port that way.'

Rob picked up the scrap of paper. He looked thoughtful as he tucked it away into his brief case.

'If Evans had killed Michael – and I'm not saying he did – how the hell did he do it?' He spoke as much to himself than to her. 'He would have had to immobilise Michael somehow, hit him, tie him up, drug him, I don't know. Then he'd have had to fit the pipe to the exhaust. Not impossible, but that would have taken some planning. And all that time, Michael, sitting there in the driver's seat …'

'Don't please Rob, don't.'

He looked up, roused from his musings.

"I'm sorry Jessie, I shouldn't be talking like this. But you do know that there's a way we may be able to find out more, don't you? It would mean exhuming …'

'No! No, never!'

'But …

'I said no! For God's sake, let him rest in peace! As far as I'm concerned, he was killed. Murdered. He didn't take his own life, he didn't choose to leave us. I've seen enough now, read enough, and I know. It's bad enough that this awful thing happened to him. And then that he should be held responsible. But exhuming him now, after all these years? What on earth could anyone possibly find now?'

'Ok, I understand. But there are a lot of tests that could be done, even now, even after such a long time. Tests that weren't available then. And some that were, but weren't judged relevant, not necessary when the verdict seemed so cut and dried. But short of a confession by Evans, we're not likely to get any sort of conviction for murder.'

Pam Groves was excited. After years of retirement she was working again. Ok, so it wasn't as a police officer. Not a proper one. But she was working on a case, as a civilian brought in by the local squad. A case she remembered well, one that had stuck in her mind. She had been nineteen years old, and a constable for just ten months.

Her first impression of Jessie Hughes, when she had arrived at the front door at the top of the impressive drive with Sergeant Dodds, had been that the wife must

430

be a stuck up snob, a spoilt middle aged lady of leisure. And when she went inside, saw the size of the rooms, the expensive furniture, the thick carpets, she was sure she was right. But then … the woman herself was young. Only a few years older than she was. And she was pleasant, polite to them. Pam had seen the shock, the horror on her face when she was told about her husband. Her late husband, as he was by then. She had felt sorry for her.

And now …now … the case was live. An old man had been charged, had been found guilty, in his absence, of a number of offences – fraud, breaching environmental laws, causing significant harm to human health, and a few others. But the reason she was being brought back, to head up a team, was a possible charge of murder. The old man was also a suspect in a case that had been judged a suicide.

She was on her way to Torrevieja, south of Alicante, accompanied by Johnny Dodds. On their way to a villa in El Chaparal, where millionaire Steffan Evans, ex council chief, ex building tycoon, expat, was living. Steffan Evans, suspect. Steffan Evans, too ill to return to the UK. Dying, they said. Didn't have long, they said. Well, she would see.

Pam was in her early sixties, slightly overweight, with hair that would be grey if she let it. But she didn't. It was the same shade of dark brown it had always been, even if it needed reminding of the fact every six weeks without fail. She had done well in her career. First woman Inspector in her neck of the woods, first Chief Inspector too. But nothing lasts. Things move on. Early retirement in the police was welcomed by most, a chance to spend time with previously-neglected family, or even to start a new part-time career. But not her. The force had been her life. She had always known she would never have a family, a husband. She had never wanted a boyfriend. She wanted a girlfriend. And that wasn't allowed. Not in the force, not in her town, not in life. Oh, the law allowed it, eventually, when she was coming up to thirty. But she'd grown used to it by then. Accepted it. Family life was not for her. So her colleagues became not only her mates, but her family. And she felt lost when she was "encouraged" to go, in the name of restructuring, reorganisation, reform, call it what you will, she thought – they're getting rid of the dead wood, the oldies.

She took it well, so it seemed. She didn't make a fuss, complain, call them all bastards before she went. She took the obligatory clock and the lump sum, made a pretty speech, thanked everyone and went home to her tidy cottage in Trefni Bridge. Where she read, and watched TV, and fed her cat. She sometimes thought that if it weren't for her cat, she might as well be invisible. Might as well not be here. Might as well … dark thought crept in late at night when she didn't sleep.

But then … she got the call. The local division was setting up a new team of ex-police, retired detectives, to clear some of the back-log of unsolved cases in the area. Cold Cases they were being called. Cases where some new information, new evidence, had come to the attention of the people at the top. And she was to head up this team. How glad she was that she had left in the manner she had.

The sun was warm on her face now, her heart light, her demeanour sober, as she sat in the cool white-walled solarium, iced fruit juice in front of her, files on

432

her lap. She glanced at Johnny, still a sergeant in her mind, despite his nearing seventy.

'All set, Sarge?'

'All set, Boss.'

They both smiled. Then in he walked. Not that they would have recognised him from the old photographs they had dug out, pictures of council events, ceremonies; pictures showing a large man, overweight, several chins and a vast belly. No, this man didn't even resemble him. Emaciated, jaundiced, stooped, folds of skin hanging where his jowls had been, this man wasn't well. No fakery there, at least. Pam and John stood up.

'Mr Evans, we're …

'I know who you are.'

His voice was a growl.

'You wouldn't have got in if I didn't.'

He sat, facing them, and they followed suit. He looked at them.

His eyes are the same, she thought. The same as in the photographs she had poured over, stored to memory.

Pam spoke first, clearly and calmly.

'Mr Evans, I think you know why we're here. You were found guilty, in your absence, of abuse of public office, and a number of environmental offences which took place from 1950 up to 1967 and possibly later. In particular the construction of seven hundred houses on contaminated land, land that you owned, and land which you knew to be contaminated, resulting in …'

'Yes, yes, I've heard all this, seen all the paperwork. Had it all from my solicitors. And now my son is paying for it. Well, he never earned it, so why shouldn't he? So why are you here then? Just to tell me what I already know?'

Pam took a breath. She'd been waiting for this.

'Mr Evans, we are here to question you in relation to the death of Michael Hughes on Wednesday August 7th 1957. Is there anything you wish to say at this point? I need to caution you ...'

'What? What do you mean? You think I had something to do with Meic's death? Thirty odd years ago? Bloody ridiculous. Now bugger off.'

'... I need to caution you that you do not have to say anything but anything you do say will be taken down and may be given in evidence. And we will be recording this interview.'

Johnny finished writing, Pam placed the small recorder on the bamboo table between herself and her suspect. It whirred into life.

'Can you tell us where you were on the morning of August 7th 1957?'

'You're joking aren't you? No-one could remember that far back!'

'I can.' Pam spoke quietly. 'I was at Michael Hughes' home, telling his wife – his widow – that he was dead. Now, think again, Mr Evans. You must remember the fact that he had died, surely? He was a friend, wasn't he? Surely you remember he died that summer?'

'Well yes, of course I do! I remember that! But it had nothing to do with me!' he was shouting now, or trying to. His voice was straining.

'He committed suicide, didn't he? Exhaust pipe, wasn't it? So why the questions?'

He rose from his seat now, clearly agitated.

'And why now? I'm an old man, an old sick man.'

'New evidence has come to our attention, Mr Evans' replied Pam, cool, calm, choosing to ignore his pacing. 'Evidence that implicates you.'

He stopped, stood in front of her, and she could see, beneath the sallow skin, the wasted body, the sunken cheeks, a glimpse of the man he was, powerful, commanding, intimidating ...

'Evidence? What evidence?'

She knew that what evidence they had was sketchy to say the least. Circumstantial. Over the weeks she had weighed it up, as she scrutinised every word of every report she could find, every morsel of information, every piece of background on Evans. All the time looking for those watchwords – Motive, Means and Opportunity. It seemed he had the motive; opportunity? Possibly. But means?

'I'm not at liberty to say, Sir. But we have been given permission to exhume Michael Hughes' body.' Her fingers were crossed under the papers she held on her lap. She knew that no such permission had been given – yet. That Rob Daly was still to convince Jessie Hughes that it was the right thing to do.

Evans sat down abruptly.

'Have you now?' he said softly. And he laughed. A grating, rasping sound.

'Incidentally, Mr Evans, I notice that you were the only boy in your year to go to university.'

Johnny Dodds turned abruptly to look at her. What was this about?

'You didn't finish your course' Pam went on. 'Although you did complete the first two years, didn't you?'

Evans looked at her. And smiled. And then, suddenly, he said

'I'm tired of this. What do you want from me? A confession? Ok. Yes, I killed him.'

Both ex-officers drew a breath. Neither spoke for a moment.

'Are you confessing to the murder of Michael Hughes on August 7th 1957, Mr Evans?'

Pam's voice was calm but her pulse was racing. She hadn't expected this. Was it a trick?

'Yes, officer, I am. Not because your exhumation will prove anything. Just because I'm tired. And I might as well.'

He laughed his humourless laugh again.

'I'm dying, you see. I'll never make it to one of your courts. You can try extradition but that will take too long. There's no treaty with Spain. And I'm not going to make it easy for you.'

'I have to correct you there, Sir' said Dodds. 'A new treaty was signed six years ago. So extradition is a definite possibility.'

Steffan Evans sank back into his chair.

'No matter. As I said, this will never come to court. I have cancer. Riddled with it. In my liver mainly, lungs too. And I have heart failure. End stage. So it's a toss-up which one will get me first. Either way, chances are I won't make three months. Probably less. So – I'll tell you what I did, how I did it. Bloody clever, if I say so myself.'

And he laughed, making that horrible sound once more.

'As to why I did it – well, you've probably worked that out.'

Then he told them how Michael had phoned him, wanting to bring their meeting forward. Demanding to meet that day, telling him that he'd seen the report on the condition of the land.

'Silly boy. Always was holier than thou. Wouldn't tell me who'd given it to him though.'

He told them he never went to his meeting in Bury Port, but it was in the council diary. A watertight alibi. In a meeting with so many others that no-one would be sure if he'd been there or not. Instead, he had driven straight to his home where he had picked up all he needed. He knew what he would have to do. When he reached the roadside café, Michael's car was already there, parked at the back.

'I tried to talk some sense into him. I knew it wouldn't do any good. I'd pushed him too far, and he was wearing his righteousness like a cloak!'

He stopped, eyes glazing over. Was he thinking back? Was he regretting his horrific actions, the betrayal of the friendship he had feigned, that Michael had believed was true? He focussed again.

'He was going to the police, he said. To the council. Anything to stop me building on that land. I'd paid good money for it! Nobody told me it was contaminated!' He was indignant now.

'It was the site of a petro-chemical works, Mr Evans' interrupted Dodds.

Evans ignored him.

'So I had to do something. It was easy. Michael would never imagine I would – anyone would – do such a thing. So when I stabbed him with the needle, he didn't know what had hit him. Literally.' He started to laugh, but coughing stopped him.

'What did you inject him with, Mr Evans?'

Pam was struggling to keep her voice neutral, non-judgemental; the revulsion she felt was more to do with his complete absence of remorse than the act itself.

'You'd call it Sux' he said. 'Succinylcholine. Wonderful drug. Starts working in less than a minute. Only lasts a short time, but that's all I needed. Pipe attached, engine on, doors and windows closed – he'd never come round. Carbon Monoxide would do the rest. And the best thing about it ...'

The self-satisfaction in his voice was clear.

'The body starts to break it down immediately. There's no Sux left to test and so testing for it wouldn't show anything. Even if they did any testing. Which they didn't. And digging up his body now won't prove a thing – waste of time.'

The silence that filled the room was full of the feelings and emotions of the three people who sat there. For the retired detectives - horror. Disgust. Relief and

438

elation that he had confessed. And for Steffan Evans –
pride. As Pam Groves and Johnny Dodds stood to make
the arrest, she spoke quietly to the old man.

'Your university course must have been
invaluable, Mr Evans. Pharmacy, wasn't it?'

CHAPTER 30

DECSION TIME

1991

The news from Spain brought a sense of closure to the family, not least to Jessie. The huge relief, knowing that she had not been abandoned all those years ago, was mixed with the wretchedness she felt when she thought of her husband's last hours, his last minutes. Now she could finish grieving for him as she had never allowed herself to do.

But the end of the investigation left a hole, an anti-climax, in all of their lives. They had been teetering on a cliff-top for a long time, not knowing if they would fall, and now they could walk away. It would take a little while to feel normal again, Anya knew. But life as an MP was a busy one, even during the summer recess. It was no holiday. Her constituents still had their problems, she was still expected to attend functions and events, and she knew that an election would be called within the year.

Her children, she felt, were doing well, moving on with their studies and their lives, socialising with their friends, all was well with them. So it was more than a shock when Emily informed her, over a Saturday breakfast when her sisters were still in bed, that she thought she might be pregnant.

Anya did and said all the things she knew, later, that she shouldn't have. She shouted, she scolded. She was disappointed, she said. How could she be so stupid, she said. How could she throw her life away like this, she said. Emily rose from the table and walked away. Anya saw her mother in the doorway. Not a word was said. None was needed.

'Byron, can I meet you please? Now? No, not Parliamentary stuff. Personal stuff.'

They met in the café where she had once told him of her own pregnancy. Now she poured out her fears for her eldest daughter, her anger, her disappointment. And Byron listened. Then he asked her what her mother had said to her, when, at eighteen, she had found she was pregnant. *This is wonderful news,* she had said. *A new life! This is something to celebrate*!

'Do you think your Mum wasn't disappointed, Annie? Do you think she was over the moon about it? Bloody hell Annie, she must have been gutted!'

And he reminded her of what Jessie had said when Anya had believed there was only one way out of what she thought was a mess, five years ago. *Maybe there's some way we can do this,* she had said.

Anya cried then. She cried as she hadn't done for a long time, tears of shame and guilt. And Byron, as always, was there to comfort her. And Gino brought more coffee.

When she arrived home, her mother was waiting.

'I know' she said, before Jessie could speak. 'I know. I was a bitch. I'm sorry Mum.'

'It's not me you need to talk to, Annie. Your little girl's upstairs.'

As she stood outside the bedroom door, Anya wasn't sure of the reception she would get. She realised she wasn't sure if she knew her girls any more. Emily was seventeen. Where had the time gone? Hadn't she noticed that they were growing up, becoming young women? Had she been too busy, too wrapped up in her own world, her world of meetings and votes and too much time away from home? She knocked tentatively on the door.

'Come in.'

Emily's voice sounded thick from crying.

Anya saw her sitting on her bed, her face streaked with tears, looking like the little girl she had been. Was still, perhaps. And they were in each other's arms, both sobbing, each apologising to the other. Then they talked. Anya told her that this needn't be the catastrophe it might seem. She told her about her own experience, about her mother's words.

'I am so sorry, sweetheart' she said again, wiping away her daughter's tears, automatically pushing the straying strands of hair away from her face, the better to see her.

And Emily talked too. She told her mother that the boyfriend was no more. That she hadn't wanted to marry him anyway. But that the idea of a baby, her own baby, thrilled her. She didn't want to go to university, she said. She never had. She wanted to work with animals, or babies.

Anya said nothing. Why didn't she know this? Why had she allowed herself to assume so much about this young woman? How could this have happened?

'You don't have to do anything you don't want to, Em. We'll sort all of this out. The baby, your future, we'll sort it out, I promise.'

442

Jessie looked relieved when the two of them came down the stairs.

'Time for tea and cake I think, Mum' Anya said.

It was two weeks later that Emily's pregnancy was discovered to be a false alarm. That should have been the end of it, Anya thought, but the truth was far from it. Relationships in the family home had shifted yet again, and would never be the same. But there seemed to be a fresh outlook by all concerned. The news that their sister might be having a baby had rocked Fran and Lucy. They were at once thrilled at the idea of the fun a baby would be, and appalled at what they saw as an end to Emily's life. Anya, aided by Jessie, put them right on both counts.

Once again, Anya asked Byron to meet her in the little café. He was surprised at this, as they met regularly in their official roles, but he agreed cheerfully.

'Always glad to talk with you about topics other than politics' he said, grinning, as she walked in.

'You're a fine one to talk! When we first met you talked about little else!' she said, sitting beside him on the old bench seat as she used to do.

'But I'm right to think this is more personal than work?'

'We'll see' she said.

'How's Em? Is she doing ok?'

'Yes, she's getting there. I can see how much she's hurting. She's grieving. Even if it is for a baby that never was.'

'Did she want a baby then?'

'When she thought there was one, yes she did. Her emotions may not have been triggered by hormones. but they were real nonetheless.'

'She's very young though' he said, as Gino brought them their coffees.

'Yes. Even younger than I was. But I've never regretted having my children, Byron. Never, not for a second. Even if I've let my eye off the ball these last few months. Years.'

'Come on Annie, you mustn't …'

'Em is too young, yes. But what about us Byron? Are we too old?'

'What?'

'Are we too old? To have children?'

Byron was clearly taken aback.

'Is that what you want, Annie? Because if it is …'

'What if it is what I want, Byron? How would you feel? Is it too late?'

He looked at her for a long time before he smiled his beautiful smile.

'If that's what you want, Cariad, then I may be the oldest dad at the school gates, but I'd be over the moon.'

She smiled, kissed him gently on his lips, and said.

'Good. Because I'm three months gone.'

Among the disbelief, amazement and eventual joy of her family at this news, Anya knew she and Byron had some serious planning to do. Not just the planning that goes into every pregnancy, especially one where the mum-to-be is working full-time. No, this was different. She worked two hundred miles away for most of the week. She couldn't expect her mother to put her life on hold, again, to look after a tiny baby, just when she was starting to enjoy a life of her own, with someone she was clearly very fond of. Nannies? Nurseries? More than all this, Anya wanted to be with her baby.

And then there was the little matter of a general election. It would have to be called within the next few months. The Labour Party had a better chance of winning this than at any time over the past thirteen years, but it would still mean long days and nights, campaigning, knocking doors, making speeches. Their baby was due in March. She wouldn't be able to be in Parliament until it was at least three months old, with an election in the middle. It was ridiculous timing. Very bad planning. But she couldn't stop smiling when she thought about it.

She and Byron talked into the night, on many nights. Then she decided.

'I think we need to go to the café' she told him one morning, and he laughed.

'That's become the place, has it?'

'Hasn't it always?' she said, and she laughed too.

He knew that she had made up her mind. So they sat, holding hands, as she told him she wouldn't be standing in the election.

'I can't, can I?' she said, looking for his reaction. 'And … and I don't want to.'

He raised her hand in his, and kissed it.

'So what will you do?'

'I'll be a mum for a while. A proper full-time mum. I'd like that. Then – I'd like to go back to the college, if they need me there. I've missed having friends, Byron. I've had lots of colleagues but no real friends. And I've missed the students, those bubbly, lively, annoying young kids who meant more to me than I realised.

'I've been living, working, in a place where big decisions are made, and it's been a privilege to be part of it. I've been involved, taken part, made speeches, argued, voted. I've seen new laws come in, on the health service, on planning, on pensions. On embryology and the environment. And on mining. I've seen the end of the poll tax, and soon there'll be huge changes to Further Education that will affect you, and all our friends in Nanty Tech. I've got to know all those people we met on my first visit to the House of Commons, some better than others, but all inspiring in their way. And now we're on the verge of taking power. Of forming a Labour government. That is so exciting.

'But that will all continue without me. Oh, don't get me wrong. I'm still as committed to the party as ever, as I was when you first converted me! But I can see that there are so many other ways I can make a difference to people's lives. Sometimes I feel that I did more for the people of Cwmdawel when I was a lecturer than ever I've been able to do as their MP. I was able to see them as individuals, do something that may seem small in the grand scheme of things, but made huge differences to their lives. Did you know that Sian has finished her degree? And that Jen is teaching? I helped that to happen, didn't I? And all those youngsters, the ones who tried their best

446

to give me grief but came to me at breaktime, sometimes crying, sometimes embarrassed … all those young people …'

She took a breath, and a gulp of coffee.

'You've made up your mind then?' He grinned. 'I knew it was a mistake to get you involved in politics. My God, you certainly know how to make a speech!'

Anya punched him in the shoulder, and he laughed.

'I agree with every word, love.' He was serious now. 'Whatever you'd decided, I'd back you, you know that. But for what it's worth, I think you're right.'

'You knew all that, didn't you?'

'What?'

'When I asked you to work full time with me …'

'For you, not with you' he corrected.

'Ok, for me. You knew you needed to keep your job, that what you were doing was important, didn't you?'

'You've caught me out! Yes, I did. But it wasn't just what I could do for them. That job has been my salvation at times. I may argue with the guys – quite a lot! - but they've supported me over the years, and seen me through some pretty dark times. And helping the students has given me a real purpose when I didn't feel I had any. I need them as much as they need me. At least, I like to think they need me.'

'None of your false modesty, Mr Jones!' she smiled at him. 'So – now what?'

There wasn't much time. October already. Finding a worthy candidate to replace Anya at the next election wasn't going to be easy. She had broken the stranglehold of Plaid Cymru in the area, but allegiances could easily change back. Part of her felt she was letting the party down, but she knew she was doing the right thing. Once again, she, Byron and Geraldine sat around a table, considering her replacement, her possible replacement, before her decision not to stand was made public. This time, the table was in her living room rather than the café.

Jessie popped in and was immediately asked to join them for coffee.

'We could do with a break, Jess' said Byron, running his finger through his long hair, and leaning back in his chair.

But the discussion continued, and Jessie listened. No obvious contender came to mind, and the pros and cons of other members were batted back and forth. Jessie continued to listen. She waited until Geraldine excused herself to have a cigarette in the garden, then she spoke up.

'I don't understand why you're not thinking about her. Geraldine. I don't get it.'

Anya and Byron stared at her.

'I mean – am I missing something? Surely she's the perfect person? Experienced, committed, well known …'

'Good God, Jessie! I could kiss you!' Byron sat up straight. 'Yes, why haven't we thought about her, Annie?'

Anya laughed.

'Do you know, it never occurred to me! I just thought – well, she's settled, she's got her council work, she's ...'

'Do you mean she's too old, Anya?' Jessie's voice was disapproving.

'Oh God! No! Well ...' and in a whisper 'how old is she, d'you think?'

'Haven't you ever thought to find out? Isn't she supposed to be your friend? After all she's done for you? She's five years younger than I am. She's fifty one. And we're both in our prime, thank you very much!'

Anya blushed.

'Oh Mum, I didn't mean she's too old. I just meant – well, she seems ageless!'

'Great! Just what every woman wants to hear!' But she laughed.

'So, Anya, what do you think?' Byron said. 'Should we ask her?'

'Wait.' Jessie held up a hand. 'Before you do – there's something you need to know. Something she would need to tell you.'

The pair had no chance other than look bemused before Geraldine came back into the room. As she tucked the cigarette packet and lighter into her brief case, she said, not looking up,

'You're all looking very shifty. Been talking about me?'

Byron looked at her.

'As a matter of fact, Geraldine, yes. We have. I don't know why we didn't think of it sooner, but we think we've found the perfect candidate.'

449

This was beginning to sound familiar to Anya. She remembered her reaction when the same thing was said to her back in their little café some years ago. She had been shocked, then annoyed, and eventually downright angry.

'Oh yes?' Geraldine sat.

'Would you, Geraldine? Would you stand for selection? And hopefully election?'

The older woman didn't seem fazed, or indeed surprised, but neither did she seem overjoyed.

'I could do the job, of course' she said. 'Whether I could muster the sort of personal support that Anya has, I'm not so sure. But – and it's a big "but" – there is a reason why I've never considered it. Jessie may have told you - I have a criminal record.'

The silence that followed seemed to last several minutes.

'It looks as though she hasn't told you then. So she won't have told you what it was for. And it's something that may affect your decision to put my name forward.'

CHAPTER 31

GERALDINE'S STORY

1956 – 1961

An unremarkable child was Gerry. Unremarkable to the point of plainness. So said her mother, so it must be true. She knew she was a disappointment to her mama, whom she adored. Her gentle papa would never gainsay his wife, who, he knew, had married beneath him. He walked each day to the colliery, to sink into the bowels of the earth to quarry the coal face for the lumps of black gold. Gerry knew he loved her. But it was her mother's approval she craved, and rarely, if ever, received.

Named after her maternal grandfather whom she'd never met, Gerry was meant to be a boy. She was meant to be talented in the arts, or on the sporting field. She was neither. And she was meant to be beautiful. But her mouse-coloured hair was straight as a line, cut short over her ears. Her skin was pallid, sallow. Her abundant freckles did nothing to adorn her. She was too tall, too thin, too clumsy. She knew that. Such a disappointment.

Largely ignored by the person she loved best, it wasn't surprising that she fell for the first boy who showed her some interest, who flattered her, talked to her. Well, not a boy exactly. Ten years her senior. Her mother was only too glad to get her off her hands, and although her father advised her to wait, to meet more people, to see something of the world as he never had, she would have none of it. Her school friends too, were wary. Jealous

451

maybe, to see their friend at sixteen off to get married, but worried too. The brightest girl in the class, the one forecast for a great future, leaving it all behind? Romantic, yes. Risky though. But she loved Len Maddox. Was devoted to him.

So they married. And she found that she wasn't too tall after all. She was just the right height. Considerably shorter than her new husband. And her hair wasn't mousey, it was a light ash brown; her skin wasn't pallid, she was fair skinned.

She revelled in being a housewife. She cooked and she cleaned, she was there at the end of each shift as he came home, and if he was sometimes a bit quiet, a bit offhand, well that was to be expected, wasn't it? He'd had a hard day. He was tired. And if he started to push her, pinch her, it was because she could be so irritating, so stupid. So she tried harder.

She must always look her best, she decided. That was the least she could do. She had very little money, only what she could save from the housekeeping he gave her. This custom was new to her. Her father had always handed over his pay-packet to her mother, unopened, and she would hand him back some pocket-money. As far as she knew, this was the norm in the little village of Cwmdawel. But what did she know? She was a stupid ignorant girl, as he told her, over and over. She believed it now.

When she had saved enough to have her hair cut and styled, properly, in a hairdresser's, she did it to please him. To look attractive for him. She waited by the door that evening, dressed in her best blouse and dirndle skirt, wearing a dab of powder and some pink lipstick. She felt beautiful, and excited.

He took one look at her and pushed her, hard, back into the room. And then he hit her, hard, across her face.

'You fucking little whore!' he whispered at her, his face close to hers, as she opened her eyes, terrified, not knowing what was happening or why.

But he told her. She was a whore and a slut, he said, a fucking bitch. Painting her face to invite every man in the village, he said. Flaunting herself, flouting the vows she had made. Each accusation accompanied by a slap, a punch, a kick, until she sat curled in a ball, her arms over her head, pleading through her sobs, telling him that she was sorry.

Later that evening, when he came home again, she backed away from him. But he was quiet now. He told her he was sorry, but she shouldn't have made him so cross. That it was her fault really, but he forgave her. That it was because he loved her so much he was afraid she would leave him. And he cried. And she comforted him, and told him again that she was sorry. The lovemaking that followed was intense, urgent, rough. But she knew that he loved her, that this was his way of showing it, so she didn't cry out, and she put witch-hazel on her bruised body when he was asleep. She was seventeen years old.

So it went on. The cycle of beatings, for any reason and none. Sometimes he would pull her from bed as she slept, dragging her by her hair, down the stairs, to show her the cup she hadn't washed or the rug she hadn't shaken. He would push his lit cigarette into her arm until

453

she screamed with pain, then hit her because the neighbours would hear. And each time he would tell her he was sorry, that he only did it because he loved her, and that she shouldn't make him so angry. And each time his lovemaking became more brutal.

Gerry's life was a fog, a terrifying one and a confusing one. He loved her, he said. She wasn't allowed to meet her friends because they weren't to be trusted, because they would persuade her to go with other men. When her parents became ill she mustn't see them, he said, in case she brought germs back to their house. And only when they died, quite suddenly, of Asian Flu in the terrible epidemic that seemed to be sweeping the country, was she allowed to visit them. At the graveside.

She was scared, and tired, and wasn't sure what the future held. But when she found she was pregnant, she was overjoyed. For herself, of course: to have someone of her own to love, who would love her too, that was enough. But, she thought, Len would be thrilled too. Surely. And he was. He said so. And she enjoyed the most peaceful time of her short marriage, for three whole months.

She never did find out what set him off that evening. It could have been that she had been too extravagant with the tea leaves, or that she hadn't scrubbed the front step as he liked it. But whatever it was, it was one of the worst. He struck her first, with the back of his hand, across her face. Across her head. As she reeled from the punch, he rained a flurry of blows on her head, her shoulders, her arms, until she was staggering from left to right, right to left, a rag doll, a puppet on a broken string. The only things stopping her from

454

collapsing to the ground were the wall he had pinned her to, and the avalanche of his attack.

He punched her stomach, hard. Too hard, she knew. And again. And again. And now she was on the floor, arms not over her head but across her belly, vainly trying to protect her baby, sobbing, begging him, her voice dying as she lost consciousness.

It was quiet when she came round. An hour later? A minute? She couldn't tell. She crawled to the door, raised herself by clutching at the door frame, stumbled down the path and, steadying herself on garden walls, made her way along the street to the phone box at the end. She dialled 999 and asked for an ambulance, then sat on the cold ground, waiting. She knew it was too late. She could feel the warm trickle of blood as the little life inside her died. As part of her died too. And all the time she sat there, all the time she was taken gently into the ambulance, wheeled into the cottage hospital, she knew that it had to end.

'You have to get away'.

That was what they told her. The nurses. And she knew this. But how? Where was she to go? She had no money, no family. Her old friends had been hurt by her snubbing, as they saw it, but anyway, they wouldn't have wanted to get involved. What had happened to her – what had been happening for three years - was an embarrassment. This sort of thing should stay behind closed doors. Between a man and his wife. What Len was doing was not illegal – he had a right to chastise his wife. The police were told this sort of thing was a family affair and they weren't allowed to meddle; reports of wife-beating were not recorded as assaults anyway. And even if she had somewhere to go – would he let her?

But something had hardened in her now. She could see clearly for the first time, and she was determined to get away. Clutching the little card she had been handed by a nurse as she was discharged, she sought advice from the Citizens Advice Bureau in Swansea. She took her bus fare from the pile of shilling coins set aside for the electricity that week. She didn't care if he beat her for it. She didn't care if they sat in the dark. She needed to know.

The word Divorce wasn't one spoken out loud very often in her world, unless it was to add to the gossip about a film star or other celebrity. But now she was talking about it as a possibility. The news that she would receive legal aid made her raise her hopes. The fact that she could sue her husband for divorce on the grounds of mental as well as physical cruelty raised them further. But it wouldn't be plain sailing. She would need evidence. And she set about getting it.

She still had bruises. She braved ridicule and humiliation, and went to a friend of her father who, she knew, not only had a camera but a dark room where he developed and printed his photographs. He was taken aback at the request, by a young woman he hadn't seen for many years, for him to take some quite intimate pictures of her. She gave as little information as she could, but her polite, dignified demeanour, and the tired world-weary look in her young eyes, made him sympathetic to her. So she stood, erect, in his back bedroom, dressed in her petticoat, while she turned this way and that, the better to show the bruising on her arms, her legs, neck and shoulders, colours ranging from black to blue, green to yellow, as newer injuries overlaid older ones. She did not expose her bitten breasts, her scarred buttocks, more for his sensibilities than hers. But the cigarette burns were clear to see on her arms and across the top of her chest, without the need to expose more.

He was shocked, but did his best to hide it. So he went about treating this poor child as he would a bowl of fruit or a bouquet of flowers, any of his still life compositions. He told her the pictures would be ready in a week, and he was as good as his word. He handed her a fat envelope, and she in turn handed him a bag of coins.

'What's this?'

'It's for the pictures. I don't know how much they cost, but this is all I've got. If it's not enough I can give you some more next week.'

'No love, no need.' He swallowed hard, his mouth formed a tight grim line, and she realised he was stopping himself from crying. He composed himself.

'No need' he repeated. 'You take it. And good luck, love.'

'That's very kind of you' she said.

She turned, and as she reached the gate he called after her.

'Your dad would be proud of you.'

And it was her turn to swallow hard, as she nodded and went her way.

She had a solicitor. She had the photographs. She had a letter from the hospital listing the injuries they had treated her for. She still needed to show that this wasn't a recent occurrence, but had been long-term, and sustained, but she would need to plead her case on that. Mental cruelty would be harder to prove, her solicitor said, but maybe the physical evidence would be enough to get a decree in her favour.

When she was told that a marriage had to be at least five years old in order to dissolve it, that was a setback. And when she was told that she should be living separately from her husband during that time, that was another. A seemingly insurmountable one.

All this time she was living with him. Of course she was. There was nowhere else for her to go. She would have to show to the courts that she had no alternative but to stay, that she had not in fact decided to "give the marriage another go". She had to convince them that they were not "leading a normal married life", not "enjoying marital relations". She had learned from the helpful volunteers at the Citizens Advice Bureau that there was no government or council help for women in her position. No accommodation, no refuge, no escape route. She arranged to meet her local county councillor, who told her that there were many other people waiting for a council house who had more reason than she did to be housed. He then advised her not to be so fussy, and to be satisfied with her lot. She met with a parish councillor too, who tutted and sympathised in a self-conscious way and said there was nothing he could do. She wrote to her member of parliament, but received no reply. But she kept a record of her attempts to move out. She kept a record of everything.

She kept quiet at home, doing as she was told, trying not to do any of the things that wound him up. As she always had. He still beat her. But now, in the time between his stalking off and the inevitable rough sexual encounter on his return, she would write down every detail of his assault, every kick and punch. And after he returned, after he had rammed himself into her, bitten her, sodomised her, she would later add one word to her daily account. RAPE.

Two more years. She had to endure this life for two more years. She decided she wouldn't waste the time, and each day, when he was at work, she hurried through her chores, not caring if the corners weren't properly swept or the washing hung out to dry neatly, because after all, he'd beat her anyway, wouldn't he? Then she would walk the two miles to the nearest library, which the Workers' Education Association had set up, where they still ran courses. She attended talks on history and politics. She read huge tomes on common law, crime and punishment. And she knew what she had to do.

So she waited, not knowing what the future would hold for her. Days, weeks, months passed and at last, she reached the time when she could set the wheels in motion. All was going as she planned. But the biggest hurdle was yet to come. The divorce papers would need to be served on Len. She didn't know if she would have a future once Len received them, but she had done her homework. She told her solicitor to go ahead, serve the papers. Then she set about putting her plan into play.

The letter arrived by the first post, just as he was leaving the house to walk to the mine. He gave the envelope a cursory glance, saw the official-looking stamp on it, and left it on the mantelpiece. She wasn't surprised. He didn't like reading, and would need to sit down to study the contents. He would never lower himself to ask for her help, and having suffered the consequences of her first offer soon after they were married, she learned not to make that mistake again.

He waited until his meal was eaten and two cups of tea drunk before he brought the letter to the table. She stood against the wall, next to the fireplace, watching him. He took his time. Then he frowned, stared, re-read it. The next thing she knew, the table was up-ended, crockery shattering onto the floor, hot tea gushing from the smashed teapot. He turned to her.

'What the fuck is this, Bitch?' he said quietly. And he slapped her.

She said nothing.

'I said, what the fuck is this?'

He slapped her on every syllable.

'Can't you read?'

This was so unexpected that he halted. She had never answered him back before. The fleeting respite didn't last long. He raised his hand, but before he could bring it down, she caught it, held it. She was no match for his strength, she knew, but she was banking on the element of surprise, again. Because there were some things she wanted him to hear. And it worked.

460

'I'll tell you what it is, Len.' Her voice was low, controlled, steady.

'It tells you that I've had enough. That you're a bully, a nasty cruel bully and a coward. And pretty soon, a judge is going to tell you that I'm not your wife any more, and ....'

That's as far as she got. His fist came crashing down, smashing her head against the edge of the mantelpiece, and for a split second she thought she might pass out before she could do what she knew she must. But she held on, even as he raised his arm again, and she grasped the knife she had hidden behind the clock, just a foot away, on the mantel. And she thrust it into his chest, under his outstretched arm, with all the strength left in her.

CHAPTER 32

CHANGING PLACES

1991

Geraldine's account of the episode was succinct to say the least. She had stabbed her husband, she said, after years of violence and abuse. Had she intended to kill him? No, she didn't think so. She still couldn't say for sure, even after all these years. She just wanted him to stop. Was she arrested? Charged? Yes, she was charged with attempted murder, she said calmly. But her time spent studying and researching stood her in good stead. Firstly, she could show evidence of his violence towards her. And secondly, she knew the law said she had a duty to retreat if she were being attacked. She also knew that she could show it was impossible for her to retreat, given that he was pinning her against the wall. She'd made sure of that. And of course he was so much bigger, so much stronger than she was. She claimed self-defence.

'Remember, this was 1961. It was another six years before the law was changed. So under common law at the time, I was found not guilty because a murder hadn't occurred, and that my actions were in self-defence. So I had a complete acquittal.'

They all took a deep breath.

'My God, Geraldine. I had no idea. All these years. I had no idea.' Byron shook his head.

'Well why should you? All the village knew at the time, but they kept quiet. And after a while, they were very kind to me.'

'What happened to your husband?' whispered Anya, still trying to take it all in.

Geraldine was silent for a moment.

'He died. Eighteen months later. It wasn't as a direct result of the wound I gave him, but the injury had caused problems. Breathing problems. And then there were complications. But I was in the clear. He hadn't died within a year and a day, so I was not held liable.'

They sat quietly, drinking fresh coffee, listening to Geraldine as she gave a resume of her life following the trauma she had been through. How she had got her divorce, found a job in a village shop, and rented a room above it. She had continued her studies at the local library, and would also sit, in her every spare moment, at a reading desk in the university library in Swansea, devouring every book she could fit into her available time. She had considered studying for a degree, but she didn't have the qualifications she would need and felt that, at twenty three, she was too old.

'No Access courses then, Anya!' she said, smiling. 'But there were other things I could do. I knew I couldn't be the only woman. The only woman to be treated like a punch bag. So I did my own research, asked my own questions. I set up little groups. There was so much these women needed. I would see them turning up when their men were at work, sneaking out of their houses, scared, a toddler in tow, a baby on the hip, maybe two. Bruised and cut and burned, they came along.

Sometimes their bruises didn't show. Sometimes the marks were inside their heads. Inside their souls.'

She stopped. Took a breath. She hadn't ever talked about this.

Then head up, strong again.

'All I could give them was space to talk and be listened to. Which was more than they were getting from the police, or their doctors, or their priests. But what they needed was housing. Protection. Somewhere to hide. Somewhere to feel safe. And then – and it took years – I heard about a wonderful woman in London who had set up what was called a Refuge. A refuge for battered women. I went up there, talked to other people like me, people who were trying to help. And I got involved with a group that became Women's Aid, setting up refuges all over the country, in secret locations. It was changing women's lives. And I was part of it.'

Her thin pale face glowed at the memory. And Anya thought – *she's beautiful.*

Geraldine cleared her throat, not used to sharing emotions like this. Not used to talking about herself.

'Go on, love.' It was Jessie, who was holding her hand, tears in her eyes. 'Go on. Tell them.'

'Not much more to tell really' she said in her usual brisk tone, although she didn't pull her hand away.

'I decided that, if I couldn't be a lawyer, or a doctor, or help in that way, I'd try to make sure I could help in other ways. I managed to get a few hours lecturing at the college. Then I thought - I'd had no help from the council, and I wanted to change their attitude, educate them. So I stood for the council elections. And I got in.'

464

'I remember you telling me' said Anya suddenly. 'Ages ago. You said "*I had my own reasons for wanting to stand for election*". Oh Geraldine.'

'I've never regretted being a councillor. In my own way I think I've managed to make things better for some people, little by little. I don't have a family ...'

'Rubbish!' Jessie's voice was firm. 'You do now. You have us.'

And Geraldine squeezed her friend's hand.

The selection process to choose a new Labour candidate was slicker and quicker than Anya remembered, and Geraldine was a match for all comers. She was in place before Christmas, and out on the campaign trail straight after. Anya did what she could to help, but her days of walking the streets were over for a little while. She found she had to finish work eleven weeks before her due date, even though she felt fine, and initially protested, but she had to admit that she enjoyed the enforced time at home. So she sorted leaflets and answered the phone, while her belly swelled alarmingly. At seven months, the midwife at her regular check-up noticed something she hadn't noticed before. A second heartbeat. The ultrasound confirmed it. She was having twins.

'Twins?' Byron and Jessie chorused.

'Twins?' Emily, Fran and Lucy were incredulous.

'Twins?' Byron repeated weakly and sat down.

Anya laughed. She was delighted, both at the news, and at their reactions, which were all she could have hoped for. But they soon recovered, and were as overjoyed as she was. And while she went into overdrive

465

in doubling everything they would need, Byron tried to split his time between acting as Geraldine's agent, and being a middle-aged first-time father, fussing and worrying and behaving quite unlike himself.

'Go home, good boy' Geraldine said at last, a week before the twins were due.

They were about to attend a hustings meeting, where candidates from all the political parties would be questioned, quizzed and interrogated. They stood at the back of the hall, watching the local residents take their seats.

'I can't do that, Geraldine, I can't leave you …

'Don't talk nonsense. Your mind's not here anyway, is it? Your dithering is putting me off. And with Neil Kinnock doing and saying all the right things at the moment, I think I can manage this lot. Now go!'

And he went. And none too soon. Anya went into labour that night, and their tiny twin girls were born the following morning.

Elizabeth and Katherine. Family names, one from each side. They were, of course, the centre of attention for the whole family, none more so than their father. Byron, for all his knowledge, his wit, his worldliness, his experience, seemed struck dumb at the little miracles they had made. He held each in turn, talking softly to them.

'I hope you're not talking politics to them!' Anya said, laughing.

He smiled at her.

'I'm just letting them know that parliament is being dissolved today' and he winked.

Labour had entered the campaign feeling confident, with **opinion polls** showing a Labour lead. They could do this, Anya thought, despite the slanging matches that people saw on their TVs. But their lead started to fall. Kinnock's American-style rally in Sheffield wasn't welcomed by all party members, and some, particularly in Wales, were downright embarrassed by it. But it was a new way of doing things, and maybe this was the future. Hopes were high.

The result when it came was a shock. The Tories back in. Under John Major, whom many had written off as a party leader, let alone a prime minister. Neil Kinnock, after all his good work and the promise he had shown, resigned. John Smith was now leader of the Labour Party. A gloom settled over party members. This was their fourth consecutive defeat. Some doubted they would ever be in government again.

Locally though, there was much to celebrate. Geraldine Mainwaring was their new MP, and took to the role as if born to it. Which maybe she was.

CHAPTER 33

ANOTHER CHAPTER

1997

Anya loved being at home with her babies, although they were growing fast. And the family was changing. The house now had a new name. Well, had reverted to its old one: Maes Ty Clyd. Emily was slowly building up a respectable smallholding, and spent half her time caring for her hens, the two pigs and a tiny flock of sheep, on which her dog Taffy kept a careful eye. The other half of her time she looked after her little sisters. She doted on them, and they on her. They had inherited their father's velvety brown eyes and their deep auburn hair was a perfect mix of both their parents' colouring.

By the spring of 1997, Fran was about to finish her degree in politics, and Lucy was in her first year at teacher training college. Anya had returned to work part-time, and Byron had taken up his full-time post again, still as argumentative as ever over the canteen table, still grumbling about the Tories. Anya fitted back in to the world of further education, even though some familiar faces had gone, and new ones had appeared. And she appreciated it more than ever. She would glance up from her lunch and catch the eye of the man she loved so much, and his smile, or his wink, still made her blush. In her forties, and still blushing, she thought. She wouldn't have changed it.

And another election was coming up. Surely, surely they had to win this one?

It had been a severe blow when John Smith had died suddenly, just two years into his leadership. But the new boy, young Tony Blair, seemed to have the right idea. He ruffled feathers, he caused much dissent within the party, with his plans for change, modernisation. But they were plans to win. And it seemed that they were working. Anya, Byron, Geraldine – they held their breath. Much of the country did the same. Then, in the early hours of the second day of May, the results were announced

And their world exploded with excitement, with congratulations, with tears of joy. A landslide victory for Labour. Byron cried as he hugged Anya, she sobbed and laughed, even Geraldine shed a tear – quickly brushed away – as she took to the podium, one of so many Labour MPs, now in government, now able to do all the things they had wanted to do for so long.

'I love you, Annie-May' Byron whispered into her hair as they clung together, surrounded by people celebrating, dancing, singing.

The bride stood erect next to the groom as the minister pronounced them man and wife. And when they turned, she looked radiant as all brides should. She walked slowly up the aisle, arm in arm with her new husband, and smiled, and chatted, and held outstretched hands of well-wishers who had gathered to hear this wonderful couple say their vows. They were followed by a white-blonde matron of honour, two bridesmaids - one brunette, one redhead - and two little auburn-haired flower girls. The entourage reached the door of the lovely old chapel, more used to hearing the Welsh language than English. They walked out into the glorious sunshine and were surrounded by their family and their friends.

'You look beautiful Mum' Anya said as she kissed her mother. 'And you too of course, Geraint! Quite the dandy in your top hat and tails!'

'Had to make an effort for your Mam, didn't I?' and he kissed his new wife on the cheek.

As they waved the newlyweds off, Byron turned to Anya.

'So what do you think, Annie-May? Do you think it's time you made an honest man of me at last?'

She looked at her family, crowding around them, laughing, chattering, Emily and Lucy each holding a twin on their hips, dancing with them. Their family, she thought. And she looked at him. She knew every inch of his face, no less beautiful now than when she'd first seen him, and she knew this was the only man she would ever love. They'd had their ups and downs, heaven knows, but here they were, together. She wasn't an innocent teenager any more. Or the naïve young woman he had first met. She knew there may be some tough times ahead, probably some rows, maybe sickness, things out of their control. She knew it may not always be easy. But she knew, too, that those heady days and months, when she had first fallen in love with him, were real. Those feelings were still there. Sometimes hidden under everyday matters, ordinary conversations, but she still felt weak at the thought of him. Not always, not every time, but enough to remind her of what they still had. What they would always have.

'So – do you? Do you, Annie-May?'

He was waiting for his answer, and she smiled at him.

'I do' she said.

THE END

Acknowledgements

There are a quite a few people I would like to thank for helping me get this book written and published. Firstly, my family, for supporting me at every stage, for telling me I can do it, for giving me a much-needed boost when I was flagging: thank you. For reading my many draft versions, which must have been tedious to say the least – thank you again!

There are many others who have encouraged me too - and apologies in advance if I don't mention you here. To my MP friends who gave me the opportunity to gain first-hand knowledge of what it's like to be a parliamentary candidate, a Member of Parliament, and an agent, thank you; to Lord Kinnock, who generously gave me permission to quote him; to the staff in various cafés across south Wales, who kept me fed and watered while I was typing away in the corner on many a morning; to Swansea University archives, and the Environment Agency, who made sure that my facts were correct – to you all, please accept my grateful thanks and appreciation.

To friends and ex-colleagues in the world of Further Education some of whom may think they recognise themselves in this book: thank you, and I assure you that they are only based on you if you feel they have an abundance of wonderful attributes!

To the mining communities across Wales, who over so many years have contributed to the education and culture of all of us.

And lastly, to the Labour Party and its members, who have, albeit unwittingly, provided me with such a rich seam of history, activity and stories. Thank you.

Alana Davies

Printed in Great Britain
by Amazon

35349824R00269